**Praise for *New York Times* bestselling author
Carla Neggers**

"Readers can feel the danger on every page and
will enjoy it from beginning to end."
—*RT Book Reviews* on *The Waterfall*

"Well-plotted, intriguing and set mostly in the
lushly described Irish countryside, the novel is
smart and satisfying."
—*Kirkus Reviews* on *Declan's Cross*

"Everything is out of control, and nothing is as it
seems, making for the intense, edge-of-your-seat
whirlwind that bestselling Neggers does so well in
her Sharpe & Donovan series."
—*Booklist* on *Liar's Key*

**Praise for *New York Times* bestselling author
B.J. Daniels**

"Super read by an excellent writer. Recommended!"
—#1 *New York Times* bestselling author
Linda Lael Miller on *Outlaw's Honor*

"Crossing multiple genres, Daniels successfully
combines Western romance, suspense and political
intrigue with ease."
—*RT Book Reviews* on *Hard Rain*

Carla Neggers is the *New York Times* bestselling author of more than sixty novels, including her popular Sharpe & Donovan and Swift River Valley series. Her books have been translated into twenty-four languages and sold in over thirty-five countries. A frequent traveler to Ireland, Carla lives with her family in New England. To learn more and to sign up for her newsletter, visit carlaneggers.com.

B.J. Daniels is a *New York Times* and *USA TODAY* bestselling author. She wrote her first book after a career as an award-winning newspaper journalist and author of thirty-seven published short stories. She lives in Montana with her husband, Parker, and three springer spaniels. When not writing, she quilts, boats and plays tennis. Contact her at bjdaniels.com, on Facebook or on Twitter, @bjdanielsauthor.

New York Times Bestselling Author

CARLA NEGGERS

THE WATERFALL

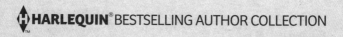

HARLEQUIN® BESTSELLING AUTHOR COLLECTION

ISBN-13: 978-0-373-01223-7

The Waterfall

Copyright © 2017 by Harlequin Books S.A.

The publisher acknowledges the copyright holders
of the individual works as follows:

The Waterfall
Copyright © 2000 by Carla Neggers

Odd Man Out
Copyright © 1995 by B.J. Daniels

Recycling programs
for this product may
not exist in your area.

HARLEQUIN®
www.Harlequin.com

Printed in U.S.A.

CONTENTS

Also by Carla Neggers

Sharpe & Donovan

THIEF'S MARK
LIAR'S KEY
KEEPER'S REACH
HARBOR ISLAND
DECLAN'S CROSS
ROCK POINT (novella)
HERON'S COVE
SAINT'S GATE

Swift River Valley

RED CLOVER INN
THE SPRING AT MOSS HILL
A KNIGHTS BRIDGE CHRISTMAS
ECHO LAKE
CHRISTMAS AT CARRIAGE HILL
  (novella)
CIDER BROOK
THAT NIGHT ON THISTLE LANE
SECRETS OF THE LOST SUMMER

BPD/FBI Series

THE WHISPER
THE MIST
THE ANGEL
THE WIDOW

Black Falls

COLD DAWN
COLD RIVER
COLD PURSUIT

Cold Ridge/U.S. Marshals

ABANDON
BREAKWATER
DARK SKY
THE RAPIDS
NIGHT'S LANDING
COLD RIDGE

Carriage House

THE HARBOR
STONEBROOK COTTAGE
THE CABIN
THE CARRIAGE HOUSE

Stand-Alone Novels

THE WATERFALL
ON FIRE
KISS THE MOON
TEMPTING FATE
CUT AND RUN
BETRAYALS
CLAIM THE CROWN

Visit carlaneggers.com for more titles

THE WATERFALL

Carla Neggers

To Dick and Diane Ballou...
for the house, the clothes, the fun
and the friendship.

Chapter 1

"The Widow Swift?" Lucy made a face as she absorbed her daughter's latest tidbit of gossip. "Who calls me that?"

Madison shrugged. She was fifteen, and she was doing the driving. Something else for Lucy to get used to. "Everyone."

"Who's everyone?"

"Like, the six people who live in this town."

Lucy ignored the light note of sarcasm. *The Widow Swift.* Good Lord. Maybe in some strange way this was a sign of acceptance. She had no illusions about being a "real" Vermonter. After three years, she was still an outsider, still someone people expected would pack up at any moment and move back to Washington. Nothing would suit Madison better, Lucy knew. At twelve, life in small-town Vermont had been an adventure. At fifteen, it was an imposition. She had her learner's permit, after all. Why not a home in Georgetown?

"Well," Lucy said, "you can just tell 'everyone' that I prefer to be called Lucy or Mrs. Swift or Ms. Swift."

"Sure, Mom."

"A name like 'the Widow Swift' tends to stick."

Madison seemed amused by the whole thing, so much so that she forgot that parking made her nervous and just pulled into a space in front of the post office in the heart of their small southern Vermont village.

"Wow, that was easy," Madison said. "Okay. Into Park. Emergency brake on. Engine off. Keys out." She smiled at her mother. She'd slipped into a little sundress for their trip to town; Lucy had nixed the flimsy slip-on sandals she'd wanted to wear. "See? I didn't even hit a moose."

They'd seen exactly two moose since moving to Vermont, neither en route to town. But Lucy let it go. "Good job."

Madison scooted off to the country store to "check out the galoshes," she said with a bright smile that took the edge off her sarcasm. Lucy headed for the post office to mail a batch of brochures for her adventure travel company. Requests from her Web site were up. Business was good to excellent. She was getting her bearings, making a place for herself and her children. It took time, that was all.

"The Widow Swift," she said under her breath. "Damn."

She wished she could shake it off with a laugh, but she couldn't. She was thirty-eight, and Colin had been dead for three years. She knew she was a widow. But she didn't want it to define her. She didn't know what she wanted to define her, but not that.

The village was quiet in the mid-July heat, not even a breeze stirring in the huge, old sugar maples on the sliver of a town common. The country store, the post office, the hardware store and two bed-and-breakfasts—that was it. Manchester, a few miles to the northwest, offered considerably more in the way of shopping and things to do, but Lucy had no intention of letting her daughter drive that far with a two-week-old learner's permit. It wasn't necessarily that Madison wasn't ready for traffic and busy streets. *Lucy* wasn't ready.

When she finished at the post office, she automatically approached the driver's side of her all-wheel-drive station wagon. Their "Vermont car," Madison called it with a touch of derision. She wanted a Jetta. She wanted the city.

With a groan, Lucy remembered her daughter was driving. Fifteen was *so* young. She went around to the passenger's side, surprised Madison wasn't already back behind the wheel. Driving was all that stood between her daughter and abject boredom this summer. Even the prospect of leaving for Wyoming the next day hadn't perked her up. Nothing would, Lucy realized, except getting her way about spending a semester in Washington with her grandfather.

Wyoming. Lucy shook her head. Now *that* was madness.

She plopped onto the sun-heated passenger seat and debated canceling the trip. Madison had already voiced objections about going. And her twelve-year-old son, J.T., would rather stay home and dig worms. The purported reason for heading to Jackson Hole was to meet with several western guides. But that was ridiculous, Lucy thought. Her company specialized in northern

New England and the Canadian Maritimes and was in the process of putting together a winter trip to Costa Rica where her parents had retired to run a hostel. She had all she could handle now. Opening up to Montana and Wyoming would just be spreading herself too thin.

The real reason she was going to Wyoming, she knew, was Sebastian Redwing and the promise she'd made to Colin.

But that was ridiculous, too. An overreaction—if not pure stupidity—on her part to a few weird incidents.

Lucy sank back against her seat, feeling something under her—probably a pen or a lipstick, or one of J.T.'s toys. She fished it out.

She gasped at the warm, solid length of metal in her hand.

A bullet.

She resisted a sudden urge to fling it out the window. What if it went off? She shuddered, staring at her palm. It wasn't an empty shell. It was a live round. Big, weighty.

Someone had left a damn *bullet* on her car seat.

The car windows were open. She and Madison hadn't locked up. Anyone could have walked by, dropped the bullet through the passenger window and kept on going.

Lucy's hand shook. Not again. Damn it, not again. She forced herself to take slow, controlled breaths. She knew adventure travel—canoeing, kayaking, hiking, basic first aid. She could plan every detail of inventive, multifaceted, multi-sport trips and do just fine.

She didn't know bullets.

She didn't *want* to know bullets.

Madison trotted out of the country store with several other teenagers, swinging her car keys as if she'd been driving for years. The girls were laughing and chatting, and even as Lucy slid the bullet into her shorts pocket, she thought, *Yes, Madison, you do have friends.* Since school had let out, her daughter had been making a point of being miserable, if only to press her case for Washington.

She jumped into the driver's seat. "Saddle up, Mom. We're ready to roll."

Lucy didn't mention the bullet. This wasn't her children's problem, it was hers. She preferred to cling to the belief that she wasn't the victim of deliberate harassment. The incidents she'd endured over the past week were random, innocent, meaningless. They weren't related. They weren't a campaign of intimidation against her.

The first had occurred on Sunday evening, when she'd found a dining room window open, the curtains billowing in the summer breeze. It was a window she never opened. Madison and J.T. wouldn't bother. But Lucy had dismissed the incident, until the next night when the phone rang just before dawn, the caller breathing at her groggy hello, then hanging up. Too weird, she'd thought.

Then on Tuesday, while checking the mailbox at the end of her driveway, she'd had the distinct sense she was being watched. Something had alerted her—the snapping of a twig, the crunching of gravel. It wasn't, she was certain, her imagination.

The next morning, the feeling was there again, while she was sweeping the back steps, and ten minutes later, she'd found one of her tomato plants sitting on the front porch. It had been ripped out of the ground.

Now, today, the bullet on her car seat.

Maybe she was in denial, but she didn't believe there

was enough to take to the police. Individually, each incident could have an innocent explanation—her kids, their friends, her staff, stress. How could she prove someone was watching her? She'd sound like a nut.

And if she went to the police, Lucy knew what would happen. They would notify Washington. Washington would feel compelled to come to Vermont and investigate. And so much for her low-profile life.

It wasn't that no one in town knew her father-in-law was Jack Swift, a powerful United States senator. Everyone knew. But she'd never made it an issue.

She was his only son's widow; Madison and J.T. were his only grandchildren. Jack would take charge. He would insist the Capitol Police conduct a thorough investigation and make sure his family wasn't drawing fire because of him.

Lucy couldn't imagine why anyone going after Jack would slip a bullet onto his widowed daughter-in-law's car seat. It made no sense. No. She was safe. Her children were safe. This was just…bizarre.

"Mom?"

Madison had started the engine and backed out onto the main road without Lucy noticing, much less providing comment and instruction. "You're doing great. My mind's wandering, that's all."

"What's wrong? Is it my driving?"

"No, of course not."

"Because I can get someone else to drive with me. It doesn't have to be you, if I make you nervous."

"You don't make me nervous. I'm fine. Just keep your eyes on the road."

"I *am.*"

Madison had a death grip on the steering wheel.

Lucy realized she'd scared her daughter, who noticed everything. "Madison. You're driving. You can't allow yourself to get distracted."

"I know. It's you."

It *was* her. Lucy took a breath. She could feel the weight of the bullet in her pocket. What if it had worked its way under the seat and J.T. had found it? She shut off the stream of what-if scenarios. She'd learned from hard experience to stick with what was, which was difficult enough to absorb.

"Never mind me and drive."

Madison huffed, annoyed now. With her blue eyes and coppery hair, her introspective temperament and unbridled ambition, she was so like her father. Even Madison's two-week-old driving mannerisms were pure Colin Swift.

He'd died, suddenly and unexpectedly at age thirty-six, of a cardiac arrhythmia while playing tennis with his father, his life and a brilliant career at the U.S. State Department cut short. Madison had been twelve, J.T. nine. Not easy ages to lose a father. Six months later, Lucy had plucked her children away from the only life they knew—school, friends, family, "civilization," as Madison would say. But if they hadn't moved—if Lucy hadn't done something dramatic to get her bearings— they'd have been in danger of losing their mother, too, and that simply wasn't an option.

There'd been nothing from Sebastian Redwing when Colin died. Not a flower, not a card, not a word. Then, two months later, his lawyer showed up on Lucy's doorstep offering her the deed to his grandmother's Vermont farmhouse. Daisy had died the previous year, and Sebastian had no use for it.

Lucy threw the lawyer out. If Redwing couldn't even offer his condolences, she didn't want his damn house.

A month later, the lawyer was back. This time, she could have the house at a below-market price. She would be doing Sebastian a favor. His grandmother had wanted someone in the family to have the house. He had no brothers or sisters. His parents were dead. Lucy was the best he could do.

She'd accepted. She still didn't know why. Sebastian had once saved her husband's life. Why not hers?

In truth, she couldn't pinpoint one clear, overriding reason. Perhaps the lure of Vermont and starting her own adventure travel business, the stifling fog of grief, her fears about raising her children on her own.

Maybe, she thought, it boiled down to the promise she'd made Colin shortly before he died. Neither had known until that day on the tennis court that he had a heart condition that could kill him. The promise had seemed like one of those "if we're trapped on a desert island" scenarios, not something she would ever need to act on.

Yet Colin had been so sincere, so serious. "If anything happens to me, you can trust Sebastian. He's the best, Lucy. He saved my life. He saved my father's life. Promise me you'll go to him if you ever need help."

She'd promised, and now here she was in Vermont. She hadn't heard from Redwing, much less seen him, since she'd bought his grandmother's house. The transaction had been handled entirely through his attorney. Lucy had hoped never again to be so desperate that she'd feel compelled to remember her promise to Colin. She was smart, she was capable, and she was used to being on her own.

So why was she packing herself and her kids off to Wyoming—Sebastian Redwing country—in the morning?

"Mom!"

"You're doing great. Just keep driving."

With one finger, Lucy traced the outline of the bullet in her pocket. There was probably an innocent explanation for the bullet and all the other incidents. She should just focus on having fun in Wyoming.

The locals still referred to Sebastian Redwing's grandmother as the Widow Daisy and the remnants of her farm as the old Wheaton place. Lucy had learned Daisy's story in bits and pieces. Daisy Wheaton had lived in her yellow farmhouse on Joshua Brook for sixty years as a widow. She was twenty-eight when her husband drowned saving a little boy from the raging waterfall in the hills above their farmhouse. It was early spring, and the snowmelt had made the falls treacherous. The boy had gone after his dog. Joshua Wheaton had gone after the boy. Later, the falls and the brook they were on were named after him. Joshua Falls—Joshua Brook.

Daisy and Joshua's only child, a daughter, couldn't wait to get out of Vermont. She moved to Boston and got married, and when she and her husband were killed in a hit-and-run accident, they left behind a fourteen-year-old son. Sebastian came to live with Daisy. But he hadn't stayed in Vermont, either.

Seven acres of fields, woods and gardens, and the rambling yellow clapboard farmhouse were all that remained of the original Wheaton farm. Daisy had sold off bits and pieces of her land over the years to second homeowners and local farmers, keeping the core of the place for herself and whoever might come after her.

It was said Daisy had never gone back to Joshua Falls after she'd helped pull her husband's body out of the frigid water.

The Widow Daisy. Now, the Widow Swift.

Lucy grimaced as she walked up the gravel path to the small, classic barn she'd converted into office space. She could feel the decades yawning in front of her and imagined sixty years on this land, alone.

She stopped, listening to Joshua Brook trickling over rocks down the steep, wooded embankment beyond the barn. The falls were farther up in the hills. Here, the brook was wide and slow-moving before running under a wooden bridge and eventually merging with the river. She could hear bees buzzing in the hollyhocks in front of the garage. She looked around her, at the sprawling lawn, lush and green from recent showers, and the pretty nineteenth-century farmhouse with its baskets of white petunias hanging on the front porch. Her gaze took in the stately, old sugar maples that shaded the front yard, the backyard with its vegetable garden and apple trees, and a stone wall that bordered a field of grass and wildflowers, with another stone wall on its far side. Then, beyond that, the wooded hills. So quiet, so beautiful.

"You could do worse," Lucy whispered to herself as she entered her office.

She had learned most of what she knew about the Wheaton-Redwing family not from closemouthed, elusive Sebastian, but from Rob Kiley, her only full-time employee. He was parked in front of his computer in the open, rustic space that served as her company's home base. Rob's father was the boy Joshua Wheaton had saved sixty years ago—one of the circuitous but inevitable connections Lucy had come to expect from living in a small town.

Rob didn't look up. "I hate computers," he said.

Lucy smiled. "You say that every time I walk in here."

"That's because I want to get it through that thick, cheapskate skull of yours that we need a full-time person to sit here and bang away on this thing."

"What are you doing?" Lucy asked. She didn't peer over his shoulder because that drove him nuts. He was a lanky, easygoing Vermonter whose paddling skills and knowledge of the hills, valleys, rivers and coastline of northern New England were indispensable. So were his enthusiasm, his honesty and his friendship.

"I'm putting together the final, carved-in-stone, must-not-deviate-from itinerary for the father-son backpacking trip." This was a first-time offering, a five-day beginner's backpacking trip on nearby trails in the southern Green Mountains; it had filled up even faster than he and Lucy had anticipated. Rob looked up, and she knew what he was thinking. "There's still time for J.T. to join us. I told him I wasn't a substitute for his real dad, but we can still have a lot of fun."

"I know. This is one he has to figure out for himself. I can't decide for him."

He nodded. "Well, we've got time. By the way, he and Georgie are digging worms in the garden."

Lucy wasn't surprised. "Madison will love that. I just sent her to check on them."

Rob tilted back in his chair and stretched. Sitting at a computer was torture for him on a day when he could be out kayaking. "How'd she do driving?"

"Better than I did. She's still lobbying for a semester in Washington."

"Grandpa Jack would love that."

"She's romanticized Washington. It's everything Vermont isn't."

Rob shrugged. "Well, it is."

"You're a big help!" But Lucy's laughter faded quickly as she slipped her hand into her pocket and withdrew the bullet. "I want you to take a look at something."

"Sure."

"And I don't want you to mention it to anyone."

"Am I supposed to ask why not?"

"You're supposed to say okay, you won't."

"Okay, I won't."

She opened her hand and let the bullet roll forward in her palm. "What do you think?"

Rob frowned. "It's a bullet."

"I know it's a bullet. What kind?"

He picked it out of her palm and nonchalantly set it upright on his cluttered desk. He'd grown up around guns. "Forty-four magnum. It's the whole nine yards, you know, not just an empty shell."

She nodded. "I know that much. Can it go off?"

"Not sitting here on my desk. If you dropped it just right or ran it over with a lawn mower or something, it could go off."

Lucy stifled a shudder. "That can't be good."

"If it went off, you wouldn't have any control over where it goes. At least with a gun, you can take aim at a target. You might take lousy aim. But if you run over a live round with a lawn mower, there's no chance to aim at anything. Thing can go any which way." He sounded calm, but his dark eyes were very serious. "Where'd you find it?"

"What? Oh." She hadn't considered a cover story and hated the idea of lying. "In town. I'm sure it's no big deal."

"It's not Georgie or J.T., is it? If they're fooling around with firearms and ammunition—"

"No!" Lucy nearly choked. "I stumbled on it in town just now. I didn't want anyone to get hurt, so I picked it up. I was just wondering if I was panicking unnecessarily."

"You weren't. Someone was very careless." He touched the dull gray metal tip of the bullet. "You want me to get rid of it?"

"Please."

"Do me a favor, okay? Check J.T.'s room. I'll check Georgie's. If I find anything, I'll let you know. You do the same. I don't keep a gun at home, and I know you don't, but they wouldn't be the first twelve-year-old boys—"

"It wasn't J.T. or Georgie."

Rob's eyes met hers. "If you won't check J.T.'s room, I will."

Lucy nodded. "You're right. I'll check his room."

"The cellar, too. I nearly blew myself up at that age screwing around with gunpowder."

"I don't have gunpowder—"

"Lucy."

"All right, all right."

Rob was silent, studying her. She'd known him from her earliest days in Vermont. He and his wife, Patti, were her best friends here. Georgie and J.T. were inseparable. But she hadn't told him about the weird incidents.

Lucy tried not to squirm. Sweat had matted her shirt to her lower back. So much to do, so many responsibilities. She didn't need some crackpot targeting her. "Just get rid of the damn bullet, okay?"

Rob crossed his arms on his chest. "Sure, Lucy."

She could guess what he was thinking—what anyone would be thinking. That she was on edge, frayed and crazed, more than would be warranted by a rapidly expanding business, widowhood, single motherhood and an impending trip west. That he wanted to call her on it.

Lucy took advantage of his natural reluctance to meddle. "I'm sorry if I seem a little nuts. I have so much to do with this whirlwind trip to Wyoming this weekend. You can hold down the fort here?"

"That's in bold print on my resume. *Can hold down forts.*"

His humor didn't reach his eyes, but Lucy pretended not to notice. She smiled. "What would I do without you?"

He didn't hesitate. "Go broke."

She laughed, feeling better now that the bullet was out of her pocket. These incidents had to be unrelated. It was kooky and paranoid to think they were part of some kind of bizarre conspiracy against her. What would be the motive?

She left Rob to his computer aggravations and bullet disposal, and went outside. She'd ask Rob later what he thought about this Widow Swift business. She had a good life here, and that was what counted.

"I made lemonade," Madison called from the front porch.

"Great. I'll be right there."

Lucy reminded herself it was only in recent months

her daughter had come to feel aggrieved by their move to Vermont.

"I'm pretending I'm living in an episode of 'The Waltons,'" Madison said when her mother joined her amidst the hanging petunias and wicker furniture. Indeed, she had filled one of Daisy's old glass pitchers with lemonade and put on one of her threadbare aprons. Sebastian hadn't taken anything of his grandmother's before he'd sold her house.

"Did you ask the boys if they want any?" Lucy asked.

"They're still out back digging worms. It's disgusting. They smell like dirt and sweat."

"You used to love digging worms."

"Yuck."

Lucy smiled. "Well, I'll go ask them. And since you made the lemonade, they can clean up."

The two boys were still hard at work on the edge of the vegetable garden, precariously close to Lucy's tomatoes. Not that she minded. She wasn't as enterprising a gardener as Daisy had been. She'd added raised beds and mulched paths to take up space and had cultivated a lot of spreading plants, like pumpkins, squash and cucumbers. She had little desire, however, to can and freeze her own fruits and vegetables. This was enough.

"Madison made lemonade. You boys want some?"

"Later," J.T. said, too preoccupied with his worm-digging to look up.

He, too, had Colin's coppery hair and clear blue eyes, although his sturdy frame was more Blacker than Swift. Lucy smiled at the thought of her kind, thickset father. She had inherited her mother's slender build and fair coloring, and both her parents' love of the outdoors. They'd recently retired to Costa Rica to run a hostel, leaving behind long careers at the Smithsonian. Lucy planned to visit them over Thanksgiving, taking Madison and J.T. with her and working on the details of a Costa Rica trip she wanted to offer to her clients next winter. It was a long, painstaking process that involved figuring out and testing every last detail—transportation, food, lodging, contingency plans. *Nothing* could be left to chance.

Flying to Costa Rica to see them, Lucy thought, made more sense than flying off to Wyoming to see Sebastian Redwing.

J.T. scooped up dirt with his hands and piled it into a number-ten can he and Georgie had appropriated from the recycling bin. "We want to go fishing. We've got a ton of worms. Want to see?"

Lucy gave the can of squirming worms a dutiful peek. "Lovely. If you do go fishing, stay down here. Don't go up near the falls."

"I know, Mom."

He knew. *Right.* Both her kids knew everything. Losing their father at such a young age hadn't eroded their self-esteem. They had Colin's optimism, his drive and energy, his faith in a better future and his commitment to making it happen. Like their father, Madison and J.T. loved having a million things going on at once.

Lucy left the boys to their worms and returned to the front porch, where Madison had brought out cloth napkins and a plate of butter cookies to go with her lemonade. "Actually, I think I'm more Anne of Green Gables today."

"Is that better than John-Boy Walton?"

Madison wrinkled up her face and sat on the wicker settee, tucking her slender legs under her. "Mom—I really, really don't want to go to Wyoming. Can't I stay here? It's only for the weekend. Rob and Patti could look in on me. I could have a friend stay with me."

Lucy poured herself a glass of lemonade and settled onto a wicker chair. Her daughter was relentless. "I thought you couldn't wait to get out of Vermont."

"Not to *Wyoming*. It's more mountains and trees."

"Bigger mountains, different trees. There's great shopping in Jackson."

She brightened. "Does that mean you'll give me money?"

"A little, but I meant window-shopping. It's also very expensive."

Her daughter was unamused. "If I have to sit next to J.T. on the plane, I'm inspecting his pockets first."

"I expect you to treat your brother with respect, just as I expect him to treat you with respect."

Madison rolled her eyes.

Lucy tried her lemonade. It was a perfect mix of tart and sweet, just like her fifteen-year-old daughter. Madison untucked her legs and flounced inside, the sophisticate trapped in the sticks, the long-suffering big sister about to be stuck on a plane with her little brother.

Lucy decided to give her the weekend to come around before initiating a discussion on attitude and who wouldn't get to do much driving until she changed hers.

She put her feet up on the porch rail and tried to let the cool breeze relax her. The trip to Wyoming made no sense. She knew it, and her kids at least sensed it.

The petunias needed watering. She looked out at her pretty lawn with its huge maples, its rambling old-fashioned rosebush that needed pruning. She'd just gone to town with her fifteen-year-old behind the wheel, inspected a can of worms and dealt with her daughter's John-Boy/Anne of Green Gables martyr act *and* a bullet on her car seat.

The Widow Swift at work.

Lucy drank more lemonade, feeling calmer. She'd managed on her own for so long. She didn't need Sebastian Redwing's help. She didn't need anyone's help.

J.T. permitted his mother to help him pack after dinner. Lucy kept her eyes open for firearms, bullets and secret antisocial tendencies. She found none. His room betrayed nothing more than a twelve-year-old's mishmash of interests. Posters of Darth Maul and peregrine falcons, stuffed animals, Lego models, sports paraphernalia, computer games, gross-looking superheroes and monsters, way too many Micro Machines.

He didn't have a television in his room. He didn't have a computer. Dirty clothes were dumped in with clean on the floor. Drawers were half open, a pant leg hanging out of one, a pair of boxers out of another.

The room smelled of dirty socks, sweat and earth. A dormer window looked out on the backyard, where she could still see evidence of the digging he and Georgie had done.

"You didn't bring your worms up here, did you?" Lucy asked.

"No, me and Georgie freed them." He looked at her, and corrected, "Georgie and I."

She smiled, and when she turned, she spotted a picture of Colin and J.T. tacked to her son's bulletin board. Blood rushed to her head, and she had to fight off sudden, unexpected tears. The edges of the picture were cracked and yellowed, pocked with tack holes from the dozen times J.T. had repositioned it. A little boy and a young father fishing, frozen in time.

Lucy smiled sadly at the image of the man she'd loved. They'd met in college, married so young. She stared at his handsome face, his smile, his tousle of coppery hair. It was as if she'd gone on, propelled forward in time, while he'd stayed the same, untouched by the grief and fear she'd known since the day his shattered father had knocked on her door and told her that his son—her husband—was dead.

The searing pain and shock of those early days had eased. Lucy had learned to go on without him. So, in their own ways, had Madison and J.T. They could talk about him with laughter, and remember him, at least most of the time, without tears.

"You can pack the extra stuff you want to take in your backpack," Lucy said, tearing herself from the picture. "What book are you reading?"

"A *Star Wars* book."

"Don't forget to pack it."

She counted out shirts, pants, socks, underwear, and debated whether to bother looking in the cellar and the garage. J.T.'d had nothing to do with the bullet in her car.

She set the clothes on his bed. "You're good to go, kiddo. Can you shove this stuff into your suitcase, or do you need my help?"

"I can do it."

"Don't forget your toothbrush."

She went down the hall to her daughter's room. The door was shut, her music up but not at a wall-vibrating volume. If Madison needed help, she'd ask for it. Lucy left her alone.

Her own bedroom was downstairs, and on the way she stopped in the kitchen and put on a kettle for tea. She'd pack later. It was an old-fashioned, working kitchen with white cabinets, scarred counters and sunny yellow walls that helped offset the cold, dark winter nights. The biggest surprise of life in Vermont, Lucy had discovered, was how dark the nights were.

She sank into a chair at the pine table and stared out at the backyard, wondering how many nights Daisy had done exactly this in her sixty years alone. A cup of tea, a quiet house. The Widow Daisy. The Widow Swift.

It was dark now, the long summer day finally giving way. Lucy could feel the silence settle around her, the isolation and loneliness creep in. Sometimes she would turn on the television or the radio, or work on her laptop, write emails, perhaps call a friend. Tonight, she had to pack. Wyoming. Good God, she really was going.

She made chamomile tea and took her mug with her down the hall to the front door, locked up. Shadows shifted on the old wood floors. She had no illusions the ancient locks would stop a determined intruder.

A sound—the wind, maybe—took her into the dining room.

She hadn't touched it since moving in. It still had the old-fashioned button light switch for the milk-glass overhead, Daisy's faded hand-hooked rug, her cabbage-rose wallpaper, her clunky dining room set. A 1920s upright piano stood along one wall.

A breeze brought up goose bumps on Lucy's arms.

Someone had opened a window. Again.

The tall, old windows were balky and difficult to open. Since she almost never used the dining room during the summer, Lucy didn't bother wrestling with them. She'd meant to have them looked at before the good weather, but hadn't gotten around to it.

She felt along the wall with one hand and pressed the light switch. It *had* to be a kid. Who else would sneak into her house and open the windows?

Light spilled into the room, casting more shadows. It could be a great room. One of these days she'd have the piano tuned, the rug cleaned, the wood floors sanded and oiled. She'd hang new wallpaper and refinish the table, and have family and friends over for Thanksgiving. Even her father-in-law, if he wanted to come.

The floor seemed to sparkle. Lucy frowned, peering closer.

Shards of glass.

She jumped back, startled. The window wasn't open. It was broken, its upper pane spider-cracked around a small hole. A triangle of glass had hit the floor and shattered.

Lucy set her mug on the table and gingerly touched the edges of the hole. It wasn't from a bird smashing into her window, or an errant baseball. Too small.

A stone?

A bullet?

She spun around, her heart pounding.

It couldn't be. Not twice in one day.

She saw plaster dust on the chair next to the piano, directly across from the window. Above it was a hole in the wall.

Holding her breath, Lucy knelt on the chair and reached up, smoothing her hand over the hole. The edges of the wallpaper were rough. Plaster dust covered her fingertips.

The hole was empty. There was no bullet lodged there.

She sank onto her hands and knees and checked the floor. She looked under the piano. She flipped up the edges of the rug. She could feel the hysteria working its way into her, seeping into her pores, sending poison into every nerve ending.

She flopped back onto her butt and sat there on the floor. So, she thought. There it is. Some bastard had shot a hole in her dining room window, sneaked into her house, removed the bullet and sneaked back out again.

When? How? *Why?*

Wouldn't someone—Madison, J.T., Georgie, Rob, the damn mailman—have heard or seen *something?*

They'd run up to Manchester last night. It could have happened then, when no one was home.

The windows faced east across the side yard and the garage, the barn, Joshua Brook. A hunter or target shooter could have been in the woods near the brook and accidentally landed a stray bullet in her dining room, panicked, slipped inside and dug it out.

"Ha," she said aloud.

This was no accident.

Lucy was shaking, sick to her stomach. If she called the police, she'd be up all night. She'd have to explain to Madison and J.T. Rob's grandmother had a scanner—she'd call Rob, and he and Patti would come over.

And that was just the beginning. The police would call Washington. The Capitol Police would want to know if the incidents had anything to do with Jack Swift. He would be notified.

She staggered to her feet and picked up her tea.

Now was she desperate enough to ask Sebastian Redwing for help?

She ran into the kitchen, dumped her tea down the sink and locked the back door. She went into her bedroom to pack. "You need a dog," she muttered to herself. "That's all."

A big dog. A big dog that barked.

"A big, ugly dog that barks."

He'd take care of intruders, and she could train him to go fishing with J.T. Even Madison would like a dog.

That settled it. Never mind Redwing. When she got back from Wyoming, she'd see about getting a dog.

Chapter 2

Sebastian slipped off his horse and collapsed in the shade of a cottonwood. He was out on the far reaches of his property where no one could find him. Still, the bastards had. Two of them. In a damn Jeep. It was bouncing toward him. He could take his horse through the river, but the idiots would probably come after him.

He sipped water from his canteen, took off his hat and poured a little water over his head. He could use a shower. The air was hot and dusty. Dry. He hoped the dopes in the Jeep had water with them. He wasn't planning on sharing any of his canteen. Well, they could drink out of the river.

The Jeep got closer. "Easy," Sebastian told his horse, who didn't look too worried or even that hot.

A man jumped out just as the Jeep came to a stop about twenty yards off. "Mr. Redwing?"

Sebastian grimaced. It was never a good sign when someone called him Mr. Redwing. Not that chasing him in a Jeep was a good sign.

He tipped his hat over his eyes and leaned back on his elbows. "What?"

"Mr. Redwing," the man said. "I'm Jim Charger. Mr. Rabedeneira sent me to find you."

"So?"

Charger didn't speak. He was a new hire, probably waiting for Sebastian to get up and act like the man who'd founded and built Redwing Associates, a premier international security and investigative firm. Instead he kept his hat over his eyes, enjoying the relief from the Wyoming summer sun.

Finally, he sighed. Jim Charger wasn't going anywhere until he delivered his message. Sebastian liked Plato Rabedeneira. They'd been friends since their early twenties. He'd trust Plato with his life, the lives of his friends. But if Plato had been the other man in the Jeep, Sebastian would have tied him to this cottonwood and left him.

"Okay, Mr. Charger." He tipped his hat back and eyed the man in front of him. Tall, blond, very fit, dressed in expensive western attire that was no doubt dustier now than it had ever been. A Washington import. Probably ex-FBI. Sebastian could feel the blood pounding behind his eyes. "What's up?"

If Sebastian Redwing wasn't proving to be what Jim Charger had expected, he kept it to himself. "Mr. Rabedeneira asked me to give you a message. He says to tell you Darren Mowery is back."

Sebastian made sure he had no visible reaction. Inside, the blood pounded harder behind his eyes. He'd left Mowery for dead a year ago. "Back where?"

"Washington."

"What's Plato want me to do about it?"

"I don't know. He asked me to deliver the message. He said to tell you it was important."

Darren Mowery hated Sebastian more than most of his enemies did. Once, Sebastian would have trusted Mowery with his life, with the lives of his friends. No more.

"One other thing," Charger said.

Sebastian smiled faintly. "This is the thing Plato said to tell me if I didn't jump in your Jeep with you?"

No reaction. "Mowery has made contact with a woman in Senator Swift's office."

Jack Swift, now the senior senator from the state of Rhode Island. A gentleman politician, a man of integrity and dedication to public service, father-in-law to Lucy Blacker Swift.

Damn, Sebastian thought.

At the reception following Lucy Blacker and Colin Swift's wedding, Colin had made Sebastian promise he'd look after Lucy if anything happened to him. "Not," Colin had said, "that Lucy will want looking after. But you know what I mean."

Sebastian hadn't, not really. He didn't have anyone in his life to look after. His parents were dead. He had no brothers and sisters, no wife, no children. Professionally, though, he was pretty damn good at looking after people. That mostly had to do with keeping them alive and their pockets from getting picked. It didn't have to do with friendship, a promise made to a man who would be dead thirteen years later at age thirty-six.

Colin must have known. Somehow, he must have guessed he would have a short life, and his wife and whatever children they had would end up having to go on without him.

When Sebastian had made his promise, he'd never imagined he'd have to keep it.

"What do you want me to tell Mr. Rabedeneira?" Charger asked.

Sebastian tilted his hat back over his eyes. A year ago, he'd shot Darren Mowery and thought he'd killed him. It was carelessness on his part he hadn't known until now whether Mowery was dead or alive. In his business, that kind of lapse was intolerable. There was no excuse. It didn't matter that Darren had once been his mentor, his friend, or that Sebastian had watched him send himself straight into hell. When you shot someone, you were supposed to find out if you'd killed him. It was a rule.

But this was about Jack Swift. It wasn't about Lucy. Plato would have to handle Darren Mowery. Given his personal involvement, Sebastian would only muck up the works.

"Tell Plato I'm retired," Sebastian said.

"Retired?"

"Yes. He knows. Remind him."

Charger didn't move.

Sebastian pictured Lucy on the front porch of his grandmother's house, and he could almost feel the Vermont summer breeze, hear the brook, smell the cool water, the damp moss. Lucy had needed to get out of Washington, and he'd made it happen. He'd kept his promise. He no longer owed Colin.

He decided to stop thinking about Lucy. It had never done him any good.

"You've delivered your message, Mr. Charger," Sebastian said. "Now go deliver mine."

"Yes, sir."

The man left. Sebastian suspected he hadn't lived up to Jim Charger's expectations. Well, that was fine with him. He didn't live up to his own expectations. Why should he live up to anyone else's?

He'd quit, and that was the end of it.

Barbara Allen fumbled for the keys to her Washington apartment. Acid burned in her throat. Sweat soaked her blouse, her dozens of mosquito bites stinging and itching. Part of her wanted to cry, part to scream with delight. Incredible! At last, she'd acted. At last!

She unlocked her door and pushed it open, gasping at the oppressive heat. She'd turned off the air-conditioning before she'd left for Vermont. Vermont had been cooler than Washington, wonderfully exhilarating. She quickly shut her door and leaned against it, letting herself breathe. She was home.

She had no regrets. None. This surprised her more than anything else. Intellectually, she knew what she'd done was wrong. Her obsession with Lucy was even, perhaps, a little sick. Normal people didn't spy on other people. Normal people didn't stalk and terrorize other people.

But if anyone deserved to live in fear, it was Lucy Blacker Swift. She was the worst kind of mother. Self-indulgent, impulsive, reckless. Colin had provided a necessary check against her worst excesses, but with his death, there was no one to rein her in.

For more than a year, Barbara had taken a secret thrill in sneaking up to Vermont on a Friday night to watch Lucy, heading back to Washington on Sunday. She was Jack Swift's eyes and ears, his confidante, his trusted personal assistant. She'd given twenty years of her life to him, suffered every loss with him. The ups and downs of his political career, the assassination attempt, the long, slow, painful death of his wife, the sudden death of his son.

Then, Lucy's galling decision to move to Vermont. It was the last straw. Barbara knew Jack was appalled at how she was raising his son's children. Madison, aching for a real life. J.T., running wild with his dirty little friends. But Jack would never say anything, never do anything to force Lucy to wake up.

Well, Barbara had. *At last, at last.*

Let people underestimate her. Let them take her for granted. She *knew.* She had the courage and self-discipline to do what needed to be done.

With one foot, she nudged her suitcase into the corner by the coat closet. She'd unpack later. She turned the air-conditioning on high and went into her living room. Like the rest of her apartment, it was simply decorated in contemporary furnishings, its clean lines and clean colors reflecting her strength of character. She despised anything cute or frilly.

She sat in a chair by the vent. Her apartment was in a nondescript building on the Potomac; it was one of the smallest units, with no view to speak of. Not that she spent much time here. She was in the office by eight and seldom out before seven.

She closed her eyes, feeling the cool air wash over her. She'd worn long pants and a long-sleeved shirt to hide her bug bites. Each one deserved a tiny Purple Heart. They were her badges of courage. It wasn't weakness that had made her act—it was strength, courage, conviction.

She'd been meticulous. She wasn't an idiot. She hadn't felt the need to do anything dramatic to conceal her presence. She'd stayed at a Manchester inn and driven a car she'd rented in Washington. She'd had a plausible cover story in case she had been discovered.

Oh, Lucy, I was just stopping in to see you and the kids. I took a few days off to go outlet shopping, do a little hiking. By the way, did you hear gunfire? I saw someone going up the dirt road over by the brook with a rifle. They must have been target practicing awfully close to your house.

It had never come to that. She'd conducted exhaustive surveillance before implementing her plan, even something as simple as the late-night hang-up. Lucy was too self-centered, too stupid, to catch her.

Firing into the dining room had been Barbara's supreme act. It was even better than the bullet on the front seat. That was just the proverbial icing on the cake. Barbara had waited until Lucy and the children left for Manchester. She was parked up on the dirt road, as if she were off to check out the falls. She crossed Joshua Brook, jumping from one rock to another, and dropped down low, working her way up the steep, wooded bank until Lucy's house came into view. She lay flat on her stomach in the brush. Mosquitoes buzzed in her ears, chewed on every inch of exposed skin. Her tremendous self-discipline kept her focused.

If she'd been caught then, at that moment, with her rifle aimed at Lucy's house, she'd have had no cover story. The risk—the challenge—was part of the thrill, more exhilarating even than she'd imagined.

Her father had taught her and her three sisters how to shoot. He had never said he wished he'd had a son, but they knew he did. Barbara was the youngest. The last, shattered hope. She'd become a very good shot. No one knew how good—certainly no one in Jack's office. Not even Jack himself. They knew her only in relation to her work, her devotion to her job and her boss.

Only after she'd fired and lay in the still, hot, prickly brush did she decide to go after the spent bullet. It wasn't concern over leaving behind evidence that propelled her across the yard behind the barn—it was the idea of further terrorizing Lucy, imagining her coming into her dining room and seeing the shattered window, then realizing someone had slipped inside to dig the bullet out of the wall.

The back door wasn't locked. Lucy often didn't lock all her doors. Perhaps, Barbara thought, this would teach the silly twit a lesson.

The acid burned down her throat and into her stomach, gnawing at her insides. The urge to scare Lucy, throw her off her stride, had gripped her for days, consuming her. With each small act of harassment, Barbara felt a little better. The pressure lifted. The urge subsided. Now, she could think straight.

"So. You're back."

She jumped, suppressing a scream. "Darren, my God, you startled me. What are you doing here?"

He stepped over her feet and sat on the sofa. "Waiting for you."

Even knowing Darren Mowery, Barbara thought, was a calculated risk. She'd heard the rumors in Washington. He'd gone bad, he'd lost his company, he'd been killed in South America. He was dangerous. She knew that much. She smiled uneasily. "You could have turned on the air-conditioning."

"I'm not hot."

"You must be half lizard."

They'd bumped into each other a few weeks ago at a Washington restaurant and ended up having dinner a couple of times, although Barbara had no serious romantic interest in him—or he in her, as far as she could tell. She didn't know where their relationship would lead, but her instincts told her he was important. Somehow, Darren Mowery would help her get off the grinding treadmill that had become her life. Perhaps it was because of him that she'd finally taken action against Lucy.

"You disappeared for a week," he said.

"I didn't disappear. I took a few days off. I told you."

"Where did you go?"

She didn't answer right away. Darren was a man who'd want to believe he was in charge, that he had the upper hand. He was very handsome, she had to admit. Early fifties, silvery haired. He could have stood out in Washington if he'd wanted to. Instead, he chose to blend in with his conservative dark suits and country club casuals, his only distinguishing feature his superb physical condition. He was in better shape than many men half his age, but his reflexes were the real give-away. This was not a man who'd spent the past thirty years behind a desk.

"I went outlet shopping," she said.

"Where?"

"New England." Let him think she was being evasive. She didn't care. She wanted him to know she was strong while at the same time believing he was stronger. It was a delicate balancing act.

He scratched one side of his mouth; he always looked relaxed, at ease with his surroundings. Yet he was observant, alert to every nuance around him. Barbara knew she couldn't make a misstep with such a man. He'd probably searched her apartment, she realized; but she'd anticipated as much.

No, she had no illusions. She wasn't yet sure of the exact nature of the game they were playing, but she knew Darren Mowery would kill her if she crossed him. She had to be careful, strong, sure of herself. And smart. Smarter than he was.

"We've been dancing around each other long enough," he said. "Let's put our cards on the table. I want to know everything. No surprises."

What did that mean? Did he know about her and Lucy? Barbara dodged the little needle of uncertainty and suppressed the surge of excitement that finally they were getting down to it. She shrugged, nonchalant. "All right. You first."

He studied her. He had very blue eyes. Stone-cold blue eyes. "Lucy Swift left for Wyoming today."

It wasn't what Barbara expected. Another, weaker woman might have panicked, but she sat back in her chair and yawned. She was the personal assistant to a powerful United States senator, a professional accustomed to managing the unexpected. She already knew about Lucy's trip to Wyoming; she'd found out when she'd checked in with Jack's office yesterday. Lucy must have told Jack, and a member of his staff had left Barbara a routine message. The unexpected was that Darren knew. "Yes, I know. Something to do with her adventure travel business, I believe."

"Redwing Associates is based in Wyoming."

"Ah, yes. Sebastian Redwing sold Lucy her house in Vermont. It belonged to his widowed grandmother. From what Jack tells me, he and Lucy aren't very good friends. Didn't Sebastian once work for you?" She was tempted to pick at an itchy mosquito bite, but resisted. "I gather his company is doing very well."

Mowery didn't react. Barbara liked that. It meant he had self-control. According to Washington gossip, there was no love lost between Sebastian Redwing and his old mentor. There was even talk that Mowery blamed Sebastian for the downfall of DM Consultants, Darren's private security firm.

Barbara supposed it was theoretically possible that Lucy would go whining to Sebastian about what had happened to her this week, but she doubted it. Lucy was quite determined to prove herself capable, independent— which, of course, she wasn't. Barbara had already calculated that Lucy wouldn't go to Jack or to the Capitol Police. Lucy wanted no part of being a Swift.

"I get the impression you don't like Lucy Swift very much," Darren said.

"I don't see what concern that is of yours."

He leaned forward. "Cards on the table, Barbie. I have a bone to pick with your boss. I want to make him sweat. And I want your help."

"My help?"

"I think you've got something on him," Mowery said, smug and confident.

"No. Senator Swift is a man of sterling integrity."

Mowery threw back his head and laughed.

Barbara pursed her lips. "I'm serious."

"Yeah, well, so am I. Barbie, Barbie." He shook his head at her, sighing. "Office gossip says you threw yourself at the old boy a couple weeks ago, and he laughed you out of his office."

Her stomach flipped over on her. "That's not true."

"What part? You didn't throw yourself at him or he didn't laugh?"

"You're disgusting. I want you to leave."

"No, you don't want me to leave. You want to help me settle a score with Jack Swift. You want to see him sweat. You want him to suffer for humiliating you."

"He—he wasn't prepared for the level of intimacy I offered, that's all. He was scared."

"Scared, huh?"

"He knows I've been there for him. Always. Forever."

Mowery's gaze bored through her. "What do you have on him?"

"Nothing!"

"Barbie, I'm going to put the squeeze on Senator Jack. I'm going to bleed him. You're going to watch, and you're going to enjoy the show." He reached over and touched her knee. "Revenge can be very sweet."

She said nothing.

His eyes narrowed, and he smiled. "Only it's not revenge you want, is it, Barbie? I get it now. You want Jack to suffer and come to you, the one woman who loves him unconditionally. This is precious. Truly precious."

"My motives," Barbara said, "are irrelevant."

"In twenty years, has old Jack ever made a pass at you?"

"He wouldn't. For much of that time he was a married man."

Mowery laughed out loud. "God, you're a riot. This is going to be fun."

She was on dangerous ground. Deadly ground.

Her stomach heaved, and she ran to the bathroom and vomited.

Oh, God. I can't do this.

But she had to. She'd given Darren Mowery all the signals. He *knew* this was what she wanted. Not just a chance to get back at Jack for spurning her, but a chance to provide him with the opportunity to come to her for help, to find solace in her strength and wisdom. She'd driven up to Vermont and harassed Lucy, hoping it would relieve the pressure of wanting to hurt Jack, too. But it hadn't. She loved him, and she wasn't one to give up easily on those she loved.

When she'd confided her love to him, Jack hadn't gotten angry with her or shown any passion, any heat, any depth of emotion. He'd been kind. Solicitous. Professional. He gave her the predictable speech about how much he appreciated her, how he felt affection for her as a member of his staff, and how together, over the past twenty years, they'd done so much good for the people of this great nation.

Blah-blah-blah. He'd even offered her a way out of her embarrassment, saying they'd all been under tremendous pressure and she should take a few days off.

Well, she had, hadn't she?

She splashed her face with cold water and stared at herself in the mirror. Her gray eyes were bloodshot from the effort of vomiting, the lashes clumped together from water and tearing. She was just forty-one, not old. She still could have children. She knew plenty of first-time mothers in their forties.

But she couldn't have Swift children. Jack didn't want her. Twenty years of dedicated service, and what did she have to show for it?

Lucy was the one with the Swift children.

Barbara dried her face. She could have had Colin. She could have had the Swift children. Instead, she'd waited for Jack.

Darren opened the door behind her, and she placed a hand on the sink to steady herself. "I'm sorry. My stomach's a little off. It must be the heat."

He was so smug. "Blackmail's not a game for someone with a weak stomach."

That *was* what they were tiptoeing around—and had been right from the beginning. Blackmail. She nodded, cool. It was to her advantage for him to think he was the security expert with the murky past, the dark and dangerous insider convinced he knew how the "real world" worked better than a super-competent, deskbound bureaucrat possibly could.

"Colin and I," she began. She swallowed, met Mowery's cold gaze. "We had an affair before he died. Jack doesn't know. Neither does Lucy. No one does."

"And?"

"And I have pictures."

Mowery nodded thoughtfully. "Kinky pictures?"

"You're disgusting."

"Well, if it's pictures of you two on his daddy's campaign trail—"

"By your standards, the pictures would be considered 'kinky.' By mine, they're proof of the physical and emotional bond we shared."

"Uh-huh."

"Do you want to see them?"

He rubbed his chin. "So you fucked the son, and the widowed daughter-in-law and the innocent grandkids don't know it."

"Must you be so coarse?"

"Listen to you, Barbie. You're the one who had an affair with another woman's husband. The boss's son. And this you tell me not two weeks after you threw yourself at the boss, presumably because you'd like to get some of him, too. Let's talk about who's 'coarse.'"

She was silent. Stricken.

"Well," Mowery said, "it's not pretty, but it could work."

"It will work. Jack will pay dearly to keep such information quiet." She straightened, eyed him coolly. She wanted him to think he was in control, not that she was a complete ninny. "If you're not convinced, walk out of here now. I'll forget we ever had this conversation."

He gave a curt laugh and started back down the hall to the living room. Without turning around, he motioned with one finger for her to follow.

Barbara joined him. She had to stiffen her muscles to keep herself from trembling. Goose bumps sprang up on her arms from the air-conditioning. She was cold now. Dehydrated. Not nervous, not afraid, she told herself. She was absolutely positive this was the best—the only—course of action.

"Here's the deal, Barbie. In for a penny, in for a pound. I don't do cold feet."

She raised her chin and met his gaze directly. "I'm not some weak-minded twit."

She sat stiffly on a chair and crossed her legs and arms, steeled herself against the cold of the air-conditioning, the itching, stinging bug bites, the insidious feeling that

Mowery knew more about her than she realized. She had to remember the kind of work he did, remain on her guard.

Slowly, her shivering subsided.

"Did you fuck the son," he asked, "or are you just making that up because Jack doesn't want you?"

She remained calm, practicing the restraint she'd learned in twenty years as Jack Swift's most trusted aide. "Men like you don't understand loyalty and service, true commitment."

"Damn right we don't." He grinned, deeply amused by his own wit. "Well, it doesn't matter. You can have whatever little fantasies you want, Barbie."

"I'm not a woman taken to fantasizing."

Indeed not, she thought. She wouldn't have gone to Jack if she hadn't believed with all her heart, soul and mind that he wanted her to speak up, finally, after all these years. She didn't invent this sort of thing, not after two decades in Washington. She hadn't misread the cues. Jack Swift simply wasn't prepared to act on his own feelings. He had run. And now she needed to turn him back in the right direction, back to her.

Darren jumped up, grabbed both her hands and lifted her onto her feet. Her breath caught. What now? What was he doing? He was very muscular and strong. She could never physically overpower him. She had to rely on her wits, her intelligence and incredible self-discipline.

There was nothing sexual in the way he held her. "How long has it been, Barbie? How long since you've had a man?" He squeezed her waist, choking the air from her. "Not since Colin Swift? Not ever?"

"That's none of your business." She kept her tone deliberately cold, in control. "Our relationship is strictly professional. We are partners in a scheme to blackmail a United States senator. That's *all*."

He squeezed harder, painfully. She couldn't move. "No surprises, Barbie. Understand? If this is going to work, I know everything."

"I told you—"

"Did you have an affair with Colin Swift?"

"Yes."

This had to be a test. She didn't know what to do to pass. Run screaming? Beg him to make love to her? Slap him?

No, she thought. Hold your ground. She wanted him to underestimate her, not to think he could roll over her.

"You stereotype me at your own peril, Mr. Mowery," she said. "I'm not some dried-up prune pining for a man I can't have."

"Where were you last week?"

"On vacation. I hit outlet stores all over New England."

"Vermont?"

"What?"

He moved his hands higher, squeezing her ribs. "Did you go to Vermont?"

"I can't breathe—"

"You can say yes or no."

She nodded, gasping. "Yes."

"Did you see Lucy Swift?"

She shook her head, unable to speak.

"She decided to go to Wyoming at the last minute. She paid top dollar for the tickets. She took her kids. I want to know why."

"I can't—breathe—I—"

He eased up, just slightly.

Barbara coughed, gulping in air. "Goddamn you—"

"Tell me about Lucy."

"I don't *know* anything. You'll have to ask her yourself. I went outlet shopping in Manchester one day. That's all."

Lying to him was dangerous, Barbara thought, but telling the truth had to be more dangerous.

He traced the skin just under her breasts with his thumbs. He had no sexual interest in her. His focus on his mission was total. He wasn't that complicated a man, Barbara thought, and she wasn't that undesirable a woman. Obviously his obsession with Jack Swift was something she needed to better understand.

His gaze was cold even as he released her. "Arnica," he said.

She rubbed her sides. "What?"

"Rub in a little arnica oil for the bruises."

She headed back to the bathroom. This time she didn't throw up. She washed her hands, closed the lid on the toilet and sat down. She was risking everything. She had a stimulating career, a nice apartment, a fabulous set of friends. There were men who wanted her. Good, successful men.

She didn't have to let a scummy Darren Mowery fondle her in her own living room.

After Jack had dispatched her, so politely, as if she were pathetic, she'd learned he was seeing Sidney Greenburg, a curator at the Smithsonian—fifty years old, never married, no children. Why her? Why not Barbara?

Sidney was one of Lucy's Washington friends.

I could have married Colin. I didn't have to wait for Jack.

"Barbara?"

Darren was outside the door. She didn't move.

"Here's how it's going to go down," he said. "I'll approach Jack. I'll put the squeeze on him. He's not going to risk his own reputation or sully his dead son's reputation. He'll pay. And you'll get ten percent."

She jumped up and tore open the door. "Ten percent! Forget it. I'll call the police right now. You'd have nothing without me. *I* had the affair with Colin. *I* have the pictures."

"You won't call the police," Darren said calmly.

"I *will*. You're threatening a United States senator."

"Barbara. Please." He was cold, supercilious. "If you make one wrong move once this thing gets started, I'll be there. Trust me. You won't want that."

Her stomach turned in on itself. She clutched it in silent agony. What if Lucy went crying to Sebastian Redwing because of her harassment campaign? "Bastard."

"Bingo. You got that one right."

Barbara held up her chin, summoning twenty years of experience at using other people's arrogance to her own advantage. And to Jack's. "Jack couldn't survive a week in this town without me, and he knows it. When he comes to me, you'd better be far away. That's your only warning."

"Oh, is it? Get this straight, Barbie." Mowery leaned in close, enunciated each word clearly. "I don't care if you fucked Swift father and son at the same time. I don't care if you made up the whole goddamn thing. We're putting this show on the road, and we're doing it my way."

Acid rose up in her throat. "I can't believe I let you touch me."

He laughed. "And you will again, Barbie. Trust me on that."

He swaggered back down the hall. She spat at his back, missing by yards. He laughed harder.

"Fifty percent," she yelled.

He stopped, glanced back at her.

She was choking for air. Dear God, what had she done? "I want fifty percent of the take."

"The take? Okay, Dick Tracy. I'll give you twenty-five percent."

"Fifty. I deserve it."

He winked at her. "I like you, Barbie. You got the short end of the stick with the Swifts, and you keep on fighting. Yep. I like you a lot."

"I'm serious. I want fifty percent."

"Barbie, maybe you should think this through." He rocked back on his heels. "I'm not a very nice man. I expect you know that by now. My sympathy for you only goes so far."

She hesitated. Her head was spinning. This wasn't a time for cold feet, any sign of weakness. "Twenty-five percent, then," she said.

Jack Swift poured himself a second glass of wine. It was a dry apple-pear wine from a new winery in his home state. He toasted Sidney Greenburg, who was still on her first glass. "To the wines of Rhode Island."

She laughed. "Yes, but not to this particular bottle. I love fruit wines, Jack, but this one's pure rot-gut."

He laughed, too. "It is, isn't it? Well, I've never been

much of a wine connoisseur. A good scotch—that's something I can understand."

It was a very warm, humid, still evening. They were sitting out in the tiny brick courtyard of his Georgetown home. Rhode Island, his home state, the state he'd represented first in the House, then in the Senate, seemed far away tonight. This was where he'd raised his son, where he'd nursed his wife through her long, losing battle with cancer. They were both gone now. He'd been tempted to sell the house. He'd bought it in his early days in Washington; it'd go for a mint. He'd even debated quitting the Senate. Barbara Allen had talked him out of both. Over twenty years, she'd saved him from many a precipitous move.

"I don't know what to do, Sidney." He stared at the pale wine. He and Sidney had been discussing Barbara Allen most of the evening. "She's been with me since she was a college intern."

"You're not going to do anything."

"I can't just pretend—"

"Yes, you can, and you'll be doing her a favor if you do."

Sidney set her glass on the garden table. That she had such affection for him was a constant source of amazement. He was an old widower, a gray-haired, paunchy United States senator who wasn't eaten up with his own self-importance. She was a striking woman, with very dark eyes and dark hair liberally streaked with gray. She wore little makeup, and she complained about carrying more weight than she liked around her hips and thighs; Jack hadn't noticed. She was intelligent, kind, experienced and self-assured, comfortable in her own skin. She'd worked with Lucy's parents at the Smithsonian and had known Lucy since she was a little girl, long before Lucy had met Colin.

"Listen to me, Jack," she said. "Barbara is not a pathetic woman. You are not to feel sorry for her because she's forty and unmarried. If she's given herself to her job to the exclusion of her personal life, that was her choice. Allow her the dignity of having made that choice. And don't assume just because she doesn't have a husband and children, she must not have a full life."

"I haven't! I wouldn't—"

"Of course, you would. People do it all the time." She smiled, taking any edge off her words. "If Barbara Allen's feeling a little goofy and off-center right now, accept it at face value and give her a chance to get over it."

Jack sighed. "She practically threw herself at me."

"And I suppose you've never had a *married* woman throw herself at you?"

"Well…"

"Come on, Jack. If Barbara's nuts unmarried, she'd be nuts married."

He held back a smile. As educated and refined as Sidney was, she did know how to cut to the chase. "I didn't say she was nuts."

"That's my point exactly." Her eyes shone, and she spoke with conviction, laughing at his frown. "You are a very dense man for someone who has to go before the people for votes. Jack, the woman made a pass at you. It's been three years since Colin's death, five years since Eleanor's death. You've only just begun dating again. I see her actions as—" She shrugged. "Perfectly normal."

He drank more of his wine. The damn stuff all tasted the same to him, whether it was made from pears, apples or grapes. "Maybe so."

"But?"

"I don't know."

"The unmarried forty-year-old in the office makes people nervous. They never know if she's a little dotty, living in squalor with twenty-five cats."

"That's archaic, Sidney."

She waved a hand dismissively. "It's true. If Barbara were married and made a pass at you, you'd be flattered. You wouldn't sit here squirming over what to do. You'd think she was a normal, healthy woman." She grabbed up his hand. "Jack, I've *been* there."

"No one could ever think you were off your gourd."

She smiled. "I have two cats. I've been known to feed them off the china."

He saw the twinkle in her eye and laughed. That was what he treasured about Sidney most of all. She made him laugh. She was quick-witted, self-deprecating, irreverent. She didn't take her job, herself, or life inside the Beltway too seriously.

But Jack couldn't shake a lingering sense of uneasiness. "There's still something about Barbara."

"Then there's something about Barbara. Period."

"I see what you're saying—"

"Finally!" Sidney fell back against her chair, as if his denseness had exhausted her. "Now, can we change the subject?"

He smiled. "Gladly."

She gave him an impish grin. "Let's talk about my cats."

Sidney didn't stay the night. They both had unusual Saturday meetings, but Jack knew that really wasn't the issue. "I'm just not ready to hang my panty hose in a senator's bathroom," she said breezily, kissing him good-night.

He remembered her counsel the next morning when he arrived in his office at eight and Barbara Allen, as ever, was at her desk. Before he could say a word, she gave him a bright smile. "Good morning, Senator."

"Good morning, Barbara. I thought you were still on vacation."

She waved a hand. "It was a few days off, not a vacation. I always planned to be back for this meeting. I know it's important."

He smiled. "Well, then, how were your few days off?"

"Perfect," she said. "Just what I needed."

She flipped around in her chair and tapped a few keys on her computer. She looked great, Jack thought—relaxed, polished, professional, with none of the wild desperation that had made them both so uncomfortable the week before.

Relief washed over him. A little time away had done the trick. He would follow Sidney's advice and pretend nothing had happened. It wasn't just a question of doing Barbara a favor—he was doing himself a favor, too. He needed her efficiency, knowledge and competence, her long years of experience.

He headed into his private office. Thank God, she was back to her old self.

Chapter 3

"Bastian Redwing saved Daddy's life?"

Madison sighed at her brother with exaggerated patience. "It's not *Bastian*. It's *Sebastian*. And he saved Dad *and* Grandpa. Some other guy saved the president."

J.T. frowned. "How come I don't remember?"

"Because you weren't born."

"Madison doesn't remember, either," Lucy said. "It happened before your dad and I were married."

"I read the articles," Madison reminded her mother.

J.T. kicked the back of her seat. They'd rented a car when they'd arrived in Jackson yesterday, and this morning Lucy had dutifully met with the western guides, who were wonderful and all but told her outright she had no business trying to expand out west. No surprise there.

Afterward, she'd almost talked herself out of following her hotel desk clerk's directions to see Sebastian. Almost. She still had time to turn around and go back to Jackson.

"Was it an assassination attempt?" J.T. asked. "Tell me!"

Madison was horrified. "Mom, how does he know something like 'assassination attempt'? That shouldn't be in a twelve-year-old's vocabulary."

J.T. snorted from the back seat. "Oh, yeah? Then how am I supposed to know about Abraham Lincoln and Martin Luther King? And President Kennedy and Julius Caesar?"

"Julius Caesar?" Madison swung around at him. "You don't know anything about Julius Caesar."

"He was stabbed in the back."

"You're sick."

"*You're* sick."

Lucy gripped the steering wheel. She was on a stretch of clear, straight road, trying to enjoy the breathtaking Wyoming scenery. The mountains surrounding the long, narrow valley, she thought, were incredible. She'd pointed out the different vegetation to Madison and J.T., explained about the altitude, the dry air. But they wanted to discuss Sebastian Redwing and how he'd saved their father's life.

Lucy gave up and told the story. "The president was giving a speech in Newport, Rhode Island. Someone got in with a gun and started firing. Sebastian knocked Grandpa and Dad to the floor, while the man he worked for at the time, Darren Mowery, tackled the shooter."

"Was anyone hurt?" J.T. asked.

"Sebastian spotted a second shooter, who'd actually helped the other guy get inside. Sebastian, your dad and

another man, Plato Rabedeneira, a parachute rescue
jumper who was being honored, went after him. The
man shot Plato in the shoulder, but it wasn't serious."

"What happened to the shooter?"

Lucy hesitated. "Sebastian killed him."

"Sebastian had a gun? Why?" J.T. was into the story
now. "What was he doing there?"

How to explain Sebastian Redwing? All J.T. knew
about him was that he'd sold them their house. Lucy
slowed the car. "Sebastian was a security consultant.
He was very young—he and Darren Mowery, his boss,
were after the shooter for some other reason. They had
no idea they'd get mixed up in an attempt to assassinate
the president of the United States."

"Dad, Plato and Sebastian all became friends," Madison added. "Sebastian was the best man at Mom and
Dad's wedding."

J.T. was hopelessly confused. "I don't get it."

His sister moaned. "What is there to 'get'?"

"Sebastian has his own company now, J.T.," Lucy
said. "Redwing Associates. It's based here in Wyoming.
He and Plato and Dad weren't able to see as much of
each other as they'd have liked."

That seemed to satisfy her son.

"At least Sebastian had the sense to get out of Vermont," Madison said.

They came to a cluster of log buildings set in a
grassy, rolling meadow. No marker announced this
was the base and main training facility for Redwing
Associates, an international investigative and security
firm with clients ranging from business executives and
government officials to high-profile entertainers and
sports figures. Many came here, to Wyoming, to learn

for themselves how to assess, prevent and manage the risks they faced, whether it was kidnapping, assassination, corporate espionage, disgruntled ex-employees, obsessed fans or computer fraud.

Security was subtle but not unnoticeable. When Lucy came to the end of the long, winding driveway, a man in casual western attire introduced himself. "I'm Jim Charger, Mrs. Swift. I'll take care of your car. Mr. Rabedeneira is expecting you."

She tried to smile. "Plato Rabedeneira?"

Jim Charger didn't return her smile. "That's right, ma'am."

What was Plato doing here? And why was he expecting her? Lucy fought off a rush of uneasiness. "Well, I guess you guys really are that good, aren't you?"

Still no smile. "Your children can stay out here with me or go in with you. Your choice."

"They'll go with me."

He motioned for her to go into the sprawling main house, its rustic log construction deceiving. This was no ordinary ranch house. No expense had been spared in its furnishings of wood, leather and earth-colored fabrics. The views were astounding. Not one square inch of it reminded her of Sebastian's roots in southern Vermont.

Plato joined her in the living room, in front of a massive stone fireplace. He took both her hands and kissed her on the cheek. "Hello, Lucy. I heard you were in the area."

"You must have spies on every corner."

"Not *every* corner."

He laughed, dropping her hands. He was a dark-haired, dark-eyed, intensely handsome man who'd worked his way out of a very tough Providence neighborhood into a very tough profession, where he'd excelled. He'd helped his mother, who'd raised him alone, earn her college degree; she was now a professor at a community college, and one of Jack Swift's constituents.

Colin, Lucy thought, had never been tempted to jump out of a helicopter into the teeth of a storm to rescue fishermen and yachters. He had been content with his work at the State Department and testing himself on the tennis court—which had killed him.

"When did you start working for Redwing Associates?" Lucy asked.

"I was injured in a rescue jump eighteen months ago. When I woke up from surgery, my summons from Sebastian was waiting for me." He turned to Madison and J.T., both obviously enthralled. "Well, you two have grown up. It's great to see you."

He was so charming, Lucy thought. She would feel safe if she had to dangle from a rescue helicopter over churning seas with him. Colin had been well-mannered and kind, a man people tended to like automatically. Sebastian Redwing, she thought, was none of the above. He wasn't charming, well-mannered, kind or likeable. He wouldn't care about making her or anyone else feel safe. That, he would say, was up to them. He was just very, very good at what he did.

"You kids want a grand tour of the place?" Plato asked. "Go back out front. Tell Mr. Charger I'd like him to show you around."

The prospect of a tour clearly excited J.T. more than it did Madison, who seemed transfixed by her father's ultra-fit, very good-looking friend. But she went along with her brother, and Lucy suddenly felt self-conscious, even a little foolish. Redwing Associates dealt with real threats and real dangers. Kidnapping, extortion, terrorist attacks. Not late-night hang-ups and bullets dropped through an open car window.

"You're looking well, Lucy," Plato said, eyeing her.

"Thanks."

"How's Vermont?"

"Great—I have my own adventure travel company. It's doing surprisingly well for a relatively new company."

"I don't get adventure travel, I'll admit."

She smiled. "That's because you've had to clean up after too many adventures gone wrong. Safety is our first priority, you'll be glad to know."

He moved to the leather chair, and she noticed his slight limp. It would never do in the demanding world he'd left, and at Redwing Associates, it would keep him behind a desk.

He dropped onto the couch, his expression turning serious. "You want to tell me why you're here?"

"I had business in Jackson. I just thought I'd stop in and say hello."

"You didn't know I'd be here," he pointed out.

"I know, but Sebastian—"

"Lucy. Come on. Since when would you or anyone else make a special trip to say hello to Sebastian?"

She sat on the edge of a wood-armed chair, thinking it would be nice if she could just sit here and visit with an old friend, reminisce about the past, forget the bullet hole in her dining room wall.

Of course, Plato would see through her halfhearted story. Cold feet were probably common in both his past and current work.

At least Plato had sent flowers and written a card when Colin died. He couldn't get away for the funeral, he said, but if she ever needed anything, she had only to let him know. He'd be there. Colin had trusted him, too. But, possibly because of the different nature of their work—or their personalities—it was Sebastian he'd made her promise to go to if she ever needed help.

"Has he changed?" she asked.

"That depends on your point of view. Look," Plato said, "why don't you tell me what's going on. Then we can figure out what to do about it."

Meaning, whether she needed to bring it to Sebastian's attention.

Lucy twisted her hands together. At home, in her business, she was at ease, confident, capable. This was foreign ground for her. Sebastian Redwing and Plato Rabedeneira had been her husband's friends. She and Colin had fallen in love so fast, marrying within two months of their first date. Madison had come along the next year. Then J.T. And then Colin was gone.

She really didn't know Plato *or* Sebastian.

"Lucy?"

"It's silly. I'm being silly, and I know it. So please feel free to pat me on the head and send me back to Vermont." She leveled her eyes on him. "Trust me, you'd be doing me a favor."

"Well, before I do any head-patting, why don't you tell me what's going on first. Okay?"

She nodded, gulped in a breath and told him everything. She kept her tone unemotional and objective, and left out nothing except her own reactions, the palpable sense of fear, the nausea.

When she finished, she managed another smile. "You see? Pure silliness."

Plato rose stiffly, his limp more noticeable as he walked to the massive stone fireplace. He looked back at her, his dark eyes serious. "You won't go to the local police?"

"If you're convinced it's the best thing to do, I'll consider it. But they'll call Jack."

He nodded. "That might not be such a bad idea."

"These incidents—whatever they are—have nothing to do with him."

"Maybe not. The point is, you don't know why they're happening."

Lucy ran a hand through her hair. She felt light-headed, a little sick to her stomach. Jet lag, the dry air and the altitude were all taking their toll. So was reliving the events of the past week.

"Either there's no connection at all between these incidents," she said, "or someone's just trying to get under my skin. If I go to the police, it proves they succeeded."

"And if they don't get the desired reaction from you, the incidents could escalate."

"Damn." She sank back against the couch and kicked out her legs. "I don't have a clue what the 'desired reaction' is. Coming out here? Fine, the bastard can declare victory and get out of my life. Running screaming into the night? Forget it." She jumped to her feet. "I won't fall apart for anyone."

"What does your gut tell you?" His voice was quiet, soothing. Plato was very good at caring.

"I don't *know.*" Lucy paced on the thick, dark carpet. "Plato, I'm not a normal person. I'm the widowed daughter-in-law of a United States senator. You know damn well Jack will send in the Capitol Police."

"Lucy—"

"I have a business to tend. I have kids to raise. Damn it, I'm all Madison and J.T. have. I'm not going to put myself in undue danger, but I won't—Plato, if I can possibly avoid it, I'd rather not have Jack and a bunch of feds mucking around in my life."

Plato placed an arm around her shoulders. "It's okay. I understand. Look, I have to be in Frankfurt this next week—"

"I wasn't hinting you should drop everything and come to my rescue. I just wanted an expert opinion." She smiled a little. "It felt good to tell someone."

He smiled back, but shook his head, giving her upper arm a gentle squeeze. "You didn't come for *my* expert opinion."

"I would have if I'd known you were here. I'd much rather tell my troubles to you than Sebastian."

He laughed. "Who wouldn't?"

"Good. Then it's settled. I'll trust my gut instincts. I'll go home and hope nothing else happens—"

"No, Lucy, you're going to see Sebastian and tell him everything."

"Isn't he going to Frankfurt?"

"No way. He's..." Plato frowned, walking her toward the door. He seemed to be searching for the right words. "He's on sabbatical."

"Sabbatical? Come on, Plato. It's not like he's some kind of professor. How can he—"

"You'll have to drive out to his cabin," Plato said. "It's not that far. I'll give you directions."

Lucy slipped from his embrace and stood rock-still

in the middle of the hall. He kept walking, his back to her. She was blinking rapidly, as if that might somehow clear her head.

"I don't want to see Sebastian," she said.

Plato turned back to her. "He can help you, Lucy. I can't."

"I told you, I didn't come here for help."

"I know why you came here." His dark, dark eyes seemed to burn into her. "You promised Colin you would."

Her throat caught. "Plato..."

"Colin was right to send you to Sebastian. Lucy, I did rescues, and now I keep this company out of hot water. Sebastian's a son of a bitch in a lot of ways, but he's the best."

Lucy stood her ground. "What if I drive on out of here without seeing him?"

"Then I'll have to tell him what you told me."

She eyed him. "I have a feeling that would be worse."

He gave her a devilish smile. "Much worse."

Plato's directions were simple. He put Lucy on a dirt road and said to keep going until she couldn't go anymore. She'd know when she reached Sebastian.

Lucy wasn't encouraged. However, not finishing what she'd stupidly started seemed to carry more risks than finishing. If he told Sebastian her story, Plato might exaggerate. Then Sebastian might end up in Vermont, and she'd really be in a mess. Sebastian might be worse than the feds. He might be worse than the occasional stray bullet through her dining room window.

So *why* had she dragged herself and her two children out to Wyoming?

The road was winding, dry, hot and dusty. The scenery was spectacular. Wide-open country, mountains rising up from the valley floor, a snaking river, horses and cattle and wildflowers. Despite its other uses, this was still a working ranch.

J.T. loved it. Madison endured. "I'm pretending I'm Meryl Streep in *Out of Africa*," she said. "That might keep me awake."

"The high altitude is probably making you sleepy," Lucy said.

"I'm not sleepy, I'm bored."

"Madison."

She checked herself. "Sorry."

The road narrowed even more, their car kicking up so much dust Lucy made a mental note to run it through a car wash before taking it back to the rental agency. Finally, they came to a tiny, ramshackle log cabin and small outbuilding tucked into the shade of a cluster of aspens and firs. The road ended.

Lucy pulled in behind a dusty red truck. "Well," she said, "I guess this is it."

"Oh, yuck." Madison surveyed the pathetic buildings. "This is like Clint Eastwood in *Unforgiven*."

From *Out of Africa* to *Unforgiven*. Lucy smiled. Madison kept the local video store in an uproar trying to track down movies for her. It was an interest one of her teachers, in the school she so loathed, encouraged.

Three scroungy, big mutts bounded out from the shade and surrounded their car, barking and growling as if they'd never seen a stranger. J.T., his seat belt off, nervously stuck his head up front. "Do you think they bite?"

"I bet they have fleas," Madison said.

Lucy judiciously decided to roll down her window and see how the dogs reacted. They didn't jump. Possibly a good sign. "Hello," she called out the window. "Anyone around?"

She checked for any venomous, antisocial bumper stickers on the truck, like Vermonters Go Home. Nothing. Just rust.

The dogs suddenly went silent. The yellow Lab mix yawned and stretched. The German shepherd mix plopped down and scratched himself. The smallest of the three—an unidentifiable mix that had resulted in a white coat with black and brown splotches—paced and panted.

"You kids hear anyone call them off?" Lucy asked.

J.T. shook his head, his eyes wide. This was more adventure than he'd bargained for, out in the wilds of Wyoming with three grouchy dogs and no friendly humans in sight. "No, did you?"

Madison huffed. "Plato should have sent us with an armed guard."

Lucy sighed. "Madison, that doesn't help."

"You're scaring me," J.T. said.

"You two stay here while I go see if we have the right place." Lucy unfastened her seat belt and climbed out of the car. The air seemed hotter, even drier. The dogs paid no attention to her. She smiled at her nervous son. "See, J.T.? It's okay."

He nodded dubiously.

"Relax, Lucy." The male voice seemed to come from nowhere. "You've got the right place."

J.T. swooped across the back seat and pointed at the cabin. "There! Someone's on the porch!"

Lucy shot her children a warning look. "Stay here."

She mounted two flat, creaky, dusty steps onto the unprepossessing porch. An ancient, ratty rope hammock hung from rusted hooks. In it lay a dust-covered man with a once-white cowboy hat pulled down over his face. He wore jeans, a chambray shirt with its sleeves rolled up to the elbows, cowboy boots. All of it was scuffed, worn.

Lucy noted the long legs, the flat stomach, the muscled, tanned forearms and the callused, tanned hands. Sebastian Redwing, she remembered, had always been a very physical man.

The yellow Lab lumbered onto the porch and collapsed under the hammock in a *kalumph* that seemed to shake the entire cabin.

"Sebastian?"

The man pushed the hat off his face. It, too, was dusty and tanned, and more lined and angular than she remembered. His eyes settled on her. Like everything else, they seemed the color of dust. She remembered they were gray, an unusual, surprisingly soft gray. "Hello, Lucy."

Her mouth and lips were dry from the long drive, the low western humidity. "Plato sent me."

"I figured."

"I'm in Wyoming on business. I have the kids with me. Madison and J.T."

He said nothing. He didn't look as if he planned to move from the hammock.

"Mom! J.T.'s bleeding!"

Madison, panicked, leaped out of the car and dragged her brother from the back seat. He cupped his hands under his nose, blood dripping through his fingers.

"Oh, gross," his sister said, standing back as she thrust a paper napkin at him.

Lucy ran toward them. "Tilt your head back."

The German shepherd barked at J.T. Sebastian gave a low, barely audible command from his hammock, and the dog backed off.

J.T., struggling not to cry, stumbled up onto the porch. "I bled all over the car."

Madison was right behind him. "He did, Mom."

Sebastian materialized at Lucy's side. She'd forgotten how tall and lean he was, how uneasy she'd always felt around him. Not afraid. Just uneasy. He glanced at J.T. "Kid's fine. It's the dry air and the dust."

Madison gaped at him. Lucy concentrated on her bleeding son. "May we use your sink?"

"Don't have one. You can get water from the pump out back." He eyed Madison. "You know how to use an outdoor pump?"

She shook her head.

"Time you learned." He was calm, his voice quiet if not soothing. "Lucy, you can bring J.T. inside. Madison and I will meet you."

She shrank back, her eyes widening.

Lucy said, "It's okay, Madison."

Sebastian frowned, as if he couldn't fathom what about him would be a cause for concern—a dusty man in an isolated cabin with three dogs and no running water. He started down the steps. Madison took a breath and followed, glancing back at Lucy and mouthing, "Unabomber."

Lucy got J.T. inside. The prosaic exterior did not deceive. In addition to no running water, there was no electricity. It was like being catapulted back a century to the frontier.

"It's just a nosebleed," J.T. said, stuffing the paper napkin up his nose. "I'm fine."

Lucy grabbed a ragged dish towel from a hook above a wooden counter. The kitchen. There was oatmeal, cornmeal, coffee, cans of beans, jars of salsa and, incongruously, a jug of pure Vermont maple syrup.

In a few minutes, Madison came through the back door with a pitted aluminum pitcher of water. Lucy dipped in the towel. "I think you've stopped bleeding, J.T. Let's just get you cleaned up, okay?" She glanced at her daughter. "Where's Sebastian?"

"Out taming wild horses or hunting buffalo, I don't know. *Mom*. He doesn't even have a bathroom."

"This place is pretty rustic."

Madison groaned. "Clint Eastwood, *Unforgiven*. I told you."

Sebastian walked in from the front porch. "What's she doing watching R-rated movies? She's not seventeen."

"That's without a parent or parental permission." Lucy stifled an urge to tell him to mind his own damn business, but since he hadn't invited her to come out here, she kept her mouth shut. "Madison's a student of film history. I watched *Unforgiven* with her because it's so violent."

He frowned at her. "I'm not violent."

Lucy had always considered him a man of controlled violence in a violent profession, but before she could say anything, Madison jumped in. "But you live like Eastwood in that opening scene with his two children—"

"No, I don't. I don't have hogs."

That obviously settled it as far as he was concerned. Lucy shook her head at Madison to keep her from arguing her point. For once, her daughter took the hint.

"How's J.T.?" Sebastian asked.

"He's better," Lucy said. "Thanks for your help."

J.T. kept the wet towel pressed to his nose. "It doesn't hurt."

"Good." Sebastian didn't seem particularly worried. "You two kids can go down to the barn and look at the horses while I talk to your mother. Dogs'll go with you."

"Come on, J.T.," Madison said, playing the protective big sister for a change. "The barn can't be any worse than this place."

She and her brother retreated, both getting dirtier with every passing minute. If the dry air, dust and altitude bothered Madison, she'd never admit it.

Sebastian grunted. "Kid has a mouth on her."

"They're both great kids," Lucy said.

He turned to her. She was intensely aware of the silence. No hum of fans or air-conditioning, no cars, not even a bird twittering. "I'm sure they are."

"Plato said you were on some kind of sabbatical."

"Sabbatical? So that's what he's saying now. Hell. I have to remember his mother's a professor."

"You're not—"

Something in his eyes stopped her. Lucy could count on one hand the times she'd actually seen Sebastian Redwing, but she remembered his unnerving capacity to make her think he could see into her soul. She expected it was a skill that helped him in his work. She wondered if it was part of why he was living out here. Perhaps he'd seen too much. Most likely, he just didn't want to be around people.

"Tell me why you're here," he said.

"I promised Colin." It sounded so archaic when she said it. She pushed back her hair, too aware of herself for her own comfort. "I told him if I ever needed help, I'd come to you. So, here I am. Except I really don't need your help, after all."

"You don't?"

She shook her head. "No."

"Good. I'd hate for you to have wasted a trip." He started back across the worn floorboards toward the porch. "I'm not in the helping business."

She was stunned. "What?"

"Plato'll feed you, get you back on the road before dark."

Lucy stared at his back as he went out onto the porch. In the cabin's dim light, she saw an iron bed in one corner of the room, cast-off running shoes, a book of Robert Penn Warren poetry, a stack of James Bond novels and one of Joe Citro's books of Vermont ghost stories. There was also a kerosene lamp.

This was not what she'd expected. Redwing Associates was high-tech and very serious, one of the best investigative and security consulting firms in the business. Sebastian's brainchild. He knew his way around the world. If nothing else, Lucy had expected she might have to hold him back, keep him from moving too fast and too hard on her behalf.

Instead, he'd turned her down flat. Without argument. Without explanation.

She took a breath. The dust, altitude and dry air hadn't given her a bloody nose like they had J.T. They'd just driven every drop of sanity and common sense right out of her. She *never* should have come here.

She followed him out onto the porch. "You're going to take my word for it that I don't need help?"

"Sure." He dropped back into his hammock. "You're a smart lady. You know if you need help or not."

"What if it was all bluster? What if I'm bluffing? What if I'm too proud and—"

"And so?"

She clenched her fists at her sides, resisting an urge to hit something. "Plato fudged it when he said you were on sabbatical, didn't he? I'll bet Madison was more right than she realized."

"Lucy, if I wanted you to know about my life, I'd send you Christmas cards." He grabbed his hat and lay back in the hammock. "Have you ever gotten a Christmas card from me?"

"No, and I hope I never do."

She spun around so abruptly, the blood rushed out of her head. She reeled, steadying herself. Damn if she'd let herself pass out. The bastard would dump a pitcher of well water on her head, strap her to a horse and send her on her way.

"I'm sorry, Lucy. Things change." She couldn't tell if he'd softened, but thought he might have. "I guess you know that better than most of us."

She turned back to him and inhaled, regaining some semblance of self-control. She was furious with herself for having come out here—and with Plato for having sent her when he had to know the reception she'd get. She was out of her element, and she hated it. "That's it, then? You're not going to help me?"

He gave her a half smile and pulled his hat back down over his eyes. "Who're you kidding, Lucy Blacker? You've never needed anyone's help."

* * *

Plato didn't come for Sebastian until early the next morning. Very early. Dawn was spilling out on the horizon, and Sebastian, having tended the horses and the dogs, was back in his hammock when Plato's truck pulled up. He thumped onto the porch, his gait uneven from his limp. It'd be two years soon. He'd have the limp for life.

"You turned Lucy down?"

Sebastian tilted his hat back off his eyes. "So did you."

"She didn't come out here for my help. She came for yours."

"She hates me, you know."

Plato grinned. "Of course she hates you. You're a jackass and a loser."

Sebastian didn't take offense. Plato had always been one to speak out loud what others were thinking. "Her kid bled on my porch. How am I going to protect a twelve-year-old kid who gets nosebleeds? The daughter's a snot. She kept comparing me to Clint Eastwood."

"Eastwood? Nah. He's older and better-looking than you." Plato laughed. "I guess Lucy and her kids are lucky you've renounced violence."

"We're all lucky."

Silence.

Sebastian felt a gnawing pain in his lower back. He'd slept in the hammock. A bad idea.

"You didn't tell her, did you?" Plato asked.

"Tell her what?"

"That you've renounced violence."

"None of her business. None of yours, either."

If his curtness bothered Plato, he didn't say. "Darren Mowery's hanging around her father-in-law."

"Shut up, Rabedeneira. You're like a damn rooster crowing in my ear."

Plato stepped closer. "This is Lucy, Sebastian."

He rolled off the hammock. That was what he'd been thinking all night. This was Lucy. Lucy Blacker, with the big hazel eyes and the bright smile and the smart mouth. Lucy, Colin's widow.

"She should go to the police," Sebastian said.

"She can't, not with what she has so far. Jack Swift would pounce. The Capitol police would send up a team to investigate. The press would be all over the story." Plato stopped, groaning. "You didn't let her get that far, did you?"

"Plato, I swear to God, I wish you were still jumping out of helicopters rescuing people. I could sell the company and retire, instead of letting some dipshit busybody like you run it."

"You didn't even hear her out? I don't believe it. Jesus, Redwing. You really are an asshole."

Sebastian started down the porch steps. He was stiff, and he needed coffee. He needed to stop thinking about Lucy. Thinking about Lucy had never, ever done him any good. "I figured she told you everything. No need to make her go through it twice."

"Lucy deserves—"

"I don't care what Lucy deserves."

Sebastian could feel his friend staring at him, knowing what he was thinking, and why he'd slept out on the porch. "Yeah, you do. That's the problem. You've been in love with her for sixteen years."

That was Plato. Always speaking out loud what was

best left unsaid. Sebastian walked out to his truck. It was turning into a beautiful day. He could go riding. He could take a run with the dogs. He could read ghost stories in his hammock.

The truth was, he was no damn good. About all he hadn't done in the past year since he'd shot a friend gone bad was kick the dogs. He'd renounced violence, but not gambling, not carousing, not ignoring his friends and responsibilities. He didn't shave often enough. He didn't do laundry often enough. He could afford all the help he needed, but that meant having people around him and being nice. He didn't have much use for people. And he wasn't very nice.

"I can't help Lucy," he said. "I've forgotten half of what I knew."

"You're so full of shit, Redwing. You haven't forgotten a goddamn thing." Plato came and stood beside him. The warm, dry air, he said, helped the pain in his leg. And he liked the work. He was good at it. "Even if you're rusty—which you aren't—you still have your instincts. They're a part of you."

Then the violence was a part of him, too. Sebastian tore open his truck door. "I hate bullshit pep talks."

"Redwing—goddamn it. You've never felt sorry for yourself for one minute of your life, have you?"

He had. The day he watched Lucy Blacker walk down the aisle and marry another man.

Sebastian squinted at the dawn. "Tell me what's going on with Lucy."

Plato told him. He was succinct and objective, and Sebastian didn't like any of it. "It's the kids and their friends," he said. "Maybe just their friends."

"It's Mowery, and you know it."

"Mowery's not my problem."

"I had your plane gassed up," Plato said. "They haven't taken your pilot's license, have they?"

Sebastian smacked the dusty roof of his truck. *Damn.* "I'd rather go through drown-proofing again than fly to Vermont."

"You never went through drown-proofing. That was part of my training. I'm the ex-parachute rescue jumper."

"You are?" Sebastian grinned at his old friend. It had been a bad day when he'd learned Plato Rabedeneira was finished jumping out of helicopters, might not even walk again. "I thought that was me."

Plato grinned back. "Lucy's prettier than ever, isn't she?"

"Shut up, Rabedeneira, before I find a helicopter and throw you out of it."

"Been there, done that." Plato stood beside him. "I'll have someone look after the dogs and horses."

"Damn," Sebastian said under his breath.

He knew what he had to do. He'd known it the minute Lucy Blacker Swift had rolled into his driveway. Arguing about it with Plato was just a delay tactic.

He climbed into his truck and followed Plato out the dirt road.

Chapter 4

Jack knew he should call the Capitol Police and have them arrest Darren Mowery and bodily remove him from the premises. There really was no question. The bastard was threatening a United States senator. This was *blackmail*.

But Jack didn't reach for his phone or stand up and yell to his staff. He just glared at Mowery, paralyzed. Like most of Washington, Jack had thought Darren Mowery dead, or at least out of the country for good. Instead, here he was in a senator's office.

"Think hard, Senator," Mowery said. "Think hard before you say anything."

Jack summoned his tremendous, hard-won capacity for self-control. "Damn you. I'd like to wipe that smirk off your face."

Mowery shrugged. "Go ahead and buzz the Capitol

Police. They look bored today. I think they'd get a kick out of bouncing a blackmailer from a senator's office."

"Don't you think walking into my office has raised a few eyebrows already?"

"That's not my concern."

Jack could feel the pain gnawing in his lower abdomen. Nerves. Outrage. That Mowery had confronted him in his office only added to the effrontery, the sheer insult of the man's presence.

What he did now, Jack knew, would determine his legacy as a United States senator. This was what his thirty years in Washington would boil down to—this moment. How he responded to blackmail.

He glanced around at the framed pictures and the letters of thanks, the awards, all the evidence of his long, proud career in public service. He wasn't an arrogant, power-hungry politician. To him, public service was a high and honorable calling.

"You're a cocky bastard, Mowery." He was surprised at how calm he sounded, how restrained. Inside, his guts were roiling. "You'll never get away with blackmailing a United States senator."

"I don't think of myself as blackmailing a United States senator. I think of myself as blackmailing a father who doesn't want the world to know his son was balling a woman who wasn't his wife, two weeks before he dropped dead on a Washington tennis court."

Jack felt a sudden, stabbing pain, a hot arrow through him. He took a shallow breath. "I want you out of my office. Now."

"I can arrange to have you see a sample of the pictures." Mowery leaned forward on his chair, confident, his gaze as cold and calculating as any Jack had ever seen. "Go ahead, Senator. Call the Capitol Police. Have them haul me off. I've slipped the noose before. I'll slip it again. And even if I don't, the pictures go out."

"You smug, insolent—"

"Yeah, yeah."

"I won't pay one single, solitary dime to you."

"Okeydokey." Mowery got to his feet. He wore a light gray suit, fitting in with the tourists, lobbyists, press and staff floating around the Senate office building. The perfect Everyman. "Consider the first batch of pictures already on its way to various media outlets and to Lucy Swift, the wronged widow."

Jack couldn't speak. His jaw ached from tension. The stabbing pain in his lower abdomen spread upward. He almost wished he could drop dead of a heart attack right here, right now. He'd watched his son collapse and die. It had been so quick, so unexpected. So easy.

Colin. Dear God. What did a father owe his dead son's memory? What did he, Jack Swift, United States senator, owe his son's widow, his son's children?

And what did he owe the people of his state? Himself?

"Remember, Senator." Mowery seemed very sure of himself. "Sex scandals are always fresh, particularly when they're about anyone or anything related to a powerful, sanctimonious, squeaky-clean senator."

"How *dare* you."

Mowery ignored him. "And, of course, no matter what the papers do, Lucy will know. You won't be able to stuff that cat back into the bag once she sees her dead husband with another woman's mouth—"

"Stop. Just stop. Colin's been dead for three years. Have you no decency?"

"He didn't. Why should I?"

"It's my decency you're preying on," Jack said, more to himself than to the man standing across from him.

"Look, Jack. You can't change what your baby boy did. You can't change that I know about it and have pictures. You can only decide if it's going to remain between us or if the whole world's going to know."

"I could kill you with my bare hands." Jack could hear his voice cracking; he sounded ancient, pathetic. He was a goddamn dinosaur. "Damn you, if I were younger—"

"Well, my friend, guess what? You're not younger. And you don't have the pictures. I do. And," he added pointedly, "I'm better at this than you are. I have contingency plans. You pay me or you lose. Period."

"I won't sell my vote."

Darren laughed. "What would I want with your vote?"

"And I won't betray my country," Jack said.

"Jesus. That's right out of a World War Two movie. Corny, Jack. Real corny. I don't want your vote, and I don't want state secrets. I want cash."

Cash. It sounded so simple. "How much?"

"Ten grand. It's not even enough to get the IRS interested."

Which meant it wouldn't end here, today. Ten thousand was pennies to a man like Darren Mowery.

Jack was silent, the pain eating away at his insides.

Mowery dropped a piece of paper on his desk. "That's where you can wire the money. With the Internet, it's easy. Shouldn't take two minutes."

"I know who you are. I can find you."

"So? I thought about doing this anonymously. You

know, the altered voice on the phone in the middle of the night telling you to stuff twenty-dollar bills in a backpack and leave it at the Vietnam Memorial. I figured, nah, too complicated. Too likely you'd hang up and go back to sleep. This way, you know exactly who you're dealing with."

"An arrogant lowlife who threw away his own reputation and career—"

"You got it, Senator. That means I have nothing to lose. If I were still an honest man and you were my client, I'd tell you to pay the ten grand and cross your fingers."

He started for the door.

Jack rose, his knees unsteady. "I want all hard copies of the pictures and all the negatives."

"That's pretty old-fashioned. I could have them on computer disk by now. Truth is, Senator, with what we can do on a computer these days, they could be fakes." He went to the door, turned and winked. "Transfer the ten grand into my account."

He left.

Jack staggered back to his chair. For thirty years, he had refused to succumb to cynicism, venom, temptation or arrogance. He did his best. He was honest with himself and the people he represented. That was all he'd ever asked of himself, all he'd ever expected anyone else to ask of him.

Now, he was facing an impossible choice.

If Colin had cheated on Lucy, she'd have known about it. That was Lucy Blacker. She looked reality square in the eye.

But this was her secret to keep, Jack thought. His son was dead and deserved to rest in peace. His widow and children deserved to go on with their lives. Maybe the affair was part of the reason she'd moved to Vermont.

Mowery hadn't gone to Lucy with his sordid blackmail scheme because she wasn't the senator; she didn't have the power, the reputation, the money that Jack had.

But what did Darren Mowery *really* want?

Ten grand was a small price to pay for his family's peace. Giving in to a blackmailer, Jack thought, was the bigger price.

If he was lucky, it would end here. But Darren Mowery hadn't walked into Jack's office because he was lucky. He wanted something, and Jack doubted it was ten thousand dollars.

When Darren Mowery walked past her desk in Senator Swift's outer office, Barbara refused even to look up. She didn't dare meet his eye. He was so brazen! Her stomach muscles clamped down painfully. He'd warned her that he believed in the direct approach.

So, the deed was done.

Barbara did her meditation breathing. She wasn't very good at it. Even at home, with her eyes shut and scented candles lit, she found it difficult to focus on her inhaling and exhaling, to let her obsessive thoughts quiet.

She was not to contact Darren. He would contact her when he felt it appropriate. Even if she wanted to, she had no idea how or where to reach him. That wasn't important, she told herself. It wasn't that she trusted him or felt she had enough hold on him—she simply didn't care if he made off with all their profits. She didn't care about the money for what it could buy. She wanted to see a frightened, desperate Jack turn to her for help. She wanted him to understand just what she meant to him.

Let him suffer for taking her for granted. Let him learn.

She suddenly couldn't breathe. Oh, God! She wanted her life back. She wanted to be herself again. If only she'd never said anything to Jack. If only she'd stayed home this past week and hadn't bothered Lucy to relieve her own tension.

Oh, but it had felt good! And if Lucy came crying to Jack, so be it. Barbara could turn it into another lesson. The only danger was if Darren found out.

And the police.

Acid rose in her throat.

"Good Lord," a staff member said. "What's Darren Mowery doing here?"

Barbara looked up as if she'd been deep in concentration. "Oh, you know the senator. He'll give anyone a few minutes of his time to make their case."

Her colleague shuddered. He'd been on Jack Swift's staff almost as long as she had, but *he* wasn't indispensable. "The guy gives me the creeps."

Barbara returned to her work. It was routine, nothing stimulating. She'd once been so ambitious, determined to become the senator's chief of staff, possibly his press secretary. Secretly, she'd hoped he'd run for the presidency.

She'd had so many goals and dreams. Somehow they had gotten away from her. Now here she was, in danger of becoming the sort of woman she loathed. Obsessive, secretive, in love with the boss. She was pathetic.

Except she *wasn't.*

Her alliance with Darren was a show of strength. It demonstrated a great belief in herself, not cowardice.

When he finally emerged from his office an hour later, Jack looked perfectly normal. He was so understated and mannerly, not a bombastic ideologue. He wasn't a rabble-rouser, which sometimes allowed people the mistaken belief he had weak convictions. The premature deaths of his wife and son only added to his mystique, his appeal. He was the last senator in Washington anyone would think could be the victim of blackmail.

He came to Barbara's desk. Her heart jumped.

But there was no sign of fear or even distraction when he spoke. "Barbara, I've decided to spend the August recess in Vermont with Lucy and the kids."

"You're not going home?"

"It's an easy drive to Rhode Island. I'll manage."

Barbara saw now that he was a little off, not quite himself. Of course. He was a strong man, and he'd want to hold on as long as he could before confiding in anyone, even her. But Vermont. This was not a good development. Darren must have triggered an urge for Jack to see his grandchildren.

"J.T.'s been wanting to show me his favorite fishing spots. Madison…" He breathed in, nodded to himself. "Yes, August in Vermont. That's what I'll do. Do you mind, Barbara?"

"Mind what?" She wondered if she'd missed something, or if Jack's encounter with Darren was making him obtuse.

He ran a hand through his gray hair, and only because she'd known him for so long could Barbara detect his agitation. "I'd like to rent a house in Vermont, close to Lucy. Could you make arrangements?"

She smiled through her agony. This wasn't going at all as she'd calculated. "Of course."

"And don't say anything to Lucy just yet. This is so spur-of-the-moment—I don't want to disappoint her and the children if it doesn't work out, for whatever reason."

Like blackmail? Barbara quickly grabbed a stack of papers, as if she had a million things to do and Jack was just giving her one more easily handled detail. "I understand. I'll start making calls right away."

"I think it might be better if you went up to Vermont yourself," he said.

"What?" She felt so thickheaded, unable to follow the logic of his thinking. Why didn't he pull her into his office and beg her to help him with Darren Mowery's blackmail scheme?

"We don't have much time before the August recess, and you'll need to rent a house and get it ready rather quickly." He smiled, looking a bit less distracted. "Unless you'd rather not seize this as an excuse to get out of sweltering Washington for a few more days."

She made herself laugh. "Oh, no, you don't. I'll tie up a few loose ends here and be off. As I recall, there are several vacation homes above Lucy's house. I'll see if one's available to rent."

Jack seemed to relax. "Thanks, Barbara. I knew I could count on you."

Did he? She wondered if this was a start. Or maybe this was just a way to get rid of her while he coped with blackmail. Why have her around, adding to the pressure on him? Perhaps it was an excuse to get her out of town.

Barbara felt sick. She'd thrown herself at him, poured

out her soul. They were pretending nothing had happened, but he knew it had, and she knew. She'd broken the bond of trust between them by saying out loud what she knew they both were thinking. She'd hoped blackmail would jolt him out of his denial about his feelings toward her. *Barbara, I'm so sorry. I need you. You know I do!*

Instead, it was off to Vermont with her.

But this was her job as his personal assistant, she reminded herself. She handled the odd details of Jack Swift's life as a senator, a grandfather and a father-in-law.

He couldn't know that by sending her to Vermont, he was sending her back into the lion's den.

She would leave Lucy alone. She *had* to. If Darren found out, he'd kill her.

"Barbara?"

She smiled. "I was just thinking that Lucy could have picked a worse place to live than Vermont. It'll be fun going up there for a few days. I'll keep you posted."

Lucy plopped a colander of freshly picked green beans on her lap and sighed happily. Two normal days. She'd been to the hardware store to replace the glass in her dining room window, she'd patched the hole in the wall, she'd reported back to Rob Kiley that she hadn't found any firearms or ammunition in her son's possession or anywhere on her property. He likewise reported that Georgie was "clean."

And after a busy day of office work, she and Madison and J.T. had picked beans.

"Do you think Daisy made Sebastian pick beans?" Madison asked, joining her mother on the porch.

Lucy grabbed a handful of fresh, tender beans and started snapping off the ends. "I don't think anyone's ever 'made' him do anything."

"Well, his horses were beautiful."

That, Lucy allowed, was true. Beautiful horses, mutt dogs, no electricity, no running water. Sebastian Redwing had never been an easy man to figure out. Luckily, she didn't have to. He was in Wyoming on his hammock, coughing dust.

While Madison helped with snapping beans, J.T. was making himself scarce. It was a warm, fragrant, perfect Vermont summer evening. In a way, Lucy thought, asking Sebastian for help and having him turn her down so unceremoniously had been cathartic, forcing her to dig into her own resources. She really was on her own.

Colin couldn't have known, she thought. When he'd extracted her promise, Sebastian Redwing had been a different man from the rude burnout she'd found in Wyoming.

"Mom," J.T. yelled from inside, "Grandpa's on the phone!"

"Bring the phone out here."

Madison dropped a half-dozen snapped beans back into the colander. "Can I talk to him?"

Lucy nodded. "Of course."

J.T. ran out with the portable phone, deposited it in her lap and jumped off the porch, taking all the steps in one leap. Talking to their grandfather, Lucy thought, always perked up both her children. He would never let them know he disapproved of their mother's decision to move them out of Washington. But he'd let her know, in his subtle, gentlemanly way. She got the message. He hadn't lasted in Washington as long as he had by being wishy-washy.

"Hi, Jack," she said into the phone. "What's up?"

"I had a minute and thought I'd give you a call."

"Well, I'm glad you did."

"How are you?"

"Madison and I are snapping beans on the front porch."

"Sounds idyllic."

She laughed, but she detected a slight note of criticism mixed with an unexpected wistfulness. "I don't know about idyllic. How're you? How's Washington?"

"I'm fine. Washington's hot."

"It's summer. Let's talk again when the cherry blossoms are out there and it's mud season here."

"J.T. said you had a good trip to Wyoming."

"It was quick, but we enjoyed ourselves."

"Did you stop in to see Sebastian Redwing?"

Lucy paused. Did Jack know about her promise to Colin? Was he suspicious that visiting Sebastian meant trouble? He didn't sound suspicious, but then, he wouldn't. Jack Swift knew how to keep his emotions in check better than most. "Yes," she said carefully. "It made for an interesting field trip with the kids."

"I gather they're not going to camp this summer."

They hadn't gone to camp last summer, either. "I don't see the need, given where we live and what I do."

Lucy kept her tone light, deciding to take his question at face value and not read any criticism into it. But she knew it was there. Her father-in-law would never openly criticize her parenting skills, but she knew he thought his grandchildren's upbringing lacking. That Madison and J.T. could kayak, canoe, hike, swim in an ice-cold stream, pick their own vegetables, climb trees, fish and wander in the woods of Vermont was all well and good—but they weren't learning sailing, golf, tennis. Their occasional lessons at the town rec department didn't count.

"They need their own lives, Lucy," Jack said softly.

Lucy was taken aback, but forced a laugh. "That's what they tell me every time I insist they clean their rooms. 'Mom, I need my own life.'"

"Do you think Colin would have wanted them raised in Vermont? Snapping beans, running through the woods—Lucy, it's a hard world out there. They need to be ready."

"Colin's not here, Jack, and I'm doing the best I can."

"Of course, you are. I'm so sorry."

He *was* sorry, but he'd said what he felt. He was a man without a wife or son, and Lucy had taken his grandchildren off to Vermont. She wasn't raising them the way he and Eleanor had raised Colin. Lucy understood, but wished he could simply say he missed having them right there in Washington instead of implying she wasn't a good mother.

"Forget it, Jack. Look, Madison and J.T. would love to see you. Any chance you can get up here during the August recess?"

"I hope so."

"We'd like to sneak down to Rhode Island for a few days, if you're available. And Madison's looking forward to her trip to Washington this fall."

Lucy glanced at her daughter, who was listening intently to every word. If there was a way to use her grandfather to convince her mother to let her do a semester in Washington, Madison would jump at it. But as much as he might disapprove of Vermont, Lucy was confident Jack would never undermine Lucy that way.

"She'd love to stay longer than a three-day weekend," Lucy said. "Here, would you like to talk to her?"

"Yes, thanks. Great talking to you, Lucy. Oh, by the way, Sidney Greenburg sends her best."

Lucy interpreted this to mean Sidney and Jack were still seeing each other. She hoped a relationship might take some of the focus off her own shortcomings, and the edge off his loneliness. "Thanks. Tell her the Costa Rica trip is coming along—she wants to be the first to sign up."

"Maybe we both will," Jack said. "And Lucy, I didn't mean to imply—you should go on with your life. I know that."

"It's okay, Jack. We miss you, too. We'll see you soon."

Madison disappeared inside with the phone. Jack was good to both her children, Lucy reminded herself. And they loved him. But if she'd stayed in Washington, they'd have stayed in Colin's world—Jack's world—and Lucy knew she wouldn't have survived. She'd needed to make a clean break.

She grabbed another handful of beans. Rob joined her on the porch, flopping down on a wicker chair. "The Newfoundland trip just filled up. Do you want to start a waiting list?"

"Makes sense."

"And J.T. told me he thinks he wants to come on the father-son trip, after all."

"Did he? Well, good. I hope he does."

They talked business, and Lucy snapped beans. She and her kids had a good life here, she thought. That was what mattered, not Jack's approval—or even Colin's.

* * *

Sebastian arrived in southern Vermont late in the day and checked into a clean, simple motel on a historic route outside Manchester. Far enough from Lucy, but not too far.

He'd made a detour to Washington first and checked with Happy Ford, a new hire Plato had put on Mowery. She was ex-Secret Service and very good, but only Plato would hire someone with a name like Happy Ford.

She said Mowery had visited Senator Jack Swift at his office this morning. And disappeared.

Sebastian warned her not to underestimate Darren Mowery. "Assume he's better at what you do than you are."

"Do you think he knows I'm on to him?"

"He knows."

Sebastian took his cardboard cup of coffee out onto the small patio in front of his motel room and sat on an old-fashioned, round-topped metal chair. It was painted yellow. The chair for the next room was lavender, then pink, then blue. Cute.

There were brochures in his room for the sites in the area—old houses, covered bridges, Revolutionary War stuff, outlets, inns, resorts. He thought about renting a big, fat inner tube and floating down the Battenkill. It seemed like a better idea than spying on Lucy.

He'd never been much of a tourist or an historian. Or much of a Vermonter. Born here, more or less raised here, generations of family buried here. Daisy had insisted she had an ancestor who'd fought at the Battle of Bennington, which actually had occurred just over the border in New York state. Daisy had liked the aura of being a native Vermonter.

He'd left his boots and his hat in Wyoming. He was an outsider there, but he really didn't give a damn.

The evening air was warm and slightly humid, but pleasant. The rounded hills were thick with trees, and as he sat with his coffee, he felt as if they were closing in on him. Or maybe it was the memories.

He threw the last of his coffee into the grass. "Lucy, Lucy."

He'd done a lot of dumb things in his life. Falling for Lucy Blacker on her wedding day was one of the dumbest. Coming out here was probably right up there with it. A bullet left on her car seat. It was kids. It wasn't Mowery.

Sebastian walked out into the fading sunlight. Tomorrow, he thought, would be hot.

He'd gotten rid of his guns. No point having one, seeing how he didn't hunt and had no intention of shooting anyone. People thought he was kidding when he said he'd renounced violence. He wasn't. Darren Mowery had been his last victim.

A mosquito landed on his arm. He flicked it off. Who the hell needed a gun? If he was going to find out who was intimidating Lucy, what he needed was some serious bug spray.

Chapter 5

Lucy grabbed her binoculars and headed across the backyard, over the stone wall and into the field. She had on shorts, a T-shirt and sneakers. The air was hot and humid for southern Vermont.

Two more days without any incidents. She was in good shape. An early start that morning had caught her up on her work, as well as freed her to agree to a local inn's request for her to lead a family on a canoe trip down the Battenkill. Madison and J.T. had gone with her, and they'd had a great time. She'd felt so...*normal.*

Madison was off to Manchester to see a movie with friends, J.T. at the Kileys to play Nintendo with Georgie and spend the night.

Lucy had the evening to herself.

The field grass was knee-high, mixed with daisies and bright orange hawkweed, black-eyed Susans, frothy

Queen Anne's lace. With a line of thunderclouds moving in from the west, she couldn't go too far into the woods. The storm should, however, blow out the heat and humidity that had built up through the day.

An old stone wall marked the far edge of the field; beyond it were woods of oak, maple, hemlock, pine and beech. Lucy climbed over the wall and stood in the shade of a huge maple, her binoculars slung around her neck. It was a perfect climbing tree. Up high in its branches, she would have a tremendous view. She could perch up there and bird-watch, enjoy her solitude.

What the hell, she thought, and with both hands, she reached up and grabbed hold of the lowest branch. She'd always loved climbing trees as a kid growing up in suburban Virginia.

When she lived in Washington, she'd had a job organizing unique trips for a Washington museum, and it had seemed such a natural way to combine her degree in anthropology with her love of the outdoors. She'd discovered a passion and a talent for understanding what people wanted and translating it into trips they couldn't stop thinking about once they opened up one of her brochures, something that had served her well when she'd decided to go out on her own. Many of her Washington clients had followed her into her own business.

She swung onto a low branch and climbed higher, the maple's rough bark biting into her hands. Bark had never bothered her at twelve. She moved carefully, having no desire to fall out of a damn tree on her evening off.

She found the perfect branch and sat down, her feet dangling. Even without binoculars, the view was spectacular— woods, fields, stone walls, brook, her yellow farmhouse tucked on its narrow stretch of reasonably flat land. Not too far from here, Calvin Coolidge was buried in a hillside cemetery so as not to take up precious flat land for farms.

Balancing herself with one hand on the tree trunk, Lucy removed the binoculars from her neck. Maybe she'd see a hawk floating in the hazy sky.

But as she put the binoculars to her eyes, she heard something in the woods around her. She went very still. The noise didn't sound like a squirrel or a chipmunk, or even a deer. A moose? The pre-Wyoming incidents came back to her, making her question what she would ordinarily take in stride. A noise in the woods. Big deal.

Without making a sound, she swiveled around to see what was under and behind her. Brush. More trees.

And Sebastian Redwing.

She gulped in a breath, so startled she lost her balance. Her binoculars flew out of her hand as she grabbed the tree trunk to keep herself from falling.

The binoculars just missed Sebastian's head. He caught them with one hand and looked up. "Trying to kill me, Lucy?"

"It's a thought." She caught her breath, but was still shaking. "Damn it, Redwing, what the hell are you doing here?"

"You wanted my help. Here I am."

The heat and humidity must have gotten to her. She was imagining things. Sebastian was konked out in his hammock in Wyoming with his dogs and horses. He wasn't in Vermont.

She swooped down to a lower branch and swung to the ground as if she were twelve again—forgetting she wasn't. She dropped in a controlled but hard landing.

Pain shot up her ankle. Her shirt flew up to her midriff. She swore.

Sebastian wrapped an arm around her lower back, steadying her. She could feel his forearm on her hot skin.

His gaze settled on her. "Easier going up than it is coming down."

"I've been climbing trees since I was a kid."

He smiled. "That's bravado. You almost sprained an ankle, and you know it."

"The key word is *almost*. My ankle's fine."

If she'd injured herself, he'd have carted her off to the emergency room. There'd be no end to her humiliation.

"What were you doing up there?" he asked mildly.

"Bird-watching."

"Birds have all hightailed it before the storm hits."

He still had his arm around her. "You can let go now," she said.

"You've got your footing?"

"Yes."

He released her and took a step back. He wasn't dusty. The dirty cowboy hat and scuffed cowboy boots were gone. He had on good-quality hiking clothes, including hiking boots. He was lean, tanned, fit—and alert, Lucy thought. That was the first thing she'd noticed when she'd met him all those years ago, just how alert he was. She could feel him taking in everything about her, from her sneakers to her wild hair.

He was worse than an ex-CIA agent. Maybe he *was* an ex-CIA agent. She suddenly realized she knew very little about him. What if she'd taken her promise to Colin out of context, and Sebastian Redwing was the last person she should have asked for help?

She adjusted her shirt. "I thought you weren't interested in helping me."

"I'm not."

"Then go back to Wyoming." She stepped past him and climbed onto the stone wall. "I didn't mean I wanted your help as in you sneaking around my woods. I wanted your opinion." She looked back at him, breathing hard, fighting for some way to assert her control over the situation. "Do note my use of the past tense."

"Noted."

She took a deep breath. "I sure as hell didn't want you scaring me out of a tree."

"I didn't scare you out of your tree. You scared yourself." He stepped over the stone wall, tall enough he didn't have to climb up over the rocks piled up by long-ago farmers, probably his ancestors. "You should find out what you're dealing with before you react."

"Yeah, well, I'm good with canoes and kayaks and snapping beans. I'm not so good with men jumping out of the brush at me."

He smiled. It was an unsettling smile, not meant, she felt, to reach his eyes. Which it didn't. "You nailed me with your binoculars."

"It wasn't deliberate."

He handed them back to her. "I used to climb that tree when I was a kid."

His words brought her up short. He was, after all, Daisy's grandson. He'd sold this place to her. It was more his turf than hers, no matter whose name was on the deed.

Lucy went out into the field, more comfortable on open ground. "How does it feel to be back here?"

He shrugged. "I'd forgotten how pesky mosquitoes can be."

She slung the binoculars over her neck. "I never meant for you to come here."

"What did you mean for me to do?"

"Tell me I wasn't in any danger."

There was still nothing she could reliably read in his eyes.

"And how was I supposed to know that without coming here?" he asked.

"Instincts and experience."

"In other words, I was supposed to release you from all your worries from the comfort of my hammock." He eyed her a moment, then added in a low voice, "Believe me, that would have suited us both."

"I don't want you going to any trouble on my account—"

"Too late."

With a groan of frustration, Lucy started across the field. She took long strides, hoping to separate herself from Sebastian Redwing as fast as possible.

He didn't say a word. He didn't come after her.

She stopped dead in her tracks and swung around. He was just a few yards behind her, as tall and immovable as an oak. And she'd all but invited him here. "You can go back to Wyoming now."

"I can do whatever I want to do."

"You're trying to spook me. Well, forget it. I've been living out here, just me and the kids, for the better part of three years. I don't spook easily."

"What about the bullet through your dining room window?"

"That's over. It was nothing. I was wrong."

He shrugged. "Maybe, maybe not. No incidents since you got back from Wyoming?"

"No. None." She frowned, wondering if she'd be less agitated if he weren't so damn calm. She was letting him get to her. She never let irritating people get to her. "When did you arrive?"

"A couple days ago."

She held her fury in check. "Where are you staying?"

"Motel."

"So you've had two days to spy on me."

He smiled. "Why would I spy on you? You're not the one who shot up your dining room."

She searched for a way to rephrase what she knew—what he *knew* she knew—he'd been up to. "You've been keeping an eye on me," she said.

He started down through the field. "Your life's pretty goddamn boring."

His way of saying she was right. "To someone like you, maybe." She marched after him, her binoculars swinging on her neck with each furious step. "Did you follow me on my canoe trip?"

"Nope. Sat up here and watched the woodchucks have at your garden."

"You did not."

He glanced around at her. "Check your beans. You'll see."

She bristled. "I do not need a bodyguard."

"Good, because I'm no good at bodyguarding. I was just getting the lay of the land. Lucy goes to work. Lucy picks beans. Lucy takes care of kids. Lucy runs errands. Lucy has a glass of wine on her porch. Lucy goes canoeing." He yawned. "There you go."

"It's better than lying about all day in a hammock."

"No doubt."

She was so aggravated, she could have hit him. Thunder rumbled in the distance. The sky darkened. The wind picked up. She reined in her emotions. She didn't want to be out here alone with him when the storm hit. "Go back to Wyoming. If I catch you on my property, I'll call the police."

"They won't arrest me."

"They will—"

"I'm Daisy Wheaton's grandson. I'll say I'm here visiting the ancestral home. They'll probably hold a town barbecue on my behalf."

She stared at him. "Have you always been this big a jerk?"

He grinned at her. "Nah, I'm a lot worse than I used to be. Plato didn't tell you?" He winked; he gave no indication of giving a damn what she thought or what she wanted. "See you around, Lucy Blacker."

Lucy turned the shower as hot as she could stand it. She scrubbed herself with a lavender-scented gel made by a local herbalist who wasn't, she was confident, related to Sebastian Redwing.

Daisy Wheaton should have willed her place to the Nature Conservancy instead of to her miserable grandson.

Then I wouldn't be here, Lucy thought.

Maybe she'd have moved to Costa Rica with her parents, or stayed in Washington and made her father-in-law happy.

Well, Colin had never said Sebastian was a gentleman or even a reasonably nice guy. He'd said he trusted him. He'd said Lucy could go to him if she needed help. It was a mistake, obviously, but Colin couldn't have known.

She dried off with her biggest, fluffiest towel and shook on a scented herbal powder that matched the gel. The thunderstorm had subsided, but she could still hear rumbling off to the east. The air was cooler, less humid. She was calmer. Her encounter with Sebastian had left her spent, drained…and feeling more alive than she wanted to admit.

She pushed aside that uncomfortable thought and slipped into a dressing gown she'd picked up for a song at an outlet in Manchester. Black satin, edged with black lace. Quite luxurious. She'd sit up in bed and read until Madison got back from her movie.

She started into the hallway, but stopped abruptly, catching her reflection in the mirror above the old pedestal sink. She turned and stared at herself in her black satin. Since Colin's death, she had seldom taken the time to think of herself simply as a woman. As a mother, an entrepreneur, a widow, an individual getting her life back together after sudden tragedy, yes. But as a woman who might attract, and be attracted to, a man, no. Not again. Not after Colin, not after the searing grief she'd endured. Never mind that she was still only thirty-eight.

"Good Lord," she breathed. "Where did *that* come from?"

It had nothing to do with leaping out of a tree at Sebastian's feet. The feel of his arm around her. She'd have to be mad to be attracted to him. Her sanity, her rationality, her common sense had seen her through the ups and downs of the past three years. She wasn't about to throw them out the window because of one little touch.

She headed into her bedroom.

Immediately she spotted something black in the middle of her bed. It brought her up short, and her knees nearly collapsed under her. *No.*

She stepped closer. It didn't move. It appeared to be organic—not plastic or rubber, not one of J.T.'s disgusting toys.

She saw the rough texture of its skin, the bits of fur. Wings.

A bat.

Her stomach lurched. Was it alive?

She tugged on the quilt. The bat didn't move.

And the horror swarmed in on her all at once. She couldn't control it. Madison and J.T. were away, and she didn't have to hold back. She tightened her hands into fists and yelled out in anger, disgust and shock. "Damn it, damn it, damn it. Whoever you are, I am not giving you the satisfaction of going to pieces. Not now, not ever!" She brushed back tears, gulped for air. No one could hear her. She was alone. "Damn it, I will not be afraid!"

She coughed, choking back tears.

A dead bat. In her bed.

She tore around her room for something to use to dispose of it. Fury and horror consumed her. Someone had sneaked into her house, slipped down the hall to her first-floor bedroom and deposited a dead animal in her bed.

She wanted to tear up the place. Rip out drawers, smash lamps, kick doors to pieces. She'd held back for so long. She was tired of being *under control.*

She found a tennis racket in her closet. A knife-cut of pain carved through her chest. Tennis. She hadn't played since Colin had died.

She snatched up the racket. She'd scoop up the bat and fling him into the woods. It wasn't *evidence*. It was a damn dead bat.

She spun around, racket in hand.

Sebastian was there as if she'd conjured him up herself. He jumped back a step. "Easy."

"Don't you believe in knocking?" She didn't lower her racket. "You're like a damn ghost. I can't—I—" She made herself breathe. "I can't have you here."

"I heard you yelling bloody murder." His voice was steady, dead calm. He was slightly damp from the rain. "I called from the back door. When you didn't answer, I came to find you."

She pointed with her racket. "There's a dead bat in my bed."

"So I see. Charming."

"Bats don't fall down dead on wedding-ring quilts."

He said nothing. It was obvious the bat hadn't fallen or crawled there to die.

"Daisy made that quilt," Lucy said. "It was in an old trunk in the attic."

"I remember it," he said softly. His eyes didn't leave her.

Her breathing steadied. Her legs were shaking under her, and she became aware of her appearance. The lace-edged black dressing gown, her damp hair, her bare feet, the spots of white powder on her throat. She remembered her reflection.

Sebastian took the tennis racket. His fingers touched hers, and it was all over. She fell against him, his mouth finding hers, her dressing gown making her feel almost as if she were wearing nothing at all. His body was hard, lean, unrelenting. Desire spilled through her, hot, aching, overpowering. It had been so long. So very, very long.

Then she was standing in the middle of her bedroom carpet, and Sebastian was staring out her window. Just like that.

Lucy quickly recovered. It was the dead bat. It had robbed her of all self-control. "Well. I don't even want to know what *that* was about."

He glanced at her, his gray eyes narrowed into slits. "Pretty obvious to me."

"The lonely widow finds a dead bat in her bed, and next thing she's throwing herself on the man who swoops in to her rescue? I don't think so."

Sebastian picked up her tennis racket. "Takes two."

"To what? Play tennis, get rid of the bat—"

"Lucy."

He'd meant the kiss. Obviously. It took two to do what they'd done. He hadn't forced her. She obviously hadn't forced him.

She winced, still tasting his mouth on her. "I'm a little addled. Don't worry about the bat. I'll get rid of it."

"I can take it on my way out."

He was leaving. Thank God.

"You'll be all right alone?" he asked.

She nodded. "Whoever left that little present here isn't trying to hurt me or the kids."

"Maybe not yet."

"You didn't see anything?"

He shook his head. If he was irritated with himself for not catching the bat-depositor in his two days of sneaking around, he didn't show it.

Lucy stared at the bat. Bats outside were fine with her. Bats inside, dead or alive, weren't. If nothing else, there was rabies to consider. "It's awfully daring, don't you think, to slip in here, drop a bat on my bed and slip out again?"

"It was daring, yes." He patted the racket with one hand. She could see his mind working. He knew how someone who wanted to harrass and intimidate operated. "But I'd say your friend here doesn't leave much to chance."

"Meaning he or she, or whoever, plans ahead, knows my comings and goings."

"Let me check out your house. It's unlikely I'll find anything, but we'll both sleep better if we know for sure no one's hiding in a closet. It'll take a few minutes."

"I'll help—"

"You'll make a cup of tea and sit in the kitchen and drink it."

"Madison's due back any minute."

"If I hear her, I'll leave. I don't think your kids need to know I'm in Vermont."

Lucy ran a hand through her damp hair. "I hate this."

"I know," he said, then scooped up the dead bat with the tennis racket, checked under her bed, checked her closet and went into the hall.

She followed him. "What are you going to do if you find someone, beat him over the head with the tennis racket?"

He pulled open the hall closet. She had to remember he knew his way around this house, but found she couldn't picture him as a twelve-year-old like J.T., digging worms in the backyard. He glanced at her. "I could shove the bat down his throat."

"Do you think it died of natural causes?"

He moved down the hall in the opposite direction

from the kitchen, where she was supposed to go and have tea as if nothing had happened. "I'm not planning to autopsy the damn thing," he said.

"I'd hate to think of someone deliberately killing a bat just to terrorize me."

He stopped. "Then don't."

"Am I distracting you?" she asked.

"Yes."

She'd meant by talking. He clearly meant something else. She motioned vaguely toward the kitchen. "I'll make myself that cup of tea. You can finish up."

He went without a word.

When he returned to the kitchen ten minutes later, he didn't linger. "Place is clean." He pulled open the back door. "I'll get rid of the bat and leave the tennis racket on the back steps."

Lucy was at the table with a cup of untouched chamomile tea. She hadn't been able to drink. She kept thinking about the dead bat, about kissing Sebastian. Neither induced calm. "That's fine. Thanks."

He looked at her. In the waning evening light, the soft gray of his eyes was even more unusual, as if warning her he didn't belong here. "Colin was a damn fool for ever sending you to me."

"He made me promise," she said.

"I know." He started out the screen door, stared out at the darkening Vermont sky. "Lucy, you don't have to worry. I won't touch you again."

She smiled and echoed him. "It takes two."

He didn't glance back, just left with her dead bat.

There was an unexpected flash of lightning, a rumble of thunder, and a few minutes later, another downpour.

Lucy thought Sebastian might come back in out of the rain, but he didn't.

She ran outside onto the back steps. In seconds, the rain drenched her gown. She could see her nipples outlined against the silky black fabric.

How had he disappeared so fast?

She returned inside, dumped out her tea and walked back to her bedroom. She changed into a prosaic nightgown and jumped into bed with a book, but she couldn't concentrate enough to read.

A few minutes later, a car sounded in her driveway, and Madison dashed in through the back door. "Hi, Mom, I'm home," she called from the kitchen. "Hey— who left the tennis racket out?"

Lucy didn't breathe. Sebastian must have seen her on the back steps, her dressing gown clinging to her against the kitchen light. "It was me." She almost couldn't get the words out.

Madison appeared in her bedroom doorway, and Lucy managed a smile. She would do anything, she thought, to protect her children—even let Sebastian skulk around her woods.

She smiled at her daughter. "So, how was the movie?"

The bat hadn't died of natural causes. Sebastian was no expert on dead bats, but that much was obvious.

And tossing its carcass into the woods in no way made up for kissing Lucy when she was in shock.

"That was pretty goddamn low," he said under his breath as he locked himself into his motel room. He had considered, and dismissed, the necessity of keeping watch on her all night. The bat-depositor had accomplished his—or her—mission for the day. Sebastian had no real sense of who was behind the nasty little deeds—man, woman, coconspirators. He was now inclined to eliminate kids as a possibility.

He wasn't sure if Lucy had initiated the kiss, or if he had. He knew for damn sure she'd wanted it. But that didn't matter. She'd just found a dead bat in her bed, and he shouldn't have taken advantage of the situation.

On the other hand, he really didn't have any regrets. All right, he was low. But he'd imagined kissing Lucy for close to twenty years, and now that he had, he felt better.

He kicked off his hiking boots and flopped on his bed.

Who the hell was he kidding? He didn't feel better. Kissing Lucy hadn't helped.

He pictured her standing on her porch steps in her rain-soaked gown. She was smart and daring, and he didn't know why the hell he'd fallen for her, a woman he couldn't have—a woman he *shouldn't* have.

He called Happy Ford in Washington. Nothing yet on Darren Mowery. "I'm chasing down a few leads," she said.

"Be careful."

"Always."

Sebastian unwrapped the tuna sandwich he'd picked up en route back to his motel. He turned on the television. He hadn't watched TV in months. He found a rerun of *Gilligan's Island* and sat on his bed, watching Gilligan and the Skipper and the gang try to get home. There's no going back, he wanted to tell them. Walking above Daisy's house the past two days, that simple, terrible truth had etched itself on his soul. No going back.

He shut off the television.

Was Mowery in Vermont? Was Sebastian's coming here playing into his hands? Would he use a young widow to lure Sebastian east?

He knew to keep speculation and facts separate. Darren Mowery's reappearance in Washington, DC, might have nothing to do with the dead bat tonight on Lucy's bed in Vermont.

"Don't start a job you don't mean to finish," Daisy had liked to tell him.

When he'd gone after Mowery last year, Sebastian had meant to finish the job. But he hadn't, and now he had to make sure no one but he paid for his mistake.

Chapter 6

The house was perfect.

Barbara stood on its rear deck above Joshua Brook. She loved being right. She'd known she'd find something close to Lucy. It was the last house on the dirt road above the stupid twit's house. Barbara had rented it on the spot. Jack would be pleased.

The house had two bedrooms, a living room with a fireplace, a full kitchen, a study and lots of glass. There was a screened porch in case of rain or too many mosquitoes. The furnishings were contemporary country, suitable should an emergency press conference be required. The landscaping needed work—it was a little woodsy for Barbara's taste.

The brook was visible through a steep bank of hemlocks and pine, its clear, ice-cold water washing over silvery-gray rocks. She closed her eyes, letting the rhythm of the water absorb her. She could feel a slight breeze on her face.

Darren doesn't know I'm here. Should I tell him?

The thought was an unpleasant intrusion. It was almost as if he'd beamed it to her, just when she was about to relax and attempt to forget she'd colluded with a dangerous man in a scheme to blackmail a senator, the man she'd loved for twenty years.

What if Darren were out there in the woods, watching her?

She shuddered. He couldn't possibly know about her longtime obsession with Lucy. If he did, he'd have killed her by now.

"Just do your job and let me do mine," he'd told her. "You screw this up, you'll answer to me."

She'd intended to leave Lucy alone. But she hadn't, she couldn't—and she didn't understand why. Barbara was a woman of great strength and willpower. She wasn't stupid or weak. She didn't lack self-discipline.

She dropped onto an Adirondack chair. It was Lucy's fault she was even here. If Lucy had stayed in Washington where she belonged, Jack wouldn't have had to send his personal assistant to Vermont to rent a house so he could see his grandchildren. Barbara wouldn't have been tempted to leave a dead bat for his ungrateful wretch of a daughter-in-law to find. She and Lucy might even have become friends.

Her cell phone trilled.

"The money's in the bank," Darren said without preamble. "We're on our way. How's Vermont?"

"How do you know I—"

"Barbara."

She licked her lips. "Jack sent me. He asked me to

rent a house for him for August recess. He wants to spend time with Lucy and his grandchildren."

"Blackmail'll do that to a guy."

"He suggested I stay an extra day or two."

"Of course he did. Come on, Barbie. Can't you feel the noose dropping around your neck? He's easing you out. You won't even know what hit you." Darren laughed. "Wishing you hadn't thrown yourself at him after all, aren't you?"

"You're disgusting, and Jack isn't easing me out. This is my job." She drew on her strength of character—*no one* intimidated her. "I don't want you to call me again."

"I don't care what you want, Barbie. Just keep your nose clean. I'll be in touch."

He disconnected.

Barbara slid the cell phone back into its designated slot in her tote bag. She could handle Darren Mowery. He just liked to play games with her to show her how smart he was. Well, she was smarter—

"Barbara? It *is* you!" Madison Swift suddenly appeared, running up the steep bank from the brook. "I can't believe it! My friend Cindy said her mother showed this place to someone from Washington, and I was hoping—" The girl laughed, delighted. "Barbara, it's *me*. Madison Swift. Senator Swift's granddaughter."

Barbara had recognized the girl immediately. She just needed a moment to recover from the shock. Surely Madison was too polite to eavesdrop—she couldn't have overheard Barbara's conversation with Darren. The girl bounded onto the deck. She had grass stains on her knees, briar tracks on her shins. Her pretty face was freckled from the sun. Her dark, copper hair was in a messy, unfashionable single braid down her back.

She was so like Colin, Barbara thought. Cleaned up and raised properly, Madison Swift would be an asset to Jack, a tribute to his son's memory.

Now, she was a reminder that Barbara's campaign against Lucy was the right thing to do. It had nothing to do with her alliance with Darren Mowery and her frustration with Jack's denial of his love for her. It was an act of courage and self-sacrifice on her part. Someone had to wake Lucy up. Someone had to force her to take responsibility for her children.

Barbara smiled at the excited girl. "Of course, it's you, Madison, Senator Swift's granddaughter. How are you, sweetie?"

"Bored out of my mind," she said cheerfully. "That's okay, I'm used to it. Is Grandpa coming up this summer?"

"You're a sly one, Madison. This is supposed to be a secret. Your grandfather doesn't want to create a circus for him or your mom."

"Does she know?"

Barbara shook her head. "He wanted to make sure he had a house before he told her. He wouldn't want to disappoint you all." The words almost made her sick. Madison and J.T. would have been disappointed if their grandfather had to cancel his visit, but not Lucy. Lucy Swift didn't care if she ever saw her father-in-law again. "He really should be the one to tell you."

Madison crossed her fingers and pressed them to her lips. Her vivid blue eyes sparkled. "Mum's the word."

"What do you think of the house he's rented?" Barbara asked, gesturing. "Isn't it wonderful?"

"This is my favorite house up here."

"It's a beautiful setting."

The girl shrugged. "I guess. Most of Vermont's beautiful. I don't know how much 'beautiful' I can take."

Barbara laughed. "Well, well. Now there's an attitude."

Madison scooted up onto the rail, paying no heed to the long drop. "I'd rather go to Washington to see Grandpa than have him come here. I'm going for a long weekend this fall, but it's not enough."

"Aha. You're one who'd like to have your cake and eat it, too."

"Yep." She grinned. "Aren't you?"

"Of course." Barbara glanced around at the wooded, isolated landscape. "You're alone? J.T. didn't come with you?"

"No, I'm escaping him. He and his friend want me to take them fishing. I refuse. I *hate* worms. I liked them when I was twelve, but not anymore."

"Not a country girl, are you?"

She seemed to take that as a compliment. "It's not that I hate Vermont—I just prefer the city." She jumped off the rail, a bundle of restless energy. "How long are you staying?"

"A few days. I'm taking a bit of a vacation and making sure everything's set for your grandfather. I'll stock the pantry, lay in some reading material, that sort of thing."

"He could stay with us at the house," Madison said.

And feel about as welcome as a roach. Lucy no longer thought of herself as a Swift—that much was obvious. But her children were Swifts, and there was no changing that fact, much as it might annoy her.

"This will work out beautifully," Barbara said neutrally. "Would you mind not mentioning to your mother and brother that I'm here? I hate to ask you to keep anything from them, but they'd put two and two together."

"J.T. wouldn't. Mom would, though."

With the memory of the dead bat fresh in her mind, Lucy might start asking the wrong questions and jumping to dangerous conclusions. As much as Barbara hated to ask a child to keep secrets from her mother, under the circumstances it was the only practical option.

The girl laughed. "This'll be great. Of course I won't tell anyone about you. I wouldn't want to get you into trouble with Grandpa."

"Oh, no, that's not your concern. I just don't want to spoil his surprise."

Madison nodded. "He's always liked to surprise us."

She swung around, asking abruptly, "Have you seen the falls yet?"

Yes, on her illicit visit last week, Barbara thought. She shook her head.

"Oh, you have to see them. They're not far. Do you have time? I can show you. It won't take long."

"I'm not dressed for a hike—"

"There's a short path off the road. It's a little longer than the path along the brook, but it's easier."

The girl seemed so eager. It was because of this pitiful life she led when she should be at a quality summer camp or studying abroad for the summer. Barbara had to contain her fury. If she could get Jack to tear down his wall of denial and see what she offered him, she could have influence over his grandchildren. She *knew* he hated to see them turning into country bumpkins.

She manufactured a smile as she got to her feet. "Go on, then," she said. "Lead the way."

Madison skipped down the deck steps, Barbara following at a slower pace. As a senior staffer of a United

States senator, she was dressed professionally, appropriately, in dark slacks, a crisp white shirt and loafers.

They took a gravel path to the front of the house and walked along the edge of the dirt road. Since the house was the last on the dead-end road, Barbara didn't worry too much about a passing car spotting them. This was a risk. But it was a tolerable risk, another act of strength on her part. Madison needed a break from the dull rituals of her summer life.

Barbara knew her way around the woods and paths of the hills above Lucy's house better than she dared let on.

Last night, she'd returned to the rented house alone, even before she'd completed the paperwork with the real estate agent and gotten the keys. The screened porch was unlocked, and when Barbara slipped inside, a bat flapped in front of her face.

It was very early in the evening for bats, and she'd thought it might be rabid.

Then she'd thought of Lucy.

Barbara didn't know anything about bats. She wasn't a killer of helpless animals. She could have left it alone, coaxed it outside in case it meant to make a home for itself on the porch.

But the impulse had taken hold of her, refusing to let go until she'd found a stick, dealt with the bat and tucked its carcass into a bakery bag from her morning coffee.

She'd parked her car under a pine tree on the side of the dirt road and slipped across the brook to her perch on the opposite bank, then looked out across the yard behind the barn. She saw Madison leave with friends, J.T. go off with his grubby little friend. When Lucy finally took off across the field with her binoculars, Barbara weighed the risks and the pleasures. She knew she wouldn't stop thinking about the bat until it was deposited in Lucy's house for her to find, wonder about, scream about. But what if Lucy spotted her with her binoculars?

She came up with a foolproof cover story. *Lucy! You caught me. Jack sent me to rent a house for him for August, and I couldn't resist peeking in on you and the kids. I thought I heard something, but it was nothing.*

If she'd already deposited the bat, she could argue it was the intruder she'd heard. If not, who would ask about her bakery bag?

Lucy hadn't caught her.

She'd found the dead bat and screamed.

Barbara, lurking in the woods on her way back to her car, had heard her. Her satisfaction was almost physical. She'd acquired seven mosquito bites. More little purple hearts.

Barbara and Madison came to a massive hemlock, its roots spreading like thick, spidery veins over the ground. The girl scooted down the narrow path, turning and motioning to Barbara with one hand. "This way," she said. "We're almost there."

Yes, Barbara thought. The risks were necessary, and she had the courage to meet them. Colin's children—Jack's grandchildren—deserved a better life.

Jack Swift sank into a quiet corner booth at his favorite restaurant. The past few days had been excruciating. He hadn't asked Sidney Greenburg to join him for lunch. They'd argued last night when she'd realized something was wrong and he'd insisted there wasn't. Now, he just wanted a martini, a plate of Maryland crab cakes, a good salad and the dark comfort of the traditional, no-nonsense restaurant.

He knew, at least figuratively speaking, he was a man hanging over the abyss by his fingernails. Blackmail. Dear God.

And Colin. His only son, his only child. Had he been the sort of man who fooled around on his wife? Jack had never thought so, but who knew what went on between two people? And the truth really didn't matter. He didn't want to see any "proof." He just wanted this sordid business to go away.

"Senator Swift." Darren Mowery greeted him with a warm, phony smile. "Fancy meeting you here."

Jack called upon his many years of public service to manufacture a return smile, even as every muscle in his body seemed to twist in agony. "Mr. Mowery."

"Mind if I join you?"

The restaurant was also a favorite with reporters and senior congressional staff, all perpetually at the ready for good, fresh gossip. There was no graceful way out. Darren had known it when he'd walked in here. Jack felt his smile falter. "Please do."

Mowery dropped onto the opposite red leather-covered bench. "Did you order the crab cakes?"

Jack nodded. Mowery was making the point that he knew the senator's habits, his likes, his dislikes, and that the supposed information he had on Colin was only the beginning. Which was exactly what Jack had feared—what he'd *known*—when he'd transferred ten thousand dollars into Mowery's specified account.

"I did as you asked," Jack said in a low voice.

"You sure did. And in short order, too. Much appreciated."

The waiter appeared. Darren ordered a beer. No time for lunch, he said. Jack felt no relief.

"Here's an address and a password." With one finger, Mowery passed his business card across the table. "They're for a secure Web site. You might want to take a look."

Jack snatched up the card and dropped it into his suit coat pocket. "Mowery, for God's sake, if you've posted pictures of my son on the goddamn *Internet*—"

"Relax, Senator. It's not that simple. Nothing ever is, you know."

"People are already asking questions about your visit to my office the other day. This won't help."

The beer arrived. Darren took a sip. He shrugged. "So?"

"What do you want from me?"

He drank more of his beer. "Check out the Web site. Then we'll talk."

Lucy relished the mundane routine of deadheading the daylilies and hollyhocks in front of the garage. After the dead bat incident, she'd loaded up everyone with chores. J.T. and Georgie were pulling weeds, Madison was cleaning the kayaks and canoes and wiping down the life preservers. Lucy had asked both her children to stick close to home today. She was still debating sitting down with them tonight and telling them why. But she didn't want to act precipitously, scare them unnecessarily.

A shadow fell across her, and she looked up at Sebastian. "God, you keep materializing out of thin air."

He touched her elbow. "I came across the side yard. I don't think anyone saw me. Lucy, I need to talk to you."

"In here."

She ducked into the garage and moved to the back, among the shadows, out of view. The room smelled of old wood and grease and was exactly as Daisy had left it. Lucy hadn't touched a thing, from the half-century-old wooden wheelbarrow to the cleaned, oiled tools hanging from rafters and lined up on shelves.

Sebastian seemed attuned to every nuance of his environment. He'd grown up here, Lucy reminded herself, and knew this place and its history better than she did. She was aware of his closeness. He could move with such silence and speed, his presence immediate and overwhelming. She never had a chance to brace herself.

"What's going on?" she asked. "Is something wrong?"

"Did you let Madison go off into the woods on her own?"

Lucy was stunned. "*What?* No! She and J.T. are both doing chores today. She's out behind the barn cleaning canoes and kayaks."

"No, she isn't. She skipped out. I just saw her up in the woods."

Lucy clenched her hands into fists. "That little *shit*."

"Kid's got initiative," Sebastian said.

"She didn't tell me. I had no idea."

"I thought about going after her." His eyes seemed distant, calculating. "I decided to check with you first. I don't like coming between parents and their children."

"She got a phone call from one of her friends. I debated making her call back after she finished—" Lucy huffed, furious with her daughter. "Where is she?"

"On her way back. I got ahead of her."

"You wanted to make sure I wasn't letting her and J.T. run around on their own when I've got some bat-killing lunatic on my case." Frustration and fear welled up in her, and she kicked at an oil stain on the concrete floor. "I'm not an idiot."

Sebastian stayed calm. "I can get a countersurveillance team in here by morning. Plato can spring a few guys loose. If someone's conducting surveillance on your place, they'll know it."

"Oh, come on."

"Lucy, whoever put that bat in your bedroom knew you weren't around. That means you're being watched."

She crossed her arms over her chest, tapped a foot in nervous frustration. She wore a sundress today, with sandals and tiny gold earrings. Her hair was pulled back with a twisted red bandana as a headband. Madison had liked the look, said it was "retro." Retro what, Lucy didn't know.

"I hate this," she said.

Sebastian didn't answer.

"If I have a 'countersurveillance' team in here, I might as well call the Capitol Police and be done with it. I don't care how discreet your guys are, Sebastian. People will notice. You know they will. We don't get many guys with no necks and earpieces skulking around the woods."

"Is that a no?"

She dodged his question. Wasn't this why she'd gone to him in the first place? So he could be the judge? She didn't know anything about surveillance, countersurveillance, dangerous lunatics.

She headed to the front of the garage, then turned back to him. "Do you know what route Madison's taking?"

"The brook path."

"I'll intercept her. She can find out what cleaning a kayak with a toothbrush is like."

Sebastian grinned. "Good. I was beginning to think you were too soft on those kids."

"If I want your opinion, Redwing, I'll ask for it."

"You did, as I recall."

"And as *I* recall, you sent me packing—and it had nothing to do with my parenting skills."

He moved to the front of the garage, but still in the shadows. She was in full sun and couldn't make out his eyes. His expression was serious, and she wondered if he ever really laughed. "No," he said, "it was about who'd leave a dead bat in your bed."

She clamped her mouth shut. The dead bat, somehow, bothered her more than the bullet hole in her dining room window.

"It didn't die of natural causes," Sebastian added.

"Big surprise."

"Lucy…"

She faced him. "No countersurveillance or whatever-it-is team."

"I can't be everywhere."

She nodded. "I know. I have to think. Give me…" She squinted, warding off an oncoming headache. "Let me find my daughter."

"Stay with J.T. and his friend. I'll see to it Madison gets back okay."

"She's a good kid, Sebastian. She's just fifteen—"

But he was gone, and Lucy walked out back to the vegetable garden, where J.T. and Georgie were busily weeding the rows of beans. They'd picked up their pace when they saw her. They hadn't touched the pumpkins. She went over to the raised bed, little green pumpkins hanging from their prickly vines. She started pulling weeds, the big scraggly weeds. She'd yank them out, shake off the excess dirt, toss the cast-off plant into a pile. One after another. Not breathing, not thinking.

"Mom, geez," J.T. said.

She didn't break her pace. "I'm mad at Madison. Steer clear."

He didn't need to be told twice. "Come on, Georgie, let's go down to the brook   "

"No!" Lucy swung around at the two boys, a pigweed in one hand. "Not now. Go into the kitchen and get yourselves something to drink. I bought Popsicles."

"What kind?" Georgie asked dubiously. "My mom always buys the fruit juice popsicles. They stink."

Lucy forced herself to smile. "These are the gross, disgusting kind with added sugar and artificial color."

He laughed and clapped his hands. "Okay, J.T., let's go!"

In another minute, she saw Madison walking up from the brook. She came in behind the barn, looking oblivious to the trouble she was in. Lucy abandoned her weeding and made herself take three deep, cleansing breaths before she confronted her daughter.

The air was warm, with a light breeze. A gorgeous summer afternoon, the grass soft under her feet. She made herself pay attention to everything her senses were taking in, not just her anger and frustration and fear.

Madison was in a good mood. "Hi, Mom. I only have two more canoes, then I'm done."

"Where have you been?"

"I took a break after I finished the kayaks. I walked up to the falls. Don't worry, I didn't get too close."

"Madison, I asked you to do a job. You didn't do it." Lucy took another breath, tried to be direct, firm, reasonable. "If you wanted to take a walk, you should have told me."

"Mom, what's the matter with you? I always go off into the woods alone."

"Not today. I specifically asked you—"

"I *know*. I'm getting the stupid job done. It's boring, that's all. I thought you'd be happy I wanted to go into the woods. I mean, it's not like I could go to a mall for a break."

Not that old song today. Lucy gritted her teeth.

Madison kicked the ground. "There's no pleasing you."

"Look, this isn't getting us anywhere."

Lucy blinked up at the sky, trying to figure out what to do. Lock her daughter in her room? Level with her about the intimidation? She didn't know. There was no playbook for this one. She wanted to protect her children. That much she knew. But how?

She looked back at Madison, noticed the scratches and dirt on her arm from thrashing through the woods. Two weeks ago, Lucy would have been thrilled at the idea of her daughter making an effort to enjoy her surroundings. "I want to be kept informed on your whereabouts, that's all. And for the next few days, I don't want you or J.T. in the woods alone."

"Okay, fine. Fine! I'll just stay here and rot."

"Madison—"

But she stormed off to the house, pounding up the back steps, yelling at her brother and Georgie in the kitchen. A minute later, loud music emanated from her room.

Lucy resisted the urge to march up there and turn down the music herself, lace into her daughter about her behavior. But that wouldn't make either of them feel any better, and more important, it wouldn't help the situation. She'd overreacted to Madison's understanding of her transgression. And then Madison had overreacted.

Lucy started back to the house. Had Sebastian witnessed that little mother-daughter scene?

Just then, Rob and Patti Kiley's ancient car pulled into the driveway, and Patti jumped out, waving happily. She was an active, smart woman with graying hair and a bright, crooked smile that inevitably soothed those around her. "We brought dinner. We decided you were looking just a tad stressed. So, dinner on the porch, then a walk to the falls. Maybe we'll throw caution to the wind and take a dip."

Lucy couldn't hide her relief. "You're a godsend."

Rob got out of the car and nodded at Madison's room, the house practically vibrating with her music. "You want me to go up and agree with her that her mother's a crazy bitch and doesn't understand her?"

Patti glared at him. *"Rob."*

He grinned. "Well, isn't that what all teenagers think of their mothers?"

"No, it's not. That's pure prejudice."

"Okay." He shrugged; it was often impossible to know when he was serious and when he was pulling everyone's leg. "I'll just go up and offer to take her driving. Lucy?"

Lucy could feel herself beginning to relax. It wasn't just Madison and whoever was trying to get under her skin. It was Sebastian, too. His intensity, his seriousness. He was one for worst-case scenarios. She understood—her business required her to plan for worst-case scenarios. But that's not how she wanted to think right now.

She smiled. "Great idea, Rob. Thank God for good friends."

Chapter 7

The path along Joshua Brook hadn't changed much since Sebastian was a boy. He preferred this route. When he'd visited his grandmother, he'd always made a point of walking up to the falls. Daisy never joined him. For her, the falls were a place of tragedy, danger and loss, not beauty and adventure.

He remembered visiting her late in her life, when the strenuous hike up to the falls was beyond her capabilities. "I sometimes think I'd have been better off if I'd gone up there right after Joshua died," she'd told him. "But I waited too long. Sixty years."

"You've had a good life, Gran."

"Yes, I have."

But she'd never remarried, Sebastian thought now as he ducked under the low branch of a hemlock. What she'd tried to tell him—he'd been too thickheaded to see it—was that by refusing to go to the falls, she'd allowed at least a part of herself to stop time and refuse to acknowledge that Joshua Wheaton was dead. She'd buried him, she'd gone on with her life. But there was still that place deep inside her where her husband was on his way up into the woods on a wet March day after a boy and his dog. He was the young man she'd married—and she wasn't a widow, even sixty years later.

The path narrowed and almost disappeared as it went up a steep hill. Sebastian had to grab tree trunks and find his footing on exposed roots and rocks. The brook was fast-moving after last night's thunderstorms, coursing over gray, smooth rock down to his right. He was below the falls, close now.

He had made sure Madison Swift was back with her mother. As she'd sneaked back from the woods, he'd noticed the kick in the girl's step and wondered at its source. He doubted it was the beauty of the Vermont woods that had her in such a good mood. A boy? Friends? A fifteen-year-old could get into a lot of mischief on her own in the woods.

The air was drier than yesterday, not as buggy, even close to the water. Sebastian went past a huge boulder almost as tall as he was, the path disappearing with the thin, eroded soil.

He was near the falls now. A large, upward sloping boulder blocked his view, but below it, he could hear the water rushing over the series of slides, pools and cascades it had carved into a huge monolith of granite.

The falls were beautiful, intimate, deceptively treacherous. Sebastian worked his way methodically up the steep hill, eased out to the edge of the granite wall. Above him, the brook started its precipitous, downward journey over, through and into the massive rock, shaping it into long, curving, picturesque slides and cascades that dropped into a series of three pools. The first was deep and unforgiving with its surrounding sheer rock wall. It was directly below him, impossible to reach except by a risky dive out over the protruding rock. But he could understand the appeal of its clear, cold water, the thrill of the dangers it presented.

Water from the pool funneled over another slide that formed a second smaller, shallower pool farther down the falls, before cascading to a final large, shallow pool. The water in this last pool went from ankle-deep to, at most, three-feet deep this time of year; swimmers were in no danger of being swept up in the current or bashed against rock. A proper Vermont swimming hole. Below it, the brook reformed, quietly continuing downstream past the Wheaton farm.

Sebastian caught himself. It was Lucy's place now.

He ducked past a scraggly hemlock, half its roots protruding out over the falls, and peered down, imagining his grandfather coming up here sixty years ago. With the snowmelt, the water would have been high, raging. Had Joshua Wheaton even noticed the power and beauty of the gushing waterfall? Was he that kind of man?

Sebastian remembered wanting to be as brave and heroic as his grandfather. Now, he wondered if Joshua had gone over the falls because he'd screwed up, because he just didn't know what else to do and was flat out of options.

A noise...

Rocks, sand, a movement. Sebastian reacted instinctively, but already he knew he was too late. He'd let his mind wander. Now, there was no time to adjust, no room to maneuver. Rocks, sand and dirt gave way on the steep hillside above him, cascading onto his narrow ledge. There wasn't enough room for him and the small landslide coming at him.

He grabbed for the hemlock, but a softball-sized rock struck him on the back of his knees. He thought he heard a grunt, an exhale, above him. Then another rock hit him in the small of his back, throwing him completely off balance.

His body pitched forward, and for a timeless moment he was suspended in air. He was the grandfather he never knew, about to tumble to certain death.

Only his would be an ignoble death, Sebastian thought. Knocked off his feet while his mind was elsewhere.

His training and experience took over, forced out all thought. He tucked his chin into his chest to protect his head and let his butt and shoulders take most of the fall. He hit rock, bounced, hit more rock, bounced again and hit water.

He went in hard in a sprawling dive that stung, and the water was cold, cold, cold. His mind flashed on Plato, who'd done this sort of thing for a living and would have his own commentary if Sebastian survived.

His momentum took him under. He tried not to suck in water. He smashed into the gravel bottom, scraped his face raw, banged his knees. He found his footing and pushed up through the water, gasped in the cool air.

The landslide fell into the pool—small stones, pine needles, black soil. Sebastian didn't wait for another rock to come flying at him. Painfully, as quickly as he could manage, he swam to the opposite bank of the deep pool. He felt along the vertical rock wall, barely able to see, until it gave way just above the next water slide. He hoisted himself onto the rock slide, blood pouring down his face, his head spinning, the thirty-foot drop to the next pool directly beneath him.

If the water had been any higher, the current any stronger, he'd have gone over. Instead, the rock slide, smoothed and curved from the endless stream of water, came at him fast. He was passing out. He couldn't stop himself.

Grandpa.

He collapsed, and the blackness took him.

He knew he'd been unconscious only seconds. Long enough. He moved his shoulders, just a twitch, and pain erupted through his head. He ignored it. Water flowed under him. He eased up onto his hands and knees, scraped and cut and bruised from the fall.

He remembered the grunt, the exhale of air as who-ever was on the hill above him had hurled those rocks at him. It wasn't kids. It wasn't an accident, fate. It was deliberate, and it meant he was still in the open, in the line of fire. Anyone above him on the ledge could see him. A well-aimed rock could finish him off.

He hadn't actually seen anything. And his mind hadn't been on the job, on the moment. It had been in the past, proof he should never have come back here. He should have sent Plato or Jim Charger or Happy Ford. On paper, he was still the damn boss even if Plato really had run things for the past year.

He grabbed for handholds along the rock, cursing himself for his inattention. Lucy, memories. A toxic combination.

He moved off into the shade and shadows, reached up with both hands and caught hold of the protruding roots of a thin pine. His head pulsed with pain. He had one chance. If he didn't pull himself up the first time, he'd end up back down in the water. Either he or the skinny tree would give out. Maybe both.

Ignoring the pain, the blood, his spinning head, he heaved himself up, pulling hard on the root. It gave way, and he quickly shot one hand out and grabbed a thicker section of root, hoisting himself up over the rock and onto dry, soft ground. He fell in the shade of the pine.

His hands and arms were bloody and badly scraped. He could feel more blood dripping down his temples. His back was at least bruised.

He swore viciously.

Then he heard voices below him, from the shallow, pleasant swimming hole at the base of the falls. Kids. Tourists. Lucy. He couldn't tell.

He dropped his face onto the dried pine needles. Screw it. He wasn't moving. The path on this side of the falls was seldom used. He'd take his chances. If someone found him and called the rescue squad, so be it. He'd think of some reason for being here besides removing dead bats from Lucy Swift's bed.

"I'll be right back," he heard a woman's voice saying not too far away. Lucy. It was almost as if he'd imagined her voice, as if it weren't real. "I *know* I heard something."

It was real. She hears something, Sebastian thought, and goes off to investigate by herself. No wonder someone had gotten away with shooting up her dining room.

"Who's the one lying here half-dead?" he muttered out loud.

He sounded terrible. *Half-dead* was an understatement.

Above the rush of the waterfall and his own pain, he could hear more laughter, kids squealing. Adult voices. At least she hadn't left Madison and J.T. on their own.

"It was probably just a squirrel," a man's voice called up to her.

"I know. I'm just curious."

Sebastian shivered, the water evaporating on his skin making him colder. He wondered if the cold was what had killed his grandfather. Joshua had gone into the falls in March, not mid-summer.

A fat mosquito landed on his bloodied arm. Sebastian didn't have the strength to swat it, but watched it crawl in the red ooze. He swore some more, under his breath this time.

He could hear Lucy thrashing her way up the narrow, difficult path on his side of the falls. It would take her along the ledge above his head, about four feet up. If he stayed quiet, she might walk right past him, assume her friend was right, that she'd heard a squirrel, and go back to the swimming hole.

Which left the problem of how he'd get the hell back to his motel. His car was tucked out of sight down the dirt road. A long way off in his condition. He'd probably pass out a few times before he made it. In the meantime, whoever had created the little landslide and thrown rocks at him could return and finish him off. It wouldn't take much, and he deserved it. On the other hand, what good would he be to Lucy?

"You're not much damn good now," he muttered.

Suddenly she was there, standing on the path above him. All she had to do was look down through the trees.

He should have followed his instincts and stayed in

Wyoming. Ridden his horse. Slept in his hammock. He hadn't gambled in months, so that was out. He could play solitaire and read poetry.

He sighed, even his eyeballs aching. "Hello, Lucy."

She jumped, although not as much as he'd have expected. Maybe she was getting used to having him around. "Sebastian? What are you—oh, *Jesus.*"

Without hesitation, she slid down the hill on her butt—intentionally—and crouched next to him, the adventure travel expert at work. She had on shorts and a T-shirt. She hadn't, mercifully, bothered with a swimsuit for her dip in the brook with the kids. The water was only up to her knees.

Sebastian tried not to look as bloody and beaten as he was. He grinned. Or thought he did. "I could use some dry clothes."

"You could use an ambulance. What the hell happened?"

"Landslide. I fell."

The pretty hazel eyes narrowed. He could see doubt. And fear. She touched a finger to a spot above his right eye. "You need a doctor. You could have a concussion."

"Nah."

"You could need stitches."

"I don't mind scars, and I'm not going to bleed to death."

She stared at him for a few beats. "A landslide, huh?"

"Yep."

"It wasn't an accident," she said.

"It could have been. Theoretically."

She nodded. "Sebastian, tell me. Do I need to call an ambulance?"

He shook his head. A mistake. Her face swam in

front of him, and all that stopped him from throwing up was the thought of it landing in her lap. She'd pitch him back in the water or get her friends up here and call an ambulance. There'd be a scene.

He shut his eyes, let the world get still again. "No," he said, eyes shut, "I'll be fine."

"I should call the police."

"They won't find anything. I didn't see anything." He'd only heard the grunt, the exhale—not enough.

"Sounds familiar," she said in a low voice.

Sebastian opened his eyes. "I just need water and a few Band-Aids."

"Bullshit."

"Lucy!" her friend called from below. "You find anything?"

She stood up, yelled down over the falls, "I'll be right there!" She crouched back beside Sebastian. "That's Rob. He's a friend. He knows first aid better than I do. I could ask him—"

"No."

"God, you're stubborn. All right. He and Patti can go back with the kids. I'll make up some excuse and help you get to my house and patch you up." She eyed him. "Unless you can't make it. If you collapse on me, I'm getting a rescue team in here and having you hauled out on a stretcher."

Sebastian grimaced. He had limited choices, none good. "I'll make it. I don't need your help."

"Ha," she said, and scooted back down the hill.

Sebastian was a slab of meat—cold, wet, bloody. Lucy had to catch him twice on their way down to her house. He would walk fifteen or twenty feet, crash

against a tree or grab uselessly at ferns to steady himself, walk another fifteen or twenty feet. He was lucky
he'd survived his fall.

They took a longer but easier path up from the brook
and slipped in through the back door of the house. Madison, J.T. and the Kileys had arrived ahead of them and
were in the side yard playing volleyball.

Lucy knew she'd have to explain Sebastian at some
point. But not right now.

He sank against the kitchen counter. He was very
pale, his eyes shut. Blood crusted on the gash above his
right eye. He looked awful. Lucy wondered if she could
sneak in a call to 9-1-1 while he was half out.

"World spinning on you?" she asked.

His eyes were slits. "Just catching my breath."

"Ha."

"Florence Nightingale, you're not."

She eased her shoulder under his arm. "Lean on me.
I still have a little *oomph* left."

"I'll crush you."

"No, you won't. I'll take most of your weight in my
legs. Come on, let's get moving before you pass out. It'd
be harder having to drag you by your feet."

"Where are we going?"

"My bedroom."

He managed a faint, ironic smile. She slipped an arm
around his back, taking more of his weight. She saw
him wince in pain. Bruises. More scrapes. Possibly a
cracked rib or two. He was a mess.

"You're not going anywhere for a while," she said.

He didn't answer. He was too far gone to argue. Lucy
half coaxed, half dragged him down the short hall to
her bedroom. Just inside the door, he collapsed onto his

knees on the flat-braided rug. She debated leaving him there. Just shut the door and hope for the best when she opened it again.

"Come on." She caught up one arm and tugged. "We're almost there."

"I like it here." He slumped onto his stomach, and, without raising his head, said, "I'll be fine—you can go."

He stopped moving. Lucy, exhausted and hot, knelt beside him. He was either asleep or unconscious. "Sebastian?"

"I'm not dead yet."

She ran to the window overlooking the side yard west of the house, opposite the barn and garage, where the volleyball game was breaking up. She'd called down from the waterfall and had told Rob and Patti and the kids to all go ahead of her, that she'd go on to the house in a bit. No explanation. Rob had looked faintly suspicious, well aware from recent days that she wasn't herself. This was just more evidence.

"Hi, guys," she called through the screen. "I'll be out in a minute."

"Forget it," Madison said. "The bugs are eating us alive."

Patti tucked the ball under one arm. "You okay, Lucy?"

"Oh, yeah. I just slipped and got my feet wet." That would explain her damp clothes from leaning against the soaked, dripping Sebastian. It didn't explain the streaks of his blood. "I'll put on fresh clothes and meet you out front."

She dashed back to Sebastian, who was still prone on her rug. "Are you conscious?"

"Unfortunately."

"I'll be right back. Don't try to get up without me."

"Don't worry."

She stepped over him, grabbed a T-shirt out of her drawer, and debated ducking down the hall to the bathroom. Forget it. Sebastian's eyes were pointed in the other direction, and he wasn't in any condition to make any unnecessary movements. She whipped off the wet, blood-spattered shirt and pulled on the fresh one. The clean, dry cotton against her skin instantly made her feel better.

When she got outside, Rob and Patti had the leftovers packed into the cooler. Lucy was breathing harder than she should be from an ordinary trek down from the falls.

Rob, who knew her capabilities, noticed. "Did you eat enough at dinner? You look whipped."

She *hated* lying. The trust she'd built among herself and her children, her friends, her staff, was based on being honest and straightforward. They might not like what she had to say, but it was always truthful. These, however, were extenuating circumstances. She had a bloodied Sebastian Redwing in her bedroom.

"I pushed it more than I realized," she said. "Thanks for dinner. My turn next."

He didn't look appeased. "Lucy..."

Patti touched his arm. "Come on, Rob, let's go. We don't want to outstay our welcome." She smiled at Lucy. "You take care. Call us if you need anything."

They both were suspicious, Lucy decided. Patti probably suspected a romantic tryst; Rob, something to do with the big, fat bullet Lucy had yet to adequately explain.

They collected Georgie, and Lucy waved as they backed out of the driveway.

"I wish Georgie could spend the night," J.T. said from the porch.

Lucy joined him, her legs heavy and aching with each step. J.T. was hogging the wicker settee. Madison was flopped in a wicker chair, her long legs hung over one side. Both kids looked beat. Good, Lucy thought. They'd sleep well tonight.

"I'll explain more later," she said, "but I want you both to know that Sebastian Redwing is here."

Madison nearly fell off her chair. *"What?"*

J.T. was instantly excited. "He is? Where?"

"He's the noise I heard up at the falls. He took a nasty fall, and I helped him back here. He doesn't want it to get out that he's in town. That's why I didn't mention him to Rob and Patti." She should have, she thought. She should have just gotten it over with. There was no way J.T. wouldn't blab.

"Why wouldn't he want anyone around here to know he's in town?" Madison asked.

"Because he's from here."

"Oh. Actually, I get that."

"He'll need to recuperate a day or two," Lucy went on. "If you two will make up the guest room upstairs, I'll sleep up there. I need to get back to him. You two can manage?"

"We'll be fine, Mom." Madison was already on her feet, her face flushed. In her dull, deprived world, Lucy thought wryly, the sudden appearance of Sebastian Redwing passed for excitement. "Let us know if there's anything else we can do."

"I will. Thanks."

When Lucy got back to her bedroom, Sebastian was on his feet, his shirt off. His jeans hung low on his lean hips. His arms, shoulders, back and chest were scraped and raw, bruises forming. His injuries aside, Lucy noted he was in impressive physical condition. He couldn't have spent all his time in his hammock.

"You can stay here tonight," she said. "I'll throw your clothes in the wash. The kids and I can run out to your motel room tomorrow and fetch anything else you need."

"I can drive myself back to my motel."

"*Don't* argue with me. I'm not in the mood."

He gave her a ghostly smile. "Yes, ma'am."

This wasn't a man who took easily to injury and incapacity, Lucy thought. "Sit down before you fall down." She tore open the closet door, pulled out a shoe box that contained her medical supplies. "Do you need help getting your pants off?"

"No. No help required."

Something in his voice caused heat to surge up her spine. But she concentrated on the task at hand, rummaging in the shoe box. Her work required first aid training. Rob had full wilderness EMT qualifications, but she'd sent him home. She'd have to make do.

She grabbed antibiotic ointment and her wilderness medicine manual, leaving the rest for now.

Sebastian had crawled under the wedding-ring quilt his grandmother had made. His jeans were neatly hung over the foot post. He pointed to them. "They can dry right there. I'm not giving up my damn pants."

"I can run them through the wash in no time—"

"Not without a backup pair, you're not. I don't see anyone in this house who'd wear my size."

Lucy shrugged. "Suit yourself."

"What's the book?"

"My wilderness medicine manual. I want to double-check and make sure I'm treating you properly."

"Lucy." His look was dark. "You're not treating me at all."

She ignored him and turned to the page that described falls on rocks. She didn't think she needed to bother with the stuff on near drownings. "First we have to make sure the bleeding's stopped and you don't have any broken bones."

"Done. Next?"

"Your head. It's possible you have a concussion."

"If I do, it's mild and there's nothing to be done about it. So." He shifted position, wincing. "That's it. You can scoot."

Her eyes pinned him down. "I could have left you to the mosquitoes."

"And you think that would have been worse?"

"Your bravado must be exhausting. Why don't you just shut up and let me do this? I have basic first aid training. Except for minor scrapes and bee stings, I've never really had to use it. Rob has more experience." She sat on the edge of the bed. "Are you sure you don't want me to have him take a look at you?"

"Speed counts, Lucy."

She laid her manual on the bedside stand, open to the appropriate page. "You're sure you didn't puncture a lung or break a couple of ribs?"

"Ribs're fine," he said. "Lungs're fine."

As annoying as he was, she could see that talking was an effort for him. She examined the nastiest gash, the one above his eye. "It probably could use a couple of stitches." But he didn't answer, and she assumed any discussion of stitches was over. "I'll need to clean your wounds."

"Brook did that."

"Brook water is not a proper disinfectant."

His eyes darkened, their many shades of gray helping to communicate in no uncertain terms the low ebb of his patience. This was not a man who liked being at anyone's mercy.

Lucy decided to trust him on the ribs and lungs. "Let me get a few more supplies. I'll only be a second."

She was all of half a minute looking through her shoebox, but when she turned back to him, he was asleep. Or unconscious. "Sebastian?"

She sat on the edge of the bed and leaned close. His breathing seemed normal enough. She decided he'd dozed off. Just as well. Trying to be as efficient as possible, she quickly dipped sterile gauze into disinfectant and cleaned the gash and the worst of his scrapes, leaving the more minor injuries. She dabbed on antibiotic ointment. The gash on his head had to be bandaged. She was as gentle as possible, touching him only where she absolutely had to.

When she finished, he opened one eye. "Nurse Lucy."

"You were awake?"

"I figured pretending to be asleep would make it easier on both of us. You wouldn't be so nervous, and I wouldn't have to sit here forever."

She stiffened. "You don't make me nervous, Redwing."

That amused him. "Sure."

"Well, I see the fall didn't knock the jackass out of you." She slid off the bed. "Should I give you a couple of Tylenol or let you macho out the night in pain?"

"So long as I can see Tylenol clearly written on the tablets."

They were extra-strength capsules, and he checked.

Lucy stared at him. "You don't think *I* pelted you with rocks and pitched you over the falls, do you?"

He didn't answer. She told herself it was because of his injuries. Even a man whose professional life could reasonably make him cynical and paranoid couldn't think she was capable of injuring or killing anyone.

She felt the blood draining out of her, shock settling now that the immediate crisis was over. "Do you really think this wasn't an accident?"

"Yes."

"But you don't *know.* It could have been kids messing around, or a spontaneous landslide—"

"Could have."

But Lucy saw that wasn't what he believed. Of course, he wouldn't. His life and the work he did had conditioned him to believe the worst. "Do you think whoever did this wanted you dead?"

"I don't think it mattered."

He drifted off. Either he was asleep, or too out of it to talk. Lucy stood at his bedside. Bruises were forming, and there was swelling, although nothing looked alarming. He was in no position to stop her from calling the police.

She turned on the fan and went into the hall, shutting the door behind her. She listened at the door, just to make sure he hadn't stirred. If he tried to get up and collapsed again, she'd have to leave him on the floor. She didn't have enough strength left to get him back in her bed.

She bit her lip at the rush of heat she felt, remembering last night's searing kiss. Well, that was over. The man couldn't even stand up tonight.

She headed upstairs. Madison and J.T. had the twin

bed in the guest room made up with one of Daisy's ubiquitous quilts. It was a small room with simple furnishings and a dormer window overlooking the front yard.

"How's Sebastian?" Madison asked.

"He'll be fine. He really took a nasty fall." She pulled out a painted yellow chair at Daisy's old pedal-operated sewing machine and sat down. Her legs were twitchy from exertion and nerves. "Madison, when you were up in the woods this afternoon...did you see anyone?"

Madison shook her head. "No."

Lucy went very still, her parental instincts telling her that her daughter was hiding something. "Are you sure?"

"Of course I'm sure."

"Not even the summer people?"

"I saw the optometrist in his car." A Boston optometrist owned one of the vacation homes on the dirt road up on the ridge. "I thought you meant while I was out walking—"

"I did."

J.T. jumped up from the bed. "Me and Georgie saw a truck turn around in the driveway."

Lucy stayed focused on her daughter. "If you remember seeing anyone else, let me know."

Madison nodded. No argument. No sarcasm. No impatience with her mother for interrogating her. This struck Lucy as suspicious. Either she looked more done in than she realized and Madison was giving her a break—or her daughter wasn't telling the truth.

"Listen a minute," Lucy said, "both of you. I've got a lot on my mind, and I need you both to cooperate. Sebastian got hurt in a landslide up at the falls. I don't want you two going out in the woods alone until further notice."

"Mom, I'm fifteen—"

"That's the way it is, Madison."

Lucy debated telling them about the strange incidents, but she knew it would frighten them. This was her burden, not theirs. She needed to tell them enough to keep them safe, not paralyze them with fear.

J.T. gave her a hug. "Do you like Sebastian?"

"I don't know. I haven't thought about it. He got hurt, and I'm trying to help out." She patted her son's back; he was sweaty from volleyball, but still, at twelve, a little boy. "I guess he's okay."

"Is he doing his Clint Eastwood act?" Madison asked.

"I don't think it was an act. Anyway, he's not wearing his cowboy hat and boots."

J.T. untangled himself from her. "Can I see him?"

"In the morning." Lucy got to her feet. "Now, I think showers are in order. I'll go first. Find a good book to read. Relax. Okay?"

She hugged and kissed them both, then, in spite of her own fatigue, went back downstairs to check on Sebastian. "Are you asleep?" she whispered from the door.

"No."

"Is there anything I can get you?"

She could feel his eyes on her. He was half sitting up, his face lost in the shifting shadows of the encroaching night. The fan whirred. "Your instincts were right. Something's going on around here." He fell back against his pillow. "You should call Plato."

"What can he do that you can't? I told you, I don't want to call in the cavalry if I don't have to."

"Plato isn't rusty. I am. He still carries a weapon." He paused, and his voice lowered. "I don't."

"Sebastian, if we're to the point you're worried about having to *shoot* someone, I'll call the police. I won't hesitate."

"I'm through with violence, Lucy."

She stared at him. "What?"

"Last year I had to shoot a man I once considered a friend. I intended to kill him—I thought I had."

"Jesus," Lucy breathed.

"I turned Redwing Associates over to Plato and quit the business." His gaze seemed to bore into her. "I came out of retirement for you, but I won't kill again."

Lucy straightened, trying to shake off a sudden sense of gloom. "Good heavens, Madison's right. You *are* like Clint Eastwood in *Unforgiven*."

She thought she saw a small smile, but with the fading light, she couldn't be sure. "I was never a drunk."

"Rest. We'll talk in the morning. I don't want you to kill anyone. Although," she added with a smile, "you could wing the bastard."

Jack Swift typed in the information on the card Mowery had given him at lunch. It was late, quiet in his second-floor study. Only the brass lamp on his desk was lit. With Sidney attending a function at the Kennedy Center, he was alone.

He waited for the images to download. His computer was old and slow, but he was from a generation that didn't "upgrade" until something stopped working, whether it was a toaster or a damn computer. He thought he was doing well having one in his house at all.

The images slowly appeared on his screen. He braced

himself. He expected illicit, pornographic pictures of his dead son and another woman.

Lucy.

Jack sat up straight, pain shooting through his chest. "Dear God," he whispered.

She was standing in front of the barn at her house in Vermont. She wore shorts and a T-shirt; flowers bloomed in a nearby garden. The picture had been taken recently.

The next pictures formed. Madison. J.T. His grand-children together with their mother. All could have been taken last week.

"Bastard," Jack said, clutching his chest. *"Bastard."*

At the bottom of the screen, in big, black, easy-to-read letters were the words "The lovely family of United States Senator Jack Swift."

The pictures were Mowery's way of proving he could reach Jack's family. Of proving he *had* reached them.

Jack shut off the computer. He waited a few seconds for the pain in his chest to subside. If he dropped dead of a heart attack, would Mowery stop? Would he go after Lucy and the kids, anyway, out of frustration and vengeance?

He couldn't call the Capitol Police. It was too late now for official channels. For doing what he should have done in the first place.

Calming himself, Jack reached for his Rolodex. He flipped to a card, dialed the number scrawled on it. His instructions had been to call anytime, day or night.

"Redwing Associates."

"Yes," he said in his best senatorial voice. "This is Jack Swift. I'd like to speak to Sebastian Redwing."

Chapter 8

Barbara was sick with fear and disgust.

Sebastian Redwing hadn't seen her. She was *sure* of it. But if he hadn't lost his balance—if he hadn't gone into the falls—he would have come after her. As it was, she'd had to pelt additional rocks at him to get him into the water.

A close call. Too close.

Thank God for her instincts. They'd warned her someone was nearby, and she'd ducked off the path and spotted him at the falls. Otherwise, she'd have bumped into him. She'd have had to scramble for an explanation.

He was still thrashing about in the water when she'd heard Lucy, the children and their low-life friends at the bottom of the falls. Barbara had crouched in the brush and ferns, itching and sweating as she'd waited, motion-less, before finally creeping back up to the dirt road.

A very close call, indeed.

Now, pacing on the deck of the house she'd rented for the senator, she couldn't believe the risks she'd taken. She was calculating and intelligent, not one to succumb to impulse. If her friends and colleagues in Washington learned of this obsession of hers, these risky escapades, they would be shocked. They wouldn't understand. *She* didn't understand. She imagined what a bulimic girl must feel like, eating away at dinner, then throwing up in secret—the satisfaction, the disgust, the inability to stop herself.

Except she didn't have a disorder, Barbara thought. She could stop herself, if only she would.

She leaned against the deck rail, listening to the brook, the cool early-morning breeze gusting in the woods. Such a peaceful, beautiful spot. She'd chosen well. Jack would enjoy his time here, even if he should be seeing to his constituents in Rhode Island.

What if you'd killed Sebastian Redwing?

Once she'd spotted him lurking in the woods, she'd known Lucy had contacted him on her trip to Wyoming. Lucy had gone crying to him about the few little things that had happened to her over the previous week. Barbara hated whiners. And Sebastian was Colin's friend, not Lucy's. Lucy had no right.

Now Barbara had to worry Darren would find out. "God *damn* you, Lucy."

Well, Sebastian Redwing had survived. Lucy had helped him down to her house. Barbara had seen them as she'd hid in the woods like a madwoman.

Would Madison tell her mother—and Sebastian— about their visit yesterday?

It didn't matter. No one would make the connection

between Sebastian's accident at the falls and Barbara's presence in Vermont. She breathed deeply, reminding herself she was the only one who knew—who could even imagine—she could do such a thing. To everyone else, she was the competent, professional, longtime personal assistant to a United States senator.

She sighed, feeling better, calmer. Sebastian Redwing was here in Vermont, and maybe she should tell Darren—but she wouldn't.

Sebastian awoke to a pounding head and the sounds of J.T. and his buddy playing *Star Wars* outside his window. He moaned, not moving, not even opening his eyes. "I hate kids."

The boys were throwing things—his guess, green tomatoes—and pretending they were bombs exploding on impact, with appropriate sound effects. Sebastian remembered playing similar games with his grandmother's green tomatoes.

"Boys!" Lucy yelled, probably from the back steps. "Those are my tomatoes!"

Explanations followed. They were the knobby tomatoes. They'd fallen off the vine. It was good to weed out the weaker tomatoes so the strong could get big and ripen.

Lucy wasn't buying. "Stay *out* of the tomatoes. Why don't you go pick blackberries? I'll make a cobbler."

"What's a cobbler?" J.T. asked. Apparently his mother didn't make too many cobblers.

She threatened to put them to work in the barn sorting mail. They grabbed cans from the recycling bin and vanished. Welcome silence followed.

Sebastian carefully rolled out of bed. It had been a

hellish night. The pain and humiliation of falling into the water. Thoughts of kissing Lucy. And memories. So damn many memories. At fourteen, in shock from his parents' sudden deaths, he'd never wanted to leave here.

He reeled, reaching out for a bedpost to steady himself.

"Mom! Sebastian's dying!"

Two boys' faces popped into the window screen facing the backyard. The little bastards were spying on him. He banged on the screen as if they were a couple of pesky moths, and they gasped and cleared out.

Lucy burst in. Her mistake. He was hanging on to the bedpost in his shorts. "Oh," she said, grinding to a halt in the doorway. "I thought—J.T. said—"

He grinned. It was a damned nasty thing to do, but he felt like it. "Be glad I still have my shorts on. Those kids need to learn some manners."

"They know their manners. They just don't always employ them." She had a portable phone in one hand. "I should have remembered to pull the shades."

"Should have thought of it myself."

"You're all right?"

"A pot of coffee and a bottle of aspirin would help."

She nodded and retreated, shutting the door behind her. Sebastian sank onto the bed. He wasn't up to catching bad guys today. He was sore as hell with a mood to match.

He reached for his pants on the footboard, and realized instantly they'd been washed. His shirt was folded next to them. Lucy had managed to sneak in and out of his room at least twice—once to get his clothes, again to return them freshly laundered. He hadn't known. This did not improve his mood.

He got dressed and found his way to the bathroom. Except for fresh paint and towels in bright, vibrant colors, it hadn't changed since Daisy's day. A look in the mirror told him why J.T. and his friend thought he was dying—and why they'd run off when he'd growled at them. Dried blood, raw scrapes, purple and yellow bruises.

And he needed a shave, but the only razor around was pink. He decided to wait.

He staggered out to the kitchen, where Lucy was at her laptop at the table. She had on a white top and shorts—simple, sexy. She barely looked up at him. "Coffee's made."

"Thank you." He moved slowly to the counter. "You stole my pants in the middle of the night."

"Actually, it was only about nine o'clock. You were dead to the world."

"What if bad guys had stormed the house?"

"I could dial 9-1-1 as easily as you could."

She kept the mugs in the same place Daisy had. He dragged one out and poured his coffee. "I hate going after bad guys in my shorts. I like having my pants. It's one of my rules." He leaned against the counter with his coffee. "Lucy Blacker, are you laughing at me?"

"Me? No way." She tapped a few keys. "Anyway, since you've renounced violence, you wouldn't have gone after the bad guys even if you were up to it."

The coffee was hot and strong, and made him feel almost human again. He took note of Lucy's bare arms and legs, their smooth muscles. She was strong and fit. No wonder she'd been able to help him down from the falls.

"The best thing to do in a dangerous situation," he

said, "is to get out of it. Having a gun can give you a false sense of security. And just because I've renounced killing," he added, "doesn't mean I can't still catch bad guys."

She licked her lips. "Have you renounced all violence or just deadly force?"

"I don't carry a gun. I don't own any firearms. When I did, I only fired my weapon when I believed deadly force was the only option." He sipped more of his coffee. "You don't shoot to wound someone. You shoot to kill."

"Uck," she said.

"Yes. It's too often too easy to see shooting as your only option when you're armed to the teeth."

"But would you hit someone?"

He smiled, which made his face ache. "As in spanking or beating the shit out of someone?"

She flushed slightly, whether out of annoyance or embarrassment, he couldn't tell. Probably annoyance. He didn't think Lucy embarrassed easily. She looked at him. "What would you have done if you'd caught whoever knocked you into the falls yesterday?"

"I don't deal in hypotheticals." He dropped onto a chair across from her. "I've done enough killing. That's my only point."

She nodded. "I understand."

"No, you don't, which is good. Can you point me to breakfast?"

"I can even fix you breakfast."

"You pulled me off the rocks and washed my clothes. That's enough."

She got up and opened the refrigerator. "I don't need you collapsing on my kitchen floor. A cheddar cheese omelette okay?"

"It would be wonderful. Thank you."

The kitchen quickly filled with the smell of eggs, butter, Vermont cheddar cheese and toast. Sebastian remembered countless sunny summer mornings here in his grandmother's kitchen. In Wyoming during the past year, while he gambled, rode his horses, walked with his dogs, bided time in his hammock and otherwise did nothing, he'd found himself haunted by his childhood in Vermont. Images, memories, smells, the hopes and dreams of the introspective boy he'd been. He'd assumed it was because of Lucy, knowing she was here. But maybe not.

He refilled his mug and reached for the bottle of Extra-strength Tylenol.

Lucy turned a lightly browned omelette onto a plate. "Why didn't you go to the funeral?" she asked quietly.

At first he thought she was talking about Daisy, but he pulled himself out of his own depths and realized she meant Colin. "I was in Bogotá. A kidnapping case."

"You didn't call, write, send a flower—"

"Would it have made you feel better if I had?"

She buttered the toast, not looking at him. "No. That's not the point."

He knew it wasn't.

She placed his food in front of him and walked out of the kitchen, leaving him to his breakfast. And her laptop. Sebastian slid it over with one finger and poked around her hard drive while he ate. Lucy Blacker Swift was a very busy lady, he decided. Her adventure travel company was an attractive mix of active sports, education and relaxation. He called up a draft of her new brochure. Autumn inn-to-inn canoe trips ranging from a long weekend to ten days. Sea kayaking on the coast of Maine. A nature and history hike in Newfoundland. And on it went. Each trip was described with the kind of rich detail that made Sebastian realize he hadn't been that many places just for fun. Tracking down kidnappers in Colombia wasn't the same as enjoying its fascinating culture and scenery.

Madison plopped onto the chair across from him. "Are you spying on my mother?"

No good-morning. No polite enquiry into the state of his health. He eyed her over the laptop's screen. "I'm checking my email."

"No, you're not. The modem's not hooked up."

"Okay. I'm spying on your mother."

She gave him a direct, no-nonsense look. "Why?"

The kid was a pain. "You're fifteen. Why don't you have a job?"

"I do have a job. I work for Mom's company."

"That's not a job. That's working for your mother."

She made a face. Probably if he weren't so bloodied and bruised and dangerous-looking, she'd have told him what was what. The kid had spirit. He shut down Lucy's money file and a financial spreadsheet he'd pulled up. Taking a look at her new brochure was easier to explain. He'd have to talk to her about password protection.

"I figure you can drive me out to my motel," he said. "I need to pick up a few things if I'm going to be laid up here."

"Me?"

"Yeah, you. You drive, right?"

"I have my learner's permit. I can't drive without an adult—"

"I'm an adult."

Her mouth snapped shut.

"Go ask your mother while I finish my breakfast."

The girl seemed taken aback. "Are you serious?"

He sighed. "Don't I look serious? I fell off a flipping cliff last night. I'm not in the mood to joke around."

She mumbled something about asking her mother, and fled. If nothing else, Sebastian figured he'd given her a good excuse to make her retreat. He'd always made kids nervous. He didn't know why.

Madison returned in a few minutes, breathless. "Mom said absolutely not."

"How come?"

She shrugged. She was a pretty kid, looked a lot like her father.

Sebastian grinned at her. "You mean you didn't put up a fight? I thought all fifteen-year-olds snapped up every opportunity to drive."

"I have things to do," she said quickly, and disappeared.

A teenager who didn't want to get behind the wheel. He had to look bad.

At least his head was clearing, if slowly. He felt better after eating. He cleaned up his dishes and poured himself a third cup of coffee, staring out at the backyard. Birds twittered in the garden, and he could hear the hum of bumblebees in the still summer air. A Japanese beetle had made its way onto the kitchen windowsill.

The air, the feel of the light, the vegetation—everything was so different from Wyoming. This was more like a dream, or an elusive memory.

"What do you need at your motel?" Lucy asked behind him.

He pulled himself back into the moment. This wasn't Daisy's house anymore. This was Lucy's house, and

Lucy was in a kind of trouble that still didn't make sense to him.

He turned and leaned against the counter, avoiding any sudden movements that could send his head or stomach into a tailspin. "I want to check out."

"And go back to Wyoming?"

"And move in here for a few days."

She didn't react. She wasn't twenty-two anymore, the happy and ambitious young woman starting a life with Colin Swift, the son of a senator, a decent human being who wanted to make the world a better place. Sebastian didn't have such high hopes for himself. Now she was the mother of two children, he realized, and a thirty-eight-year-old widow. She was making a name for herself in the competitive world of adventure travel. If the years had made her stronger, they'd also taken some of the spark out of her. She knew life could kick her in the head.

"I've been thinking," she said. "If your fall yesterday wasn't an accident—"

"Which we don't know."

"Granted. But if it was deliberate, why you? Why not Rob or Patti or me?"

"Two immediate possibilities. One, our little friend saw me checking on you and your place, didn't know who I was and worried I'd mess up their fun. Two, our little friend recognized me."

"How?"

"I grew up here, and I have my share of enemies from my work."

"But your work has nothing to do with me," Lucy said.

Sebastian chose not to tell her about Darren Mowery. "True."

"Could it be someone I'd know, too?"

"Maybe."

Her brow furrowed. "Who?"

"If I knew who," he said, "this'd be over."

She gave herself a small shake. "This'll make me crazy. All right. I'll go check you out of the motel. You can bunk in my room. I'll move upstairs to the guest room."

"I don't mind the guest room."

"Are you kidding? If someone leaves another dead animal in my bed, I'd much prefer you be the one to find it." She grabbed her keys off a wall hook. "You'll look after the kids while I'm gone? Rob's putting Madison to work this morning, and J.T.'s hanging out with Georgie. They have chores to do."

"My childhood revisited," Sebastian said drily.

She smiled over her shoulder at him. "A little normalcy will do you good."

She pushed open the screen door, felt the morning air warming up fast. "I don't like the idea of you going out to my motel by yourself," he said.

"Oh, sure. Big help you'd be." She turned and shook her head at him through the screen. "Sorry, Redwing, but you look as if you took a header off a waterfall. I know, even beaten and broken, you can probably still take half the men on the planet, but—" she flipped him another smile "—I'll take my cell phone and call 9-1-1 if I run into trouble."

"Have the desk clerk go into my room with you."

She trotted down the back steps, calling back, "Why? If anyone's hiding under your bed, I wouldn't want to endanger some poor innocent desk clerk. If not, then there's no reason to worry."

He went to the door. "Lucy."

She looked up at him. "I'll be fine, Sebastian. Back in an hour." She frowned suddenly. "Oh, wait."

For a moment, he thought she'd changed her mind about going alone. But she ran back into the kitchen, grabbed her laptop, and, as she walked past him again, said, "I'll remove temptation."

Two minutes after she left, J.T. and Georgie made their way into the kitchen. They kept their distance, checking him out like a couple of wary dogs.

"He looks scary," Georgie half whispered to his buddy.

J.T. licked his lips and asked Sebastian politely, "How are you feeling this morning?"

"All in all, I'd rather be in Wyoming. What're you boys up to? I thought you had chores."

"We're done," J.T. pronounced.

"I'll bet. Let's go take a look at your mother's garden, see if it's weed-free."

They didn't like that idea, but they weren't going to tell him. They scampered back outside, Sebastian following at his own reduced speed. He hurt like hell. Pure, dumb luck had saved him worse injury. He couldn't afford to let his mind wander again.

But when he stepped into Lucy's garden, it was as if his past reached up out of the ground and grabbed him by the throat. The feel of the warm dirt under his feet, the sounds of the birds and the wind, the smell of flowers and earth and mown grass. Skinny beans hung from bushy plants. Green tomatoes slowly ripened in the sun. Five varieties of lettuce were at various stages of growth, and prickly vines of cucumbers, summer squash, zucchini and pumpkins spread in their raised beds.

Daisy hadn't had raised beds or mulched paths. She'd planted more vegetables. Her garden hadn't been just a hobby, it had been a way of life for her. What she couldn't use herself, she'd given away. And she'd always had garden work for Sebastian. It wouldn't have occurred to her not to.

She'd never assumed he didn't want the place. Even when she was old and dying, and he was starting his own business and buying a ranch in Wyoming, she'd told him, "You'll get the farm after I die."

"I don't want it," he'd said.

"So what? Once you get it, you can do with it as you please. I don't have anyone else."

"You could donate it to the Nature Conservancy."

She'd scoffed at that idea. "If you get yourself killed before I die peacefully in my sleep of natural causes, then I'll consider giving it away. I worked too hard to hang on to this place. If I'd wanted to give it away, I'd have done it fifty years ago."

He hadn't tried to follow her logic. Daisy Wheaton had a mind of her own, and she'd do what she meant to do, regardless of what he thought. She'd lost a husband and her daughter, her only child, and gone on without them, living by a code that made sense to her.

"You'll know what to do with the place, Sebastian," she'd told him later, when she walked with a cane and could no longer tend her gardens. "I know you will."

He'd sold it to Lucy.

"Can we go fishing?" J.T. asked.

Sebastian shook off the onslaught of memories. This was why he'd gotten rid of the damn place. It stole his mind, invaded his senses. "No. Weed the squash. Then you can go fishing."

"Mom didn't say we had to—"

"I'm saying it."

J.T. stood his ground. "You're not our boss."

Sebastian smiled. It was about the first time the kid had impressed him. "So? You're still weeding the squash. I'll sit up on the back steps and watch you."

"Mom trusts us."

"Good for her. I don't. First chance you get, you boys'll be sneaking off to the brook. Did she tell you no fishing without adult supervision?"

They didn't answer, which meant she had.

"Yeah," Sebastian said, smug, and headed stiffly to the back steps.

Madison appeared in the back door. "Sebastian, there's a call for you. Your friend Plato Rabe—I can't say his last name."

"Rabedeneira."

"He was calling for Mom. I told him you were here, and he said he'd talk to you."

She looked at him expectantly, as if he'd explain, but he took the portable phone from her without comment. Being her mother's daughter, she stayed in the door. He sat on the steps and glanced up at her. "You going to listen in?"

She blushed. "I wasn't—"

"I thought you were working in the barn."

"I was. I'm on break."

These kids. "Your brother could use help weeding."

"I don't weed," she said. His look must have done the trick because she added quickly, "But I will today.

It's not like I don't have chores in the garden. I picked beans the other night."

"That was the other night." He pointed with the phone. "Weeds're waiting."

She slid off down the steps, and Sebastian put the phone to his ear. "I'm here."

"I don't even want to know what that was all about," Plato said. "Sounds like goddamn *Rebecca of Sunnybrook Farm.*"

"Tell me you've ever read *Rebecca of Sunnybrook Farm.* What's up?"

"Jack Swift called for you."

Sebastian was silent.

"Blackmail," Plato said.

"Mowery."

"He wouldn't give me the details, just that someone's blackmailing him and he wants to talk to you."

"Did you tell him where I was?"

"No."

It was a stupid question. Of course, he wouldn't. Plato was a talker, but he wasn't indiscreet. "No details on the blackmail?"

"None."

What could the intrusive and determined Darren Mowery find on a squeaky-clean senator like Jack Swift?

"The girl said something about you slipping into a waterfall?"

Sebastian sighed. No secrets in this family. "I had help."

"Let me know when you need me," Plato said. "I'm scheduled to leave Frankfurt in the morning. I can leave tonight."

"I'll let you know. Thanks, Plato."

"Happy Ford hasn't picked up Mowery's trail. I put her on Jack Swift."

Sebastian nodded. "We won't find Mowery unless he wants us to."

"You found him a year ago."

"Yes," Sebastian said, "but I didn't finish the job."

Lucy parked in front of Sebastian's motel room and let herself in with his key. The room was hot and dark, the curtains and shades pulled, and she felt as if she were meeting a lover. She quickly reminded herself the man who'd occupied this room was in no condition for a romantic tryst or whatever it was her mind was conjuring. And besides, he was Sebastian Redwing.

"Enough said," she muttered and got to work.

His clothes and personal items were simple, functional and obviously expensive. He was a man accustomed to travel. There was nothing frivolous, just exactly what he needed for a few days or even a few weeks.

Nor, Lucy thought, was there anything to satisfy her growing suspicion that he had other reasons for being in Vermont. It wasn't just her. It wasn't just some sense of obligation to Colin. She wasn't sure what had triggered her doubts, but last night, waking up in her guest room with the eerie sounds of an owl in the nearby woods, she'd latched onto the idea that Sebastian was holding back on her. He knew things, he had suspicions that he was keeping to himself.

She was so convinced last night she almost marched down to his room to demand an explanation. But common sense intervened, and this morning her suspicions seemed a little more far-fetched. Not that Sebastian wouldn't withhold information, but that he had anything to withhold. What could he possibly know that concerned her? Certainly nothing *bad*, not at the level he was used to. Assassinations, bombings, kidnappings, extortion. This was just someone trying to spook her.

Pushing back the flood of questions, Lucy dashed into his bathroom for his shaving gear. She was struck by the intimacy of her chore. Sebastian must have known what she'd be handling. Maybe he was too out of it to care.

"Sebastian is never too out of it," she said out loud.

That was his job. Staying alert, on task. Even, she thought, if he had managed to fall into Joshua Falls.

She wished she could call her friends in Washington for the scuttlebutt on him. What did they know about his "sabbatical"? What rumors had they heard? But she didn't dare, because her questions would give them something to gossip about, and it could get back to Jack.

She stuffed everything into her car and walked over to the small building housing the front desk. The clerk was a no-nonsense woman in her sixties. She wouldn't have been much help with any desperadoes hiding under Sebastian's bed.

The woman complained about her bad knee while she flipped through handwritten cards for the appropriate bill. "I hurt it last winter cleaning out Mother's attic. It's been a year since she died, but I couldn't bring myself to do it." She found the right card and set it on the counter, adjusting her reading glasses. "The owner keeps threatening to computerize, but I don't see the need myself. Well, I'll be! Sebastian Redwing. Daisy Wheaton's grandson?"

"That's right," Lucy said. "Do you know him?"

"Not since he was a boy. I don't know if I'd recognize him now. He came to live with Daisy after his parents were killed. That was horrible. Just horrible. I'll never forget it. That poor woman outliving her husband and her only child." She shuddered. "I was just a little girl and didn't really know what was going on when Joshua Wheaton died, but I've been afraid of waterfalls ever since. I've never even been to Joshua Falls."

"Really? They're very beautiful."

She pursed her lips in disapproval. "I thought it was morbid to name the falls after him. If I get run over by a truck, I don't want anyone naming the truck after me!"

Lucy smiled. "I think it was to honor him because he saved a little boy from drowning."

"He was reckless. He didn't think about his wife, his own little girl."

"Maybe not, but in that situation—I don't know, it would be hard not to try to do something to help. I imagine Joshua thought he could handle the risks he was taking. You can't stand by and watch a little boy drown, but you can't be totally reckless, either. That's suicide."

The clerk nodded grudgingly. "People do say Joshua knew what he was doing, and it was just one of those things. The conditions were worse than he expected, and there he was, committed, with no way out."

"Yes," Lucy said, distracted, wondering if in a way that explained her situation with Sebastian. Committed, no way out.

"Well, it's a sad story. Mother said Daisy never really got over Joshua."

"They were friends?" Lucy asked. She was curious about Daisy Wheaton, whose spirit was so much a part of her life. But she'd never asked many questions of townspeople about her for fear of seeming too nosy, prying into the life of one of their own. And she'd never considered asking Sebastian.

"They were in the quilting club together." The older woman sighed wistfully, tears coming to her eyes. "But that was a long time ago. Mother was ninety-two when she died."

And her daughter missed her, Lucy thought, touched. Would her own children still miss their father when they were in their sixties, after all those years without him? They'd think about him, remember him. That much she knew.

"What did you do with her quilts?" she asked suddenly.

"I saved them, of course. I gave one to each of my children and grandchildren. What else would I do with them?"

Sell them with your mother's place, Lucy thought. That's what Sebastian did. She didn't think he'd saved even a single one of Daisy's quilts.

With all the memories and tragedies associated with Vermont, and specifically Joshua Falls, he could have been distracted yesterday, the landslide thus catching him by surprise. It could have been an accident, after all. Under the circumstances, how reliable a witness was he?

Lucy paid his motel bill and thanked the clerk for her time. "I'm Lucy Swift, by the way. I bought Daisy Wheaton's house from her grandson a few years ago."

"Yes! I've heard of you. You've got that adventure travel business, right?"

"That's right. I hope you'll stop in one day. The house came with a bunch of Daisy's quilts. I'd love to have you tell me about some of them."

"I'd be happy to. I'm Eileen, by the way—Eileen O'Reilly. I'll take you up on your offer one of these days."

"Soon, I hope."

Lucy headed straight home. When she turned into her driveway, she stopped at the mailbox and stared down at Joshua Brook. It was wide and easy here, its water clear and coppery. Placid, beautiful. Soothing. She loved to sit on a rock on a warm afternoon and watch the water course over her feet. It was always cold, and even amidst a mid-summer dry spell, it had never gone dry.

And yet upstream, these same waters had claimed Joshua Wheaton's life and made his wife a widow. The Widow Daisy.

The Widow Swift, Lucy thought again.

She dumped Sebastian's stuff in her bedroom and found him stretched out on a blanket in the shade of an old apple tree in the backyard. J.T. and Georgie were playing checkers on the far edge of the blanket. Lucy pushed aside any lingering thoughts of Sebastian's motel room.

"Boys," she said, "would you mind getting me something cold to drink?"

"Can we have something, too?" J.T. asked.

"Of course."

"Milk shakes?"

"Not right now. Just whatever's in the fridge."

They scooted off. Sebastian eyed her, his head propped on a couple of pillows. "Madison's in the barn. She's pissed at me. Now she says I'm more like Humphrey Bogart in *The African Queen*." He squinted up at Lucy. "Do you think I'm more Bogie than Eastwood?"

"I think my daughter has an active imagination."

He sat up, wincing. In the midday light, she could see that his wounds, while unpleasant and painful, really were superficial and would heal quickly. He narrowed his eyes at her, again giving her that sense he could see into her soul.

"What's on your mind, Lucy Blacker?"

He'd always called her Lucy Blacker, from the day they'd met. "Nothing."

She realized she was pacing, and stopped. She stared out at her garden. It was lush and healthy, and it had her stamp on it. Yet it still felt like Daisy's garden. People in town thought of her as stepping into Daisy's life. Exchanging an old widow for a young widow.

Was that what Sebastian thought?

Suddenly Lucy couldn't breathe, and she knew he was watching her, trying to read her mind. Possibly succeeding.

She turned to him. "Did Daisy ever go back to the falls?"

She could see he knew what she meant. He didn't react in any obvious way, just seemed to slide deeper inside himself. His past must have taught him that—to stay in control, bury his feelings, choose what he wanted someone else to see. The past three years had taught her similar skills.

He shook his head. "No, never."

"The falls must not be an easy place for you to be."

"My grandfather died long before I was born. Daisy never liked me going up there, but she didn't stop me, except in winter." The unusual gray eyes stayed on her.

If he could read her mind, penetrate her soul, she didn't have the slightest idea how to read him, get inside his soul. She wasn't sure she wanted to.

He added, enigmatically, "It's a beautiful spot."

"Then you weren't distracted yesterday?"

He shrugged. "No, I was distracted."

"And?"

"And what?"

She groaned. "You know damn well what I mean."

"You're fishing, Lucy. What else is on your mind?"

"You didn't come here just because of me." She spoke without thinking, analyzing, debating. Enough already, she thought. She stepped closer to his blanket, knew that what her instincts were saying to her were right. "You had other reasons, too."

"Such as?"

The man was maddening. "Why should I guess when you can just tell me?"

He gave the smallest of smiles. "I don't know, I like the idea of seeing how far-fetched your guesses are."

"Is that a yes, you do have other reasons for being here?"

"You think too much."

And here she was, not thinking at all. She gave him another few seconds, but that was the end of it. Lucy crossed her arms on her chest, considered a moment. "Okay. Fine. Well, here's how it is. From this point forward, you are to keep me informed of where you are and what you're doing, what you know, what your plans are. This is my house, my town, my family—*my* life. Understood?"

"Sure, Lucy." He clasped his hands together behind his neck and settled back on the blanket. He shut his eyes and yawned, making himself comfortable. "By the way, your son cheats at checkers. When Georgie figures it out, there'll be hell to pay."

Chapter 9

Sidney pressed both hands on Jack's shoulders to keep him in his chair in the courtyard. "You sit," she told him. "I'll make the martinis."

He smiled up at her, could smell her fresh perfume as she stayed close behind him. She was so beautiful, so kind. "You don't need to wait on me."

"This isn't waiting on you." She headed off toward the kitchen, laughing over her shoulder at him. "This is snapping you out of your funk. You have one chance— one martini—then I'm out of here, and you can wallow."

In another minute, Jack heard her humming, clinking glasses. His eyes welled with tears. She was such a good woman. Smart and decent, comfortable with herself. He wished he had the courage to tell her about Darren and the blackmail. About Colin. About how he'd sniped at Lucy for living in Vermont, as if somehow the blackmail, his loneliness, was her fault.

But he couldn't bring himself to tell anyone. It was as if speaking the details out loud made them real and true, unavoidable. He supposed he was still in denial, as the pop shrinks would say. Yet his silence ate at him, chewing away at his gut like an acid leak. Except for the day he'd stood over his son's body, he'd never felt so isolated and alone, so goddamn helpless.

Sidney blamed his work. His schedule was jammed with last-minute political jockeying before the August recess. He was using every ethical tactic he knew to garner support for legislation he and another two senators were sponsoring.

To have it all end like this, he thought. He tried to be optimistic. He wanted desperately, horribly, to believe that Darren Mowery would give up his blackmail campaign without bleeding Jack completely dry or asking him to compromise his oath of office. He could only afford another ten or twenty thousand before someone started to notice, before someone talked. It could be anyone—a bank teller, his accountant. Word would get out, questions would be asked. What secrets was Senator Swift hiding? His political enemies would jump. The media would be overzealous in their watchdog role. Truth would mix with gossip and rumor, and the politics of personal destruction.

And that was the best-case scenario. The worst was if Mowery asked Jack to compromise his oath of office, the ethics by which he'd tried his damnedest to live and work his entire adult life, even before he'd taken public office. Then, who knew what would happen.

He was on his own. Sebastian Redwing hadn't returned his call. Jack wished he hadn't given in to impulse and contacted Redwing Associates. Plato had warned him Sebastian probably wouldn't call back if Jack wasn't willing to be more forthcoming. "Call me back if you want to talk details," Plato said. "I'll get word to him."

He'd refused to say where Sebastian was or to put Jack's call through to him, and finally Jack hung up in frustration. Admitting he was the victim of blackmail had made him physically ill. What difference did the details make? It was Mowery. Sebastian knew Mowery's tactics, had been Colin's friend. The honorable course of action would be to go get the bastard and never mind the sordid details.

So, here he was. Waiting.

Sidney swung out from the kitchen with two martinis. He smiled. "I'll make the next round."

"You're on." She sank onto a chair and tasted her handiwork. "Marvelous, if I do say so myself." She raised her glass to him. "To love, friendship, the United States Senate, and getting out of this town in one piece."

Jack laughed. "Amen." He had to agree, it was a superb martini. "Imagine, in just a few days, we'll be sitting on a deck in Vermont sipping martinis and looking at nothing but trees."

Her dark eyes flashed. "We?"

"You can sneak off for a week or so at least, can't you?"

"Yes, but—" She set her martini on the table. "I realize Lucy knows we're seeing each other, but you and she and your grandchildren—it's just been the five of you for the past three years."

"Lucy's parents—"

"Are in Costa Rica. Yes, I visited them in January.

But you're Colin's father. You're their only connection to him—and they're the only family you have."

"They live in Vermont now," Jack said, wincing at how bitter he sounded. "It's not as if it's been 'just the five of us' for the past three years."

"Ah," Sidney said knowingly.

He managed a smile. "'Ah' what?"

"You're angry with Lucy for moving away. Jack, she's not responsible for your happiness. She's had to get on with life without Colin, just as you have. It's different for you. Colin was your son, not your husband."

"I lost everyone, Sidney. Eleanor, Colin, my grand-children."

"Your grandchildren are in *Vermont*. It's not the end of the earth." Sidney shook her head—so kind, so indulgent. She disagreed with him, but wouldn't belittle him. "Oh, Jack. Jack, their moving isn't a rejection of you any more than Lucy's parents' move to Costa Rica is a rejection of her."

"I know that intellectually, but in my gut—" He sighed. "Sidney, in my gut they rejected me."

"That must feel awful."

He smiled, rallying. "Thank God for you. Lucy likes you, you know."

"As a friend and a former colleague of sorts. I don't know about as your lover. And," she added seriously, "I'm not just talking about how Lucy would react having me in Vermont. I'm talking about you, too, Senator Jack Swift."

He frowned. "I don't understand."

"Of course, you don't. You haven't had a 'girlfriend' in forty years."

"Ouch."

Sidney leaned forward in her chair and brushed her fingertips across his chin. "Think hard, Jack, before you invite me to Vermont with your family. I like what we are together. I don't want that to change."

"Why would it change?"

"Just think, okay?"

"Okay."

She laughed. "You are so thickheaded. But never mind." She swept up her martini and took a big sip. "Whether it's to Vermont or the beach, I'm getting out of the city for a few days. I love Washington, but summers do get trying."

With the martini, the quiet, steamy evening and Sidney's gentle, intelligent company, Jack felt more comfortable. When it came to Washington, he understood what she meant. For all its problems, dangers and frustrations, he loved living and working here. Although Rhode Island was home, Washington was where he was at his best.

He couldn't imagine how Lucy lived in Vermont, no matter how beautiful. Was she at her best there? Or was she just hiding from reality? That, he could understand. He would do anything to hide from reality now, was trying his damnedest to get away with it. Losing Colin had been a terrible blow for all of them. But a short-lived frenzy over senatorial blackmail and a sordid affair could drive Lucy even farther away from her dead husband's father.

Sidney was right. Lucy, Madison and J.T. were his only family. He couldn't act in haste.

"Jack—oh, Jack." Sidney smiled and pretended to knock on his forehead. "You're distracted tonight, aren't you?"

"Just tired," he said. "Barbara reports she's rented a house on the ridge above Lucy's farmhouse. It's within easy walking distance, just above a notorious waterfall."

"Ah, and how is Barbara?"

He shrugged. "Back to her old self."

Sidney looked dubious. "Don't count on it."

"She's worked in my office since she was a college intern. She's not going to rock the boat again. She lost it for a second, that's all. It happens. With the pressure we're under, people lose it every now and then."

"Jack, Jack," Sidney said, incredulous, shaking her head. "The woman's in love with you."

"No, she isn't. She just got carried away. And, even if she is, what can I do about it? She's a valuable member of my staff."

"Oh, God. You sound as if you're talking about your favorite pen."

"I don't mean to. Sidney, I'm not going to fire Barbara Allen because she got a little goofy on me. If she becomes a problem, I'll deal with it."

"I'm sure you will. Excuse me for meddling."

She was matter of fact, not hurt. Jack smiled. "Meddle away. It's nice to have someone with your clear eye to talk to." He sighed; the martini was relaxing him. Or maybe it was just Sidney's company. "I suppose I should tell Lucy I'm coming. She knows I want to come up for a visit, but she thinks it's just for a day or two, not the entire month."

"She and Barbara haven't run into each other?"

He shook his head. "Barbara says not. We spoke earlier today. I want this to be my surprise."

Sidney got to her feet, kissing him lightly. "You're an odd man, Senator Swift."

And jumpy, Jack thought when his cell phone rang and he nearly fell off his chair. Sidney sank back into her chair, obviously assuming his startled response was a result of his distraction over her kiss.

"Hey, Jack." Darren's voice, instantly recognizable. "How's Ms. Sidney tonight?"

Jack ignored the twist of pain in his gut. He kept his voice calm, professional. "We're both fine, thank you. What can I do for you?"

"Remember the number I gave you that day in your office?"

"Yes."

"Let's do another ten-thousand-dollar transfer. Keep things nice and friendly, build a little trust between us."

"I thought—"

"That's your problem, Senator. Don't think. Just do." Mowery gave a sick little laugh. "Didn't Yoda say something like that?"

And he disconnected.

Jack shakily set the phone back on the table. He knew he was pale. He could feel it. Sidney watched him, brow furrowed. "Jack?"

He managed a small smile. "July is always ulcer time in Washington. Another martini?"

Lucy woke up early and made sure she was out of the kitchen before Sebastian wandered in. He was on his own this morning. His presence in her house was throwing her off in unexpected ways. She didn't sleep well, she had unsettling dreams when she did sleep, and she felt constantly on edge—not irritable, just aware, alert, as if her senses were on overdrive.

This morning, she was scheduled to conduct a canoe

lesson with local kids on a nearby pond. She had no intention of canceling, or, she thought, of getting Sebastian's okay. That was the other thing about having him around. She was used to being in charge. She didn't like the idea of him thinking he was in control just because she'd asked for his help. She hadn't abdicated any responsibility for herself and her children.

J.T. helped her get together paddles and life vests. Some of his friends were in the group, but he liked to think of himself as a co-teacher more than a student. "Remember," Lucy warned him, "no one likes a know-it-all."

"But if I know something, I know it."

"That doesn't mean you have to be obnoxious about it. We all have our gifts," she said, hoisting paddles into the back of her car, "and yours is to have a mother who taught you how to paddle when you were a tot."

"Mom."

She grinned at him. "Was I being obnoxious?"

Madison floated across the lawn. "Do you mind if I join you? No point hanging around here. Sebastian will just put me to work."

"He could use the time to rest," Lucy said.

His bruises had blossomed, making him look worse, although he was actually doing much better. He hadn't taken any Tylenol yet today. Lucy wondered if having him around was a deterrent, sort of like having a big, mean dog lying in the shade.

Except he was sexy, and last night she'd tossed and turned imagining him in her bed. Not good. Dangerous thinking. *Crazy* thinking.

He came out to the car before they left, wearing jeans

and a dark polo shirt, no shoes. Lucy's mouth went dry at the sight of him.

"I'm just making sure both kids are in the car with you," he said. "I don't want any surprises."

"We thought you could use some quiet time."

His mouth twitched. "Toddlers get quiet time. You going to the pond or the river?"

"The pond."

"How many kids?"

"About a half-dozen, not counting my own. It's a very public spot."

He peered into the car, and both J.T. and Madison tried not to stare. His face wasn't as bruised as it could have been, but ugly purple and blue splotches had formed around the cut above his eye. He seemed more energetic and focused this morning, less as if he might pass out at any second. He'd gone to bed early. Lucy had sat up in the living room reading, wondering what it might be like to have him to talk to.

Not that he talked, she reminded herself. He was succinct, closemouthed or antisocial, depending on one's point of view—or mood. In his work, no one cared about his personality, just his competence.

"All right," he said, straightening. He swept her with a humorless glance. "Don't be late."

Lucy bristled. "I answer to myself, Redwing."

His voice lowered so Madison or J.T. wouldn't hear. "You don't want me coming after you."

Actually, she didn't. A hot, almost electric current ran up her spine. She thought she concealed it well, but Sebastian smiled knowingly before retreating to the house. The man noticed *everything*.

A couple of hours on the pond renewed her spirits.

The kids she taught were eager to learn, and Madison and J.T. were skilled enough Lucy didn't really have to worry about them. She relished the feel of the paddle dipping into the water, the occasional small splashes on her arms and legs, the sounds of birds and laughter. Her doubts and questions receded, and the heightened state of awareness—almost frenzy—finally quieted. By the time they packed up and headed home, she felt centered again.

But it all went to hell when she pulled into her driveway and saw Sebastian and Rob Kiley chatting on her front porch.

It was as if her two lives—the one in which she was in control versus the one in which she had lost control—had collided in a blinding crash. The two men waved and smiled, but she could see Rob's smile was forced.

"How's the pond?" Sebastian asked, sounding calm, not as pain-racked.

Lucy faked a smile of her own. "Probably much the same as when you two were kids. Catching up on old times?"

Rob got to his feet stiffly, his normal easygoing demeanor lost to obvious tension. "Sebastian never knew my grandmother gave Daisy a fruitcake every Christmas in honor of Joshua Wheaton for saving my father's life." He managed a faint glimmer of humor. "Daisy always fed it to the birds. Sixty years of fruitcakes literally out the window."

"It was good seeing you, Rob," Sebastian said. He, too, rose, and, without even a glance at Lucy, he retreated inside.

Rob sat back down. "Okay, Lucy. Talk."

So, she was right. The two men had colluded. "Talk about what?"

"Sebastian Redwing."

She sighed.

Rob shook his head, biting off any irritation. If he hated one thing, Lucy knew, it was feeling any kind of negative emotion toward anyone. "Okay, here's what I know so far," Rob said. "He's Daisy's grandson, his grandfather was killed rescuing my father from the falls, his parents were killed in a hit-and-run accident when he was fourteen. He went on to become some kind of shadowy security guy. He saved your husband's and father-in-law's lives during that attempt to assassinate the president a bunch of years ago, and he sold you this place." Rob settled back in his chair; he was so tall and lanky, he barely fit. "He lives in Wyoming. And you were just in Wyoming. As I recall, you went at the last minute."

Lucy sighed again, wishing she could be back out on the water. Maybe that's what she should do—pack up the kids and head to Canada, paddle lakes and streams and coastlines and just wait out whatever was going on here. Hide. Retreat. The passive approach, she thought.

"Rob, I'm sorry." She shook her head, her voice tight and tense. "I should have told you what was going on before now."

"Lucy, I deserve to know. My kid hangs out here."

"You're right." She leaned back in her chair and gave him a direct look. "Rob, the truth is, I'm not sure what's going on. *Something*, yes, but I could be putting incidents together that are unrelated—"

He held up a hand, stopping her. "Start at the beginning and take me through it, step by step. I'm not good at piecing things together and reading between the lines. Just give it to me straight."

She told him everything, start to finish. She only left out the volatile chemistry between her and Sebastian. "If you want to pack up Georgie and clear out—"

"No. It has to be business as usual. We're not going to let this sick bastard win." Rob was adamant, if a little shocked. "I'm just sorry you've put up with this for so long on your own. Why the hell didn't you say something? You didn't suspect me, did you?"

"No! I just—" She threw up her hands, at a loss. "I guess I'm just used to handling things on my own."

"Maybe too used to it," Rob said quietly.

Lucy didn't answer.

"This Redwing character's good?"

"He used to be. He's been retired or on sabbatical or something for the past year."

"Why?"

She frowned. "That's a good question. I'll ask him."

"I'm not much on cloak-and-dagger shit myself. Look, I don't blame you for not wanting to bring in the police, but if you get any hard evidence—you have to take it in, Lucy."

She nodded. "I will. I promise."

He smiled a little. "Grandpa Jack will calculate his political advantage and decide whether to keep the lid on this thing or not."

"That's so cynical."

"Practical."

Lucy laughed, feeling better. "Thanks, Rob."

"For what?"

"For not jumping down my throat for keeping this to myself for so long."

He waved a hand. "I figure your just punishment was helping Redwing down from the falls the other night. Serves you right when you could have had a strapping guy like me carry him down on my back."

"You'd have called the EMTs."

"He was in that bad shape, huh?"

She nodded.

"Think he fell?"

"I don't know. It was his first time back to the falls since his grandfather's death. He was distracted."

"Mini-landslides don't just happen up there. Maybe after heavy rains, but not this time of year when it's this dry." He got to his feet. "I think I'll go check on the boys."

Sebastian decided to make dinner. He got Madison and J.T. to pick whatever was ripe in the garden. What he didn't steam or throw into a salad, he chopped up and grilled. He found some chicken in the refrigerator and tossed that on the grill, too. It was a charcoal grill, and he had a couple of false starts before he got the damn thing lit. His life-style had never called for much charcoal grilling.

The smell of the charcoal, the feel of the heat on his face, the long, quiet day in a place he loved and yet had tried to forget—all helped him to feel more centered, calmer, steadier. He could go deep inside himself, where he was still and balanced, and think. Darren Mowery. Jack Swift. Blackmail. Lucy and her weird goings-on. They all fit together. He just had to find out how.

And he had to keep his mind on the job, not on what it felt like to be back home, definitely not on what it felt like to be with Lucy. He didn't know what it was about her, but she'd crawled under his skin and buried herself there fifteen-plus years ago. There was nothing he could do except live with it. Last year, he'd let emotional involvement cloud his judgment with Darren Mowery. He hadn't seen the changes in Darren, the creeping cynicism, the loss of empathy. Maybe they'd always been there, buried under a veneer of professionalism, and only last year had they surfaced, taking over.

Sebastian flipped a piece of chicken. Maybe it was like the way seeing Lucy again had taken him over, made him capable of doing who knew what. Thinking about her while grilling chicken and vegetables, for one.

He needed to think about what to do about Jack Swift. Understanding his leverage was the first step. In his experience, United States senators didn't like to talk about what a blackmailer had on them.

The screen door creaked open and banged lightly shut, and Lucy joined him, plopping down in an old Adirondack chair. She had two bottles of Long Trail beer and handed him one as she stretched out her legs, crossing her ankles. She had very good legs, tanned, slim, strong.

She smiled. "Smells good."

"That's the charcoal and barbecue sauce. I could grill up a pile of skunk cabbage and it'd smell good."

"I don't think I'd like skunk cabbage. I haven't even worked up the courage to try dandelion greens. People in town tell me they were a favorite of Daisy's."

Sebastian remembered his grandmother pointing out the tender leaves, instructing him how to pick them without bruising them. "They were," he said.

"Did you eat them?"

"With salt, pepper and vinegar."

"Gross."

He laughed. "Daisy and one of her old friends used to make the occasional batch of dandelion wine. God, it was awful."

Lucy smiled again, watching him as she sipped her beer from the bottle. It was a move that struck him as incredibly sexy. Her eyes seemed darker, even more vivid, against the deepening blue of the early evening sky. "So," she said, "did you ever think you'd stay here when you were a kid?"

"I never thought I'd leave."

"Then you didn't hate it here?"

"No, never." He looked around at the fields of tall grass and bright flowers, the wooded hills, the apple trees and maples and oaks. He could hear the brook and the wind, and remembered thinking that here, it was as if he were inside his own soul. He shook his head. "I couldn't imagine not being here."

"Why did you sell, then?"

"Things change."

He flipped vegetables, and he could feel her watching him, wondering what kind of boy he must have been. The orphan. Daisy's grandson. A child of tragedy and incalculable loss.

"What changed?" Lucy asked quietly.

"I did."

She was silent, but he knew she wasn't letting him off the hook. Not Lucy. She would dig in, probe, commit for the long haul. He'd known that about her the day she married his best friend.

He glanced back at her, drank some of his own beer. "Daisy lived here. It was her home. For me, it was a refuge, a place to hide. And one day I knew I couldn't hide anymore."

"You had to go out and learn how to save people. You couldn't save your grandfather—he died before you were born. And you couldn't save your parents. You weren't there."

He looked at her. "No. I was there."

She almost spilled her beer. She paled slightly, then whispered, "I'm sorry. I didn't know. No one's ever said. Did Colin know?"

"We drank too much one night after the assassination attempt, and it came out." Sebastian shrugged. "We were young. We never spoke of it again."

Lucy rallied, but he could see she was touched. "Nothing like bullets and booze to bond a couple of guys together. Was Plato there?"

"He drank wine. Merlot. We never let him forget."

She smiled, and Sebastian remembered how much she'd loved her husband, how much Colin had loved her. She was different now, and yet the same. Strange. Impossible to articulate.

She set her beer in the grass. "So, you saw your parents get killed, and you came here to live with your grandmother. Then you left. You went into security and investigative work, started your own company, made a lot of money and retired for the past year to a hammock and a shack without electricity or running water."

"My life in a nutshell."

She studied him, eyes narrowed. "And you renounced violence."

"Yes."

"Why?"

"A man named Darren Mowery."

"I know the name. You worked for him when you and Colin first met. DM Consultants. He saved the president's life."

"That's who Darren was. He changed."

"Tell me," Lucy said quietly.

"There was a kidnapping case a year ago. A Colombian businessman—a client—and his wife and their three children, all under ten. I took on the case myself."

"What happened? The children weren't—"

He shook his head. "They lived. DM Consultants had just gone bankrupt. I knew Darren blamed me. I knew he was desperate. Tempted."

"He was involved in the kidnapping?" Lucy said.

"He helped engineer it. He damn near got off with thirty million dollars."

Her eyes widened. "My God!"

"It was a wealthy Colombian businessman," Sebastian said with a small smile.

"What happened?"

"I foiled their plans. I had to shoot three of Mowery's Colombian cohorts in front of the children." He could hear their screams now, see their horrified faces. Children. Little children. "The men were pawns."

"Would they have killed the family?"

"Yes. And Darren would have taken the money. I caught up with him in Bogotá. He went for his gun, and I shot him. Pretty straightforward. The Colombian authorities arrived, and I went back to Wyoming."

Lucy's face had gone pale again. There was a slight tremble to her hands. "Do you know if he's alive or dead?"

She was unnerved enough. Sebastian didn't need

to tell her Darren Mowery was sneaking around her father-in-law's office. "He's alive."

"But in prison," she said. "The Colombians must have—"

He shook his head. "There was no way to prove his role in the kidnapping. I knew that when I left him for dead. Lucy, I didn't finish the job. There's no excuse."

"So that's why I found you in a hammock."

"That's why. I leave operations to people Plato and I have hired and trained, men and women we trust. The company requires a lot of attention at what Plato likes to call the 'desk level.' I've ignored that, too, for the better part of the past year."

"No wonder Plato was glad to get you out of Wyoming," Lucy said, obviously struggling to insert some humor. "What are you, Sebastian—forty, by now?"

"About."

"No wife, no kids? Ever?"

"Never as yet."

"Almost?"

He thought of her in her wedding gown so long ago—young, pretty, beaming with a kind of hope and optimism he wasn't sure he'd ever felt. "Not quite."

"I guess 'not quite' and 'almost' are two different things."

He let his gaze settle on her until she uncrossed her ankles and sat up a little straighter. "I haven't been much good to anyone in a long time, Lucy. If you want Plato to come out here and see to whoever's trying to get under your skin, I'll get him."

"No," she said, "I want you."

He grinned and drank more of his beer. "Well, finally we're on the same wavelength."

"In your dreams, Redwing." But he could see she was twitchy, aware. She jumped up, obviously needing an outlet for her restless energy. "Where are Madison and J.T.?"

"In their rooms." He scooped zucchini onto a chipped Bennington Pottery platter left over from Daisy's day. "I was going to have them sweep the porch, rake the yard, caulk the windows and deadhead the flowers, but I figured I'd give them a break."

"Daisy never made you work that hard, and you know it."

"How do you know?"

"Because I live in her house. Some nights... I don't know, it's as if her spirit's still here. I imagine she was hardworking and frugal, but I also think she was very kind and knew how to have fun."

"She was a hard-bitten old Yankee."

"Ah," Lucy said, not taking him seriously, "so that's where you get it."

He pointed his spatula at her. "I could have sold this place to a Boston lawyer."

"Why didn't you?" she asked evenly.

"Because I sold it to you."

She dropped back into her chair and stared out at the vegetable garden. Everything about her, Sebastian thought, was a mix of strength and femininity, and he knew he'd be stupid to underestimate her.

She turned, squinting at him. "The locals are starting to call me the Widow Swift. They used to call your grandmother the Widow Daisy."

"That bothers you?"

"I don't know. I have a good life here. I like to think she did, too."

"She did because she stayed here so she could live, not so she could hide. She never married again, but she had a good, full life."

"Do you think I'm hiding out here?"

He shrugged. "It doesn't matter what I think."

"That's true, it doesn't." She grinned at him, taking the edge off their conversation. "At least not about my life. Dead bats in my bed—that's another story."

He slid the chicken onto the platter with the vegetables. He hadn't done anything this domestic in years. Maybe ever. It felt good. If he didn't keep busy, his mind would spin off in too many directions. He'd start thinking things about Lucy that he'd been repressing for more than fifteen years. Kissing her the other night might have been low, but he couldn't bring himself to regret it.

She was frowning at him.

"What is it?" he asked.

"Something about your face. You haven't found anything else in my bed, have you?"

He looked at her, and she slid down a bit in her chair, one foot twitching madly. And he knew. She was thinking about their kiss, too—and more. "Lucy, I promised it wouldn't happen again. It won't."

"I don't mind that it did happen."

They were on dangerous ground. "Good."

But she jumped up, avoided his eye. "We should get dinner on the table."

Chapter 10

After dinner, J.T. slipped off. Lucy and Madison were out driving, and Sebastian made the mistake of not locking the kid in his room. J.T. had been quiet through dinner, eating his chicken and salad and pushing the grilled vegetables around his plate. Then all of a sudden—no J.T.

Sebastian checked the garage. The kid's fishing pole was missing.

He went around the back of the barn and took a gently sloping but more roundabout footpath down to the brook. There was a steeper path on the other side of the barn that led straight down the embankment. It was short and direct, and if he hadn't fallen into a waterfall yesterday, Sebastian would have taken it because it would get him more quickly to the brook's best fishing spot.

The air was cool, damp and still, the brook shaded with hemlock and pine, the coppery water shallow and clear. He headed downstream. He was sore and stiff, but it felt good to move.

He spotted J.T. on a rock at the edge of the brook. His fishing pole lay on the ground beside him. He glanced up as Sebastian came toward him, then quickly tucked his face back in his hands.

Sebastian swore under his breath. What did he know to say to a crying kid?

"Catch anything?" he asked, coming closer.

J.T. shook his head without looking up.

"Mind if I share your rock? Tramping down here's given me a headache. Blood's rushed to my head."

The shoulders went up and down again.

Sebastian took that as a yes, and lowered himself onto the rock. It was big, unchanged from when he was a boy. The trees and undergrowth were thicker, reminding him of the passage of time.

"This was my favorite fishing spot as a kid," he said. "I never caught much. Mostly, I came down here to get away by myself."

No response.

"J.T." Sebastian sighed. He hated this. "It's this father-son canoe trip, isn't it? Rob told me about it. He wants to take you. But he's not your father."

The boy looked up. Tears streamed down his cheeks, carving a path through the dirt. He smelled like Deet and sweat, and he'd been crying for a while. "I want—I want to go with Rob."

And therein lies the rub, Sebastian thought. "Then why don't you? Your mother would let you."

The kid cried harder.

Damn, Sebastian thought. This time, he hated being right. He leaned back against his arms and gazed at the constant stream of water over rock and mud. "J.T., your father was my friend. We didn't see as much of each other as we'd have liked before he died, but one thing I know. He would want you to have men like Rob in your life."

"I know—that's not it."

Sebastian knew it wasn't. He said quietly, "You won't forget him, J.T. You won't ever forget him."

The kid tucked up his knees and buried his face in them, sobbing loudly. Sebastian had known such inconsolable grief. As a boy, he, too, had come here to cry, where no one could find him, where no one could ever know.

"If I stop missing him…"

He couldn't finish. Sebastian sat up and brushed a mosquito off a scab on his forearm. This was why he avoided victim work. He never knew what the hell to say. Daisy had pretty much left him alone to sort things out.

J.T. Swift was a deceptively intense and introspective boy, already thinking deep thoughts at twelve. Sebastian hadn't thought such deep thoughts at that age. He'd cry his heart out and then push the deep thoughts away, as far away as he could.

"Wounds heal," he said lamely. "If they're deep, like losing a father, they take time, and they leave a scar. After a while, the scar may not hurt anymore, but it reminds you of what you lost. And of your courage in facing that loss."

The boy shook his head. "I'm not brave."

"J.T., I've done a lot of things. I've been shot and shot at, and I've gone after kidnappers, extortionists, terrorists and every kind of creep and scum and mad zealot you can imagine." He paused, then gave it to the kid as straight as he could. "But I think the hardest thing I ever did was watch my grandmother cry after my parents died."

J.T. sat up, sniffled. "How did they die?"

"They were hit by a car right in front of me. That was hard, too, but it was Daisy's tears that did me in, that reminded me of what I'd lost. My grandfather was killed when she was young, and she only had me left."

"What happened to your grandfather?"

"His name was Joshua," Sebastian said.

"He was named after the falls?"

"No, the falls were named after him. He fell into the falls and drowned saving a little boy—Rob's father."

"He did? Georgie never said!"

"Georgie might not know. People around here are pretty stoic. They don't like to talk about these things, dump it on kids. It was March, in the midst of the snow-melt. The water was high and cold. The kid was going after his dog. He fell in. My grandfather jumped in and saved him."

"My mom won't let us near the falls in the winter."

"You listen to her," Sebastian said.

"Did your grandmother blame Rob's dad for killing your grandfather?" J.T. asked in a hushed voice. His eyes were wide and fascinated in a good way, taking on the best of both his parents.

"He was an eight-year-old boy, and he made a mistake. Joshua had two choices. He could let the boy drown, or he could do what he could to save him."

"Mom knows about swift-water rescue. She's going to teach me someday. I don't think you're supposed to jump in after someone."

Sebastian nodded. "Sometimes life doesn't present you with a good choice and a bad choice. Sometimes you just have bad choices. You do the best you can."

The boy gave that some thought. Finally, he jumped to his feet and grabbed his fishing pole. "Bugs're bothering me."

And that was that. Their conversation was over.

J.T. bounded up the steep path. Good, Sebastian thought. He was exhausted. If someone had tried to talk to him at twelve the way he'd just talked to J.T., he wouldn't have known what the hell he was talking about. J.T. had followed right along.

Neither he nor J.T. mentioned their conversation to Lucy when she and Madison returned. "If it's run over the chipmunk or lose control of your car," Lucy was saying, "you run over the chipmunk."

"I couldn't," Madison said. "I'd just *die*."

J.T. leaned toward Sebastian and whispered, "Two bad choices?"

"Tougher to have to run over a chipmunk than go on a father-son canoe trip with Rob and Georgie, don't you think?"

J.T. grinned, and Sebastian retired to his room. Lucy's room, he amended. He surveyed the bed, the furnishings, the rug for anything out of the ordinary—dead bats, bullet holes, live rounds. He dropped down and checked under the bed. Nothing.

He kicked off his shoes and fell back onto the worn, soft quilt.

Lucy knocked. "I need to get a few things."

"Be my guest."

She went straight to her dresser and opened drawers, discreetly pulling out a nightgown—no black silky thing tonight—and underthings, socks, an outfit for to-morrow. Her back was to him. He observed the curve of her hips, the shape of her legs, the way her hair fell carelessly past her shoulders. Without looking at him, she said, "I hope today wasn't too deadly for you."

"I've had worse. You could use a couple of horses, though."

She turned to him. "I can barely manage two kids, a company and this place. What would I do with horses?"

"Loan me one. I'd rather ride a horse than pick squash." Except he'd enjoyed picking squash. He couldn't explain it and didn't want to try.

"You're in no condition to go horseback riding."

"Nah." He was stretched out on her bed, watching her. The scene struck him as scarily intimate. "I'm right as rain. Or close to it."

"Sure," she said dubiously, and breezed to the door. But she stopped, one hand on the knob. "Thank you."

"For what?"

"J.T. He told me he's decided to go on the father-son canoe trip."

"That was his doing, not mine."

"You talked to him."

He sighed. "I should have just fished with him. Kids are too intense these days. It's this damn therapeutic culture."

"Right. Nevertheless, thank you."

"Lucy." He let his gaze settle on her, felt her change in mood. "Don't let today fool you. I needed a day or two to recover from my fall. I talked to J.T., picked squash and fired up the grill to kill time."

"Are you trying to tell me you're not a nice man?"

He said nothing, and she smiled.

"I already knew that," she said, and left.

Moron, Sebastian thought. He'd had her right here in his room, thinking kindly toward him, and he'd had to remind her of what a son of a bitch he was. It was Daisy's ghost, he decided.

Back in Wyoming, he'd have had Lucy Blacker Swift in bed with him by now.

A noise woke Sebastian early, just after daylight. It came from outside. He glanced at the bedside clock: five twenty. This was an early family, but not a crack-of-dawn family. So who—or what—was in the backyard?

He rolled out of bed and peered through the window as he pulled on his pants.

Madison was climbing over the stone wall on the other side of the vegetable garden. She jumped down and, ducking low, ran up through the field.

Sebastian swore under his breath. What would get a fifteen-year-old out of bed at five in the morning?

"A secret," he said to himself.

He ducked down the hall and made his way soundlessly up the stairs to Lucy's room. The door was open a crack. He slipped inside and dropped beside her bed. "Lucy."

She bolted upright, sank her fingers into his arm. "What is it?"

"Madison's sneaking out across the field," he said. "You know how teenagers love their secrets. I'll go after her. You stay here with J.T."

"What?" She was half asleep, trying to figure out what was going on. "Madison's *where*?"

She pushed back the covers. Sebastian felt his mouth go dry. Her nightgown wasn't silky, but it was little.

The V-neckline was askew, revealing almost her entire breast. The fabric was pulled tight across the nipple. He tried not to stare, but something in his expression tipped her off—she looked down, sucked in a breath and adjusted her position.

"She doesn't have much of a head start," he said. "We'll probably be back before you and J.T. are even up. I didn't want to chance your waking up and not finding us."

The covers dropped off her legs; the nightgown just barely covered her hips. Her thighs were smooth and tanned. If her daughter wasn't charging off to God-knew-where, there'd be no stopping him. Desire fired through him, stealing his breath, his senses.

"It'll be okay, Lucy," he whispered, and kissed her, but held back, giving just a hint of how badly he wanted her. She fell against her pillow, her short nightgown riding up to her hips. He pulled away, every fiber of him throbbing with the need to make love to her, now. It was all he could do not to leave Madison to whatever mischief she was making. "I'll be back."

She slipped her sheet over herself. "You'll find her?"

"Yes. Lucy—"

"Go."

He nodded without a word and went.

The morning dew was cold, soaking his shoes and pants below the knee as he tore up through the field. He could distinguish mourning doves and crows in the flurry of bird calls, saw a bluebird swoop toward a bluebird house he'd put up for Daisy years ago at the edge of the field.

He felt better. A good night's sleep and a morning kiss had helped. His head was clear, and the pain of his bruises had lessened. He was stiff, but the soreness wasn't as raw-edged.

He wasn't worried about following Madison's trail. He knew the route she was taking, and wasn't surprised when he found her footprint in a low, muddy spot just into the woods beyond the stone wall. He took the narrow path up a hill, moving carefully and quietly but not making an effort to make no sound at all. If Madison heard him and scurried home, all the better.

The path ended at the dirt road. Sebastian had already investigated the occupants of the homes up on the ridge: a Boston optometrist, two New York florists. A local real estate woman rented out the third.

He found Madison at this last house, a glass-and-wood contemporary.

She was talking to someone on the screened porch. Sebastian couldn't see who it was as he crept under the sweeping branches of a huge, gnarled hemlock.

"Madison, you can't sneak up here at this hour." A woman's voice, low and urgent. "It's wrong. What would your grandfather think?"

"I know—but I had this terrible nightmare, and I had to get out of the house. I couldn't breathe! And my mother's not herself since…" The girl coughed, as if she were choking on her own drama. "I can't explain."

"Try," the woman said calmly.

"Do you know Sebastian Redwing?"

Sebastian remained very still. Who was this woman Madison had snuck out to see?

"Not personally. I know he saved your father and grandfather from an assassin some years ago and has his own investigative and security firm. He's widely respected in that community."

"Well, he's here," Madison said, pumping each word full of as much drama as she could.

"Sebastian Redwing?" The woman remained cool. "Really? Why?"

"Mom took us to see him when we were in Wyoming, and—and I didn't think he liked us at *all*. He was such a jerk."

Actually, Sebastian thought, he didn't think he'd been that bad.

"Now he's here," Madison went on, "and I don't know, I just think it's so *weird*. He almost killed himself at the falls the other night. He slipped or something, and Mom found him."

"Sebastian sold your mother your house, didn't he?"

"Yeah, it used to belong to his grandmother."

"Perhaps your visit in Wyoming got him thinking about Vermont, and he decided he wanted to see his grandmother's house again."

"But Mom—she doesn't want J.T. or me going off into the woods alone. She'd *kill* me if she knew I was up here."

Sebastian knew this to be untrue. If Madison really thought her mother would "kill" her for disobeying, she wouldn't have sneaked off. He wasn't sure if this meant mother and daughter really did trust each other or that the kid was a spoiled brat.

"Does your grandfather know Sebastian's visiting your mother?" the woman asked.

The criticism in her voice was almost undetectable, but still unmistakable. Sebastian frowned. This was someone who believed she had Jack Swift's best interests at heart—and believed Lucy didn't.

Madison, however, was oblivious. "I don't think so. She doesn't tell Grandpa much."

"No. I'm sure she doesn't."

Whoever this woman was, she didn't like Lucy Blacker Swift.

"Mom's very independent," the girl said in grudging defense of her mother.

"That she is. Well, you should be running along before she wakes up and doesn't find you. She'll worry."

Sebastian ducked deeper under the branches of the hemlock. He could hear creaking floorboards as Madison and the woman walked, presumably toward the door of the screened porch.

"I can't wait for Grandpa to come up this summer," Madison said. "It'll be so cool. None of my friends believe I have a grandfather who's a United States senator."

"Your friends in Washington did, didn't they?"

"I mean up here."

Madison went out onto the deck and took the steps down to the driveway, which was on the opposite side of the house from where Sebastian was hidden.

"Come see me again," the woman called from the deck. "You'll keep our secret, won't you?"

"Of course."

Sebastian didn't like secrets. It was one thing to keep your own mouth shut about something, another thing to ask someone else to keep their mouth shut. Especially a fifteen-year-old. A sure sign of something afoot was an adult telling a child to keep a secret. If it didn't involve Christmas or birthday presents, it usually wasn't good.

He wanted to know about the woman on the deck, but his first priority was seeing Madison Swift safely home. He eased down the wooded hill, making as little noise as possible, and came onto the path several yards behind her. She was walking briskly, practically skipping. Whoever this woman was, Madison certainly thought she was something.

They were almost to the field when Sebastian announced his presence. The girl jumped, startled, then turned sullen. "You *followed* me?"

"Yep. A kid sneaking out of the house at the crack of dawn is asking to be followed."

"That's not true."

She looked as if she might throw a fit. They were out of earshot of the rented house, but not if the kid started screaming and stomping around. Sebastian sighed. "Now don't start yelling bloody murder. It won't go over well if you do."

Madison snorted at him, out of breath and furious at being caught. "What'll you do, tie me to a tree?"

"It's a thought."

"My mother—"

"Your mother would tie you to an anthill."

The girl's mouth snapped shut.

"Who's the woman at the house?" he asked.

She didn't answer.

"Okay, I'll just go up there, knock on her door and ask her myself—"

"No! She'll get in trouble!"

"Is that what she told you?"

Madison obviously didn't care for his tone of voice. "It's what I *know*," she said snottily and marched a few steps ahead of him.

He was still feeling pretty good—she couldn't outrun him. He thought of his hammock in Wyoming. His horses. His dogs. He could pull together a poker game with the ranch hands. Five-card stud, cigars and a couple of six-packs.

Damn, what was he doing here?

"The woman works for your grandfather," he said to the girl's retreating back.

She refused to answer, kept walking.

Sebastian easily caught up with her. "I can call him, find out who's out of town—"

She stopped abruptly and spun around at him, her face pale. "No, don't. Please. I *promised*."

"Promised what? Your firstborn?"

"No, but I gave my word—"

"Well, you can un-give your word and tell me what's going on."

"Why should I?"

"Two reasons. One, if you don't, I'll still find out, but I won't be as pissed off if you go ahead and tell me yourself. Two, if you do tell me, I can tell your mother and hold her down and let her cool off before she tans your hide."

"My mother doesn't believe in corporal punishment."

This was no surprise. Sebastian kept his cool. "I was speaking metaphorically."

She licked her lips. "Barbara's here renting a house for my grandfather. He's spending August in Vermont. He asked her not to tell Mom. He wanted to make sure everything worked out first, then tell her himself."

"Why?"

"I don't know, that's the way he is. It's a surprise, I guess."

"Barbara who?"

"Barbara Allen. She's my grandfather's personal assistant. She's worked for him forever, since even before you saved his life."

So, as far as Madison was concerned, Barbara had seniority on him, and he wasn't such a big deal. Sebastian was amused. Little snot. But there was real fear in her eyes, not for herself but for a woman to whom she'd given her word. That mix of loyalty and kindness was more like her mother than Madison would probably want to know.

"I accidentally saw her the other day," Madison went on, "and she asked me not to tell."

"Madison, Barbara Allen isn't going to get fired because you caught her renting a vacation house for your grandfather. She must know that." And if she did, he thought, she was deliberately manipulating a fifteen-year-old girl. Why?

Madison nodded, not happy about having to tell him anything. Her blue eyes fastened on him. She wasn't afraid of him any more than anyone else in her damn family was. He was out of practice. People used to be afraid of him.

"Anything else?" she asked sarcastically, as if he were the inquisitioner.

"Nope. Now we can go back and tell your mother."

She said something under her breath. He was pretty sure it was "bastard," but she was only fifteen and shouldn't be using that kind of language. He let it go. Then she said something about being glad he'd tumbled into Joshua Falls. She spoke a little louder, wanting him to hear, wanting him to react. He didn't. In her place, he'd be pissed, too.

Which was nothing compared to what Lucy was.

She greeted Madison at the door, white-faced and

scared and too angry to speak. She had on shorts, a T-shirt and sandals. No more little nightgown. She pointed at the ceiling. "Upstairs."

"Mom, I can explain. I—"

Lucy held up her hand, and the girl shut up and flounced off, pounding up the stairs.

"A wonder she doesn't get shin splints." Sebastian slid onto a chair at the table. He was breathing hard; his head was pounding. He needed coffee and food, maybe one more day before he was fit to tackle desperadoes instead of Lucy's kids. "It wasn't a guy, if that makes you feel any better."

Lucy was slightly less pale. "Who was it?"

"A woman named Barbara Allen. She's renting a house on the sly for your father-in-law. He wants to come up in August. Know her?"

Lucy nodded. "*Damn* Jack. He's always doing things in secret. He says it's because he likes surprises and wants to avoid publicity. He thinks he's the president, I swear."

"What about Barbara Allen?"

"Barbara? She's been Jack's personal assistant for—I don't know, twenty years or so. She's devoted to him. If he says, 'Jump,' she says, 'How high?' She's always been fond of the kids—she's wonderful to us whenever we're in Washington. Gets us tickets, restaurant reservations, things like that."

"She shouldn't have told Madison not to tell you—"

"I know." Lucy took two mugs down from a cabinet, her movements jerky, betraying her agitation. "But that's Jack, and Barbara would want to please him. She probably didn't think. And she wouldn't know about the incidents."

Sebastian made no comment.

She set the mugs on the counter and looked around at him. "Sebastian, don't even think it. Not Barbara." She shook her head. "I wouldn't want to spend ten *seconds* inside your brain."

He leaned back and kicked out his legs. The trek up into the woods had done him good, but he could feel it. He smiled. "No, you wouldn't. Tell me what you know about Barbara Allen."

"I just did."

"Her personality," he said, "her sense of loyalty, what she thinks of you, your children, your move to Vermont. Anything."

"I don't know a lot. My contact with her over the years has been mostly about Jack, not her. She's very professional—she's never said much about her personal life around me. I think she has an apartment on the river."

"Not married?"

Lucy shook her head. "She's about my age, maybe a year or two older. Now, don't be thinking she's your weird, mousy, stereotypical spinster, because she's not."

"I wasn't thinking that. I wonder why you did?"

"I didn't. I was just—"

"The thought was there, Lucy. Something about this woman made you think 'weird, mousy, stereotypical spinster.' Think of how many single women in their late thirties and forties you know. Would you immediately warn someone not to think of them in stereotypical terms?"

"I don't know. Maybe."

"I doubt it. Something about Barbara Allen made you want to defend her against stereotype."

Lucy frowned. "I suppose there is a neediness about her. You'd never notice it right off, but I've known her for years. Who knows, I could be projecting."

"There's nothing needy about you."

"I don't know. After you left this morning—"

He grinned. "That's different."

She filled the two mugs with coffee, and with her back to him, said, "Sebastian, I can't be attracted to you. It'll never work, and the timing couldn't be worse."

"I agree."

She spun around to face him. "You agree?"

"Bad timing. Won't work. Can't be attracted. That's pretty much what I was thinking, too."

"After what happened upstairs."

"No, before, actually. I thought about it all night." He walked over to her and picked up one of the mugs, sipped the hot, black coffee. "Obviously I wasn't convinced."

"I am."

"Good. That'll give me ammo for talking myself out of kissing you again."

She nodded. "Right. We can't—" She turned, facing him, and leaned against the counter with her coffee. "I have a sneaky daughter and a son who's worried about forgetting his father, and a business to run, and this person to find—and now Jack Swift coming for August. So, yes, please talk yourself out of kissing me again."

"And what are you going to do?"

"About what?"

"Kissing me. Because if you know I want to kiss you, and would at the drop of a pin, then you don't have the kind of ammo I have. I know you don't want me to kiss you. You don't know that about me."

She stared at him. "You're not making any sense."

"Sure I am. I want to kiss you again. Very much." He touched her hair. "I have for a long, long time."

"How long?"

And suddenly she seemed to know. He could feel it. "Years," he said, and he touched her mouth, traced her lower lip with his thumb.

Her gaze held steady, but he could see her swallow. "I'm sorry."

"I'm not." He smiled. "Now go see about your daughter."

"She's a good kid, Sebastian."

"I know."

He moved aside, and she crossed the kitchen with her mug of coffee. At the doorway, she turned back to him and smiled. "But I am going to lock her in her room for the next hundred years."

While mother and daughter had it out, Sebastian took his coffee to the back steps. J.T. was still asleep; outside the air was warm and still, and the birds were twittering. He thought about Barbara Allen and Jack Swift, a rented house, a dead bat in Lucy's bed, a landslide that had nearly killed him, Darren Mowery, the August congressional recess and blackmail.

And kissing Lucy. He thought about that, too.

Chapter 11

Madison acted defiant and put-upon when Lucy confronted her in her room. "I'll be a junior in high school next year. I don't have to tell you everything."

"That's true," Lucy said, "and I don't need to know 'everything.' But sneaking out of the house at five in the morning after I specifically asked you—"

"There was *no* reason to worry!" Madison slammed her pillow onto the floor. She was sitting up in bed, looking misunderstood and furious. "You don't make any sense. If you had a life, maybe you'd leave me alone." She caught herself immediately and gasped. "Mom, I'm sorry. I didn't mean that."

Lucy stayed calm, even though she could feel the sting of her daughter's words. "Madison, I have a life. I have my work, I have you and J.T., I have my friends, hobbies I enjoy. I like living here. I get away just often enough. But whether or not I have a 'life,' in your eyes, isn't your concern. My happiness is my responsibility, not yours or J.T.'s."

"I just—I just don't want you to give up everything for us. I don't want us to stand in your way…" She didn't finish.

"You aren't standing in my way of doing anything."

Madison raised her chin. "Then why can't I spend a semester in Washington?"

Lucy smiled. The kid never missed an opening. "Your brother would miss you."

"No, I wouldn't!"

Madison threw another pillow at her door, where her little brother was eavesdropping. *"J.T.!"*

"J.T.," Lucy said, shooting him a warning look. He laughed without remorse and ran down the hall. She turned back to Madison. "You have lots of time for Washington. Right now, I'd like you to think about what it means to be trustworthy. If I can't trust you here, at home, how can I trust you on your own in Washington or anywhere else?"

"I'd have Grandpa—"

"He's a busy senator, Madison. He won't have time to make sure you're not sneaking off. First, you have to know you can trust yourself to make good decisions. Then I have to know. Then we might be able to discuss Washington."

"I'm sorry," Madison said simply.

"Find something to do in the house."

Her daughter nodded, if not contrite, at least rethinking her conduct.

Lucy didn't leave. "Madison, I know I didn't convey this adequately the other night—" She breathed, went on, "But I don't want you and J.T. out alone, not because I'm an overprotective lunatic mother with no life, but because I'm afraid you might become targets of someone who's been harassing me."

Madison paled. "What?"

"Right now, I seem to be the only target. And the incidents—I don't know what else to call them—seem to be tapering off. I hope they're over. I hope I've exaggerated their significance. But until I'm sure, I ask you *please* not to go off on your own."

"What kind of incidents?"

Lucy told her. She left out none of the possibilities. "I don't know if they're all related—I don't know if any of them are related."

"That's why Sebastian's here?"

That and something else, which he wouldn't explain. She expected it might have to do with Darren Mowery, an unnerving prospect. She nodded. "Yes."

"J.T. doesn't know, does he?"

"No." Lucy smiled a little. "He's still young enough that he'll do as I ask without five million questions and arguments."

Madison didn't smile. "This is spooky."

Wrung out, Lucy headed downstairs, refilled her mug with stale coffee and joined Sebastian on the back steps. She sat close to him, but not touching. She sipped her coffee. After a long silence between them, she said, "I'm not Colin's wife anymore. One of the hardest things I did after he died was to take off my wedding ring."

She jumped up before Sebastian could respond and ran into the kitchen. J.T. had wandered down from his room. They made pancakes and sausage, heated up pure Vermont maple syrup and filled the kitchen with homey smells. Madison was allowed down for breakfast, but declined.

This is my life, Lucy thought. It wasn't with a burn-out like Sebastian Redwing, a man who'd had to renounce violence, not because he was a pacifist, a gentle man by nature, but because he wasn't. He had killed people. People had tried to kill him. Maybe as recently as two days ago, someone had tried to kill him.

She sat back, stared at her hands. She wore no rings now. She and Colin had been young and broke, and they hadn't spent much on their wedding rings. But that was okay, they'd had such faith in their future together.

Daisy Wheaton had worn her wedding ring until the day she died. Rob had told Lucy, not that he'd needed to. She'd known, somehow.

I am not Colin's wife anymore.

Her chest was suddenly tight, aching, and she could feel tears welling, because it was real this time, not symbolic. She'd kissed Sebastian. She *wanted* Sebastian. Never mind that he wasn't right for her, he'd somehow managed to set her physically on edge, fill her mind with thoughts of making love to him. It was madness.

But maybe, she thought, necessary.

She didn't want to be known as the Widow Swift. As good as Daisy's life might have been, it wasn't *her* life.

She poured herself a fresh cup of coffee and took it out to the barn with her. Sebastian wasn't on the back steps. She didn't know where he was. Just as well, she thought, and settled in to work.

Barbara went for a run on the main road, past Lucy's house. She'd left her car at the end of the dirt road because she didn't want to walk back up the steep hill.

It was Sunday, but no one was around. Still, she could feel Sebastian Redwing's eyes on her as she ran. She wasn't paranoid. He was *there*. He would wonder who she was. Perhaps Madison had already told him. Barbara didn't know why she was baiting him. Why not stay up on the hill? Why go for a run?

But she knew why, and she kept up her pace, hoping the impulse would subside. She ached with the need to act. She couldn't think, could hardly breathe. She wanted the relief that came, even momentarily, with action.

No.

Pain shot up her shins from pounding too hard. She eased up. She was a strong runner, a fit, disciplined woman.

Did Sebastian Redwing suspect her of toppling him into Joshua Falls? The landslide had worked out even better than she'd anticipated. She remembered her mix of horror and fascination as she'd watched him plunge headfirst over the rock ledge. Oh, God! What if she'd killed a man?

It would have been Lucy's fault. *Lucy's fault, Lucy's fault.* She was the one who'd brought Sebastian Redwing to Vermont.

Barbara turned around at an old one-room schoolhouse, now boarded up, and headed back. Her stomach hurt. She was afraid of throwing up. It was tension, she knew. And hatred. She'd never known such pure hatred, didn't understand it. Lucy had never done anything to her.

But, of course, she had—just not directly. If Barbara followed the winding path to where Jack went wrong, where he'd moved away from openly declaring his love for her to this stubborn denial, it landed at Lucy's feet. She hadn't seen that Colin had a heart condition. She'd stolen Jack's grandchildren away. She'd made him give up Barbara, the one woman who loved him totally, un-conditionally. *Lucy's fault*. It was that simple.

Barbara abruptly stopped to pick flowers on the side of the road, grabbing them by the handful, pulling them up by their roots. Black-eyed Susans and daisies, a few purple, spiky things she didn't know the name of. She ran with them, their dirt-laden roots slapping against her shorts and sweaty thighs.

When she reached her car, she grabbed a pad and pencil.

No. She had to do this right.

She dumped the flowers onto her front seat and, panting and sweating, climbed in behind the wheel. She should take time to cool down and stretch, but she didn't.

There was nothing from Darren at the rented house. No messages on her cell phone voice mail. Nothing from Jack. Nothing from anyone.

She blinked back tears and carefully cut the roots off the flowers. Some were a little beaten up. She didn't care. She found a piece of string in a kitchen drawer and tied it around the flowers. Downstairs in a closet, she found an old typewriter. She typed a short note. She would have to get rid of the typewriter; it probably could be easily traced. But she didn't touch the paper directly, didn't leave a handwriting sample for Mr. Security Man.

"He should have died in the falls," she said. "He really should have."

Wrapping her hand in a dishtowel, she tucked the typed note into the flowers.

She smiled. "How romantic."

After the sugar and adrenaline of her morning had worn off, Lucy called her father-in-law. She used her portable phone while she deadheaded hollyhocks and daylilies in front of the barn.

"Jack? Hi, it's Lucy. Why didn't you tell me you'd sent Barbara up here to rent you a house? I could have helped! We could at least have had Barbara to dinner." She kept her tone cheerful, half teasing. "I hope you weren't afraid we wouldn't want you."

"No—no, that's not it at all." He sounded tense and awkward, his sonorous voice unable to mask his feelings. "I wasn't sure I could find anything at this late date, and I didn't want to get Madison's and J.T.'s hopes up. And you know how I love surprises."

"Well, Barbara's found you a great house just up the hill from us."

"She told me. That's wonderful. It's okay with you?"

Lucy tossed a handful of wilted blossoms into the dirt and rubbed her forehead. She could feel a headache coming on. Awakened by Sebastian in her room, thrown into fits by his kiss, her daughter acting up, too many pancakes—all had her going. "I've told you before, Jack, you're always welcome here. The kids will be thrilled to have you around."

"Barbara's rented the house for a month. I'll have to go home a few times—"

"Jack, she could have rented the house for a year. You're family."

"Lucy…" He seemed to choke up, but rallied. "Thank you. I'm sorry I went off the deep end on you the other day."

"Jack, we've known each other too long and have gone through too much together to worry about that sort of thing. Look, you sound tired. Is everything all right?"

"Yes, fine. It's just bloody hot here. Lucy—there's

something else I should tell you. Sidney Greenburg will be spending some time in Vermont with me."

"That's great. Sidney's wonderful." Lucy understood immediately what he, in his almost prudish way, was trying to tell her. "Jack, I'm so pleased for you."

"And you? Is everything all right with you?"

Not by a long shot, she thought. "Nothing a few quiet days won't cure. Is Barbara heading back to Washington? I can still have her to dinner—"

"I urged her to take a few extra days to relax. You know Barbara. This place would fall apart without her."

Lucy smiled. "Do you mean your office or all of Washington?"

He laughed, sounding more like himself.

When she hung up, Sebastian materialized behind her. "How's the good senator?"

"Eavesdropping isn't polite. I had a talk with J.T. about that very subject this morning."

"No one's ever suggested I was polite."

She swallowed and pinched off a pale yellow daylily blossom. His mood, she sensed, was not good. He was serious, the teasing sexiness and the depth of emotion of earlier replaced by a kind of dark calm.

"He was tense," she said. "This time of year is always hard in Washington. Everyone wants to get home, it's hot, and the back-channel pressures and deals come fast and furious. Jack's a plodder. He likes to think through issues, not jump on some half-baked compromise."

"I'd like to talk to him."

"Jack? Why?"

He shrugged, but nothing about him was nonchalant. "For the same reasons the local police would want to talk to him if you'd gone to them instead of me. He's a United States senator. If someone's bothering you, maybe it's to get to him."

Lucy tossed more dead blossoms into the back of the flower bed. It needed weeding, too, and a shot of organic fertilizer. "That doesn't make any sense."

"Maybe not."

"You're thinking if he's rented a house here for August, it could mean something's up."

"I'm not thinking anything. I just want to talk to him."

She plunked the phone in his hand. "Go ahead. I'll listen in."

"Lucy—"

"You're hiding something, Redwing. You're not here just because someone shot a hole in my dining room window. So, what is it? What do you know that I don't know?"

"I don't like to talk on the phone with someone breathing down my neck."

"I don't, either."

"You didn't know I was there."

"If you don't want to use my phone and have me listen in, you should have brought your own."

She yanked at a browned, soggy hollyhock blossom, and the plant, which she hadn't staked and was already leaning too far forward, fell. She tore it up and flung it onto the driveway. It lay there like a dead animal.

Sebastian watched her without comment. The man worked on her nerves, got to her senses, made her feel on edge and half-crazy, as if she couldn't think straight—or could think *too* straight. Everything seemed more alive, more energized when he was around. Even deadheading her damn flowers. There were no half-measures with him. No *peace*.

"You're a goddamn liar," she said and marched back to the barn.

He didn't follow her. She kicked a wastebasket and stormed over to a side window, one she'd added in her renovations. He was already dialing. The *bastard*. He'd gotten his way. What did he care if she was in a turmoil?

She picked up the extension.

"Hang up, Lucy. I'm better at this than you are."

"The kids could listen in," she said.

"Not and get away with it. Hang up."

She heard a voice say, "Senator Swift's office."

Sebastian disconnected without a word. Lucy watched him toss the phone into the flower bed like one of her dead blossoms, then he was coming toward her, taking long strides that put her at a disadvantage.

She was alone in the barn. J.T. was playing Nintendo in his room, Madison was confined to quarters, and it was Sunday, so her staff had the day off.

He was there.

"I was thinking about hiding under a canoe," she said, "but I figure you're the expert. You'd just find me and it'd only reinforce the big, bad wolf ideas you have about yourself."

"Lucy. Damn it."

His voice was ragged, his gray eyes flinty. He caught her around the middle, paused just long enough for her to tell him to go to hell—but she didn't—and his mouth found hers. His hands splayed on her back. She could feel the imprint of his palms and each finger like a hot spike as he drew her against him. He was fully aroused. She could feel him straining, pressing as his kiss deepened, his tongue probing erotically, telling her, in ways that words couldn't, just what he wanted.

He lifted her shirt and slid one hand down her pants, squeezing gently, then easing around the front, between her legs, where she could hide nothing from him. "Don't stop," she whispered. "Don't stop."

"I have no intention of stopping."

And he didn't, until she was quaking against his fingers. It happened so fast, so explosively, she was stunned. But she wasn't embarrassed. He pulled back, let her sink into her chair. She licked her lips, still tasting him. "What about you?"

"I'll wait."

"I don't usually—I haven't—" She cleared her throat; it would take a while before she could think properly. "I'm not usually that reckless."

"That wasn't reckless." He grinned, kissed her softly. "One day I'll show you reckless."

Impossibly, desire spurted through her again, just as searing and furious. He winked, as if he knew, and headed back toward the door. "Where are you going?" she asked.

He smiled. "To make my phone call."

Jack Swift refused to talk details. "I told Plato all you need to know. As it was, I took a huge risk. You know Darren Mowery. You know he'll do exactly what he's threatened to do if I don't cooperate."

"Which is?" Sebastian asked.

"Reveal his lies and filth."

Lies and filth. They were making progress. "Senator, my advice is for you to take everything you have to the Capitol Police. Let them do their job. They can put a round-the-clock security detail on you. Mowery doesn't have to know."

"But he will," Jack Swift said.

Sebastian felt fatigue tug at his eyes, settle into the small of his back. He'd done too much today. Kissing Lucy at dawn, chasing after her daughter, damn near making love to Lucy in the barn. He stood in the shade of one of the big old maples in the front yard, her portable phone almost out of range. She was right. He should have brought his cell phone.

The senator went on. "You know I'm right."

"Yes," Sebastian acknowledged. "I know."

"I'm not in any physical danger."

"Did you pay him?"

Jack Swift hesitated. This, too, was more than he wanted to admit. "Two installments."

"How much?"

"Ten thousand each."

Sebastian gripped the phone hard. "Twenty thousand total? Senator, Darren Mowery tried to steal millions last year. He's not planning to settle for twenty grand."

No answer.

"But you already know that," Sebastian said.

"I don't know what he wants. I only know what he'll do if I don't cooperate, and I've already decided that's intolerable." Swift sighed deeply and added, "And now that I've already cooperated twice, the bastard knows he's got me by the short hairs. There's no going back."

"Then what do you want from me?"

"I want you to stop him."

"No, Senator," Sebastian said. "You want me to kill him."

He disconnected while Swift was still gasping. The

senator, Sebastian decided, needed a little more time to think over his situation. It was damn cruel to exacerbate his already acute sense of isolation, but from hard experience, Sebastian knew that blackmail victims never liked to divulge what their tormenters had on them. They just wanted all the unpleasantness to go away by itself. Usually, it didn't.

Madison joined him on the porch and sat down next to him with a cardboard box. "I found this in the attic. It's what I do when I'm under house arrest—I poke around in the attic. Look." She opened the lid. "It's quilting pieces. Hexagons. Do you think they were your grandmother's?"

Sebastian lifted out a stack of the hexagons. He nodded, recognizing the soft, worn fabric of his grandfather's old shirts. He remembered Daisy cutting them up years after he'd died. Waste not, want not. But she'd never made the quilt.

"Yes," he said. "They were Daisy's."

"I guess she never got around to piecing the quilt."

"I guess not."

"I was thinking about asking Mom to help me—I've never sewn a quilt before. You wouldn't mind?"

"Why would I mind? Your mother bought the house. She owns everything in it."

"But…" She gave an exaggerated shrug. "If it was my grandmother's, I'd want it."

He smiled. "Consider yourself Daisy's honorary great-granddaughter."

She laughed, delighted. "Of course," she amended, "this is just because I'm bored out of my mind. If I were in Washington this summer, I wouldn't have to resort to sewing a quilt."

"People in Washington sew quilts."

"Only because they *want* to, not because they *have* to because there's nothing else to do."

"Madison, if you could, tell me everything you and Barbara Allen talked about. Just pretend you're a reporter and recorded your conversation."

"Why?"

"Because I don't trust her," he said, giving it to her straight.

"You don't trust anyone."

"I trusted Daisy."

"What about my mother?"

"Your mother?" He leaned back against a step and looked out at shaded lawn. "Well, Madison, I've loved your mother for a very long time. I don't know as I trust her."

The girl gaped at him. Sebastian was unrepentant. The kid needed to learn that if she asked impertinent questions, she'd better be prepared for impertinent answers. Let her figure out if he was serious.

"Barbara Allen," he said.

"Oh. Right." And she told him what she and Barbara had talked about. It wasn't much.

"That's everything?"

She nodded.

"Good report. Thanks."

"You don't think she's the one bugging Mom, do you?"

"I don't know. I like to keep an open mind." He glanced at her. "I suggest you do, too."

She jumped up with her box of fabric pieces. "I've known Barbara *forever*. She's worked for my grandfather since before I was even born. She *couldn't* do those things to Mom."

"Look, under the right set of circumstances, people can do just about anything."

She shook her head, adamant. "Not me."

Sebastian hated arguing with a fifteen-year-old. "Good. Okay. Not you."

She stomped off. She knew when she was being patronized. He considered going after her to apologize, but decided against it. He'd been nice enough until she started talking about forever. What the hell did a kid her age know about forever?

But he liked her. She was humiliated, annoyed, grounded, probably at least a little scared, and still she was trying to make the best of it. Quilting. The kid had guts. Like both her parents.

He thought of Colin and smiled. His dead friend would have been proud of his family and the way they were carrying on without him.

Lucy found him on the steps. She sat down next to him, folded her hands in her lap. "Looks as if Madison and I will be sewing the quilt Daisy pieced. Madison's at that age where she pushes me away and then pulls me to her, until I don't know what to do. Take it a day at a time and keep loving her, I suppose." She smiled suddenly. "Teenagers really are wonderful."

"You have great kids, Lucy. You've done well."

"So far. Fingers crossed."

"I want to go up and talk to Barbara Allen," he said. "It should only take thirty minutes or so."

"Are you asking me if I'll be okay here by myself? If so, the answer's yes. I'll be fine."

He stretched his legs down over the steps. "I don't

know. When Daisy left me here alone, I'd get spooked, especially during a thunderstorm. That thunder would echo in the hills. I'd hide under a pillow."

"You were just a kid."

"Hell, I was scared of thunderstorms until I was eighteen."

She laughed and placed a hand on his thigh. "Sebastian, about earlier—I'm not embarrassed, and I have no regrets, except that we didn't have more time. I knew when I went to see you in Wyoming that inviting you into my life was a risk. I've never been neutral about you. I'll say that much."

She started to remove her hand, but he covered it with his, keeping it in place. "After my mother died, Daisy said it was a cruel fate to lose both her husband and only child. She was angry, and she thought it would only add insult to injury if she lived a long life. But she was all I had, and she knew it, and she made the best of it. And after a while, she stopped being angry and started living again."

"I was never angry," Lucy said.

"Yes, you were."

She was silent, her hand still under his. She could have slipped it out, but she didn't.

"Colin left you with two small children and a life you didn't want to lead. Then your parents retired to Costa Rica when you needed them most. And Jack Swift was no good to you, wrapped up in his own grief, his work, his ideas about how you should raise his grandchildren." Sebastian paused, but Lucy didn't jump in to correct him, agree, tell him to go to hell. "If I'd shown up for the funeral or had seen you afterward, I would have wanted to take that anger on."

"I wish you had," she said quietly. "I would have loved to have dumped it on someone else. I guess in a way I did dump some of it on you, in absentia."

"Cursed me to the rafters, did you?"

She smiled. "Pretty much." She wiggled her hand free and gave him another pat. "You're right. I was angry. I didn't know it at the time—I had so much to do, so many emotions to sort out. Anger seemed like the least of my worries. And I felt so guilty. I still do."

"I know."

"Yes. You do, don't you?" She got to her feet, and as he looked up at her, he noticed her slim body, the muscles from her paddling and hiking. She took a deep breath. "It's a gorgeous day. Well, off to Barbara's with you. If you find any dead animals tucked away, you have my permission to haul her to the police station."

"You want to lay odds she's the one?"

"Not me. I've always liked Barbara, and I've always thought she liked me."

"Maybe it doesn't have anything to do with you."

"A dead bat in my bed?"

Sebastian nodded, rising. "You're right. That has everything to do with you."

She crossed her arms over her chest, and he could see she was nervous, rattled at the idea—however far-fetched—that her father-in-law's longtime personal assistant could wish her ill.

"I'm jumping ahead of the facts," he said. "Barbara Allen isn't even a suspect. She could have an airtight alibi, for all we know—or information that could point us in the right direction."

"Well, watch your back. I don't want to have to scrape you off the rocks again."

Chapter 12

"I want out," Barbara said. "I want out *now*."

Darren Mowery smirked at her from his chair in front of the cold stone fireplace. He'd shown up ten minutes ago, without warning. "Barbie, Barbie."

"Don't call me that. I'm Barbara, or Ms. Allen, or Miss Allen. I'm not 'Barbie.'"

She was on her feet, pacing, trying to look calmer than she felt. He'd swooped in so silently, so unexpectedly, catching her coming from the shower. Again, she'd detected no physical interest in her. He was single-minded, totally focused on his mission: the blackmail of a United States senator. Of her boss. She shuddered, horrified.

"Okay, *Barbara*." He drew it out, sarcastic, laughing at her without humor. He wore tan chinos and a white polo shirt, nothing that made him stand out. "You won't call the police."

"I will. If you don't leave me alone, I'll call the Capitol Police. I never should have gone along with you. I wasn't thinking." She'd been caught up in wanting to lash out at Jack, *force* him to acknowledge his love for her. But this was an unholy alliance. There were other ways to get to Jack.

Darren scratched the side of his mouth, looking unworried. "I warned you, if you'll recall. No cold feet, no surprises."

"That's not my problem."

"Oh, it is. You see, Barbie, if you go to the police, they get my pictures of you stalking Lucy Swift."

At first she didn't understand what he meant. Pictures of her stalking Lucy? What was he talking about? She wasn't a stalker. Then she digested his words. Understood. She didn't move, didn't breathe. She could feel him watching her with satisfaction.

"You don't understand—" Her voice cracked. "You couldn't possibly understand."

"Oh, no, I understand. It's simple. You hate her guts, and you took it upon yourself to scare the shit out of her. I tell the Capitol Police how I've been on your case for the past month. I tell them everything, start to finish."

"Jack will know the truth. He knows you're a blackmailer."

"And he'll know you're a stalker, a nutcase lurking in the bushes to get at his daughter-in-law. It'll all make sense to him. He won't say a word about me. You know he won't, Barbie. He's too scared. He doesn't care what I do so long as I don't squeal about Colin and his little shenanigans." Mowery smiled smugly. "I'll be the hero."

Barbara tried to stand up straight. "You followed me? You've known all this time—"

"Barbie." He was chastising, indulgent, arrogant. "You forget what I did for a living for the better part of thirty years."

"Oh, God," she whispered.

Darren crossed one leg over the other, as if to emphasize that he was relaxed, in control. "If I talk, you lose everything. Your job, your reputation, any hope you have of snaring your boss. At best, you get sent to the loony bin for a little head-shrinking. If the jury's like me and doesn't buy a nutcase plea, you're up the river for a good, long stay."

Barbara ignored the pain that swept through her. "There's nothing wrong with my mind."

"So you go for a plea bargain. Barbara Allen, the stalker." He yawned. "I thought the bullet on the car seat was goddamn brilliant, myself. Made Lucy's skin crawl, I bet."

Barbara sniffed, regarding him as if he were an insect on her carpet. "I don't have to explain myself to you. I was merely trying to shock her into doing right by Jack's grandchildren."

"Uh-huh."

"I'm hardly the first woman to despise a phony like Lucy."

"Yeah, right. You hate Lucy because she's everything you're not."

"That's not true."

He ignored her. "She married a Swift, she has Swift children, she has a fun, challenging career, she has a house. You hate her, *Barbara*, because she has a life and you don't."

"I do have a life! It's Lucy who has no life."

"When our buddy Jack told you to take a hike, you

let your obsession with her get away from you." Darren smiled, supercilious, almost enjoying himself. "It relieves the pressure, doesn't it? Upsetting Lucy, throwing her off her stride. Makes you feel better, at least for a little while."

Barbara held up her chin, summoning every last shred of pride she had. "I gave up everything for Jack. I've worked night and day for him for twenty years. I've put his interests ahead of my own. Lucy's not half the woman I am."

"But she signs her checks 'Swift,' and you don't."

"Bastard."

"See? I know these things, Barbie. I'm an expert."

She tried to swallow, but her throat was too constricted. He could never understand. No one could. "I just want out." God, she sounded pathetic.

Darren dropped both feet to the floor and leaned forward. "Get this straight, Barbie." He enunciated each word precisely, as if he were talking to a dunce. "I don't care about your dirty little secret. You can turn Lucy Swift into a babbling lunatic for all I care. You are in this for the long haul. Understood?"

"I hope Sebastian Redwing finds you and kills you."

Mowery grinned. "That'd be kind of fun, wouldn't it? He tried to kill me once. I'd like to see him try again."

"Darren," she said, sinking onto the floor in front of him, knowing she looked pitiful—the obsessed spinster in love with the boss. God! But somehow, some way, she had to get through to him. "Listen to me, I don't care about my share of the money—I don't care about any of it. You can do whatever you want to do. I won't say a word. I just want to stop."

"Barbie."

"Please go on without me. *Please.*"

"I don't think so."

So cocky, so arrogant. She got to her feet, hoping she wouldn't crack, throw up, cry. Her stomach hurt. She pushed back her hair with both hands and went to the windows that looked out on the woods, the brook. Lucy should have stayed in Washington. *None* of this would have happened if she'd stayed.

"I've gotten all the satisfaction I want from hurting Lucy," she said, and added in a small voice, "And I can wait for Jack."

"Yeah, so?"

She turned back to him. "I'm done. I won't say a word to anyone about what you're doing. Just go on about your business and leave me out of it."

"I can't do that."

"You mean you won't."

"Either way."

She started to shiver. He would see it as a sign of weakness. He had used her, manipulated her. Now there was no way out. It was Lucy's fault. All of it, Lucy's fault. Barbara could feel a fresh wave of rage building. She was trapped, and it was Lucy's fault.

"All right," she said. "What do you want me to do?"

"Right now, you're doing fine just being up here." Mowery walked over to her, stared out the windows at the picturesque scenery. "Vermont gives me the fucking creeps. I hate the woods. You okay, Barbie?"

"Yes. Certainly." No more being mealymouthed. It hadn't gotten her anywhere with him. She would hold her head high. "I have no apologies for what I did to Lucy. She deserved it."

He shrugged. "Sure."

"You've known from the beginning?"

"Why do you think we're in this gig together?"

"You had to have something on me so you knew you could manipulate me when the time came."

"So I could use your fucked-up little mind to my advantage." He winked at her. "So far, so good. You forget, Barbie. I'm better at this than you are."

"That was my mistake."

"There's only one man who's ever outsmarted me. He'll be knocking on your door before too long."

"Sebastian Redwing," she said.

Darren winked at her, patted her on the butt and left.

Fifteen minutes later, as he'd predicted, Redwing walked up onto the deck where Barbara was still contemplating her options. She had few.

Darren knew. Darren would have his way. So, what did she want? *Jack.* At the very least, satisfaction. Lucy suffering. Lucy miserable.

Sebastian introduced himself. He was, Barbara thought, breathtakingly sexy. He wore jeans and a faded polo shirt, but it would be impossible for him to blend into a crowd, even if he wanted to. She was aware of her own prim attire, simple slacks and a blouse, casual yet still professional.

"I'm staying at the house with Lucy and the kids," he said. "It belonged to my grandmother. I sold it to them after Colin died."

"Yes, I know."

His eyes were an unusual mix of grays, she saw. He seemed to take in more of her than she'd have liked—an unsettling quality. But even if he knew she had secrets, he would never guess what they were. That was what was so unnerving about Mowery: he knew, only because he was incapable of trust.

"Do you mind if I talk to you a minute?" Sebastian asked.

"No, of course not." She recovered, reminded herself she wasn't a woman who played up her physical attractions to manipulate men; that was for weaker, less intelligent and capable women. She smiled, poised, professional. "I suppose Madison told you I was in Vermont renting a house for her grandfather?"

"She didn't plan to tell anyone anything. She got caught sneaking up here this morning and came clean."

Barbara nodded. "I never meant for her to lie for me. I suppose asking her not to say anything was bad enough. A sin of omission rather than commission. I hope Lucy isn't too annoyed with me."

"Madison's fifteen. She knows the score."

In other words, Lucy was punishing her daughter. Acid rose in Barbara's throat. The woman was disgusting. "How long do you plan to stay in Vermont?" she asked, keeping her tone conversational.

"I don't have any firm plans. Lucy stopped in when she was in Wyoming, and I decided to come on out, see my old haunts."

"Had Colin mentioned anything about buying your grandmother's house and moving to Vermont one day?"

Sebastian shook his head. "Not Colin. He loved Washington."

"Madison's like that," Barbara said, smiling to take the edge off her words.

"That's what I understand. I didn't get to see a lot of Colin in the four or five years before he died."

"It's easy to take the young for granted."

Barbara couldn't help the subtle criticism in her tone, but Sebastian didn't react. She was thinking of herself and Jack, too, and how he'd taken her for granted for years…and years. She was always there, always capable, always willing to do whatever he asked, without complaint. Unlike too many of his senior staffers, he could rely on her without worrying about her stabbing him in the back.

And what had her loyalty gotten her? Nothing.

Jack *had* to love her.

"When do you go back to Washington?" Sebastian asked.

"In a day or two. I'm open. I'll have to help Jack tie up a few loose ends before he comes up for August."

"I'm surprised he can manage without you right now. Isn't this a busy time of year in Washington?"

"Usually, yes."

He didn't comment, and she wondered if he could see through her. Did he know? Did he suspect? Lucy, the sniveling coward, would have told him about the incidents by now. That was why he was here, of course. Not to see his grandmother's house, but to protect her. It was sickening.

Barbara didn't need a man to protect her. Maybe that was why Jack was afraid to admit his love for her—he knew she didn't need him for protection, an income, all the things an ordinary woman wanted in a man. She was different. Stronger.

Sebastian smiled, and it was spine-melting. It would be so easy for someone as weak as Lucy to turn her problems, her individuality, over to a man like Sebastian Redwing. Barbara was more self-reliant. Tougher. "Well," he said, "I don't pretend to know the workings of Washington. Lucy asked me to invite you to dinner tonight."

"How sweet. Please thank her for me, but I have other plans." Of course, Lucy would think Barbara was up here longing for her company, incapable of managing on her own. "And I hope she won't be too hard on Madison. I put her in a difficult position."

"No problem."

He started down the steps, but stopped halfway and glanced back up at her. His expression was impossible for her to read, and she was very, very good at reading people. "A former colleague of mine might be in the area. Darren Mowery. Know him?"

So this was the reason for his visit. Not Madison, not Lucy. "I've heard of him."

"He went bad last year. It's a long story. I hope I'm wrong and he's nowhere near here. If he tries to contact you, find me or call the police." His gaze leveled on her, probing, uncomfortable. "He's dangerous. I can't emphasize that enough."

"I understand. Thank you for the warning."

Lucy, Madison and J.T. had sorted the quilt pieces by color. Now they had three hundred little hexagons in piles on the dining room table. The colors were faded, the fabric worn. "It'll look like an antique quilt when we're done," Madison said happily.

"It's called a 'grandmother's garden' quilt. It'll be pretty."

"It'll be *perfect*."

Lucy fingered a blue-and-white striped broadcloth, imagining Daisy carefully cutting her dead husband's shirts into hexagons. Had the work helped her make peace with his death? Or was it frugal Daisy Wheaton making use of what was at hand? "Joshua died sixty years ago. This fabric's old."

J.T., who'd given up on sorting after the first hundred pieces, wandered out to the front porch with a couple of his *Star Wars* Micro Machines. He was making war noises, totally into his own twelve-year-old world.

"Mom!" he called excitedly. "Someone left flowers!"

Madison dropped a stack of hexagons. "Flowers? Oh, cool. I wonder—"

Lucy stopped her in mid-sentence, grabbing her arm. "Stay here."

"Why? Mom, you should see your face. You're white as a sheet! Over flowers?"

"Just stay put."

Lucy ran to the front door and banged it open, catching J.T. by the arm before he could pick up the bouquet of flowers. Black-eyed Susans, daisies. They were scraggly, wilted. If she'd spotted them first, she'd have thought they were from J.T. or Georgie. "Go inside with your sister."

"Mom, what's wrong? You're scaring me!"

"It's okay, J.T. Just go inside."

He started to cry, but did as she asked. Lucy could feel her legs giving way. She had to make herself calm down. She was scaring her children, scaring herself. Maybe she was wrong. Maybe the flowers were Georgie's doing, even if he hadn't been around today. Maybe he'd stopped by while they were inside sorting hexagons and had just wanted to surprise them.

The flowers were tied with a string. There was a note. Lucy plucked it out carefully, unfolded it.

To Lucy,
I love you with all my heart.
Forever,
Colin

It was as though the words reached up from the paper and choked her. She couldn't breathe, couldn't see. She tripped on her own feet, stumbled down several steps, reeling.

"Lucy." Sebastian's voice. His arms came around her. "Lucy, what is it?"

She gulped for air. "The son of a bitch. The son of a bitch!" Every muscle in her body tensed. She glared up at him. "Is it Barbara? Is it? Because if it is, I'm going up there now and—and—" She couldn't get the words out. "Goddammit!"

Sebastian half carried, half pushed her to the porch steps. "You're hyperventilating. If you don't stop, I'm getting a paper bag and putting it over your head."

Hyperventilating. Too much oxygen in the blood. She knew what to do. She snapped her mouth shut, counted to three, breathed through her nose, let it out slowly through her mouth.

"Two more times," Sebastian said.

"Madison and J.T."

"Two more times, Lucy. You won't do them any good passed out cold."

She knew he was right. In another minute, she was calmer, breathing normally. He snatched up the note and read it. A slight tightening of the jaw was his only visible reaction.

"I didn't expect it," she said. "I knew it was something, but not this. What kind of sick person would do something like that?"

She got to her feet, held on to his arm to help steady herself. Maybe he didn't have running water or electricity, maybe he'd renounced violence, maybe he had his demons to fight, but he was there, rock-solid.

When she regained her balance, she climbed the steps. *Forever, Colin.* Sick, sick, sick. She got to the front door. "Madison, J.T.—it's okay, you can come on out."

"I'll get rid of the flowers," Sebastian said.

Lucy nodded. "Thank you."

"And I'll call Plato."

Sebastian's take on Barbara Allen was direct and to the point. "She's up to her eyeballs in something."

Lucy smiled. "Is that your professional opinion?"

"Gut."

They were at the kitchen table, drinking decaf coffee long after dinner. Madison and J.T. had gone up to bed. Lucy asked, "Is your gut always right?"

"About whether or not I want a cheeseburger. With who's lying, hiding, contriving, plotting to rape and pillage—" He shrugged. "It's almost always right. I've been wrong on occasion."

"I sometimes forget what you do for a living. When you're here, you seem so normal."

"I'm not," he said quietly.

She ignored a warm shudder, remembered pulling up to his shack with the dogs and the dust. No, not normal. "How does Redwing Associates manage without you?"

"I hired good people."

"About Barbara." Lucy sipped her decaf, which was

a little stale. "Up to her eyeballs in what? You have an idea, don't you?"

Nothing.

"Sebastian, I deserve to know."

"It's not a question of deserving. It's a question of what you'll do with the information."

"You don't trust me."

He frowned at her. "I don't know what that means. Do I trust you to sit back and do everything I tell you? No. Do I trust you to do what you think is right for the sake of your children? Yes."

"That's too specific. I mean trust in general."

"There's no such thing."

"Yes, there is. It's when you trust someone to have an internal compass that will always point them in the right direction, not toward no mistakes—everyone makes mistakes—but toward at least trying to make good decisions."

"I'm not sure your idea and my idea of a 'good decision' are the same."

"That's not the point, either. It's not about thinking alike. It's about trusting a person to be who they are."

He drank his coffee. If he thought it was stale, he gave no indication. "You've been sitting out here in these hills too long and talking to too many crunch-granola types. Lucy, I trust you. There."

"Good." She sat up straight. "Then tell me what you think Barbara's up to her eyeballs in."

"Blackmail."

She dropped her mug, coffee spilling over her hand and onto the table. He got up, tore off a couple of paper towels and handed them to her. She was shaking. She blotted the spilled coffee, not looking at him. "My

God. Blackmail?" Then the realization hit. "Not Darren Mowery. Sebastian, please tell me—"

"I wish I could, Lucy. I've been holding back on you, hoping I could tell you Darren's not involved in what's been happening to you. But he is."

Lucy nodded, breathing rapidly. "I understand."

"No, Lucy, you don't. Darren was my boss, he was my mentor, and he was my friend. He went bad, and I went after him. I knew I might have to kill him." Sebastian returned to his seat; he was calm, as if they were discussing whether the tomatoes were ripe enough to pick. "I should have made sure he was dead or in jail before I left Colombia. I didn't."

"And now—" Lucy frowned, trying to make sense of the bits and pieces she had. She left the coffee-soaked paper towels in a mound on the table. "Is he blackmailing *you*?"

"Would that he were. That'd be easy. No, he's blackmailing your father-in-law."

"What?"

"Darren contacted him while you were in Wyoming. Jack paid him off, and when it wasn't enough and Darren came back for more, he got in touch with my office."

"And they got in touch with you," Lucy said, her head spinning.

"Yes."

"When?"

"Before the falls."

"Well, you're a hell of a better liar than I am. Or Madison, even. Jesus. You've known that long?"

"Jack wouldn't give Plato the details. I let him sweat a few days. He still won't budge."

"But you know it's this Darren Mowery character," Lucy said.

Sebastian nodded.

"Then arrest him!"

"That's the thing about blackmail, Lucy. The victim doesn't want to go public. He doesn't care about whether the blackmailer goes to jail. He just wants him to keep quiet."

Unable to sit still another second, Lucy jumped to her feet. She ran outside, down the back steps, into the grass. It was cool on her bare feet. She could hear crickets as she fought back tears. Blackmail! Jack was being blackmailed!

Sebastian followed her out into the grass, not standing too close. The more he had to think about, Lucy thought, the more he seemed to go deep inside himself and maintain an outward calm. It was a skill she didn't have, except on the water. When a crisis hit while kayaking or canoeing, she operated on training, instinct, skill. She couldn't afford to panic.

But this was what he did, she remembered. He dealt with blackmailers. Blackmail victims.

"How much did Jack pay—do you know that much?"

"Twenty grand in two installments."

"That's all?"

"For now."

She exhaled toward the starlit sky. "I just want to make a quilt with my daughter. I want to take my son fishing. I want to live my life. *Damn.*"

"Plato will be here tomorrow."

She nodded.

"Lucy." He touched her cheek with one finger. "Oh, God, Lucy. If I could make this all go away, I would, even if it meant you never came to Wyoming and I didn't get to see you."

She shut her eyes, squeezed back tears. "Do you think Barbara's involved in the blackmail?"

"Yes."

"Do you think it has anything to do with me?"

"Yes. I don't know how, but yes."

She sank her forehead against his chest and let her arms go around him. He held her. She recovered slowly, stopped crying. "I hate crying," she said. "I haven't cried in years, except when I stubbed my toe last summer, and really, it was more because I was pissed."

"Lucy, you're one of the strongest women I know."

"I'm not. I just get up every day and do the best I can."

"There," he said, "you see what I mean?"

She opened her eyes and saw his smile, and she kissed him lightly, savoring the taste of him, the feel of his hands and the night summer breeze on her back. "If I could," she whispered, "I'd ask you to make love to me tonight."

"Lucy—"

"My children are upstairs in bed. They're afraid, and they need to know where I am."

"I love you, Lucy Blacker." He touched her hair, her mouth, then kissed her in a way that made her know he meant what he said. "I always will."

"Thank you."

He laughed suddenly, so unexpectedly it took her breath away. "Thank you?"

"Well—I don't know. Yes, thank you."

He smacked her on the behind. "Go upstairs to your

kids before I toss all honor to the stars and carry you off to bed."

"That's very tempting, you know."

"Believe me, I know."

J.T. was asleep when Lucy entered his room. As if drawn by an invisible force, she turned to the picture of him with his father. "Colin," she whispered, touching his image. "Thank you for what you were to me. For Madison and J.T. and our years together. Thank you."

She went down the hall and listened at Madison's closed door, then slipped into the guest room. She gazed out at the darkening sky, thinking of blackmail and Jack and a dangerous man who wasn't dead, and when she crawled into bed and pulled her quilts up to her chin, she thought of Sebastian. And she smiled. The Widow Swift was falling in love again.

The memo came across his desk late, around nine, and at nine fifteen, Jack Swift gave up on working until midnight as he'd planned and got a cab home. It was a routine memo. His staff was aware Sebastian Redwing had once saved his life and had been Colin's friend, and they regularly passed along pertinent information on Redwing Associates.

Happy Ford, a Washington, DC-based consultant for Redwing Associates, was shot this evening here in the city. She's in critical condition. Prognosis optimistic. Unknown if injury sustained in work-related activity. No suspects at this time.

Mowery.

In his bones, Jack knew Darren Mowery had shot this woman.

He got to his house, ran upstairs, started throwing clothes into his suitcase. Lucy, the children. He had to get to them. Somehow, he'd crossed Mowery. Somehow, he'd screwed up.

"I did everything the bastard asked!"

His suitcase fell off his bed, its contents spilling across the floor. He collapsed onto the thick rug amidst boxer shorts and chinos and sobbed. He pulled his knees up under his chin, wrapped his arms around his ankles and cried like a two-year-old. He couldn't stop. Colin, Eleanor. Gone. Dead. Buried. Everything he'd lived and worked for about to go up in smoke.

He had nothing left. Nothing.

And now Lucy and his grandchildren—he didn't know. He didn't know what Mowery would do.

"Jack?" Sidney's voice, calling from downstairs. "Jack, are you here? I called your office, and they said you lit out like a bat out of a burning cave. What's going on?"

In another minute, she was in the doorway.

She gasped. *"Jack."*

"Oh, Sidney. Sidney, what am I going to do?"

Chapter 13

Lucy ignored J.T.'s protests and made him go blueberry picking with her first thing in the morning. "Wild blueberries make the best muffins," she told him. "They're just starting to ripen."

"Why can't Madison go?"

"She's still asleep, and you're right here, bright-eyed and raring to go."

He made a face and slumped his shoulders, dragging his heels. If she'd told him he could go play Nintendo or watch TV, she knew he'd perk up, which only made her more determined. She handed him a coffee can. "You can be miserable or you can be cheerful. Your choice."

"I wish Georgie could come over."

She'd called Rob and Patti last night and suggested they keep Georgie home today. Lucy slung an arm over her son's shoulder. "You're getting so big. Are your feet bigger than mine yet?"

He liked that idea, and they walked up along the western edge of the stone wall that bordered the field, finally climbing over it to a cluster of low-bush wild blueberries. They squatted down, the sun already warm on their backs. It was supposed to rain later on, but now the air was humid and so still that Lucy swore she'd be able to hear a spider move.

"They're still green," J.T. said.

"Not all of them. We only need a cup for muffins. They'll be perfect when Grandpa's here next week. We can have him down for blueberry pancakes, blueberry pie, blueberry ice cream."

"I hate blueberry pancakes."

"J.T."

He smiled at her over the blueberry bushes. He still thought his cute smile could get him out of trouble. Just like his father. Lucy noticed there wasn't the usual pang of regret, the ache of realizing that her son would never really know his father. It wasn't okay—she hated it. But they'd be all right.

"Look! Mom, look, I've got one, two, three—*five* blueberries! Look at this one, it's huge." He plucked them fast, tossed them into his can as he reached for more. "Wow, I'm in the right spot."

"Good for you, J.T. Just keep picking."

He lost interest three handfuls of blueberries later, but Lucy decided they had enough for muffins. They clambered over the stone wall, her life, at that moment, back to normal.

She saw Sebastian walk out onto the back steps and sit down. He waved to her, and her heart skipped a beat, just as if she were a thirteen-year-old with a crush. Except this was different. She and Sebastian weren't kids.

She was thirty-eight; he was thirty-nine or forty. Colin was the right man for the woman she'd been, but she wasn't that woman anymore. The past three years had changed her. She'd lost a husband, she was raising two children on her own, she'd started her own business and moved to the country.

J.T. skipped ahead of her. "Hey, Sebastian!"

"Hey, J.T. You're up with the roosters."

"Mom and I picked blueberries." He stuck his can under Sebastian's nose. "Look."

Lucy followed at a slower pace, knowing push was coming to shove. She had a plan. She was tired of waiting for the next shoe to drop. But she knew Sebastian wouldn't like what she had in mind.

"We're making muffins," J.T. said.

Sebastian eyed her as she got closer. It was as if he could sense she was up to something he wouldn't like. "Muffins, huh?"

"Yes," Lucy said. "I thought we'd take some muffins up to Barbara and surprise her."

His eyes darkened just slightly, but enough. She was right. He didn't approve. "J.T., you've got a few stems in your berries. Why don't you take your can into the kitchen and pick them out while your mother and I talk."

"Don't argue with her," J.T. warned. "She's not in the mood."

He pounded up the steps, never one to make less noise when he could make more. Sebastian stood, his bruises and scrapes even less noticeable today. "You're going to take muffins to Barbara?"

"Yes, it's what I'd do if I didn't suspect her of being involved with a blackmail scheme and leaving me mean-spirited presents."

"They were more than mean-spirited, and the point is, you do suspect her."

"Well, *you* do. I don't know if I do. I'm not the one with twenty years of experience with creeps and desperadoes. I take people on adventures. Fun adventures. Nothing extreme, nothing scary. I mean, the unforeseen can happen and does." She squinted at him against the morning sun. "But we have contingency plans."

"Lucy, whoever left those flowers yesterday knew you were here with the kids. If it was Barbara, she knew I was here. She took a huge risk. When I see something like this escalate, I don't like it."

"I didn't like it when it hadn't escalated. Sebastian, Barbara knows I know she's here. If I don't go up to see her, she's going to wonder why."

"Let her wonder."

"What if she's innocent? Then I'll have hurt her feelings for no good reason."

"No, for a damn good reason. If she's innocent, she'll understand."

"That I thought she was capable of leaving me flowers from my dead husband? I don't think so."

"J.T. was right. You aren't in the mood to argue."

Lucy pounded up the steps almost as hard as J.T. had and tore open the door. She looked back at Sebastian and caught her breath at how the sunlight struck his hair, brought out the hard lines in his face. Maybe she was jumping the gun to think she could have a relationship with him. It was one thing to fall in love, another thing to have a relationship that worked. "I'm bringing Barbara wild-blueberry muffins."

"Plato will be here by noon."

"Good. In the meantime, you can hover."

The door slammed shut behind her.

And he laughed. In another minute, he was making coffee and picking stems out of the blueberries with J.T. as if he'd admitted defeat, which Lucy knew he hadn't. Maybe defeat had driven him out to the edges of his ranch and into a shack, but it hadn't driven him into her kitchen. The man had burrowed under her skin, and he meant to stay there.

She wrapped the muffins in aluminum foil and drove up the dirt road while they were still warm, because that was what she ordinarily would have done. She wouldn't have walked for fear of squishing the muffins, and she wouldn't have waited until they were cold, because they were no good cold.

The only difference was not taking Madison and J.T. with her. They stayed at the house with Rob.

Sebastian, she knew, was on the prowl in the woods. Hovering. She could almost feel his presence when she got out of her car at the rented house. There still was no breeze, the air warm and humid even up on the ridge. She followed a shaded gravel path and took the stairs to the deck. Sebastian had suggested she not go inside. Made sense to her.

"Barbara? Hello, it's me, Lucy!"

"I'm here," Barbara said from the screened porch.

"Oh, I didn't see you. J.T. and I made muffins this morning, and I brought you some. We picked wild blueberries bright and early."

"Sounds lovely."

Barbara pushed open the screen door, smiling as she came out onto the deck. She looked perfectly normal to Lucy. A bit formally dressed for Vermont, perhaps, but that wasn't out of the ordinary for Jack Swift's assistant. Lucy tried to place when they'd first met. It was when she and Colin were dating, for sure—not long after the assassination attempt. Barbara Allen had been a fixture in Jack's office for as long as Lucy could remember. Could she feel taken for granted and resent it?

But when Barbara smelled the muffins and seemed so genuinely delighted, Lucy couldn't imagine her stalking and harassing anyone, much less her boss's daughter-in-law. If nothing else, it would be dumb, and Barbara wasn't dumb. "Thank you so much," she said. "I love wild blueberries."

"There might be a few bushes up here." Lucy noticed blueberry and flour stains on her T-shirt and wished she'd changed. "You could probably get enough at least for a batch of pancakes."

Barbara laughed. "I'm afraid I'm not that domestic."

"I don't know, just about anyone can manage Bisquick and a handful of blueberries. Well, I hope you enjoy the muffins. Are you here long?"

"Just another day or two, I imagine. Thank God for cell phones. Otherwise I wouldn't be able to spare so much time away from the office."

"Yes, I know what you mean."

But Lucy regretted her words, irritated at herself for being defensive. She enjoyed making muffins and pancakes, picking berries, puttering in her garden, hanging out with her children; she had a business, she worked, she knew her way around Washington. She had nothing to prove. So what if Barbara had to make sure Lucy knew how important and indispensable she was? Why get defensive?

"I hope I didn't get Madison into trouble," Barbara said.

"You didn't." Madison, Lucy thought, got herself into trouble. "She's looking forward to her visit to Washington this fall. We all are, actually."

"Fall's my favorite time of year in Washington. It's so vibrant, so alive. I love the country, but—" She looked around at the still, quiet woods, and smiled. "I guess all this peacefulness would get on my nerves after a while."

"My first few months here, I was so restless, I didn't know if I'd stay. Then, I don't know, I started to enjoy the pace of life. Vermont isn't as isolated as it sometimes seems. There's so much to do."

"With so many tourists and second-home owners from the city, I imagine so. Your adventure-travel business is going well?"

Lucy nodded. This woman was driving her nuts. Maybe Sebastian's suspicions had colored her perceptions, made her hypersensitive to what she might ordinarily have treated as a normal conversation. "It's going very well, thanks. I have a great staff, and we have so many ideas. Did Madison tell you we're putting together a Costa Rica trip?"

"No, actually, we didn't really get a chance to talk about you."

It was as if Lucy had just been stuck with a thousand poison needles. This woman did not like her. "My parents retired there, you know."

"Jack told me. An odd thing to do, don't you think?"

So, now not only was she selfish and inferior, but her family was odd, too. She shrugged and made herself smile. "A natural thing for them, considering their background. I'm trying to get Jack to go with us on the dry run. Wouldn't that be fun? Maybe Sidney Greenburg can go, too. She and my parents are friends—"

"Yes, I know." Barbara set the muffins on an Adirondack chair and took in a long breath, staring out at the woods. For a moment, she seemed to forget Lucy was there, but she caught herself. "I'll check Jack's schedule. I don't know if he can spare any time for Costa Rica."

For frivolities, her tone said. Lucy pretended not to notice. "I hope he can, although I understand. Life as a senator must be awfully hectic and demanding."

"Well, one must prioritize. Jack would spend all his time with you and his grandchildren if he could. You know that. Unfortunately, I have to rein him in, help him stay on track. There's very little thanks in telling someone no all the time, but he understands."

"You don't think he should spend August up here?"

"Not the entire month, frankly, no. Personally, I can understand. You're his only family. Professionally—he's a Rhode Island senator, not a Vermont senator." Barbara smiled sweetly. "If you'd moved to Providence or Newport, it would be a different story."

If she'd been a good daughter-in-law, in other words. Lucy gave a lighthearted laugh. "No one offered me a house on the cheap in Providence or Newport. Well, I should be going. We're pulling together the last details for a father-son backpacking trip."

"It must be nice to have such a flexible schedule," Barbara said. "I'm so used to my dawn-to-dusk hours!"

"Nice seeing you, Barbara."

"You, too." When Lucy was halfway down the steps, Barbara added, "Oh, and I'd keep my eyes wide open around Sebastian Redwing."

Lucy turned. "Sebastian? Why?"

"I think he has another agenda aside from seeing his childhood home again."

Yeah, Lucy thought. The blackmail of a United States senator. "I'm not worried. I've known Sebastian for the better part of twenty years."

Barbara walked to the top of the steps. She was a handsome woman, Lucy thought, but annoying. "It's obvious, Lucy. You're his hidden agenda."

"What?"

"He's been in love with you for years. Everyone knows but you."

"Washington." Lucy laughed off her uneasiness. "I sure don't miss the gossip. See you, Barbara. Enjoy the muffins."

When she got back to her car, Lucy got in behind the wheel. She was furious with herself, furious with Barbara, and sickened by the idea of what this woman had done to her. "I wish I had proof. I'd drag the bitch by the hair down to the police," she said aloud.

"Well, well, well." Sebastian grinned as he opened the passenger door and slid in. "I like your spirit, Lucy Blacker."

"You weren't supposed to hear that."

He slumped low in the seat. "Eavesdropping is an unappreciated art."

"You listened in on my conversation with Barbara?"

"Yep. Female version of a pissing contest."

"I don't know what got into me." Lucy started the engine, backed out in a fury. "I don't care if she works twenty-four hours a day and thinks I'm a frump. Really, I don't."

"She sucked you into measuring yourself by her standards instead of your own."

Lucy shifted into Drive, hit the gas pedal and tore off down the dirt road. It needed grading, and her car bounced over the washboard ruts. "It's tempting to say she has to make more of her position with Jack and work 'dawn to dusk' because she has no life." She gulped for air, relaxed her grip on the wheel. "But then I'd be as bad as she is, judging her for her choices. Well, you're right. It was a pissing contest."

"You want to slow down? If we get wrapped around a tree, Plato will end up raising your kids." Sebastian leaned back in his seat, not looking as if her driving bothered him at all. "You don't want that. He used to jump out of a helicopter in the middle of a nor'easter."

She slowed, but not because she was worried about hitting a tree or Plato Rabedeneira raising her children. She glanced over at Sebastian. He had on a black polo shirt and jeans that fit closely over his thighs, and even the fading scrapes and scratches on his arms struck her as sexy, evidence of his hard life, his hard thinking. His choices. She sighed. "What are we going to do about Barbara?"

"We?"

"She's not going to stop. Whatever she has against me, I'm pretty sure I just made it worse."

"You couldn't have said or done anything to make it better. She's determined to hate you. She likes it. Hating you makes her feel better about herself."

"Do you really think she's in cahoots with Mowery?"

"I'd say there's a high probability."

"Meaning," Lucy added, "whatever he has on Jack could be something that would also hurt me."

Sebastian regarded her with a steady, reassuring calm. "Would Jack jeopardize his reputation and his bank account to protect you?"

"Yes. Yes, I think he would."

"Because of Madison and J.T.?"

"No, not just because of them—but they're a factor, absolutely. We're all the family he has. After Colin died—" She stepped on the brake, stopping the car. "Oh, my God. Sebastian, what if it's something to do with Colin?"

"If you know something," Sebastian said quietly, his tone professional, deadly, "if you even suspect something, now's the time."

"I don't. There's *nothing*. Jack and Colin both—with both of them, what you see is what you get. Colin had no secrets, not from me. He died suddenly, without any warning at all. We had no idea he had a heart condition. He didn't have time to hide anything. I went through all his stuff."

"Did he keep a journal?"

She nodded.

"Did you read it?"

"No. I burned it without reading it. Wouldn't you?"

"Probably not."

She shot him a look and realized he wasn't kidding. "You'd read a dead person's journal?"

"I might. I wouldn't rule it out and just burn it. What if it contained the secret to cold fusion?"

She found herself biting back a laugh. "You're full of shit, Redwing."

He grinned at her. "You needed to lighten up. What about Jack? What could he have to hide?"

"He might have some unpaid hospital bills. That's about as nefarious as he'd get." She took her foot off the brake and stepped on the gas pedal. "Maybe Mowery and Barbara made up something."

"That's possible," Sebastian said.

She sighed at him. "How can you be so calm?"

"Who says I'm calm?"

When they reached the house, Lucy put Madison and J.T. both to work with her in the barn. Rob wore a look that told her he wanted to interrogate her, but he wouldn't do it in front of her kids. So they actually managed to get some adventure travel work done.

And at noon, on schedule, Plato Rabedeneira arrived.

"Holy shit," Rob breathed, peering out the barn window at Plato and his big, shiny black car. "You know, Lucy, sometimes I start thinking you're just this ordinary adventure travel person, this widow with two kids, and then the cavalry rolls in."

"This is nothing. You should see what would happen if I called Washington."

"Grandpa Jack."

She nodded.

Plato got out. Apparently he'd parked his plane next to Sebastian's at the local airstrip and had the car waiting. He wore a black suit and dark glasses, and his limp was more pronounced, probably from the long hours in the plane.

"Think he's armed?" Rob asked.

"To the teeth."

Lucy went out to the driveway and practically felt Rob's shudder when Plato kissed her on the cheek. "Hey, kid."

"Hi, Plato. Thanks for coming out here. Just one thing before I let you into my house." She crossed her arms and gave him the kind of look she'd given J.T. and Georgie when she caught them playing war with her tomatoes. "I can't believe you sicced Sebastian on me knowing—" She faltered, realizing she was already in over her head, and finished lamely, "Knowing what you knew."

Plato grinned. "You mean that he's a reprobate or that he's in love with you?"

"Both."

"I was thinking I'd sicced you on him."

"Ha."

His dark glasses made him even harder to read. "He's still the best."

"I hope so. I need the best."

"Where is he?"

"Right here," Sebastian said, walking down from the front porch. "What's with the car and the dark glasses? You're lucky I didn't shoot you."

"You don't have a gun," Plato said, "and you wouldn't use one if you did."

"Maybe I've changed my mind."

"Good. Your sabbatical's over. You can get back to work."

"Sabbatical. Jesus, Plato."

But the joking ended, and Plato said, "I have news."

He glanced at Lucy, who shook her head, adamant. "Oh, no, you don't. I'm not going anywhere. Whatever you two have to say, you can say it in front of me."

"Sebastian?"

Lucy gritted her teeth but didn't jump in and argue her point further. Technically, Sebastian was Plato's boss, and his military training would compel him to follow the chain of command—but they were *friends*, and who the hell had given Sebastian the last word? She was agitated, frustrated, and it was entirely possible what they were discussing was none of her business.

"Go ahead," Sebastian said.

"It's not good news," Plato said. "Happy Ford was

shot last night in Washington. She's critical, but she should pull through."

Sebastian had no visible reaction. "She's getting everything she needs?"

"Everything."

He looked out across the road at the lush, wooded hills. "Mowery?"

"We haven't been able to talk to her."

"Then we don't know where he is," Sebastian said.

"No. She thought she'd picked up his trail yesterday afternoon. That's the last we heard."

"If she dies, it's my fault."

Plato shook his head. "If she dies, it's the fault of whoever pulled the trigger."

"I should have killed Mowery a year ago."

"Only a year ago? Why not fifteen years ago? Why not the day you met him?"

Madison and J.T. bounded out from the barn. Lucy felt her heart flip-flop at their energy, their youth, their obliviousness. Her babies. Dear God, she had to protect them!

Sebastian's eyes had narrowed into slits. "You're on kid watch."

Plato grimaced. "I was afraid of that."

"Take them out of here. Keep them safe."

Sebastian walked back up the porch steps and disappeared into the house. The door banged shut behind him, and Lucy jumped. She tried to smile. "I'm a little on edge."

"Good," Plato said. "It'll keep you alert."

"What do you want me to do?"

"Help your kids pack up. Two changes of clothes, two pairs of shoes, no animals."

"Sleeping bags? I have a ton of freeze-dried provisions—"

His unsmiling mouth twitched. "I'm not taking them into the outback, Lucy. We'll find a motel somewhere."

"You'll call me?"

"No. If I call you, it means there's trouble."

Her knees went out from under her, but she held steady. "Plato, I don't know if I can…"

"You can come with us."

She shook her head. "No. I have to figure this out. I trust you."

He tucked a finger under her chin. "Trust Sebastian."

"Mom," Madison said, and Lucy could feel her terror. "What's going on?"

"Cool car," J.T. said.

Lucy didn't know how to explain. She composed herself, and plunged in. "I want you two to go with Plato. It could be for a few hours or a couple of days, until I get things sorted out around here. He'll take care of you."

The color drained out of Madison's face. "*Mom.* What about you?"

"I'll be fine. I'll be here with Sebastian, and with any luck, I'll just get a lot of work done."

J.T. was still enthralled with the car. "Can I ride up front?"

Plato grimaced. "Sure, kid."

Madison tried to smile. She was older, and she knew more, guessed more. But she was determined to be brave. Lucy could see her struggling not to panic. "Um—can I take my quilt?"

Lucy knew she meant the hexagons she'd found in the attic.

Plato didn't. He sighed. "Quilt? Yeah, sure. Take your quilt."

Chapter 14

Plato leaned in the doorway of J.T.'s room. "Kid's packing for the new millenium," he said to Lucy. "Your daughter's worse. Maybe you better go on downstairs and pour yourself a glass of lemonade, Lucy. I'll supervise."

She nodded. "They're nervous."

"They're packing too much. I didn't bring the moving van. Go on. We'll get it pared down in no time." He unfolded himself from the doorway and joined J.T. by his bed. "J.T., where'd you get all this crap?"

"It's not crap, it's my stuff."

"Well, it's a shitload of stuff." He picked up a Micro Machine. "Hey, I like this little helicopter here. I used to jump out of one of these babies."

"Really?"

Lucy could see her son was smitten. A tough, handsome ex-parachute rescue jumper who swore and knew helicopters—Plato would end up paring him down to a change of undershorts. He'd probably find some way of working his charms on Madison, too.

Lucy slipped downstairs to the kitchen. She didn't know where Sebastian was. Rob had gone off to Manchester on a supply run.

There was no lemonade made. She took out a frozen can of concentrate and set it in the sink, turning the hot water on to a trickle.

The phone rang, making her jump.

"Lucy? Thank God. It's Sidney Greenburg." She paused for air. "Jack's in trouble."

Blackmail trouble, Lucy thought. She wondered what her father-in-law had deigned to tell Sidney. "What kind of trouble?"

"He told me about the blackmail. How much do you know? Damned little, right? He's such an ass. He thinks he's being noble. Lucy…" Sidney groaned. "I hate this. I hate every single minute of it."

"I know." Lucy calmed herself by watching the ice melt on her can of frozen concentrate. "Tell me, Sidney. I can take it."

"Of course you can. I told Jack you could. Some jackass named Darren Mowery is blackmailing him over an affair Colin may or may not have had shortly before he died. There are supposedly pictures. If Jack knows the name of the woman, he won't tell me. I assume it's someone who'd interest the media, but who the hell knows."

Lucy stuck her finger in the hot trickle, ran it over the top of the still-icy can. An affair. Colin. "This is ridiculous. Colin didn't have an affair. Even if he did, he's dead, and it was a private matter."

"I know! That's what I told Jack! He said once something like this gets out in Washington, it can take on a life of its own. I said bullshit and told him to call you at once. He was so upset. He really thought he was protecting you and the kids by paying this bastard."

"I don't need him or anyone else to protect me from the truth. He can protect me from lions, tigers and bears if it comes to it, but never the truth."

She could almost feel Sidney's sad smile. "He meant well. He cares about you and his grandchildren so much. He'll never get over Colin. He couldn't save him on the tennis court—he can at least save his reputation."

"Where's Jack now? Did he put you up to calling me?"

"Lucy, there's more." Sidney took a deep breath. "Jack showed me. This Mowery character put up pictures of you on a secure Internet site. Recent pictures. Like from last week."

"Jesus," Lucy whispered.

"Jack was horrified. He took it as an implied threat that if he didn't cooperate and follow instructions to the letter, this guy could get to you."

Lucy shut off the hot water. "Sidney, he can get to me if Jack *does* cooperate!"

"I know. I have to say, when I saw those pictures of you, I didn't think, either. I'd have cut Mowery a check for every dime I have. Now—" Her voice faltered, and she fought back a sob. "Lucy, Jack's missing. I don't know what the hell to do."

"Missing? What do you mean, missing?"

"He was supposed to meet me at my office an hour

ago. We were going to call you together. He didn't show up. I called his office, and he never showed up there today. I went to his house—that's where I am now—and he's not here."

"Call the Capitol Police, Sidney. Tell them *everything.* Okay? Tell them to send someone up here right away. Damn it. *Damn it.*" Lucy scooped up the frozen concentrate and banged it down onto the counter. "Jack and I both waited too long, trying to protect ourselves, Madison and J.T., each other. Colin. Oh, Sidney... I'm so sorry."

"Lucy?"

"I've got a stalker," she blurted. "I thought it was Barbara, but now—I don't know, maybe someone's using her as a decoy." She rubbed her forehead, tired, frustrated, too much coming at her at once. "I can't figure it out. I've got Plato Rabedeneira and Sebastian Redwing here. They're like a couple of big, mean guard dogs."

"Listen to me, Lucy. Listen!" Sidney spoke briskly, taking charge. She was a brilliant, kind woman Lucy had always admired. "A couple of weeks ago, Barbara Allen went a little nutty on Jack and told him she's been secretly in love with him for twenty years."

"Oh, no."

"I wouldn't be surprised if this Mowery character had taken advantage of her. She thinks she's tough as nails, but she's kind of like a turtle. Her hard outer shell protects a soft, mushy inside. She won't be happy when she realizes Mowery's manipulated her. My bet is, she'll lash out before she admits a weakness. She'll do anything to keep people from seeing that mushy inside."

Lucy managed a smile. "I'm impressed."

"Forget it, my mum's a shrink, and I'm an anthropologist. I come from a family that thinks too goddamn much. You take care, do you hear me?" She spoke fiercely, her intensity palpable. "I'm counting on Costa Rica."

Sidney hung up, and Lucy stood in the middle of the kitchen, shaking.

Sebastian fell in behind her. "I don't know about you, but lions, tigers and bears would be fine with me right about now."

Lucy whirled around at him. "You listened in? Goddamn it, Redwing! How dare you? How—" She slammed her foot into a cabinet. "That was a private conversation. *Damn* you!"

He grabbed her wrists and held them up close to his chest, nothing about him calm, nothing retreating deep inside him. "Damn me all you want, Lucy. I'm not here to make you feel comfortable or to live according to your rules. I'm here to keep Darren Mowery from killing anyone else."

"This isn't about you!"

"It is about me. It's about me and a mistake I made a year ago. Mowery isn't blackmailing Jack Swift over an old affair he and Barbara Allen cooked up. He isn't after twenty grand or Jack's vote on legislation. Jack doesn't know this man. *You* don't know him."

"And you do?"

"Yes."

"He wants you," Lucy said abruptly. "Oh, my God. This is about revenge, isn't it?"

Sebastian's grip softened, and he released her, caught up one hand and kissed it. "Lucy, when I'm whitewater kayaking, I'll do everything you say. I promise."

She nodded, tried to smile. "I'll hold you to that. Any guess where Mowery is?"

"Not here. Not yet. My guess is he's already reined Barbara back in, recommitted her to the program. Sidney's calling the Capitol police. They'll get things into motion."

"We should call the local police. They're not a bunch of yokels. If I tell them to be discreet—"

"Lucy, I know who they are. I went to school with half of them. Let the Capitol police get them involved. Right now, if Mowery does have Jack, he has the advantage."

"He'll kill Jack—"

"He'll kill everyone if it suits him."

Lucy started for the back door. "I'm going up to warn Barbara she's in over her head."

"She won't thank you for it."

"I don't care."

She plunged out the door, leaped down the back steps even as she fought for calm, for control, for one quiet space in her mind where she could think.

Sebastian followed her. He didn't seem to be moving as fast as she was. Longer legs, she thought, but she felt like a whirling dervish, spinning, spinning, but not centered.

"I'll go with you," he said.

She ground to a sudden halt in the warm grass. Dark clouds were sweeping in from the west, and she could feel the humidity gathering around her. "You only want to come along because you don't want me going alone. You're a loner, Sebastian." She tilted her head back, gave him a long, clear-eyed look and saw him as he was. "It's easy to love me from a distance."

He touched her mouth and, with no warning whatso-ever, he kissed her, a quick, passionate kiss that almost sank her to the ground. He stood back and smiled. "It's not easy to love you at all."

"Sebastian—"

"Later. Let's go." She saw he'd grabbed her cell phone off the counter. He dropped it in his pocket. "Tough to believe Larry the Lump from ninth grade is the chief of police."

Barbara slipped through the back door of Lucy's con-verted barn, past the canoes, kayaks, life vests, rescue equipment and office supplies, and into her work space. How pathetic. Lucy had given up a job with a presti-gious Washington museum for this, Barbara thought. Her desks were nothing but hardware-store doors set onto handmade trestles. Cows and horses had once trod across the wide-board floor. There was a woodstove to supplement the electric heating unit, and the walls were covered with posters of northern New England, the Canadian Maritimes, Costa Rica. Only because of her Swift connections in Washington could Lucy have survived in business this long.

She had one of those plastic cubes on her desk, filled with pictures of Madison and J.T. None of Colin, Bar-bara saw. None of Jack. It was as if Lucy had wiped them out of her life. She'd come to Vermont to start over, and start over, she had.

Now she had Sebastian Redwing wrapped around her little finger, and no doubt Plato Rabedeneira, too. Didn't they see through her? But Barbara knew bet-ter. People were stupid. Men were particularly stupid. Twenty years in Washington had taught her that much.

If only Jack would admit he loved her, Barbara thought. If, when she'd finally come forward, he'd had the courage to say, as she'd fantasized countless times, "Oh, Barbara, I've been waiting all these years for you to give me the slightest hint you cared. Even when Eleanor was alive, I dreamed of us being together one day."

Sentimental nonsense, of course. In real life, Jack had patted her on the head and sent her off. Good Barbara. Reliable Barbara. What if he were just another stupid man, after all? Twenty years of her life, gone!

She stroked the barrel of the Smith & Wesson .38 she'd appropriated from her father years ago. It was the same one he'd used to teach her and her sisters how to shoot. He still wandered around the house, grumbling about what had happened to it. "I hope some stupid bastard doesn't hold up a gas station with my goddamn gun!"

A crude man, her father. It was an old gun, hopelessly out-of-date in a world of semiautomatics. But she had a silencer that fit it, and she knew it would do the job.

Plato Rabedeneira.

Madison had called from the phone in her room. "I'm packing," she'd told Barbara. "Don't tell anyone I called, okay? I just didn't want you to think we were ignoring you. All kinds of weird things have been going on around here, and my mom's friend Plato's taking J.T. and me off somewhere."

"Are you scared?"

"I'm trying not to be. We're leaving in a few minutes."

Barbara eased to the front entrance of the converted barn. Plato was out by his car. He was so handsome, but slowed down by his limp and out of his element in the hills of Vermont. She remembered his dropping to the ground when he was shot during the assassination attempt on Jack and the president. He hadn't made a sound.

She tucked her gun into her waistband and pulled her shirt over it. She didn't have a focused plan. She'd seen Sebastian and Lucy walking up along the edge of the field. Did they all suspect her? Had Lucy poisoned them against her?

Refusing to rush, Barbara walked out of the barn and across the yard toward the front porch. She would say she'd come to thank Lucy for the blueberry muffins. Maybe she'd invite them to dinner. Spaghetti. Kids always liked spaghetti.

They couldn't leave.

She wouldn't let them.

Madison stomped down the front porch steps. The hanging petunias needed watering. Lucy neglected them, just as she did her children.

The girl was complaining bitterly to Plato. "You're not making J.T. leave his Micro Machines."

Plato swore under his breath. "All right. Hurry up."

"I'll only be ten seconds." Victory sounded in her voice. "This is going to be a *fabulous* quilt."

A quilt? Dear God, Barbara thought. Madison would never be ready for the real world if she stayed here sewing quilts, snapping beans, wandering off in the woods by herself. *Someone* had to bring these people to their senses.

Barbara removed the Smith & Wesson from her waistband. She didn't know why. A precaution, a necessity. She was following her instincts.

Plato saw her. "Madison, get down!"

The girl leaped at him, pulling on his arm as he reached for his gun. "No, no, it's Barbara! She's a friend!"

Plato backhanded the girl into the dirt. "Stay put."

She scrambled to her feet, wild, out of control, then charged him. "You're a maniac! You're all maniacs!"

Barbara fired before Plato could get to his weapon. With the silencer, the shot hardly made a sound. Madison screamed, her interference and Plato's quick reactions throwing off Barbara's aim so that she only caught his upper right arm. She fired again, grazing the side of his head.

The girl went nuts, shrieking when Plato, semiconscious, collapsed onto the dirt driveway. Blood streamed down his face.

Barbara marched over to Madison and snatched her by the elbow. "Get up. Stop your screaming."

The girl sobbed, her face streaked with tears. "You killed Plato!"

"I *will* kill him if you don't shut up and come with me. Right now." Barbara inhaled. Her head ached, but now she had a clear purpose. She knew what she needed to do. "Where's your brother?"

"J.T.! Run! Run get Mom and Sebastian!"

Barbara slapped the girl across the face, half with her hand, half with the butt of her gun. Madison gulped back a scream. Barbara could see the fierce anger behind her terror. So like Colin, but corrupted by her mother.

Plato lay motionless on the driveway, blood from his wounds spilling into the dirt.

How like Lucy to abandon her children to a stranger.

There was no advantage to killing him. Barbara was more interested in the missing boy. He could be a problem.

Madison's teeth were chattering. "Don't—don't kill Plato. *Please.* I couldn't live with myself. It's my fault. I *trusted* you!"

"Well," Barbara said, "let's not give Plato a clear shot so he can kill me, shall we?" She placed her father's Smith & Wesson at the girl's head. "Your mother doesn't care about you, Madison. I'll prove it to you. She rescued Sebastian Redwing from Joshua Falls. Do you think she'll rescue you?"

Madison squared her jaw. "I'll rescue myself."

"There, you see? You're used to being on your own, even at fifteen. Come on, Madison. That's it. One step at a time."

Jack held up his head, trying to retain his dignity. "You will never get away with kidnapping a United States senator."

Darren Mowery grinned at him. "So?"

He was driving, and he was armed with a semiautomatic. They were within minutes of Lucy's house. Jack still didn't know exactly what had happened. A Senate colleague and personal friend had loaned him his private plane, which Jack, an experienced pilot, would fly to Vermont, where he planned to tell Lucy what had been going on and discuss their options.

Instead, Mowery intercepted him at the airport, and blackmail quickly turned to kidnapping. He'd piloted the plane. He had a car waiting in Vermont.

His threat to keep Jack in line was simple. He repeated it now, as he had every ten minutes since the start of this ordeal. "I'm the expert, Jack. You're the pompous senator. If you try anything, it'll just piss me off. I'll kill you. Then I'll kill Lucy. Then I'll kill your grandchildren."

"What do you want?" Jack croaked.

"You haven't figured that out yet, have you, Jack?"

"If it's money—"

"If it was money, I'd have fucked with a senator with a bigger trust fund than you have. Jesus, Jack. You're not worth much by Washington standards, you know?"

"I have devoted my life to public service."

"Yeah, and it pays shit."

"Then what is it? Power? My vote? Is someone else paying you? If I knew, maybe we could work something out."

"Nope. I had my chance at the brass ring. It was a once-in-a-lifetime deal. I knew it when I started down that road." He drove smoothly, steadily; nothing seemed to bother him. "Redwing Associates had already cut into my business. Sebastian put the word out I was losing my edge."

"That's not what I heard," Jack said.

"Who the hell ever tells a senator the truth? That's why you have all those goddamn hearings. You have to dig through everybody's bullshit to get at something." He glanced over at Jack. "Doesn't that get to you after a while?"

"No. No, it doesn't."

"Well, aren't you fucking holier-than-thou. So, here I was, going broke, that son of a bitch I trained pulling in millions—I mean, we are talking *millions*. He lives like a goddamn monk, but he's worth—well, shit, he didn't have to borrow a plane to get here."

Jack thought Mowery was exaggerating, but he chose not to say so. The man seemed to relish how put-upon he was. "It's an old story, isn't it? The student bests the master."

"The bastard didn't understand. I got wind of a kidnapping and ransom scheme and dealt myself in, but I always planned to make sure the real bad guys didn't get away."

"Weren't you one of the 'real bad guys'?"

"No, asshole, I was going to see to it the family got back safe."

"What about the ransom money?"

"That was my only sin—wanting to take the money. I figured I'd deserve it for saving the family."

"But if you put them in danger in the first place—"

They'd come to Lucy's road. Darren made the turn. "You know, Jack, why don't you shut the hell up?"

"It's Sebastian you want?"

"Well, Jack, you did it. You figured it out. If I ever move to Rhode Island, you get my vote. Now, shut up."

Chapter 15

Lucy touched Sebastian's arm, but he'd already stopped on the steep, narrow path. A few yards above them, through a screen of trees, was the dirt road. "I thought I heard something."

"I did, too."

A car sounded on the road. Sebastian shot up the path and crouched down as it passed above him. It wasn't Barbara's sturdy rental, and it wasn't Plato's shiny black car.

Lucy dropped low. "Did you see who it was?"

He eased back down to her and placed the cell phone in her hand. "It's Mowery. Lucy, he has Jack." He curved her stiff fingers around the phone. "Call the local police. Tell them they've got a probable hostage situation with a U.S. senator. Have them get in touch with the Capitol Police."

"Jack—was he okay—did he look—"

"He was in the passenger seat. He looked fine."

She nodded. "Should I tell Plato?"

"If he's still there. If not, get your butt over to the police station or a friend's house and stay put." He smiled grimly, a glint of humor coming into his eyes. "Not that I'd tell you what to do."

"Under the circumstances, feel free. What about you? If Mowery's bent on revenge, you'll just be playing into his hands. You don't even have a gun."

But he'd already slipped into the woods, off the path. Lucy watched him make his way around a huge boulder and disappear. She quickly retraced her steps down the path, dialing the police as she went. She got patched through to Larry, the chief of police, and gave him the facts as succinctly as she could. "I'm on my way back to my house," she said.

"Good. Stay there."

"For God's sake, don't come up here with guns blazing. This guy will kill my father-in-law."

"Jesus Christ," Larry said. "All right, I'll meet you at your place. Where you live, it's going to be a while before we can get there."

"I know. I'll be okay."

She disconnected and picked up her pace, coming soon to the stone wall on the far edge of the field. Plato materialized out of nowhere and caught her around the middle. "Lucy." Blood poured down the side of his head. He'd ripped off his suit coat, and blood had soaked through his white shirt; the fabric on his upper right arm was torn. He was sweating and ashen-faced, and he was heavily armed. "Lucy, she's got Madison, maybe J.T., too, by now."

"Oh, no. Oh, God." Lucy held on to him, pushed back the panic. "You mean Barbara? Where?"

"Waterfall. She shot the shit out of me. I'm going to pass out. Call the police." He grimaced, catching his breath. "Where's Sebastian?"

"He took off."

"Good."

Lucy shook her head. "Mowery's got my father-in-law."

Plato sank into the ferns growing up close to the stone wall. "Shit."

"The police are on their way. Go meet them."

"Your kids—"

"You're in no condition to help them, and you don't know the way. I'll go. I know a shortcut from here to the falls."

"I screwed up," Plato said. "I didn't realize Madison knew Barbara, liked her. I should have."

"I didn't think to tell you. I'm sorry."

"Luckily the bitch is a lousy shot."

Lucy quickly checked his wounds. They were unpleasant, but she didn't believe they were life-threatening. She shoved the cell phone at him. "I just called the police. Call them again. Can you make it back to the house? You'll be okay?"

He pushed her toward the path. "Go. The woman's a nut. Be careful. Buy time for the police to get here." He held up his gun—a black, sleek thing—with a shaking, blood-spattered hand. "Take this."

"And do what with it?"

The barest ghost of a smile as he dropped the gun. "You're right. You'll just shoot your foot off. Now, go."

Barbara's legs ached from the steep climb up to Joshua Falls. "You'll see your mother doesn't care about you. You'll see."

Madison was still defiant. "My mother never held a gun on us."

"She's done far worse. If she hadn't brainwashed you against me, I wouldn't have to hold a gun on you. It's her fault. And I'm just doing this for your own good. You have to see what she's done to you."

This time, Madison kept her mouth shut. She was even worse now that they had J.T. with them. Barbara had caught him hiding in the back of the barn. She'd had to fire at him. He got the point. He hadn't said a word since. He was scared. Brainwashed. Barbara would make sure he and Madison both got appropriate therapy in Washington. She didn't want them to have lasting scars from what their mother had done to them.

Yes, she thought, she could see a future for herself. She would take care of Colin's children, Jack's grandchildren. She would see to their upbringing, their education. She would raise them the way Swifts should be raised.

Lucy's fault they were frightened and defiant now. All Lucy's fault.

She could hear the water rushing over the falls. The rain had started, a steady, cold drizzle. Madison and J.T. didn't seem to notice. Country bumpkins.

J.T. slipped on a wet rock and skinned his knee, but he scrambled back to his feet and didn't complain. Barbara was pleased. He was stoic, like his father and grandfather. "Good boy."

"Just keep going, J.T.," Madison whispered to him. "It'll be okay. I promise. I won't let her hurt you."

Barbara resisted the impulse to strike the girl. "You sound like your mother. Don't fill the boy with negative ideas about me, poison him against me."

"I don't need to poison him against you. You've poisoned him yourself!"

That mouth. Barbara gritted her teeth and called upon her heroic self-discipline. She remembered her purpose. They had to see the truth. Both these children did.

"All right." They'd reached the top of the falls; the rain was steadier now. And colder, autumn-like. She preferred Washington heat to this dank misery. She nodded to the children. "Stop. Now, listen. Madison, I want you to take the rope." She tossed the length of rope she'd removed from Lucy's supply room. "If you do anything stupid, I will shoot you or your brother—possibly both of you, if it's really stupid. Do you understand?"

The girl nodded, pale, the rain glistening on her coppery hair. Barbara liked its color. So pretty. They'd have to get it trimmed at a good salon.

She pointed to the rope. "Take it and tie one end around your waist. Your mother taught you knot tying, I assume? I hope so. You won't want to get this wrong."

"Let J.T. go," Madison said, shivering now as she tied the rope around her waist. "This is all my fault, he didn't do anything. If I hadn't tackled him, Plato would have shot you. J.T. didn't know anything—"

Barbara waved her gun. "Tie the rope."

J.T. stood on the rock ledge, trembling and sobbing. Oh, Lucy, Barbara thought, look what you've done to your little boy!

Madison secured the rope. She tested it, and even Barbara, who admittedly knew nothing about knots, could see it was tight. "Very good," she said. "Thank you for cooperating. You'll see I'm a fair-minded, disciplined professional. Now, tie the rope around that tree right there." She pointed with her gun at a thick, mis-shapen hemlock, its roots growing out over the abyss of the waterfall. "Be careful. Don't slip."

"Why do you want—"

"Just do it."

The girl nodded. The rain had soaked through her shirt and shorts and was making her shiver even more. She crouched down and tied the rope to the tree.

"I thought about getting a rock-climbing line with one of those harness things," Barbara said, "but I think this will do. It's more dramatic. You'll see." She leaned forward, over Madison's shoulder. "Don't dawdle."

"You've made your point." Madison looked up at her, her blue eyes and spray of freckles heart-stoppingly like Colin's, like Jack's. "My mother's awful. I hate her."

Barbara smiled. "I know, love. I know. Now, lower yourself over the edge."

"First let J.T. go."

"Madison, you're not in charge. I am. I've been doing the bidding of the Swifts for twenty years. It's my turn." She stood up straight, ignoring the rain pelting down on them, and leveled the gun at the girl. "Now lower yourself over the falls."

Barbara stepped back while Madison dutifully stood up and eased herself to the edge of the hemlock's twisted, gnarled roots. She took a breath, so pale, and gave herself more length on the rope. She tugged at it, making sure the end on the tree held.

"Don't take forever," Barbara said. "If you make me push you, it'll hurt more. The rope will cut into you. You'll smash into the rock."

The girl nodded. "I know. I'm just a little scared. My stupid mother should be here."

"Yes, yes, that's right."

Madison edged her heels out over the abyss. Barbara could hear the water rushing, swirling beneath them. She wasn't quite sure how long the rope was, but she thought it wouldn't reach the water. Madison would dangle several feet above the deep, cold pool. She and Barbara would just have to take it from there.

What to do about J.T.?

"Madison, *don't*," he cried. "Don't."

Such a big baby, Barbara thought. They'd have to work on that. It was good for him to see his older sister be brave in the face of adversity.

"J.T., listen to me."

Madison's voice was calm and intense, and Barbara expected she was rallying her brother to the cause. Instead, she swooped out from the edge of the roots, kicked herself off the tree and used her momentum to carry herself toward Barbara. She kicked wildly, knocking Barbara flat onto her behind. Her gun went flying.

"Run, J.T., run! Get Mom! Go, go, go."

Barbara pushed the monster off her. The cold rain made her slippery. "I trusted you!"

"My brother's smarter and faster than you are, you *bitch*."

Barbara recoiled, seeing this stupid girl for what she was. Poisoned. Too far gone. She caught the rope with both hands and pulled hard, shoving Madison back to the edge of the ledge. The girl kicked and fought and struggled, but Barbara was too strong, too furious for her to prevail.

She went down fast. Barbara could see her trying to get her balance to rappel, but she banged against the rock wall, hitting her arm and shoulder. She yelled out in pain.

"It serves you right," Barbara called down to her.

She sank onto the wet ground. Her hands and wrists were rope-burned, stinging and bleeding as if she'd been in a violent tug-of-war. She was exhausted, but she remembered the boy. She had to rally, find him.

She reached backward, feeling for her gun, rain pouring into her eyes.

Lucy. Holding Barbara's gun. The rain pelted down on her. "You'd better pray my daughter isn't badly hurt."

Barbara saw the fear in Lucy's eyes. It wasn't fear for Madison. It was a selfish fear—fear for herself and what she would lose. From the way she held the gun, it was obvious she didn't know how to use it. She peered over the falls.

"Mom," Madison sobbed, "oh, Mom, thank God!"

Barbara sighed. She was right. The girl was lost.

"Are you hurt?" Lucy called. "Can you find a hand-hold?"

"My arm. I think it's broken."

Lucy glared at Barbara, her .38 steady. "Why? What did she ever do to you?"

"Not her," Barbara said. "You."

"Jesus," a man's voice said behind them. She looked up, and Plato, bloodied and soaked, fell against a hemlock. "You're one sick puppy, you know that?"

Lucy was obviously relieved to see him. Of course, Barbara thought. A man to the rescue. Lucy nodded to the rope still tied around the tree. "Madison's hanging over the falls. I have to get her out. J.T.—did you see him?"

Plato shook his head. "Lucy, all hell's breaking loose

down at your house. Cops're everywhere. We can get a rescue team up here to pull her out."

"Call Rob. He's the best." She peered down at her daughter, the rain easing to a drizzle. "Madison, how's the rope? Will it hold?"

"Mom, I can't hang on. My arm. I *can't.*"

Barbara was disgusted at the girl's whining. "I could have killed you and Madison when I had the chance," she told Plato.

"Well, you didn't. It's okay, Lucy," he said softly. "I've got a gun on our Ms. Allen. She's not going anywhere."

Lucy placed the .38 next to the hemlock root and dropped onto her hands and knees. She hung herself partially out over the rain-soaked ledge, inspecting, as if she knew what she was looking at. Barbara wasn't impressed. This was all for show.

"Madison." Lucy cleared her throat. "Here's the situation. I can't come down there and get you, not without equipment. I wouldn't do you any good. And I don't have the strength to pull you up by myself. Plato's here, but he's injured. You can either wait for Rob, or you can try to work your way up a little higher, then I can help."

"I can't. My arm hurts."

"What about your other arm? Use it and your feet. Find hand and footholds. Steady yourself."

Barbara sniffed. "Of course, you're too much of a coward to go after her yourself."

"You know, Ms. Allen," Plato said, dropping down beside her. He was a bloody mess. "Seeing how you've shot me twice today, I wouldn't do or say one damn thing that's going to piss me off. Right now, consider yourself lucky I'm good with pain."

"You wouldn't shoot me. You're a professional. You only shoot to kill."

"I'm right-handed. You shot me in my right arm. Holding a gun in my left hand—who knows?—it could just go off and put a bullet in your bitching leg."

"I loathe your kind," Barbara said.

"Yeah, you hold that thought. What's your pal Mowery up to?"

Barbara snapped her mouth shut. She wished it would stop raining. It was so damn cold.

"That's it," Lucy was saying, still hanging over the falls. "One step at a time. God, I'd give anything to be there instead of you."

"Tell her to pretend her injured arm got cut off," Plato said. "That's what I did with my leg when I got hurt."

Lucy glanced at him dubiously. "Thanks, Plato. She's doing fine."

Barbara could feel the cold of the rock seeping into her, the dankness of the day. She held herself stiff against shaking and shivering. In another minute, Lucy was pulling on the rope with all her might. Plato transferred his gun into his right hand, his wince of pain barely detectable. He edged over to the tree, grabbed the rope with his left arm and pulled, adding his strength to Lucy's.

Madison came up and collapsed into her mother's arms, sobbing. "J.T.," she said. "I told him to run. Is he all right? Oh, God, this is all my fault!"

"It's not your fault, Madison. You're *fifteen*."

Plato touched Lucy's shoulder. "Go ahead. Cops'll be here in no time. Find your kid."

Barbara sighed. Of course, of course. Lucy would abandon the daughter for the sake of the son. Of course.

* * *

Sebastian had the situation under control, if not to his liking. He was tucked behind a nice, fat sofa inside the house Barbara Allen had rented. Darren Mowery and Jack Swift were out on the screened porch, discussing her.

"Barbie made up the affair with Colin just to get back at you," Mowery said. "And you fell for it. Makes you feel kind of stupid, doesn't it?"

"Where is she now?"

"My guess, she's making Lucy's life miserable. Hates her guts. Totally obsessed with her. Amazing. Miss Super-Professional with a deep, dark secret."

"You used her. You manipulated her."

"Don't feel sorry for her."

"I don't," Jack said.

"Sebastian Redwing hasn't done you much good, has he?"

"If I'd told him the truth from the beginning—"

"Yeah, well. You didn't."

Sebastian didn't plan on letting them leave. He'd already disabled Mowery's car. A clump of mud in the exhaust pipe did the trick. Now, he would wait. So far, Mowery hadn't made a move against the senator. If he did, Sebastian would act. If he saw his window of opportunity, he'd act. Otherwise, he'd wait for Larry and the Capitol police to get there. Whichever came first was fine with him. With the situation stable, he had no intention of lighting a fuse.

Then J.T. came screaming up out of the woods. "Grandpa! Grandpa!" He pounded up the deck steps. "She's got Madison!"

Sebastian reacted instantly, shooting out through the

sliding glass door onto the deck. He had to get to J.T. before Mowery did, even if it meant he'd lost his advantage. He grabbed J.T. The boy was hysterical, traumatized, gulping for air. He clawed Sebastian's arms. "J.T.," he said. "It's okay. I've got you."

"Madison—we have to save her. Barbara's going to kill her. She hung her over the waterfall. She'll cut the rope. Sebastian!"

Sebastian stayed between the boy and the screened porch, where he knew Mowery would be quickly calculating his options. "Listen to me, J.T. Go back down the road. Run your ass off, you hear me? Your mother will be looking for you."

Being Lucy's son, he argued. "Grandpa—"

"I'll take care of your grandfather. Go, J.T. Trust me. Your mother will be there." That much Sebastian knew. Lucy would be there for her kids.

"Well, well, well," Mowery said behind them. "Daddy Redwing."

Sebastian stayed focused on the boy. He grabbed J.T. up and dumped him off the deck, several feet to the ground. J.T. scrambled to his feet, and yelled, "Grandpa! He's got a gun!"

Jack Swift pushed away from Mowery and leaned over the rail. "Run, J.T. I'll be fine. *Go.*"

J.T. hesitated, then darted into the woods, down the hill, moving fast. He was twelve and energetic, and he knew the woods. Sebastian had done his job. J.T. wasn't in Mowery's hands.

"What?" Mowery said. "You two think I'd shoot a kid?"

"I know you would," Sebastian said, turning to Mowery. The minute he'd heard J.T., Sebastian knew Mowery had him. He had a gun, a Glock. "It didn't used to be that way."

"Sure it did, you just never noticed. And I wouldn't shoot a kid in the back. In the head, as part of a business arrangement, only if necessary. I'm not a fucking monster."

Jack Swift, gray and breathing hard, collapsed against the deck rail. "I can't—if anything happens to Madison or J.T. I don't think I could go on."

Mowery snorted. "Enough votes, you'll go on." He walked over to the senator and put the Glock at his temple. "No whining, okay? I need to think."

"Darren." Sebastian didn't move; he was centered, focused. Plato was right. This was work he knew, even if he'd come to hate it and distrust himself. "You're on a dead-end road. I've disabled your car. The local police are probably here by now. The Capitol Police are on their way. Everyone's coming. Let Jack go and get out now while you can."

"Why would I do that?"

"Because you're good. You know my first priority is saving the senator and his family. This is your best chance to get away."

"Sebastian, in case you haven't noticed, I'm the only one here with a gun. Suppose I just shoot you both and take off?"

"If you'd wanted to shoot me, you could have come out to my place in Wyoming and shot me in my hammock." Sebastian sat on an Adirondack chair and stretched out his legs. "You don't just want me dead, Darren. You want me ruined, the way I ruined you. You want me to suffer, the way you've suffered."

"I want the senator dead. I want Lucy and her kids

dead and you held responsible, ridiculed, run out of business."

"Well, Darren. If you shoot both the senator and me, you have no hostages left. Then what? You're still on a dead-end road with no car."

"Up on your feet."

Sebastian did as instructed. He wondered where Lucy was, what had happened to Plato if Madison was dangling from Joshua Falls and J.T. was tearing through the woods on his own.

Mowery got Swift to stand beside Sebastian, then he marched them both off the deck. Sebastian wasn't too worried. He figured he had about ten minutes to figure something out before J.T. found Lucy, and all hell broke loose.

Lucy charged down the path from the falls, slipping in the wet pine needles, oblivious to her fatigue, the pain in her side from running.

"Mom!"

"J.T." She sank onto her knees, caught him in her arms as he almost ran over her. "Are you all right?"

"Sebastian," he croaked. "Grandpa. Mom!"

She realized he was incapable of talking. He was out of breath, in shock. "It's going to be okay, J.T. The police are on their way. Come on."

She half carried, half pulled him up the path back to the falls. Plato, pale and bloody, had two guns on Barbara Allen, his and hers. Madison was shivering next to him, cradling her arm in pain, not looking at the woman who'd nearly killed her.

Lucy knew that, for her children's sake, she had to appear to have command of the situation. She urged J.T.

down next to Madison. "Sit here by your sister. Don't move. Don't look at Barbara."

"Mom, that man had a gun pointed at Grandpa," J.T. said breathlessly. "And Sebastian—he—he was right there."

"Don't think about it. Just think about breathing." She put her palm on his chest. He was wet and cold with rain, terrified. "In, out. Come on, J.T. Think about it. Breathe in, breathe out. Slow and controlled."

But he whimpered like a lost puppy, and her heart broke. Madison, gray-faced, fell back on a bed of hemlock needles as she dealt with her terror and the pain of her injuries.

Lucy steeled herself against her own rush of emotions. She had to think. "Plato, I need to borrow one of the guns."

"Better idea." His voice was soothing, steady, professional. "You stay here, I go with the gun."

She shook her head. "You won't get three steps before you pass out."

He smiled feebly. "Bet I get six steps."

"Plato…"

"Go, kid." He flipped her Barbara's gun, barrel first, and kept his. "Mine's high-tech. You'll shoot up the woods with it. You know how to pull the trigger?"

"I think so." She felt the weight of the gun in her hand. "I've seen a lot of movies. Is there a safety or anything? Do I have to cock it?"

Plato looked at her with his bloodshot eyes. "Just pull the fucking trigger."

Lucy nodded. "I will if I have to."

"And trust Sebastian." Plato cleared his throat; he

was weak, in need of medical attention. "He does things in his own time, and in his own way. Trust him, Lucy."

"If he's renounced violence—"

"He's renounced gratuitous violence. If Mowery's got a gun on him and a senator, we're not talking gratuitous. Lucy, if Sebastian can't go through a brick wall, he'll go around it. He'll find a way."

She blinked back tears. "I hope you're right."

J.T. shivered violently. His lips were purple, and dark circles had formed under his eyes. "Mom, don't go. I'm scared."

Lucy looked at her son and daughter. Their father was dead, their grandfather was being held hostage. If something happened to her, Madison and J.T. would end up in Costa Rica with her parents. She couldn't be reckless or take unnecessary chances. It wasn't a question of courage. It was a question of responsibility.

She had to trust Sebastian, the way she'd had to trust Madison to get herself into a position from which Lucy could pull her up out of the falls.

"I love him," she said to Plato. "Sebastian. I love him."

Plato leaned against his rock. "I don't know which one of you has it worse. Sebastian, loving you, or you loving Sebastian. You're both a couple of stiff-necked pains in the ass."

Lucy smiled and bit back tears. "I'll go down and meet the police, make sure they get the rescue squad up here."

He nodded, satisfied, too spent to talk.

"J.T. can come with me. You up to it, kiddo?"

He sniffled and put his hand in hers, and she kissed

her daughter and told her it wouldn't be much longer. "Hang in there, okay?"

Madison didn't open her eyes. "Sure, Mom."

Barbara Allen didn't say a word, didn't acknowledge Lucy's presence or her own imminent arrest.

Plato was sinking fast. He managed one last smile. "Tell your local yokels to hurry it up. I'm about ready to push Ms. Barbara here over the falls and call it a day."

In spite of his fatigue and terror, J.T. kept up with Lucy. She took the path to the dirt road, assuming the police would come that way instead of along the brook path.

When they emerged onto the dirt road, J.T. gasped and tightened his grip on his mother's hand. Then she saw, too. Just down the road, Jack and Sebastian were walking a few feet ahead of another man who she presumed was Darren Mowery.

"That's him," J.T. whispered. "That's the man—"

Lucy bent down to him. "Go back and tell Plato."

Plato was in no condition to help, she knew, but he could hold on to her son. J.T. hesitated. She gave him an encouraging hug, and he summoned his last reserves of energy and ran back up the path.

Mowery must have heard them or sensed their presence. He half turned to her. "Put the gun down, Lucy, or I shoot Sebastian."

She'd almost forgotten she had a gun. She glanced up the path. She raised it. "If you shoot Sebastian, I'll shoot you."

Sebastian eased around slowly, without a word, and Jack inhaled sharply. Lucy didn't know what to do. She wasn't a marksman. She hated guns. She held her breath, met Sebastian's eyes just for an instant. He didn't speak. He didn't give her even the smallest sign as to what she should do.

Mowery moved, and she fired.

Blood spurted from his right buttock, and he swore viciously. Sebastian pounced, tackling Mowery with blinding efficiency and ferocity, knocking the gun from his hand as if he'd been waiting for just this moment, just this mistake.

Jack snatched up the gun. Lucy kept Barbara's gun pointed in their direction, in case she was misreading the situation and Sebastian wasn't winning.

Sebastian pushed Mowery facedown on the ground and yanked his hands behind his back in what looked like a professional hold. He shook his head at her. "You shot him in the ass?"

"I guess I did."

"Lucy, for God's sake. You don't shoot someone in the ass. If you're in a situation that requires you to fire your weapon, you're shooting to kill."

"I was shooting to shoot. It's not like I was aiming!"

"Well, hell. That makes me feel better." He motioned to her with one hand. "You want to lower that baby, then?"

She lowered the gun. She knew Sebastian was half teasing, half lecturing to keep her mind off what she'd just done—how close they'd all come. She saw how serious his eyes were. "Did you have the situation under control?" she asked.

"No." He grinned. "But I was working on it."

Jack handed Mowery's gun to Sebastian and turned to his daughter-in-law. "Lucy," he sobbed. "Oh, God, Lucy."

"The kids are okay." Suddenly tears were streaming down her face. "Madison, J.T.—they're okay."

Sebastian held the gun on Mowery, moaning in pain. "Go, you two." He spoke to Lucy and Jack without looking at them. "Go to your kids."

Lucy walked over to him, the dirt road squishy under her feet. The rain had stopped altogether now; the air was close and yet refreshing, as if it had been washed clean. Her eyes met Sebastian's. His were still deadly serious. This, she reminded herself, was his job, work he knew how to do—work that had brought her to him in the first place.

"Are you okay?" she asked quietly.

"You mean, am I going to put a bullet in Mowery's head the minute you and Jack turn your backs?" He gave her a ragged smile. "I'm the one who renounced violence, remember?"

Lucy managed a smile back. "Well, don't tell *him* that."

"Go on. I'll get Mr. Mowery to the police. No loose ends this time."

Jack took her hand, and together they walked up to the falls. She told him what Barbara had done.

"My God, Lucy." His voice cracked, tears spilled down his wrinkled cheeks. He squeezed her hand. "I had no idea. I didn't put it together. I should have spoken up sooner."

"Water over the dam now, Jack. We both made mistakes."

"I'm shattered," he said, "and I'm stunned. I never expected this. Never, not in a million years. I'd have done anything—anything—to spare you and the kids this ordeal."

"I know you would. That's the hardest thing, isn't it?" She pictured her injured daughter, her terrified son. "Realizing no matter how much you want to, how hard you try, you can't protect your kids from life."

"It is. It's the hardest thing." He tucked his hand into hers. "But you've given Madison and J.T. the skills they need, the good judgment. Lucy, when I saw J.T. running up those steps straight at Mowery—"

She shuddered. "It's over, Jack. It worked out."

"Thank God."

As they came to a curve in the path, Lucy glanced back. Sebastian was in the same position, alone with his gun drawn over an enemy who had once been his friend.

"He won't shoot him," Jack assured her.

"No," Lucy said, "he won't. But I think it's how he likes life best, don't you? Alone with a gun on a bad guy."

"Actually, no. I think he likes life best with you. I think he has for a long, long time." Her father-in-law pulled her arm around him and hugged her fiercely. "It just wasn't possible until now."

Chapter 16

The Capitol Police and the local police weren't too happy with the Swifts. "They chewed my ass off, too," Rob said, as he and Lucy lined up supplies for the father-son backpacking trip. It was four days later, and they had work to do.

Lucy sighed. "Well, I was right about them crawling all over the place, wasn't I?"

Rob grinned at her. "A kidnapped senator does bring the men with guns out of the woodwork."

The Capitol Police had assigned a detail to Lucy, Madison and J.T., until they completed their investigation and were satisfied Darren Mowery and Barbara Allen had no other accomplices. Straightforward greed, one detective told Lucy, was often an easier motive to sort out than vengeance and obsession.

Sebastian had found another car—a getaway car

Mowery had put in place—in a small clearing on the western edge of Lucy's property. He'd meant to use Jack as a shield until he no longer needed him, then shoot him, shoot Sebastian and take off. Mission accomplished, Sebastian Redwing dead and discredited. Money was never the point. The freedom from hating Sebastian was.

Rob stood over a row of water bottles. "I wish J.T. could come with us."

"Next year."

He smiled gently. "Maybe Sebastian will take him."

Lucy couldn't think that far into the future. Right now, it was enough to count water bottles. Madison and J.T. were with their grandfather and Sidney Greenburg, who'd flown up from Washington. They were all picking wild blueberries—even Madison with her broken arm in a cast. "We all need simple, healing tasks," Sidney had said in that kind, firm way of hers.

After Rob headed for home, Lucy walked across her yard to her front porch. She paid attention to the soft grass under her feet, the warmth of the sun, the smell of the flowers and the sounds of the birds. Simple, healing tasks. Walking across the yard. Breathing in the clean summer air.

Plato Rabedeneira was sitting on a wicker chair on the porch. He looked less ashen and weak, but still wasn't a hundred percent. The bullet wound on his head was lightly bandaged, bruising at its edges.

Lucy laughed as she came up the steps, delighted to see him. "I didn't know you were getting out of the hospital. When did this happen?"

"I fought my way out this afternoon." He grinned

at her. "I thought the bastard'd never spring me. I hate hospitals."

"How did you get here?"

"An FBI detective I know."

"The FBI's here, too?"

"Lucy, everyone's here."

"Well, they can all go home. I want my life back."

His dark, handsome eyes settled on her. "Do you?"

She knew he meant Sebastian. "I can't leave here," Lucy said quietly. "This is my home. Madison and J.T. need to be here."

"Lucy, Lucy." Plato shook his head at her. "There are two things in Sebastian's life that are permanent. This place and you."

"His ranch—"

"He almost lost the damn thing in a poker game."

"Redwing Associates," she said.

"He's done his bit. He can do something else, maybe leadership training. You get the right kind of leadership in place, you can prevent a lot of trouble down the line." He stretched his long legs. "Of course, sometimes you just run into bastards and wackos. Keeps us in business, I guess."

"Bastards and wackos. Are those technical terms?"

"Absolutely." But his grin faded, and he said softly, "Lucy, I'm sorry I didn't do better by your kids."

"You did fine by my kids. Madison's got good-looking men with guns watching over her, and J.T.'s named one of his Micro Machine helicopters after you. I'm sorry you got shot looking after them."

"Yeah. Not your everyday baby-sitting job."

"You're welcome to stay with us as long as you want."

But he shook his head, rising stiffly to his feet. "I need to get down to Washington and check on Happy Ford."

"She's okay?"

"She's got a long recovery ahead of her, but she's tough."

"Then it's back to Wyoming?"

"Work's piling up." He took both her hands and pulled her to her feet. His dark eyes sparkled with a humor that was pure Plato Rabedeneira. "Don't tell Sebastian, but I had his cabin bulldozed. Packed up his poetry and maple syrup and mowed that sucker down."

Lucy bit back a smile. Plato, Sebastian and Colin had always had an unusual friendship, the rules of which she didn't understand. "What about his dogs and horses?"

"Moved them up to the main part of the ranch. I think the yellow Lab might do okay out here. The other two are western dogs. Sebastian can get new horses."

"Plato…"

"He's staying, Lucy. Trust me."

"I don't know. It's as if he's gone inside himself. I don't even know where he is."

Plato laughed. "Are you kidding? He's out playing detective with the big boys and checking out the talent in case he sees any good prospects for the company. I said he was staying, Lucy. I didn't say he was quitting."

Sebastian took them up to the falls that evening after dinner. Jack and Sidney promised to have hot cocoa and cookies waiting when they got back.

The sun was low on the horizon; the air warm and dry, without a breeze. At Lucy's side, Madison shook visibly. "Mom, I don't know if I can do it."

"You don't have to do it. We can turn back."

She nodded. There didn't seem an inch of her that wasn't bruised. Her cast was already covered with signatures, drawings of hearts and flowers, smiley faces. When the news of her ordeal spread through town, her friends came up by the carload.

"I'll do it," she whispered.

Up ahead, J.T. held Sebastian's hand. He had his Plato helicopter in his other hand. He kept looking up at Sebastian, as if taking his cue from him. Sebastian focused on the task at hand. Mind the tree roots, step over the rocks. He'd been thoroughly no-nonsense since the police had carted off his former mentor and friend, a man he'd thought he'd killed a year ago.

They stopped when they could hear the falls. "Listen," Sebastian said.

Madison frowned, then managed a small smile. "It's beautiful."

J.T. looked around at her. "What?"

"The sound of the waterfall."

"It's just water," he said.

Sebastian tugged on his hand. "Come on."

They walked all the way to the top of the falls, to the ledge where Barbara Allen had dangled Madison. The scraggly hemlock was still scarred from the rope. Madison was breathing rapidly, and Lucy worried about her going into a panic attack or hyperventilating. But she said nothing, and her daughter squared her jaw and pushed ahead of her mother, her brother and Sebastian. Madison placed a hand on the tree and looked down into the deep, cold pool.

"*Don't*, Madison," J.T. sobbed. "You'll fall."

"It's just water and rock," she said over her shoulder at him. "Come on, J.T. I didn't fall the other day. I was pushed."

Tentatively, he went and stood next to his sister, but kept back from the very edge of the ledge. Sebastian looked at Lucy, his hard gaze impossible to read. "What about you?"

She remembered her terror and helplessness at seeing her daughter hanging over the waterfall, knowing she was hurt, frightened, one wrong move away from not coming out of there alive. Her baby. She blinked back tears, could almost feel Madison's little head against her shoulder as she'd rocked her as an infant. Madison wasn't a baby anymore.

"Come on, Mom," J.T. said.

Lucy walked up the sloping rock and stood next to her children. The water of Joshua Falls ran clear, a mix of sunlight and shade dancing on the surface. "We did good that day," Lucy said. "All of us."

Madison smiled at her mother. "It's beautiful here. It's just so beautiful."

On the way back, J.T. skipped ahead to catch tree toads, and Madison counted the names on her cast. Lucy smiled at Sebastian. "At least we managed to do that without the Capitol Police on our tails."

"No, you didn't."

"You mean—"

"They shadowed us. I just didn't tell you." He grinned at her. "Jack's leaving in a couple of days. They'll go then, too."

"Good."

"I will, too."

She swallowed, kept walking. "Back to Wyoming?"

"Yes. I have things I need to sort out, Lucy."

"I know you do. I'll be here."

He smiled and said nothing, and Lucy decided not to tell him Plato had had his cabin bulldozed.

"Lucy has a good life here," Sidney said, "a damn good life."

Jack nodded, holding Sidney's hand as they sat on the back steps waiting for Lucy, Sebastian and the kids to return from their trip to Joshua Falls. "Yes, she does. I'm happy for her."

"But you weren't, not for a long time."

"No," he admitted. "I guess I thought if she stayed in Washington and didn't move on with her life, somehow it kept a part of Colin alive. I miss him, Sidney. Some days it's so hard, even now."

She turned his hand over and kissed his palm. "You'll have those days for the rest of your life. Be grateful for them. They tell you how much you loved your son. They tell you that you don't have to be afraid you'll ever forget him."

"I couldn't protect him, Sidney. I couldn't protect Eleanor."

"No, you couldn't."

He smiled and brushed her cheek with the tips of his fingers. "How did you get to be so smart?"

She laughed, her dark eyes crinkling. "By not really and truly falling in love until I was fifty. Now." She sprang up and dusted off her bottom. "If you don't mind, I'm not your romance-in-the-country sort of person. Too damn many mosquitoes."

"You're not going to want to move to Vermont?"

"God, no." She grinned, and Jack's heart melted.

"Don't look at me like that, Senator Swift. I am not making love to you in the pumpkin patch."

He pulled her close. "Does this mean you're willing to hang your panty hose in my bathroom?"

"Jack, *Newsweek* has us as an item. The cat's out of the bag. I'll hang my panty hose in your Senate office."

"I don't know about that."

She laughed and kissed him. "I do."

His heart jumped. "Sidney?"

"Yes, Jack. I'll marry you."

"Goddammit, Plato," Sebastian said two days later when he arrived back in Wyoming. They stood in the dust where his cabin had been. "You bulldozed my place."

"Not me. I'm the boss. I delegated the job."

"To whom? I want a name."

"I promised anonymity."

Sebastian glared at him. They'd met in Washington to visit Happy Ford, now recuperating at home, and Plato had never mentioned the cabin. "My stuff?"

"Packed up."

"Where?"

"In your truck. I figure you'll have to drive back to Vermont. The yellow Lab won't take to flying."

Sebastian nodded. "I'll need a truck in Vermont."

The other two dogs rolled on their backs in the dust. They wouldn't do well with kids and easterners. Definitely western dogs.

Sebastian grinned at his friend and partner. "I'll let this one go, seeing how you got shot in the head."

"That barely counts as a bullet wound. Now, the one in my arm hurt. Lucky there was no nerve damage. Do you know that crazy bitch thought she was an expert marksman?"

"Ms. Allen had a lot of lofty ideas about herself."

"She operated according to a logic all her own." Sebastian knelt beside the shepherd and rubbed the old dog's stomach. He breathed in the cool, dry air. He loved this place—it had restored his mind and body. But his soul wasn't here. "If Lucy hadn't shot Mowery in the ass, I'd have killed him."

"If you had no other choice. You're a professional, Sebastian. This was personal, but you kept your cool. Your mistake," Plato said, "was in letting Mowery take the credit for thwarting that assassination attempt all those years ago."

"Thwarting?" Sebastian got to his feet, grinning at him. "What kind of word is that?"

Plato's eyes darkened. "You know what I'm saying. Darren Mowery didn't have it. The instincts, the keen sense of right and wrong, the ability to stay focused and not get cynical. He just didn't have it."

"He wanted to, at least in the beginning."

"You, on the other hand. You never wanted it."

"No, I never did. I wanted to be happy the way Daisy was happy, with a patch of dirt, her birds, the woods." He squinted out at the incredible Wyoming landscape. "I suppose I needed the last twenty years to sort that out."

"Yeah, well, you're not throwing in the towel. I figure, a nice addition to Lucy's barn, and we've got our eastern leadership training center. Invite me to the wedding?"

"I'll need a best man."

Plato rocked back on his heels. "You have a ring?

You can't be asking Lucy to marry you without a ring. I know she does all this adventure travel stuff, but she'll want a ring. Trust me."

Sebastian sighed and dug in his jeans pocket, producing a simple diamond ring. "There."

Plato frowned. "That's it? You can afford a bigger rock than that."

"It was Daisy's. My grandfather gave it to her. They didn't have much money."

"I thought you didn't take anything of Daisy's after she died."

Sebastian shrugged. "I didn't. I appropriated this from the attic before I left."

"You mean you stole it?"

"It wasn't stealing. Daisy meant for me to have it, only I was too stupid to take it."

"You never thought Lucy would fall for you," Plato said. He shook his head. "You're right, you were stupid."

"Keep it up, Rabedeneira. I've already got you earmarked for kid duty during the honeymoon."

"Ha. Me and what army?"

"They adore you."

"Yeah, well, those two get me shot again, that's it for me and kids."

Sebastian arrived in Vermont unshaven, jittery from too much road food and sick of his damn dog. The dog was sick of him, too. When Sebastian opened the door of the truck, the dog bounded out and immediately laid ruin to Lucy's hollyhocks and daylilies.

Well, what the hell. They'd plant more.

Lucy walked down off the front porch. She had on a long sundress and sandals, and her hair was down, shining in the late-afternoon sun. "I heard you were in town."

"Spies everywhere."

"You stopped at the store for something. My spies wouldn't tell me what. They recognized your Wyoming plates. They didn't recognize you. They said you were—" She pretended to search her memory. "Disreputable looking. That was it."

"Am I?"

"Around here, disreputable is a euphemism for sexy."

"Ah. I see."

She glanced over at the yellow Lab, now chasing a gray squirrel across the yard. "Think he'll ever learn the rules?"

"Not a chance."

"Hell of a nerve, bringing your dog."

Sebastian leaned against his truck. She wasn't twenty-two anymore, and neither was he. But she was the woman he'd always loved. "Where are the kids?"

"Rob and Patti Kiley took them to their place for the night."

"Convenient."

"Hmm. The feds have finally left us to our own devices. The media have decamped. The bad guys are in jail without bail." She smiled at him. "I'm alone."

"No, you're not."

He kissed her, long and slow and gently, and after a while he got the champagne out of the truck. It was what he'd bought in town. He'd told the woman at the counter, who had a spying-for-Lucy look about her, to keep her mouth shut. It was probably all over town by now—Daisy's grandson and the Widow Swift having champagne together up at the old Wheaton place.

They went into the kitchen, and he popped the cork and filled two glasses.

"What are we celebrating?" Lucy asked.

"Well, we can celebrate anything we want. We can celebrate getting the bad guys. We can celebrate living another day. Or," he said, "we can celebrate Lucy Blacker falling in love again, or making love again, or anything you want, because I'll take whatever you can give me."

She smiled. "Can I celebrate all of the above?"

He didn't think he could manage to carry two glasses of champagne and her, but it wasn't far to the bedroom. Then she threw back her head and laughed; it knocked him off balance and the champagne spilled all over her. Both glasses. He started to lay her on the bed.

"My antique quilt," she said.

He whisked it off, the old wedding-ring quilt Daisy had stitched so long ago.

Lucy dangled her arms around his neck. "I smell like champagne."

"You taste like champagne, too."

"You taste like...dog hair."

He laughed, kissing her. "Do you want me to shower first?"

"No, shower second."

"We'll shower together."

"I was just kidding." She rubbed the back of her hand on his beard stubble. "You taste like a man who's driven hard across country to—" She smiled, her eyes alive, happy. "To make love to me."

"It's all I've thought about for days."

"Years, I think."

He could see the shape of her breasts against her

champagne-soaked dress. "You've a fine opinion of yourself, Lucy Blacker."

"Of you," she said. "I love you, Sebastian. I think I always have in one way or another. You've been there for me all along. It's different now. I love you as a partner, not just as a friend. I love you as an equal, not just as my protector. I love you up close." She pulled him to her and said as her mouth found his, "Never again from a distance."

He licked the champagne from her throat, and when they dispensed with her dress, he licked it from her breasts and stomach, until she was quaking with urgency. He made short order of his clothes, too, and when he came back to her, curving his hands over her hips, her stomach, her breasts, he could feel his own urgency, his unstoppable desire for this woman he'd loved for so long.

"I can't hold back, not anymore."

"Then don't," she said, and pulled him into her.

It was cool in her room, and he could hear the birds outside, his dog panting after a fresh scent, and in the distance, Joshua Brook tumbling out of the hills. He was home, and when he made love to Lucy, he knew this was where he belonged.

"I've always loved you," he whispered. "I always will."

* * * * *

Visit the Author Profile page
at Harlequin.com for more titles.

ODD MAN OUT

B.J. Daniels

To Kathrina,
who showed me the way,
and Kitty and Judy,
who read every word along the way.
Special thanks to Neil and Dani.

Prologue

Rain pelted the tops of the parked cars like rocks hitting tin cans. Rivulets of the icy stuff ran off the brim of J. D. Garrison's gray Stetson as he hung back in a stand of snowy pines on a hillside overlooking the tiny Fir Ridge Cemetery. Hidden from view, he eyed the funeral service taking place beneath the swollen dark clouds covering the valley below. He'd been away far too long. He hunched deeper in his sheepskin coat, his head bent against the cold wetness of the Montana spring day, as he wished it hadn't been death that had brought him home again.

Half the county had turned out for Max McCallahan's burial even in the freezing downpour. Snatches of the service reached J.D. on the hillside. He had to smile at the priest's portrayal of the old Irish private eye. Max must be turning in his grave to hear such malarkey. Too

bad the good Father didn't just tell the truth—that Max
had been a big, loud, red-faced Irishman and damned
proud of it. That he'd loved his ale. And that, if the need
arose, he hadn't been one to back down from a good
brawl. The truth was, the devil had danced in the old
Irishman's eyes most of the time. But there'd also been
another side to Max, a gentle, loving side, that a young
girl had brought out in him.

As the priest led a prayer, J.D. studied that young
girl—Max's niece, Denver McCallahan. She was no
longer a girl but she would always have that look because of her slight build. She stood under the dripping
canopy at the edge of the grave, a large black felt hat
hiding most of her long auburn hair and part of her face.
Her manner appeared almost peaceful.

J.D. wasn't fooled. He knew Denver's composure
was an act. Max had been her only family; she would
have killed for him. J.D.'s jaw tensed under his dark
beard as the tall cowboy beside Denver slipped an arm
around her shoulders. He'd have recognized the man
anywhere, not only because of his blond hair and his
arrogant stance, but by his trademark—the large, white
Western hat now dangling from the fingers of his right
hand. J.D. swore, surprised by his reaction. He didn't
like seeing Denver in the arms of his childhood friend,
Pete Williams.

J.D. looked up as an older woman joined him in the
seclusion of the pines. She wore a worn wool plaid hunting jacket, Max's, no doubt, jeans, a flannel shirt and
boots.

"I've never been so glad to see anyone in my life,"
Maggie said as she stepped into his arms. He hugged
her to him, feeling her strength. Sturdy. That was what

Max had called her. Sturdy, dependable Maggie. She'd been Max's friend, his lover, his confidante. Although they'd never married and had lived in separate houses, Maggie had been the love of Max's life.

Maggie stepped back, brushing a wisp of graying brown hair from her face, a face that belied her fifty-five years. She glanced at the cemetery below them, her expression as grim as the day. Dark umbrellas huddled around the grave like ghouls. Denver moved closer to drop a single bloodred rose on her uncle's casket. Even from the distance, J.D. could see that she'd grown up since he'd been gone. A lot of things had changed, he thought, watching her with Pete.

"Shouldn't we be down there at the funeral?" J.D. asked, still surprised that Maggie had suggested meeting here instead.

"Max knew how I felt about funerals," she said softly. "And I'd prefer Denver didn't know you're back in town yet."

His eyebrow shot up. "Why is that?"

"There's something you need to know before you see her." Maggie took a breath and let it out slowly. "Denver's in trouble."

He almost laughed. Ever since they were kids, Denver McCallahan had been in some sort of trouble; blame it on her fiery spirit, but it was one of the things he'd always admired about her. "What kind of trouble?" The moment he said it, he could guess. "She's heard the rumors you told me about Max being involved in something illegal and she's determined to clear his good name, right?"

"You know Denver. And while she's at it, she intends to bring his killer to justice, as well."

That didn't surprise him in the least. "And I suppose you want me to keep her out of trouble while she's doing all that?" He shook his head. "You don't know what you're asking."

Maggie met his gaze and he glimpsed an expression in her eyes that startled him. Anger. Cold as the granite bluffs in the distance. "I'm asking a lot more than that, J.D. I want you to keep her away from Pete Williams."

"You can't be serious." The rain fell harder, dimpling the spring snow's rough surface. He stared at her with a puzzled frown, and realized she *was* serious. "Why would I do that?"

"I know things about Pete—" She looked away. "You just have to keep him away from Denver."

"You're asking the impossible." He'd been gone for nine years and he hadn't left on the best of terms.

Maggie pulled her jacket around her. "Denver knows I've never liked Pete. She won't listen to me."

J.D. watched Denver lean into Pete Williams's embrace as the two stood alone beside the grave. "Denny won't—" he stumbled on the childhood name he'd always called her. "Denver wouldn't appreciate any interference in her life from me."

"Oh, J.D., you know how she's always felt about you."

"She had a crush on me when she was sixteen, Maggie! Believe me, it didn't last." He remembered only too well how angry Denver had been that afternoon at Horse Butte Fire Tower when he'd told her he was leaving town. And how hurt. She'd been like a kid sister to him. He'd never forgiven himself for hurting her.

"If anyone can handle her, it's you," Maggie argued.

"I'm not sure there's a man alive who can handle

Denver McCallahan." The umbrellas suddenly dispersed like tiny dark seeds across the snow. The rain turned to snow as the mourners headed for their cars.

"Just promise me you'll do everything you can to keep Pete away from her," Maggie said. "If you don't—" She turned to leave.

"Wait, what are you saying?" J.D. demanded. Surely she didn't believe Denver had anything to fear from Pete. "Give me a reason, Maggie. A damned good reason."

To his surprise, her eyes filled not with their usual resolve but with tears. That anger he'd glimpsed earlier mixed with pain and burned red-hot. "Pete Williams killed Max."

Chapter 1

Denver ducked her head to the cold and the pain as she let Pete lead her away from the cemetery. The rain had turned to snow that now fell in huge, wet flakes. She walked feeling nothing, not the ground under her feet nor Pete's steadying hand on her elbow.

"You're Denver McCallahan, right?" A woman in her fifties in a long purple coat and a floppy red wool hat stepped in front of her; the woman didn't wait for an answer. "I'm Sheila Walker with the *Billings Register*." She flipped open her notebook, her pen ready. "I need to ask you some questions."

Pete put his arm around Denver's shoulders. "Ms. McCallahan just buried her uncle. Now is not the time." He tried to pass, but the reporter blocked his way, ignoring him as she turned her full attention on Denver.

"This has to be the second worst day of your life.

First your parents, now your uncle." From a web of wrinkles, she searched Denver's face with dark, eager eyes. "You think there's a connection?"

Denver stared at the woman. Her bright red lipstick was smeared and her hat drooped off one side of her head, exposing a head of wiry black-and-gray curls. A scent of perfume Denver couldn't place hung over her like a black cloud. "My parents were killed more than *twenty* years ago." The murders connected? Was the woman crazy? Pain pressed against her chest; she fought for breath. Pete pulled Denver closer and pushed on past the woman.

"Who do you think killed your uncle?" the reporter asked, trotting alongside Denver. "Do you think it was that hitchhiker they're looking for?"

"Please, I can't—" Denver fought the ever-present tears.

"Leave her alone," Pete interrupted in a menacing tone. They'd reached his black Chevy pickup. He opened the door for Denver and spun on the woman. "Back off, lady, or you'll wish you had." Climbing in beside Denver, he slammed the door in the reporter's face.

She tapped on the window. "The rumors about your uncle, is there any truth in them?"

Pete started the pickup and peeled away, leaving Sheila Walker in a cloud of flying ice and snow.

"You don't believe it."

J.D. watched Pete leave with Denver in a fancy black Chevy pickup, then turned his attention back to Maggie. "That Pete murdered Max? No, I don't believe it." He and Pete had been friends and as close to Denver and Max as family. Through the falling snow, he could see workers pushing cold earth over Max's casket with a finality that made his heart ache.

"I don't want to believe it, either," Maggie said. "Max loved Pete. He loved you both like the brother he lost."

"Then how can you suspect Pete of murder?"

She took a long, ragged breath. "The morning after Max's murder, Denver and Pete came over. I'd made coffee and sent them into the kitchen. You remember the photograph Max took of you, Pete and Denver at the lake on her sixteenth birthday?"

J.D. nodded; it had been right before he'd left town. He could still see Denver in the dress Max had bought her. A pale aquamarine. The same color as her eyes. "You gave me a copy of the photo." He still had it. It reminded him of those days at the lake with Denny and Pete. Sunlight and laughter. A long-lost happiness twisted at his insides.

"It was Max's favorite photograph. He always carried it in his wallet," Maggie said. "I saw it the day before he died. It was dog-eared and faded and I wanted to put it away for safekeeping, but Max wouldn't hear of it." She stopped; he watched her fight the painful memories. "When I went to hang up Pete's coat, I saw a piece of the photograph sticking out of his pocket."

"Didn't Pete have a copy, too?"

She nodded. "But I'd written on the back of the one I gave Max. I could still make out the writing. It was the photo from his wallet. Only…it had been torn." She met his gaze. "Someone had ripped you out of the picture."

"That's not enough evidence to convict a man of murder."

"I know, especially since Pete has an alibi for the day of the murder. Supposedly he was in Missoula with his band. But I called to check. The Montana Country Club band was there, but when I described Pete to one of the cocktail waitresses, she didn't remember him. If Pete's good looks didn't make an impression on her, that blue-eyed charm of his would have."

"That's pretty weak, Maggie."

"Pete wasn't in Missoula. I'd stake my life on it."

"I hope you won't have to do that." J.D. tugged at his collar; he wasn't used to this kind of weather anymore.

"I have to go," Maggie said.

J.D. walked with her to her Land Rover parked along the edge of the road in the pines. "It still doesn't make any sense," he said. "Why would Pete want to kill Max?"

"Max wasn't part of anything dishonest if that's what you're thinking." She hugged herself against the cold wetness. "I'll admit something was bothering him."

"What?"

She shrugged and opened her car door. "If Pete finds out that I called you or that I suspect him—"

"Dammit, Maggie, tell me why you're so frightened. It has to be more than a hunch and an old ripped photograph."

She nodded, fighting more than grief. "That last week, Max was…afraid."

J.D. had never known the man to be afraid of anything, or anybody—no matter how big or tough they were.

She slid into the front seat and shoved her hands into the pockets of Max's hunting jacket. "He seemed to be looking over his shoulder as if—" She broke off and shivered. "As if something had come back to haunt him.

He was obsessed with death and kept talking about his brother's murder."

J.D. fought the chill that stole up his spine. "Denny's father?"

She nodded. "He felt responsible for encouraging Timothy to become a cop. He blamed himself for Timothy's death."

"Maggie, what does that have to do with Pete?" J.D. asked.

She shook her head as if to chase away the memories. "I haven't told anyone this because I was afraid of what Pete would do," she said, her voice barely a whisper. "The last time I saw Max, he was furious at Pete." She bit her lip. "I've never seen Max like that. He said he had to stop Pete...before someone got killed."

"I'm sorry about that reporter," Pete said as they headed south toward the town of West Yellowstone. "Are you all right?"

Denver nodded, wondering if she'd ever be all right again. Leaning back in the seat, her hat in her lap, she watched the pines and snowfall blur by outside the window. Max dead. Murdered. It wasn't possible. But worse yet were the rumors. She ran a finger through the water droplets beaded up on the brim of her hat, fighting the pain.

"You know, that woman was right..." Her voice broke. "People are saying that Max was dirty. That he'd gotten himself involved in something illegal."

"Denver, why do you listen to it?" Pete demanded angrily. "You knew Max better than anyone. If your uncle had a fault, it was being too honest. Naively so."

It wasn't that she believed the rumors. She just

couldn't stand seeing Max's name dragged through the dirt. But more than that, she knew the rumors were somehow tied in with the way Max had been acting the past few weeks. Secretive. Something had been bothering him. And Denver felt that if she knew what it was, she'd know who killed him.

"He's gone, Denver," Pete said, taking her hand as if he could read her thoughts. "As much as we both hate it, he's gone. Leave it alone."

Concentrating on the click-clack of the wipers, she closed her eyes. Now wasn't the time to let grief blind her, not when there was something much more important that had to be done—no matter what Pete said.

"I think it would be a good idea if you stayed at my place and didn't go back out to the cabin tonight," he said.

Denver opened her eyes, tempted to take him up on it. Since Max's death, she'd been having the nightmare again. "Thanks, but the cabin's home and I need that right now."

Pete's look reflected a mixture of annoyance and worry. "I don't like the idea of your being out there alone. It's too deserted this time of year."

"You know how I feel about the lake. I love this time of year *because* it's quiet out there." She touched his arm. "I'll be fine."

"I wish you'd change your mind." He sounded angry.

And she wondered if he was talking about her staying at his place or about the argument they'd had earlier.

"I swear, sometimes you're as stubborn as—"

"As Max?" she asked. Max McCallahan had given stubborn a new definition.

Pete's smile faded. "Yeah. Max." She could see him

fighting painful emotions as he turned on the radio. Intermittent snow flurries, the newsman said. A slow, sad Western song came on. Pete took her hand. "I just worry about you."

"I know." She smiled, feeling the familiar tenderness she'd felt for him since they were kids. Pete, Denver and J.D. Max had called them the Terrible Trio because of all the trouble they'd gotten into. Pete and J.D. had been the older brothers she'd never had; now Pete was her best friend. She chastised herself for arguing with him earlier; he was just trying to protect her the way he always had.

She studied him, forgetting sometimes how good-looking he was—tall, handsome with his blue eyes and blond hair, and capable of being utterly charming. If only she'd fallen in love with him all those years ago. Instead of J.D.

Another song came on the radio. Denver saw Pete tense and her own heart lurched as it always did when J. D. Garrison's voice filled the airways. "Number ten on the country and western chart and climbing," the radio announcer cut in. "Our own J. D. Garrison with his latest hit, 'Old Friends and Enemies.'"

Pete snapped off the radio. "I can't believe he didn't make the funeral."

Just the thought of J.D. brought back the hurt and disappointment. In her foolish heart, she'd always believed J.D. would come home if she or Max ever needed him. Well, they'd needed him. And he hadn't come.

"I doubt J.D. can just drop everything at a moment's notice," she heard herself say. "Maybe he didn't get the message you left him."

Pete shot her a look. "Still making excuses for him?"

She looked away. Loving J.D. had always been both pleasure and pain. And all one-sided. J.D. had never seen her as anything more than a kid. But sometimes his gaze had met hers and—And then he'd ruffle her hair or throw her into the lake. No, he'd never taken her seriously, even when she'd promised him her heart. Instead, he'd teased her. Just a schoolgirl crush. Puppy love. She'd get over it.

He'd been gone nine years, but she still saw his ghost lounging on the sandy beach beside the lake, heard his laugh on the breeze that swept across the water and felt his touch on a hot summer's night as she stood on the dock, unable to sleep. She'd just never met anyone who made her feel like J.D. had.

But if J. D. Garrison were here right now, she'd wring his neck. For missing Max's funeral. For breaking a young girl's heart. For still haunting her thoughts.

It began to snow harder as they dropped down to the Madison River. A soft mist rose from the water, cloaking the bridge in a veil of white fog and driving snow. A local teenage superstition prophesied that if you didn't honk as you crossed the bridge you'd be in for bad luck. Pete didn't believe in superstitions. "You make your own luck," he'd always said. Denver honked, partly out of superstition, partly out of tradition; J.D. had never crossed the bridge without honking.

As they crossed the bridge, Pete didn't honk. The snow fell in a thick, hypnotizing wall of white in front of the pickup. Denver realized she could barely make out the Madison Arm sign as they passed it. She glanced in the side mirror and was startled to see a huge semitrailer barreling down on them.

"Pete?" Her voice cracked. Her heart caught in her

throat. "Pete!" He looked back, his eyes widening as he saw it. At the last moment, the truck swerved into the passing lane. Denver thought it would head on around them, but instead, she realized with growing horror, the truck was edging over into their lane.

"Son of a—" Pete yelled.

Denver could see the huge semitrailer wheels right next to them. A scream lodged in her throat; the truck would either force them off the road or—

Pete hit the brakes. The back of the semi just missed the front of the pickup by inches as it swerved the rest of the way into their lane.

Snow poured over the cab in a blinding rush as the semi roared past. Pete brought the pickup to a skidding stop sideways in the middle of the highway. Denver stared through the falling snow, expecting another vehicle to come along and hit them before Pete got the pickup pulled over to the edge of the road.

He sat there gripping the steering wheel. "Are you all right?" he asked. His voice sounded strained as if the shock of their near mishap was just sinking in.

Denver took a shaky breath. Now that the danger had passed, she was trembling all over. "I think so. What was that guy doing?"

Pete shook his head as he looked at her. "I don't know, but I could kill the bastard."

Denver looked at the highway ahead, half expecting the trucker to come back and finish the job. "I can't believe he didn't even stop to see if we were all right."

Pete swore as he steered the pickup back onto the highway and headed toward West Yellowstone again.

"Did you recognize the truck?" she asked. It had

happened so fast she hadn't even thought to look at the license plate.

"I'm sure it was just some out-of-stater who's never been in a snowstorm before." But Pete kept staring at the highway as if he expected to see the truck again, too. And Denver knew she wouldn't feel safe until they reached town. No, she thought, she wouldn't feel safe until Max's killer was caught.

Chapter 2

Pete slowed on the outskirts of town. At first glance, West, as the locals called it, appeared abandoned. They drove down the main drag, past the Dairy Queen, a row of T-shirt and curio shops and Denver's camera shop. All were still boarded up behind huge piles of plowed snow. A melting cornice drooped low over Denver's storefront. Out of a huge drift peeked a partially exposed homemade sign. See You In The Spring!

The only hint of spring was in the rivers of melting snow running along the sides of the empty streets. Dirty snowbanks, plowed up higher than most of the buildings, marked the street corners they drove by. Everywhere, a webbing of snowmobile tracks crisscrossed the rotting snow still lingering in the shadow of the pines. Down a muddy alley sat a deserted snowmobile, its engine cover thrown back, falling snowflakes rapidly covering it.

Only a couple of gas stations had their lights on. Near a mud puddle as large as a lake, two locals sat visiting, with their pickups running.

It was April. Off-season. Snowmobiling was over for another winter and the summer tourist trade wouldn't officially begin until Memorial Day weekend. Denver usually cherished this time of year, a time for the locals to take a breather before the tourists returned. But today, the town seemed to echo her lonely, empty feeling of loss.

"I'm going to get you something hot to drink," Pete said, touching her arm.

Since the near accident with the semi, she hadn't been able to quit shaking. Pete pulled up to a convenience store and came back a few minutes later with two large hot chocolates. "It's beautiful, isn't it?" he said, motioning toward the falling snow. "I love this time of year." His gaze turned from the storm to her. "And I love you."

"Pete, don't—"

"When are you going to stop fighting it, Denver? I love you." He put his finger to her lips when she tried to protest. "I know you don't love me. At least not enough to marry me. Not yet. But you will, very soon."

As she looked at Pete's handsome face, she wished he were right. Marrying Pete was safe, and Max had made no secret of the fact that he had liked Pete for that very reason.

They finished their hot chocolates and drove farther on into town, finally stopping in front of a house on Faithful Street. The place was typical of the older West Yellowstone residences: rustic log with a green metal roof, surrounded by lodgepole pines.

"Let's get this over with," Pete said as he parked in front of Maggie's house.

* * *

J.D. stood at the window of his room in the Stage Coach Inn, watching snowflakes spin slowly down from the grayness above. He blamed his restlessness on being back in West Yellowstone after all these years, on the weather, on Max's burial service.

Jeez, Garrison, you've been lying to yourself for so long, you've started believing it. He stepped away from the window and went to the makeshift bar he'd set up on the dresser. *It's seeing Denny again that's thrown you.* He frowned, still surprised at his reaction. Denver. He swore under his breath as he ripped the plastic off one of the water glasses and poured a half inch of Crown Royal into it.

All these years he'd remembered Denny as the little freckle-faced girl he'd had water fights with on the beach and beat at Monopoly. Not that there hadn't always been something about her that made her special to him. A fire in her eyes and a spirit and determination that had touched him. But she'd been just a kid. Now he couldn't help wondering about the woman he'd seen at the cemetery—the woman Denver McCallahan had become. How much was left of the girl he'd once shared his dreams with?

The window drew him back again. His dreams. He sipped the whiskey and looked out at his old hometown. It was here he'd picked up his first guitar, a beat-up used one. He'd fumbled through a few chords, a song already forming in his head. It had always been there. The music, the knowledge that he'd make it as a singer—and the ambition eating away inside him.

He stared at the town through the snow. It had been here that he'd performed for the first time, here that he'd dreamed of recording an album of his own music, here that he'd always known he'd end up one day. But not like this.

Nine years. Nine years on a circuit of smoky bars and honky-tonks, long empty highways, flat tires on old clunkers and cheap motel rooms. Somewhere along the way, he'd made it. Even now, he couldn't remember exactly when that happened, when he realized it was no longer just a dream. J. D. Garrison was a genuine country and western star. Grammys and Country Music Association awards, his songs on the top of *Billboard*'s country charts. Since then, there'd been more awards, more songs, more albums, more tours. And better cars, better bars, better motel rooms.

But one thing remained the same. That distant feeling that he was drifting off the face of the earth, that he'd become untethered from life. A few weeks ago, he'd awakened in a strange motel room and forgotten where he was, and when he'd looked at himself in the mirror, he realized he'd forgotten who he was, as well. He was losing the music. The songs weren't there anymore—and neither was the desire to make them.

J.D. spread his fingers across the cold windowpane. The white flakes danced beyond his touch; a tiny drift formed on the sill. "Oh, Denny," he whispered. There was no doubt in his mind that she would try to find Max's murderer. The question was how to keep her safe. And how to keep Pete away from her until he could sort it all out.

But he knew one thing. He'd do whatever he had to do. *Like hell. You're looking forward to coming between the two of them. But is it because you believe Pete might have changed so much in these nine years that he could kill someone? Or is it simply that you don't want Pete to have Denny?*

He frowned as he remembered the woman he'd glimpsed at the cemetery. Denver McCallahan was definitely a woman worth fighting for. And if he were Pete Williams, he'd fight like hell for her.

Maggie met Pete and Denver on the screened-in porch in worn jeans, an old flannel shirt that could have been Max's, and a pair of moccasins. She hadn't attended the burial, saying she preferred to remember Max the way he was. A bag of groceries rested on the step, and from her breathlessness, Denver guessed she'd just come from the store.

The buzz of the going-away party spilled through the door behind her as she hugged Denver. "You okay?"

"I need to talk to you," Denver whispered.

Maggie handed Pete the bag of groceries and asked him to take them inside where friends had already started Max's party—their version of an Irish send-off.

"What's the matter?" Maggie asked after Pete was out of earshot. "Pete isn't pressuring you again, is he?"

Maggie was always quick to blame Pete. She disapproved of him, not because he was a musician with the band he and J.D. had started, the Montana Country Club, but because he'd never gone beyond that. "He's as talented as J.D. but he lacks J.D.'s inner strength," she'd said. "Behind all that charm is a very disappointed, angry young man." It was one of the few things Max and Maggie had ever argued about.

Denver wished Pete and Maggie could get along, especially now that Max was gone.

"Pete's fine. It's about Max," Denver said. More

guests arrived. She'd known Max made friends easily, but Denver was astounded at the number of people who'd come hundreds of miles to pay their respects to him.

Maggie told Denver to go on through the house to the kitchen, where the noise level was lower and the temperature definitely warmer, and wait for her. "Cal Dalton was here earlier," Maggie said. Since the party was an all-day kind of thing, people kept coming and going. "I just got back so I don't know if he's still here or not."

"Thanks, I need to talk to him."

Denver worked her way through the guests, stopping to accept words of sympathy and visit a moment with friends. She didn't see Cal. In the kitchen, she stood watching the snow fall and thinking of Max. She didn't even hear Maggie come in.

"Has Deputy Cline found some new evidence?" Maggie asked hopefully.

"No." Denver pulled off her hat and coat, and hung them on a hook by the back door. She wandered around the familiar kitchen, too keyed up to sit. "Cline is still convinced Max was killed by a hitchhiker."

Max's body had been found at the old city dump; according to Sheriff's Deputy Bill Cline, he'd been stabbed once in the heart. Cline was looking for a hitchhiker Max had bought lunch for at the Elkhorn Café earlier that day.

Maggie sat down at the kitchen table, her eyes dark with pain. "I can't believe Max was killed by someone he helped."

"I don't think that's what happened." Denver bit her lip, watching for Maggie's reaction. "What if it was connected to one of his cases? Maybe an…old case."

"You aren't suggesting it might be——"

"No." Denver fought off a chill. "Even Max had given up on that one." The one old case that had haunted Max for years was the unsolved murders of Denver's parents. Denver stopped beside the table, settling her gaze on Maggie. "I've been having the nightmare again."

"Oh, Denver." Maggie took her hand. "Max's death must have brought it back."

It had been years since she'd had the nightmare, not since Max had brought her to live with him in West Yellowstone. She'd been five at the time and could remember very little of her life before then. Except for images from the nightmare of fear and death from that day at the bank. She'd been with her parents the day the bank robber had killed her father and mother. Her father had just gotten off duty; he was still in his police uniform. Max said that was what had gotten him killed—walking into the middle of a robbery in uniform.

"I thought maybe Max might have mentioned a case," Denver said, changing the subject.

"You know the kind of work he did, small-time stuff, insurance fraud, divorce and child custody, theft—nothing worth getting murdered over."

"What if he'd stumbled across that once-in-a-lifetime case he'd always dreamed of?"

Maggie smiled. "I wish he had, honey. But you know Max. He couldn't have kept that a secret from us."

Denver ran her fingers along the edge of the kitchen counter. "He could if it was too dangerous or confidential or…" The word *illegal* sprang into her mind. Surely Maggie had heard the rumors.

"The last time he mentioned a case, he was tailing a husband whose wife thought he was having an affair,"

Maggie said. "I remember because Max was keeping odd hours. He wouldn't get in until the wee hours of the morning." She laughed. "I asked him if *he* was having an affair."

"How did the case turn out?" Denver asked.

"He never told me." Maggie looked past Denver, her gaze clouded. "There is one thing, though. A few days before he was…before he died, he brought some file folders home from the office. Old ones."

"Where are they now?" Denver asked as she sat down across from Maggie.

"He burned them."

"He what?" Denver couldn't believe her ears.

"That night we were sitting by the fireplace. He was sorting through some things. That's when I saw the folders—right before he tossed them into the fire."

"Did you see what they were?"

Maggie frowned. "I wasn't paying much attention, but a newspaper clipping fell out of one of the files. I don't even remember what it was about, just that it was old. I'm sure that's why Max was throwing the files away."

"Still, that doesn't sound like Max. He never threw anything away."

"I didn't think it was strange at the time…" Maggie's voice trailed off. "You know, he did keep one of those files. I guess he took it back to his office."

"There are too many strange things. Like Max's will. Not even his lawyer's seen it. It seems Max drew it up himself and said he'd put it in a safe place." Denver shook her head. "I wonder what Max would consider a safe place? Probably the middle of his kitchen table."

Maggie laughed softly, her eyes misty with private

memories of Max. "The police didn't find it in either Max's apartment or office. Do you think he could have left it at your cabin?"

"I haven't looked yet," Denver said. "And Max's gun is missing, too. Deputy Cline says the killer must have taken it when he took Max's wallet. But you know Max hardly ever carried a gun."

Maggie brushed at her tears. "Max would have given that hitchhiker money before the guy could even ask, and given him his shirt and shoes, as well. Even his car."

"That's just it, Maggie. Why didn't the guy take Max's car? The keys were in it." Denver turned and was startled to find Pete standing just inside the kitchen doorway. She wondered how long he'd been there, listening.

"I thought we'd already settled this." He glared at her, his gaze hard with anger. "You were going to stay out of the murder investigation and let Cline do his job."

Denver drew in a deep breath. Obviously she hadn't made herself clear when they'd argued about this earlier. "I can't stay out of it. How is the killer ever going to be caught when Cline isn't even looking into Max's cases?"

"What cases?" Pete demanded. "Come on, Denver. You're clutching at straws. It was a hitchhiker. You know how bad Max was about picking up strays."

No one knew better than she did just how Max was about helping people in trouble, she thought as she fingered her mother's gold locket at her neck. Fortunately, Max McCallahan had been that kind of man.

"No, it simply doesn't make sense," Denver said, standing her ground. "Maggie said he burned some old files right before he was killed. Doesn't that sound suspicious to you?"

Pete raked his fingers through his hair, not bothering to hide his exasperation. "So what are you going to do? Go after this murderer by yourself?"

"Pete's right," Maggie interrupted, surprising them both, since she seldom agreed with Pete on anything. "Listen, honey, Max wouldn't have wanted you getting involved in this. Obviously it's dangerous. I think you'd better leave it to the deputy sheriff."

Denver stared at her. It wasn't like Maggie to tell her to run from trouble; Maggie had always encouraged her to join Max in the investigation business. It had been Max who wouldn't hear of it, who had insisted she stick to photography, even though she'd helped him by taking photos on some of his cases.

"I'd better get back to my guests," Maggie said, slipping past Pete.

The tension in the kitchen dropped a notch or two in the moments after Maggie left; Denver knew it was because Pete thought he might be able to dissuade her. She looked out the window. The day had slipped away into dusk.

"I'm sorry," Pete said, crossing the kitchen to put his arms around her. "I know you're upset about Max. I just don't want to see you get hurt."

The worry in his eyes startled her. If he believed Max had been killed by some stranger passing through town, why would he be so afraid for her? Clearly he didn't believe it any more than she did.

"Just promise me you'll stay out of this," Pete whispered into her hair. "I want to help you get through it, if you'll let me."

Denver buried her face in his shoulder. She felt protected in his arms. Maybe Pete was right. She was a photographer—not an investigator. But that knowledge did little to cool the fever burning deep within her. She had to see Max's murderer behind bars; she owed Max at least that. And after all those years of hanging around him, she'd picked up a little something about investigative work. She wasn't going after the killer blind; she knew of the danger. But the danger didn't scare her as much as the thought that her uncle's murderer might get away.

"I'm sorry, Pete," she said, lifting her cheek from his shoulder. "I can't make that promise." She felt him tense. He dropped his arms and stepped back, his expression one of disappointment and anger. "I'm going to find Max's killer if it's the last thing I do."

Pete nodded. "It just might be."

J.D. couldn't shake the feeling that Denver was already in trouble, more trouble than just being involved with Pete—a possible killer.

He picked up the phone and dialed Maggie's number. Someone pretty well sloshed answered. A moment later, Maggie came on the line. "Is Denny all right?" he asked, feeling foolish.

"She's fine," Maggie said. "She's here and Pete just left." Her voice sounded muffled as if coming from inside a closet. From the party noise in the background, he guessed she probably was.

"Good. I won't worry about her for the moment anyway." He hung up and reached for his coat, trying to shake off the ominous feeling he had.

His options were limited. Confront Pete with what little "evidence" Maggie had against him and have Pete just deny it? Or try to talk to Denver about him. Maggie hadn't taken that route for two good reasons. One was that Denver knew Maggie had never liked Pete, and adding suspicion of murder to that list would only alienate her. The other was that the Denver he remembered would fight to the death to defend a friend, let alone a lover. And it was obvious she and Pete were very close.

J.D. cursed the thought. Nor did he doubt what Denver would do if he told her his suspicions. She'd go straight to Pete. Head-on. That was the way she operated. He assured himself Pete would never hurt her. At least, not the Pete he used to know. He considered Maggie's evidence against Pete flimsy at best. But Maggie's obvious fear for Denver made him think twice about dismissing it. If for some reason Pete *had* killed Max, then what would he do if he thought Denver suspected him? It wasn't a chance J.D. was willing to take with Denver's safety. And sitting around a motel room wasn't going to get him the answers he needed.

After Pete left her alone in the kitchen, Denver stood staring at the snow falling in the darkness outside, thinking of Max. The need to avenge his death tore at her insides, holding her grief at bay most of the time. Except tonight. Tonight she felt alone and frightened.

As a girl, when she'd been afraid, she'd fantasized about J.D. rescuing her. Nothing quite as dramatic as being tied to the railroad tracks with the train coming—but close enough. Always at the last minute, J.D. would appear and save her. But this wasn't a fantasy now. Max was dead. Not even Pete was on her side this time. And J.D. certainly wasn't coming to her rescue.

The noise from the other room had reached a rowdy pitch, music blasting. Denver heard the kitchen door open behind her only because it increased the volume. At first, she thought it might be Pete coming back.

Cal Dalton closed the door behind him and leaned against it. "I hear you've been looking for me."

He reminded her of a coyote, a wild look in his eyes, his body poised for flight. And instantly she wondered what he had to be afraid of; he frightened her much more than she ever could him. Everything about him was cold, from his graying pale blond hair to his icy blue eyes. He had to be hugging fifty but he hung around the bars with men half his age. Cal was known in town as a womanizer and a mean drunk, always getting into fights. One jealous husband had even shot him, and Cal liked to show off the scar, according to local scuttlebutt.

"I'm trying to find out what cases Max was working on," she said. For reasons Denver could not fathom, Max had befriended Cal in the weeks before his death, something she could only assume meant Max was on a case.

"You think I hired your uncle?" Cal scratched his neck. "What would I need with a private eye?" Good question. "Max and I were just drinking buddies."

"He didn't mention a case he might have been working on?" she asked. "Or maybe hire you to do some legwork for him?"

"Legwork?" Cal shook his head. His gaze took her in as if he realized for the first time she was a woman and certainly no threat. "Speaking of legs, yours aren't half-bad," he said, making her feel as if he'd just peeled off her black slacks.

This had been a mistake. "Well, I'm sorry I bothered you."

"Max did talk a lot about you," he said.

She found that more unlikely than their being drinking buddies. "If you'll excuse me, Pete is waiting for me." She tried to get past him, but he blocked her way.

"I don't think so. I saw Pete leave." He was close now. She could feel his breath on her face, smell the reek of beer.

Pete wouldn't leave without telling her, would he?

Cal leaned his hands on either side of her, trapping her. "I'm afraid Pete's thrown you to the wolves, darlin'." His eyes traveled over her with a crudeness that turned her stomach. "How about a little kiss for old Cal?"

"No, and if you touch me—"

He moved closer. "I like feisty girls." He bent to kiss her. Denver dived under his arm, shooting for the space between his body and the counter. He caught her, swung her into him and gave her a smelly, slobbery kiss that made her gag. "How'd you like that?" he asked, leering. "Better than that pansy boyfriend of yours, huh?"

She jerked her arm free and slapped him with a force that drove him back a step.

He rubbed his jaw; a meanness came into his eyes. "You shouldn't have done that. All I wanted was a little kiss."

Denver grabbed the first thing she could find as Cal moved toward her. A pottery pitcher.

"Denver?" Cal turned at the sound of the voice behind him, and Denver looked past him to see Max's old friend, Taylor Reynolds, standing in the doorway. "Is there a problem here?"

Denver set down the pitcher and pushed past Cal to step into the big man's arms.

"It's okay," Taylor said, holding her awkwardly. The old bachelor wasn't a man used to a physical display of sentiment. "Buddy, don't you think you'd better get back to the party?"

Denver heard Cal leave but she didn't look up; she found herself crying, crying for Max, for herself.

"Hey, easy. This is my best suit," Taylor kidded, then pulled back to look at her. "What was going on in here? If he's bothering you—"

She stepped from the shelter of his arms, trying to regain control. "Cal was just being Cal."

Taylor pushed out a chair for her at the table and pulled down some towels from a roll. He handed them to her and joined her at the table.

Denver took a deep breath, wiped her eyes with a towel and looked at the man before her. She remembered Max talking about his buddies from the army, but she'd never met this one before. Taylor Reynolds was a powerful-looking man much like Max had been. Only unlike Max, Taylor was soft-spoken and shy. He'd shown up right after Max's murder.

"Max saved my life in the army—I owe him," Taylor had said, standing with his hat in his hands on Maggie's porch. "I'll be staying at the Three Bears if you need anything."

Denver had taken to him immediately, and so had Maggie. Denver knew it was because he and Max had been so close; in Taylor a small part of Max still lived.

"It's tough, but we're all going to get through this," Taylor said now. He didn't seem to know what to do with his big hands. He took a toothpick and spun it between two fingers.

"Who do you think killed him?"

Taylor's face clouded. "A damned fool."

"Do you think it was the hitchhiker Deputy Cline's looking for?" She had a sudden flash of Max, the flicker of sunlight on the water behind him, the gentle lap of water against the side of the boat, the sound of his laugh floating across the lake. When she looked up, she realized Taylor had been talking to her.

"Denver?" He studied her, his eyes dark with concern. "You're having a rough time with this, aren't you, kid? Be careful. Don't let Max's death become more important than living."

Denver looked away. The noise of the party seemed at odds with the silence of the darkness outside.

Taylor reached across the table and patted her hand, then quickly pulled back, obviously embarrassed by the gesture. He got to his feet. "I think that Cal fellow has had enough to drink. Why don't I see he gets home where he won't be bothering you anymore tonight."

"Thank you."

"We're all going to miss Max, kid," he said as he left.

For a few moments, Denver stood in the quiet kitchen, thinking about what Taylor had said. She knew he was right; Max would have wanted her to get on with her life. And he would have liked her to marry Pete.

"I want to know there's going to be someone around for you when I'm gone," he'd said the last time they'd talked.

Denver closed her eyes. And now Max *was* gone. Had he known there was a chance he might be killed?

The kitchen suddenly felt as if it were closing in on her. Denver took her coat and hat and slipped out through the side door into the night. A chilly wind spun a weathered wind sock on the end of the eaves. She ducked her head against the cold and pulled her coat more tightly around her. The snow had stopped; now it was melting, dripping from warm roofs and dark pine boughs along the street.

Cal had told the truth, she realized with a shock. Pete's pickup was gone. "Men," she groaned as she started the four-block walk to her car.

For days she'd told herself that it was all a mistake, that Max wasn't really dead. Now as she walked the familiar streets, she acknowledged that he was gone. The truth came like a swift kick to the stomach. All the values she'd believed in, Max had taught her. She owed him her very life.

Her Jeep was parked in front of Pete's apartment, where she'd left it earlier before the service. Pete's pickup was nowhere to be seen. As she drove down Firehole Avenue, she realized how tired she was. All she wanted to do was go to the lake cabin and get some sleep. But as she looked down the dark street to Max's office, she wondered again about what cases Max might have been working on, something Cline wouldn't have recognized as a clue since he was so busy looking for a hitchhiker. Finding Max's killer couldn't wait, she realized. And nothing was going to stop her. Nothing. And nobody.

Chapter 3

Pete stood in the snowy shadows of the old log building at the edge of town listening to the night. Normally he loved this hour, when darkness settled in, cloaking secrets and regrets. Tonight, though, he felt vulnerable and afraid. Softly he knocked at the rear door. It opened a crack, then fell open. A hand grabbed his jacket and jerked him inside.

"I've told you not to come here. It's too risky."

Pete stumbled into the dimly lit room; the door slammed behind him. He followed the man to the front of the cabin. "I want to talk to the boss." The man swaggered into the living room. Pete followed, realizing he'd been drinking. "Let me talk to him. Now. Or I'm walking."

The man scowled. "So walk. You're the one who wanted in on this operation."

"If I walk, I walk to the feds," Pete said.

"That would be real smart." The man slumped into a chair before the fire roaring in the small fireplace. He picked up a whiskey bottle from the floor and took a long swig. "But that would be one way to meet the boss. He'd kill you."

Pete looked into the fire. What little he knew about their boss reminded him of hell and the devil himself. "You going to call him?"

"You're signing your death warrant if you mess with him." But he got to his feet and went into the kitchen to the phone. Pete listened to him dial. A long-distance number. It took a moment and Pete knew the call was being forwarded somewhere else. Then he heard the man in the kitchen talking in a hushed tone, apologizing, explaining. Finally, he called Pete in and handed him the receiver. The look on his face warned Pete he'd stepped over the line.

"You have a problem?" the synthesized voice asked on the other end of the line.

"Look, Midnight, I'm tired of putting up with this bozo," Pete said of the man standing next to him. "I want a number where I can call you. And I want to know why you had someone try to run me off the road this afternoon."

Midnight laughed, the synthesizer turning it into a midway sideshow. "You certainly want a lot, don't you?"

Midnight. How perfectly the code name described a man both dark and dangerous. "I've proven myself in your little organization, haven't I?"

Silence. He could tell Midnight didn't like the "little" part. "So you have."

"I don't like being threatened. You could have killed us both!"

Midnight's voice turned deadly serious. "Yes, I could have. But I didn't. Did it convince you how important it is to keep Denver from looking into Max McCallahan's death?"

"I was always convinced." Pete decided honesty might be the best policy, even with a man like Midnight. "But Denver's determined to find Max's killer."

Midnight let out another carnival laugh. "Well, she doesn't have to look too far, does she?"

Pete glared into the fire. The flames licked at the logs with hot fury.

"You said you could control her," Midnight continued. "I don't like problems."

"I'll take care of Denver. That was the arrangement."

Midnight's voice turned raspy with anger. "Arrangements can be changed."

Pete knew if anyone would renege on a bargain it was this man. Hadn't the truck episode proved that today? Denver had no idea what she was getting herself into if she persisted in searching for Max's murderer.

"You're sure the case file I'm looking for wasn't at Max's office?" Midnight asked.

"Yes."

"Then that leaves the cabin. You haven't said what you found out there. And don't tell me you haven't looked yet."

Pete wanted to tell him to do his own search but knew Midnight hired other men to do his dirty work while he hid on a phone line, behind a synthesizer. Why so much secrecy? All he could figure was that Midnight had to be someone he knew; it made him nervous not knowing with whom he was in business. "I tried to get Denver to stay at my place tonight so I could search the cabin, but she's determined—"

"She's determined?" Midnight let out a string of oaths. "I'm determined. No more excuses. I want that cabin searched *tonight*."

"And how do you expect me to do that with Denver there?" Pete asked in frustration.

"I've left a prescription in your name at the drug-store."

"Pills?" Pete gasped. "You don't want me to—"

"Kill her?" Midnight groaned. "No. A couple of tablets and she'll sleep like the dead, though. Make sure you don't overdo it or you could kill her." His voice seemed to vibrate with an evil that chilled Pete even in the hot room. "Hit the cabin tonight. And you'd better find that file."

"I told you how Max was. He didn't think like other people. Who knows where he's hidden it, if it even exists?"

"It exists." Midnight sighed. "You realize if Denver finds the file first, we'll have to kill her."

And if anyone could find the file, it would be Denver, Pete thought. She already had her suspicions; it was just a matter of time before she figured it out. "I'll take care of it tonight."

"If you don't—" Midnight paused "—I'll find someone who can."

Pete started to hang up, but Midnight stopped him.

"We have another problem that needs to be taken care of," he said. "It's that kid, Davey Matthews. You know the one who was always hanging around Max's office? I'm afraid he knows too much."

"Just what we need, another murder."

"I'll call you later at the cabin and we can discuss what to do about Davey. He's young and foolish. Young and foolish men have accidents. Put the bozo back on," Midnight said. "Then you'd better get to the drugstore before it closes."

Max Mccallahan's detective agency filled the bottom floor of a small two-story log house on Geyser Street; he had lived in a tiny efficiency apartment upstairs. Denver could never understand why he hadn't married Maggie. He'd spent most of his time over at her place, but refused to give up the apartment because he didn't want people to talk. Well, people were talking now, Denver thought bitterly.

A snow-filled silence hung over the street as she walked past Max's old blue-and-white Oldsmobile station wagon parked out front. She'd forgotten the police had left it there. Like everything else, the car reminded her of her loss. She headed up the unshoveled walk, steeling herself for the memories she knew waited inside, but stopped abruptly. Someone else had already climbed these same steps tonight. There were fresh boot prints in the newly fallen snow—coming and going.

Shadows came to life as the large pines flanking the house swayed and creaked in the wind. Water dripped from the eaves and the old house sighed forlornly under the weight of the wet snowfall.

Denver stopped, fighting to shake off the spooked feeling in her stomach. She suddenly thought of a dozen good reasons why she should come back in the morning. She cursed her lack of courage. After her parents died, Max had brought her to West Yellowstone, offering her a safe place to live so she'd never have to be afraid again. For Max—and for herself—she had to find his murderer or she'd never feel that kind of security here again.

With renewed determination, she ascended the steps, her boot heels thudding across the wooden porch. On the window in the old oak front door a sign was painted in gold letters: McCallahan Investigations. Behind the letters, the drapes were drawn. Nothing moved. She dug for her key, then reached to unlock the door.

But it was already open. The hinges gave a sigh as the door swung into the dark room. With fingers cold and shaking, Denver flipped on the light. She feared what she'd find, but nothing prepared her for this.

File cabinets lay over on their sides, folders sprawled everywhere, their contents crumpled and strewn across the floor. All the drawers on Max's big oak desk were upside down. Even the photographs she'd given him had been pulled from the walls and thrown into the pile of debris.

Denver clung to the doorjamb fighting for breath. Why would anyone do this? For several moments, she just stared. What had the burglar been looking for? No doubt the same thing she was. That was some consolation. Maybe there *was* something to find. Or had been, anyway.

She glanced around the office, wondering if it could still be here. If Max was on a hot case, something explosive, what would he have done with the evidence he'd collected? Good question.

Max had no concept of organization. His files were always a disaster with some filed by first names, others by nicknames, even a few by last names. He had once hired a part-time secretary to straighten them, but when she had gone to lunch, he couldn't find a thing and made such a mess of the file cabinet that she finally gave up and quit.

Denver bent to retrieve a handful of folders from the floor. It would take hours to make any sense out of this mess. And she had to face the probability that any clues Max might have left had already been stolen. Not only that, she might be destroying evidence that could lead Deputy Cline to the culprit who did this, she realized, dropping the files on the edge of Max's desk.

She righted the huge oak office chair and sat down, more certain than ever that Max had left something behind to help her solve his murder. *Think like Max*, she told herself. She put her feet up on the desk and leaned back with her hands behind her head, imitating Max's favorite pose when he was pondering a case.

Where, Max? Where would you put something that would incriminate the person you were after? She surveyed the ceiling lights. Max jotted down everything; that was how he worked through his cases. Usually it was just a lot of scribbles. Sometimes it might be only a few words. Then he filed the notes until he solved the case. If Max was working on a job, there'd be scribbles and there'd be a case file.

And that was what the burglar had been looking for. That had to be it. And the same person was probably spreading those rumors about Max. Muddying the waters. But why bother, with Cline convinced that Max was killed by a hitchhiker for no other reason than robbery?

Denver was so preoccupied that at first she thought she'd imagined the sound. Then it happened again—a floorboard creaked overhead, followed by the scraping sound of wood. It was coming from upstairs in Max's apartment. She froze. Why hadn't it crossed her mind that the burglar could still be in the house?

Carefully she slid her feet off Max's desk and, slipping off her boots, tiptoed to the bottom of the stairs. No sounds, except the thunder of her pulse in her ears. She picked up the nearest object from the floor—the telephone—and unhooked the cord, then, carrying it as a weapon, started up the stairs.

Halfway up, one of the steps creaked under her weight and she stopped, afraid to move. Reason invaded her brain. What was she doing?

Why didn't you think to call Deputy Cline *before* you unplugged the phone, the rational little voice in her head asked.

Nice that you should suggest that *now*, Denver retorted silently as she looked from the disconnected phone in her hand to the creaky steps behind her. And Max used to think she was a little too impetuous. If he could see her now.

She stood on the step, listening. Silence so strong it seemed alive answered her back. She shifted the phone to her right hand and continued up the stairs, willing herself to remain calm, knowing she wouldn't.

At the top of the steps, she cautiously pushed open the door to the apartment, phone ready. When nothing jumped out, she reached in hesitantly and switched on the lights. She expected the apartment to resemble Max's office; she hadn't expected it to be destroyed. An overstuffed chair was upended, the mattress hung off the side of the bed, its guts spilling out on the floor. The contents of all the dresser drawers had been thrown around the room. She hoped the destruction meant that the burglar hadn't found what he was looking for.

She exchanged the phone for a brass lamp base, checked the closet and started to breathe a little more easily. Across the room, a shutter banged softly against the side of the house. That explained the noise she'd heard. No ghosts. No burglars. Just the breeze.

The state of the apartment and Max's office reinforced her theory that Max had left something that would incriminate his killer. All she had to do was figure out what it was and find it before the killer did. If he hadn't already found it.

That was when she noticed the partially closed bathroom door. She headed for it, thinking about what she'd tell Deputy Cline. Surely when he saw this place, he'd have to give up his hitchhiker theory. Reaching into the bathroom, she fumbled for the light switch with her free hand.

Cold fingers clamped over her wrist in a deathlike grip. Denver let out a cry of total terror as she was jerked into the darkened bathroom. She swung the lamp. It connected with something solid and veered off. She heard a male voice swear as the fingers on her wrist let go, and a loud thud followed. Denver retreated, fumbling for the bathroom light switch on her way out, this time with the lamp in her hand ready to swing again.

She found the switch. The bathroom light flashed on. Denver blinked. At first because of the sudden brightness, then out of disbelief. Sitting crosswise in the bathtub swearing and holding his head was none other than J. D. Garrison.

Denver stumbled backward and fell over, tripping

on the overturned chair. She landed on her bottom in a pile of mattress stuffing. J. D. Garrison leaned over her.

"Hello, Denny," he said, offering her a hand. "It's been a long time."

Chapter 4

Denver lay staring up at the man standing over her, unable to move. J.D. J. D. Garrison. After all these years.

She'd envisioned the day he returned thousands of times, always in Technicolor, always with the same basic plot. He'd come riding in like John Wayne, all handsome and charming. He'd beg her to forgive him for not taking her with him, sweep her off her feet, promise his undying love, maybe play a few songs on his guitar. And then she'd tell him to drop dead.

Never would she have imagined it quite like this.

She ignored his offer of help and got to her feet on her own power, dusting herself off. The gesture gave her a few moments to compose herself; J.D. was the last person she'd expected to see in that bathtub.

"What are *you* doing here?" she demanded, her pride as well as her bottom still smarting. Damn. The effect he had on her! Her heart was pounding and not from fear anymore; she felt sixteen again. The feeling made her all the more angry with him.

"It's nice to see you again, too," he said, his smile widening.

She'd practiced at least ten thousand times what she'd say to him if she ever *did* see him again. But nothing came to her lips. He'd changed; he wasn't that lanky young man she remembered. A dark mustache and neatly trimmed beard nearly hid his deep dimples. His eyes, always a blend of moonlight silvers and midnight grays, seemed darker, but there was an older look about them, almost a sadness...

She realized he was holding his head where she'd hit him with the lamp. His gray Stetson dangled from his other hand. "Are you all right?" she asked guiltily.

He nodded and tried to get the hat back on his head over the lump she'd given him. "My head's too hard for most lamps. But the fall into the bathtub I could have done without." As he rubbed his backside, she noticed the flashlight stuck in his belt. "I'm sorry I scared you. I heard a noise and thought the prowler had returned." He grinned.

Prowler indeed. His grin sent her heart racing around in circles. Just what she needed. "So you're back in town," she said, before adding, "you missed Max's funeral and you better have a damned good reason."

He leaned back and laughed. "You had me worried for a moment there. I thought you'd lost that charming way you've always had with words." Those wonderfully deep dimples were now just a hint under the beard, and little wrinkles had been added around his eyes. It didn't matter. He still had that same heart-thumping effect he always had on her.

She frowned and turned away from the look in his eyes. What was it? Affection on his part? Or imagination on hers? Without another word, she hurried down the stairs; she could hear J.D. right behind her.

"Don't you want to hear my damned good reason?" he asked.

"I didn't really expect you'd make it anyway," she said, pulling on her boots. "I figured you were probably busy making a new album or performing for all those fans of yours." Bitterness and hurt crackled from her words and she wished she could bite her tongue. She bent down to pick up files and loose papers from the floor, forgetting all about saving evidence for Cline. "I told Pete not to bother calling you."

"Pete called?" J.D. sounded surprised.

"Don't pretend you didn't get the message." She heard the soft tread of his boots on the floor as he came up behind her.

"Denny, I was so sorry to hear about Max." His voice was soft. So was the touch of his fingers on her shoulders. "I wanted to be at the funeral for you."

She shrugged his hands away and spun on him. "I thought you cared about Max. I thought you cared about—" Tears brimmed in her eyes. She fought the culprits, determined not to cry. She'd shed enough tears for J. D. Garrison. Damned if she'd cry in front of him.

"I do care," he said, lifting her chin to meet her gaze. "I caught the first plane out. But getting to West Yellowstone this time of year is kind of tricky. You might remember the airport's closed until Memorial

Day weekend." He flashed her a sheepish grin that beseeched her to give him a break. "I'm here now, though."

She wished he'd just take her in his arms and hold her, but he didn't, and she stepped back, all the hurt flowing out of her in place of tears. "I'm sure we'll probably read in the tabloids next week just how hard it was for you to get back for the funeral." The tabloids had followed his exploits with one woman after another for years now. "I suppose there'll be flight attendants involved this time."

J.D.'s jaw tensed as he shook his head at her. "I'm surprised you read the tabloids, let alone believe them." He met her gaze and held it as gently as a caress. "Come on, you know me better than that."

Know him? She thought she knew him. She'd shared his dreams. And a lot more. She'd given him her heart. No, she'd given her heart to J. D. Garrison, the boy she had grown up with, not this stranger in designer Western wear.

"Did you find what you were looking for?" he asked, motioning to the mess in the room, probably thinking a little humor would soften her up.

Fat chance. "Don't you remember? This is the way Max liked his office. Everything out where he could find it."

J.D. nodded, his eyes darkening. "Yeah, I remember that about Max." He stood, just staring at her. "You've changed."

Her chin went up instinctively. "I've grown up, if that's what you mean. I'm not a kid anymore."

"I can see that." The look in his eyes blew the devil out of her theory. Those weren't the eyes of a stranger.

She looked away. "I assume you won't be staying long?" she asked, bracing herself for his answer.

He tipped up one of the drawers with his boot toe, and then let it back down gently. "I've taken a room at the Stage Coach Inn for a few days."

She nodded. In a few days he'd be gone again. That old pain gripped her heart. What had she expected? "A few days? And Max's funeral is what brought you home?" She wanted to clarify it for her heart, just in case the silly thing wasn't getting it straight.

"I came home because of you, Denny."

Her head snapped up.

He grinned at her surprise. "I know you, Denver Mc-Callahan. And I know what you're thinking."

"You do?" She let her eyes travel the length of him. If he knew what she was thinking, he'd be blushing.

But when her gaze returned to his silver-eyed one, she realized with a shock that he *did* know what she was thinking. She felt her face flush red-hot and looked away first.

"I'm worried about you," he continued, his voice gentle. "You think I don't know what you're doing here tonight?" She watched him step over a pile of papers on the floor. "You're looking for Max's killer, and if you'd arrived a little earlier, you might have found him."

"I can take care of myself," she said, her chin coming up again.

He smiled. "I don't doubt that for a moment—under normal circumstances." The smile faded. "But Max is dead and someone tore this place apart with a desperation that scares me even if it doesn't you. You could be in a lot of danger."

Danger? She'd just gone up the stairs after a burglar

with only a phone. Her heart pounded harder, her pulse raced faster just being this close to J. D. Garrison. "I have to go." She glanced at her watch, seeing nothing. She had to get away. She couldn't bear spending another minute in the same room with him, wanting to touch him, to feel his arms around her, to kiss those lips. "I promised Pete—" The lie caught in her throat. Who was she kidding? She didn't even know where Pete was.

A shadow flickered across J.D.'s eyes as he turned to look at her. "I guess you and Pete are pretty close?"

She crossed her fingers. "Just like that." It didn't bother her at all to let him think they were more than friends. He frowned. "You've made a lot of…friends yourself," she said, unable to stop herself. "Weren't you engaged to a Hollywood starlet, if I remember right?" Which she did. "And not six months after you left Montana." She glared at him. "Didn't take you long, did it, Garrison?"

His grin was the old J.D.'s. "You haven't called me Garrison since the last time you were mad at me. I've kinda missed it."

"I'll just bet." She edged her way toward the door, trying to put space between them; she felt like an out-of-balance washing machine.

As she passed J.D., he reached out and grabbed her arm. His gaze settled on her, solid as a rock. "Where do you think you're going?"

"I beg your pardon?" She shook off his hold.

"Look at this place, Denny," he said, sweeping an arm out. "What do you think the burglar was looking for?"

"How should I know?" If she knew that, she wouldn't be standing here talking to *him*.

"Then let me ask you this. Do you think he found what he was looking for?"

"No," she said, not sure why she felt so confident that the burglar hadn't.

"So, Denny, where do you think he'll look next?"

She stared at him, all cocky and sure of himself, standing in the middle of the mess in Max's office. But he was right. Why hadn't she thought of it? Because seeing J.D. again had put her mind on a permanent spin cycle.

"You bet," J.D. said. "Your burglar will more than likely head straight for the lake cabin because that's the next logical place to search. He'll probably be waiting for you when you get there." He raised an eyebrow at her. "Unless you aren't going home tonight?"

"I *was* planning to go to the cabin." His gaze narrowed. "Alone."

A grin played at his lips. "I thought you promised Pete—"

Oh, what a tangled web we weave… "I promised… I'd call him when I got home."

He looked pleased to hear that was all there was to it. "Then change your plans and stay in town at the hotel. I'll get you a room and you can call him from there."

She glared at him. "And just let the burglar have the cabin for the night?" No burglar or even a murderer was going to force her out of her home. And no man was going to start running her life—especially when that man was J. D. Garrison. "Guess again."

J.D. let out a long sigh. "Then I'm coming out to the lake with you." She started to argue but he stopped her. "If there's no sign of trouble, I'll just stay for a while."

She relented, seeing how hard that concession was

for him to make. Unfortunately he was right; it made sense that the cabin would be the next place the burglar would hit. "All right."

J.D. held the door open for her. "I'm glad to see you're not as impossibly stubborn as you used to be."

She made a face at him as she swept past. "Don't push your luck, Garrison." She could hear his laugh as he walked to a pale green Ford pickup parked down the street.

Denver climbed into her Jeep and started the engine, thinking how funny life could be. Well, maybe not funny. No, not funny at all.

She made a U-turn and headed toward the lake. A few miles out of town, she glanced in the rearview mirror to see the lights of the pickup right behind her. J.D. was home. Just like in her dreams. Almost. It made her want to laugh. And cry.

"Dammit." J.D. followed Denny out of town, telling himself that it wasn't seeing her again that had him in a tailspin. But he couldn't get over his reaction to her. Or hers to him, he thought with a grimace. The woman he'd seen in Max's office certainly wasn't the girl who'd had a crush on him at sixteen. No, she'd definitely gotten over her infatuation with him.

He tried to concentrate on the problem at hand. The destruction to Max's office and apartment had convinced him of just how much danger Denny was in. But not from Pete. J.D. just didn't believe Pete capable of tearing apart a place like that—let alone murder.

And keeping Denny away from Pete was even more impossible than he'd first thought, now that he knew how Denny felt. About Pete. And about J. D. Garrison.

He smiled ruefully to himself. He'd hoped to charm her as a last resort. Ha. That would be like trying to charm a hungry grizzly bear away from a Big Mac.

As they neared the lake cabin, J.D. realized his only hope would be for Max's killer to be found. And fast.

The lights from Denny's cabin spilled from the windows and shot like laser beams through the pines. "Damn." The burglar had already been there, he thought as he followed Denny up the narrow, snowy driveway.

What if the burglar was still in the cabin ransacking it? Denver slowed, and he knew she must be thinking the same thing. Her headlights lit up a vehicle parked at the edge of the driveway. J.D. stared at Pete's black Chevy pickup. "Double damn." He pulled in behind Denny.

Before he had a chance to get out, Denny walked back to talk to him. He rolled down his window.

"Pete's here," she said, resting her hands on the window frame. "There's no reason for you to stay now. I'll be perfectly safe."

Right. "Then you won't mind if I make sure." He opened the pickup door, and with obvious reluctance, she stepped back.

"You should talk about stubborn," she mumbled as they walked up to the cabin.

A slice of moon peeked through a break in the clouds and splashed the partially thawed lake with thin metallic light. In the crisp night air, he smelled pine and lake water and…smoke. He looked up to see smoke curling up from the chimney. "Looks like Pete built you a fire."

She scowled. Clearly she hadn't expected Pete to be here nor did she seem that happy about it.

"Looks like he made himself at home," J.D. added,

fighting a grin. He heard Denny mumbling under her breath.

The moment they entered the cabin, J.D. smelled peppermint. Denny looked puzzled by the scent, too, as she closed the door behind them. The cabin was as J.D. remembered it. The living room had a fireplace at the entrance and huge glass windows at the other end, looking out on Hebgen Lake. To the left was an adjoining kitchen and down the hall was a bath, small office and laundry room. Max had converted the laundry room into a darkroom before he gave the cabin to Denny, Maggie had told him. Upstairs were two bedrooms along with another bath.

J.D. was glad to see that the place hadn't changed. He was even more delighted to see that it hadn't been ransacked. In fact, everything appeared perfectly normal. Except maybe for the man-size pair of cowboy boots by the front door.

Denver called out a tentative hello. J.D. wasn't sure what he expected. But it wasn't Pete coming out of the kitchen in his stocking feet and carrying a teapot.

"Surprise!" Pete said, then stopped in his tracks as he spotted J.D.

"Surprise," J.D. said. Pete hadn't changed at all; he still had those boyish looks J.D. had always envied. Nor did he look like a murderer, standing there in one of Denny's aprons holding that teapot. Feeling foolish for suspecting Pete, J.D. extended his hand to his former best friend. "How have you been?"

Pete didn't move. Something J.D. couldn't quite read flickered across his face. He quickly covered it with a smile and reached to take J.D.'s hand. "J. D. Garrison. Boy, has it been a long time."

Out of the corner of his eye, J.D. saw Denny frown.

"I guess I should have made more tea?" Pete directed the question to Denny. There were already two cups and saucers on the coffee table in front of the fire. And a single red rose.

How touching, J.D. thought and growled softly to himself. "Yeah, let's have some tea and catch up on old times."

Pete didn't look thrilled by the idea, to put it mildly.

"Not tonight," Denver said. She motioned to the orderly state of the cabin and lowered her voice. "As you can see, I'm in good hands."

"Yeah," J.D. said, unable to come up with a reason not to go. Blurting out that Maggie thought Pete was a murderer didn't seem like a great idea at the moment. And even if Pete were Jack the Ripper, it was doubtful he'd do anything to Denver with J.D. knowing he was there. "If you need me—"

"I have more than enough baby-sitters for one night, thank you." She opened the door for him.

But he still didn't want to leave her there alone with Pete. And not because of Maggie's suspicions. He tried not to think of Pete and Denny in front of the fire, or the single red rose on the coffee table, as Denny closed the door in his face.

He stood for a moment in the dark, lost. The idea of sitting outside the cabin posting guard seemed ridiculous as well as emotionally painful. Denny was right; she didn't need him. He stalked to his pickup, trying to remember something important he'd meant to do at Max's office earlier. All he could see in his mind was that cozy little scene back at the cabin. *What's wrong with you, Garrison? You're acting jealous as hell.* He jerked open his pickup door. *Jealous? What a laugh.* But as he climbed into the cab, he couldn't get Denny out of his mind. Or Pete's damned little tea party for two.

That was when he recalled what had been so important. He'd spotted what looked like a wallet wedged behind the old radiator in Max's apartment. He had started to work it out of the hole when he'd heard what he thought was the burglar returning. Later, when he'd looked up from the bathtub to find Denny standing there…well, he was just lucky he remembered his name.

He turned the pickup toward West Yellowstone and Max's office, promising himself he'd be back within the hour to check on Denver. As he raced toward town, he realized he was humming the same tune over and over again as he drove. With a curse, he recognized the song—"Tea for Two."

Denver turned to find Pete looking a little guilty as he set the pot on the coffee table by the two cups and saucers and the sugar bowl.

"So J.D.'s back, huh?" he asked. "Did he say how long he's staying?"

Exhaustion pulled at her. All she really wanted was to go to bed and sleep.

"I know you said you wanted to be alone and I promise I won't stay long." He brightened. "I made tea."

"Tea?" Max used to make her tea when she couldn't sleep.

Pete sat down and proceeded to pour the tea. Denver had to stifle a smile as she took off her coat and hung it in the closet. The teapot appeared so small and fragile in his hands. She'd bet money this was the first tea he'd ever made.

"I mixed the spiced kind with some other one that sounded good," Pete said, confirming her suspicions. It also explained the peppermint scent. He bent over, the spoon clicking against the china cup as he stirred.

"No sugar for me, please," Denver said, feeling like the visitor. J.D. was right; Pete had certainly made himself at home. She could see that the laundry room door was ajar. She'd closed it before she left for the service, having souped some photos that morning to keep her mind off Max. What had Pete done? Searched every room to make sure Max's killer wasn't here waiting for her? It would have been funny, if he wasn't so determined for her to stay out of Max's murder investigation.

"Oh, a little sugar never hurt anyone," he said, handing her the china cup and saucer, her treasured rose-patterned dishes Max had brought her back from Canada. "Anyway, I'm afraid I put sugar in them both. I hope you don't mind."

She didn't have the heart not to drink the tea after he'd gone to so much trouble—sugar and all. Sitting down across from him, she said, "I looked for you at the party but you'd left."

He grinned sheepishly. "I thought I'd come on out and surprise you. I remembered where Max hid his spare key so…here I am."

Yes, here he was, even though she'd told him she wanted to be alone, she thought resentfully as she got a whiff of the strange brew. The last thing she wanted to do was drink it.

"Do you like it?" Pete asked, sounding hopeful.

The truth was she hadn't even tried it. "It's good." She took a sip; it was too hot to taste, fortunately. The warmth seemed to take away some of the day's pain.

Max was gone. She'd have to learn to accept that. If only she could throw off the memory of J.D. in Max's office. Max's ransacked office. And J.D. grinning at her.

Realizing Pete was waiting for her to drink her tea before he left, she took another sip and burned her tongue. Exhaustion had numbed her muscles and made her feel as if she were sinking into the chair. All she really wanted to do was put this day behind her.

"So J.D. followed you home?" Pete asked.

She saw his jaw tense and remembered the animosity she'd felt between the two of them earlier. "He's like you, worried I might be in some sort of danger."

"Oh, really?"

The phone rang. Pete offered to get it, but Denver was only too anxious to have an excuse not to finish her tea. She put her cup down and went to answer it.

It was Taylor. "Denver?"

She smiled. He always sounded a little embarrassed.

"I was thinking about that trouble you had earlier with Cal. You're all right out there, aren't you?"

Another man worried about her. If only they'd just let her get some rest. "I'm fine," she said, thinking how much Taylor reminded her of Max.

"I gave Cal a ride home but I was afraid he might decide to show up at your cabin. No trouble?"

Denver thought about Max's ransacked office. And J.D. "What kind of trouble could I get in?" She laughed guiltily but didn't want to mention either problem in front of Pete. "No trouble. Pete's here with me."

"Good." He seemed to hesitate. "You know, if you need anything…"

"I know. I appreciate it." She hung up the phone and returned to the coffee table but didn't sit. Pete was in the kitchen washing the teapot. Denver thought of excusing herself, but decided it would be rude not to at least drink some of her tea.

Hurriedly she picked up the cup from the table and drank it down, trying not to gag. When she went to replace the cup in the saucer, though, she realized she'd finished Pete's instead of her own. She was switching the cups when Pete came back into the room. Quickly she handed him the full cup.

"Who was that?" he asked.

"Taylor."

He seemed annoyed that Max's friend had interrupted their little tea party. "What did *he* want?"

"He was just checking on me."

Pete frowned. "It seems I'm only one of a long line of men concerned about your welfare."

She let that pass. "I think I'm going to call it a night," she said with a wide yawn and a stretch.

Pete glanced at Denver's empty cup on the coffee table and smiled. "I can take a hint." He drank his; from the face he made, he didn't like it any better than she had. "I'll just throw a few more logs on the fire and make sure both doors are locked before I leave."

Denver started up the spiral log stairs to her bedroom. "Good night, Mother Hen."

Pete looked sad to see her go. "Good night, Denver. Sleep well."

J.D. parked in the darkness of a lodgepole pine outside Max's office. Denny had locked the front door, but thanks to the burglar, all he had to do was put his shoulder against the old door and it fell open. He took the stairs two at a time to Max's apartment. Images of

Denny in the middle of the mess made him smile. He rubbed the lump on his head in memory. Hadn't he always known she'd grow into a beautiful, strong, determined woman with a helluva right-handed swing?

He went to the old radiator. Sure enough, there was something down there. He picked up a thin bent curtain rod and worked to pry what looked like a wallet from the radiator's steel jaws.

The wallet tumbled out onto the floor. He picked it up and opened the worn leather. Max's face looked up at him from a Montana driver's license. J.D. thumbed through the rest of the contents. There was no doubt it was Max's wallet. The question was: how did it get behind the radiator? J.D. shook his head, remembering what Max had been like. Absentminded about day-to-day things.

He took the wallet downstairs and dumped out the contents on Max's desk. There wasn't much—a few receipts, some business cards he'd picked up, Denny's graduation photo, a yellowed, dog-eared photo of Denny and her parents, forty dollars in cash and a MasterCard.

J.D. stared at Denny's photo for a moment, realizing how many years he'd missed by leaving. Then he looked at the picture of Denny and her parents. She couldn't have been more than two at the time. Denny's father, Timothy McCallahan wore his police uniform, and the threesome stood on the steps of the Billings Police Department. Timothy looked like Max, only younger. Denny had his grin. Her mother was the spitting image of Denny, the same auburn hair, same smattering of freckles and identical intense pale blue-green eyes.

J.D. stared at the happy family, unable to accept the fact that someone had killed Denver's parents. Somehow Denny had escaped being hit in the gunfire. He hoped that same luck held for her now.

It took him a moment to realize what finding the wallet meant. Maggie's strongest evidence against Pete was the photograph from Max's wallet because she assumed Max had the wallet *and* the photo on him the day he was killed.

If the wallet was behind the radiator the day of the murder, then Pete didn't get the photograph at the murder scene. But the fact that Pete even had the photo made him look suspicious. How had he gotten the photo and why had he taken it?

J.D. just hoped there might be a clue to Max's murder among the receipts, scraps of paper and business cards as he stuck the wallet inside his jacket pocket. Maybe Denny could make some sense of it.

On the way out, he turned off the lights and closed the door. As he stepped into the darkness of the porch, he felt a chill on the back of his neck.

Denver.

A premonition swept over him. He had to get to her; she needed him. As he hurried across the porch, he caught the slight movement of something in the night. He turned, but too late. An object glistened in the streetlight for an instant, and then there was only pain and darkness.

Chapter 5

J.D. woke, cold and confused. He glanced around, surprised to find himself on Max's office porch. He was even more surprised to find he was alive. His head ached and he couldn't remember a thing. Except Denny. He could see the light in her auburn hair, hear the sweet sound of her voice. And...feel the lamp as she knocked him into the bathtub. He groaned. It was all starting to come back.

Rubbing the bump on the side of his head, he tried to get up. A wave of nausea hit him and forced him back down. Where was Denny now?

As he stumbled to his feet, bits and pieces of the night began to return, ending with him leaving Denver at the cabin with Pete. He swore—and reached into his coat. Max's wallet was gone.

Except for his pickup parked at the curb, the street

was empty. His watch read 3:52 a.m. Damn. One thing was for sure. Investigating Max's murder was turning out to be more dangerous than he'd realized—than he was sure Denny realized. He had to protect her. He smiled at the humor in that; he wasn't even doing a very good job of taking care of himself. But now more than ever, he feared for Denny's safety.

As he headed for the lake cabin, he wished he could come up with a logical explanation for waking Denny and Pete at this time of the night. Instead he knew he was about to make a first-class fool of himself. At least it was something he was good at. But he had to make sure Denny was safe. A vague uneasiness in the pit of his stomach warned him she wasn't.

In the dream, Denver skipped through the bank door ahead of her parents, singing the song her mother had taught her. The words died on her lips; her feet faltered and stopped. Everyone inside the bank lay on the floor on their stomachs. A silence hung in the air that she only recognized as something wrong. As she turned and ran back to her parents, she saw the other uniformed policeman on the floor. Her father's hand came down on her shoulder hard. He shoved her. She fell, sliding into the leg of an office desk. She heard her mother scream. Then the room exploded.

The phone rang.

Don't answer it, her father said in the dream. He wore his police uniform and he was smiling at her. The phone rang again. Don't answer it unless you want to know the truth. But as she looked at him she already knew—

Denver sat up, drenched with sweat. The phone rang again. For a moment, she couldn't remember where she was. Then familiar objects took shape as her eyes adjusted to the dark. The phone rang again. She fumbled for it. "Hello?"

Silence. Heavy and dark as the night. The dream clung to her. Alive. Real.

"Hello?" Denver shivered. Just nerves. And that damned dream. "Is anyone there?"

"Denver McCallahan?" a voice whispered.

The dream had left her with an ominous feeling. She tried to shake it off. "Yes?"

"I have information about your uncle."

"Who is this?" The voice sounded familiar. She sat up straighter and rubbed her hand over her face. The dream and the last remnants of sleep still hovered around her like a musical note suspended in the air. "You know something about Max's murder?" Her head started to clear a little. It was just a crank call. "If you know anything, why haven't you gone to Deputy Cline?"

The caller coughed. "You'll know when you meet me at Horse Butte Lookout under the fire tower. But hurry."

Now fully awake, Denver clutched the phone. "You can't expect me to come to an abandoned fire tower *now*." The voice sounded even more familiar; if only she could keep the person talking.

"Look, if he finds out I called you, I'm dead meat." The caller sounded genuinely frightened. "The fire tower. Hurry. I won't wait."

"Please just tell me—"

But he'd already hung up.

"Damn."

Denver stared at the receiver in her hand. Then at the clock beside her bed. It read 4:05 a.m. She hung up the phone and hurriedly pulled on warm clothes. The fear in the caller's voice made her think he really might know who murdered Max. That hope ricocheted around in her head, forcing out everything else. If he really knew...

Denver opened her bedroom door and started down the stairs. Her heart thudded. Someone was downstairs. She listened, trying to recognize the noise floating up from the living room. It sounded like—Cautiously she crept down the stairs and stopped, staring in surprise.

The fire had burned down to smoldering embers. The warm sheen from the firebox radiated over the living room, bathing the sleeping Pete Williams in a reddish wash. Sprawled across the couch, Pete snored loudly.

Denver shook him gently; he didn't stir. She tried again, a little more forcefully. He groaned and started snoring again. Well, she'd tried, she told herself as she covered him with the quilt from the back of the couch. She knew he would have tried to stop her from going, anyway.

Hastily she wrote him a note—"Gone to Horse Butte Fire Tower"—and propped it against his teacup. Trying to protect her must have worn him out, she thought with a laugh as she closed the front door behind her. Just as she reached her Jeep, an arm grabbed her from the darkness. Only someone's hurried words stopped the scream on her lips.

"Take it easy, slugger," J.D. said. "It's only me. You don't have a lamp with you, do you?"

"What are you doing?" Denver demanded in a hushed tone as he released her. "Trying to scare me to death a second time?" As her eyes adjusted to the darkness, she could see his pickup parked in the trees.

"I think the question is where are we going at this hour of the night? And why are we whispering?"

Denver planted her hands on her hips. "I thought you left."

"I did." He gave her an embarrassed shrug. "I came back. I had a feeling you might need me."

She liked the sound of that. And, although she'd never admit it to him, she was glad he was there.

"Maybe I'm psychic when it comes to you." He grinned. "Or maybe I just know you."

She mugged a face at him. "Well, as you can see, I'm fine." She reached for the Jeep's door handle. J.D.'s gloved hand covered hers.

"'Fine' isn't going for a drive at four in the morning, Denny. What's going on?" He glanced at Pete's pickup. "Where's Pete?"

Out like a bad light bulb, she thought. "I don't have time to argue—"

From inside the cabin, the phone rang. Denver started to run back to answer it in case it was her mysterious caller changing his mind. But it stopped on the third ring. Maybe it had been the caller, checking to see if she'd left yet.

She turned to find J.D. already in the Jeep. He grinned at her. Maybe it was the grin. Or the late hour. Or just plain common sense. She might need him when she got to the fire tower. But at that moment, she didn't mind the idea of the two of them in the close confines of the Jeep together.

As Denver backed down the driveway and started up the narrow road through the pines, she realized she hadn't thought about where her caller had phoned from. There was no telephone near the fire tower. She'd just assumed he was calling from West Yellowstone, but he wouldn't be able to reach the tower quickly if he'd phoned from town. No, he either had to call from a private residence near the lake, or—

As she tore up the road, she remembered the phone booth at Rainbow Point Campground.

"Where exactly are we going in such a hurry?" J.D. asked. Denver smiled as she took a corner in a spray of snow, ice and gravel, and he fumbled to buckle up his seat belt.

"Horse Butte Fire Tower."

His gaze warmed the side of her face. "Really?"

She'd made the mistake of kissing him at the tower the day he said he was leaving. She'd foolishly thought one kiss would change his mind. She shot him a look. "I can promise you you're not going to get as lucky as you did the last time." She couldn't believe she'd said that.

To her surprise, he laughed. "That's too bad."

But she could feel him studying her, and when she glanced over at him, she saw what could have been regret in his gray eyes. Probably just lack of sleep, she assured herself as she concentrated on the next curve, waiting for the campground phone booth to come into view. As she came around the corner, her foot pulled off the gas pedal unconsciously.

The phone booth stood in the darkened pines, door closed. The overhead light glowed inside. She stared at it half expecting someone to materialize inside it. The pines swayed in the wind. The booth stood empty. Had that been where he called from?

"I think you'd better tell me what's going on," J.D. said, frowning at her as she hit the gas again and barreled past the campground. Denver glanced back into the darkness, then took a sharp curve on the snowy, narrow road with the familiarity of someone who'd driven it for years. J.D. hung on. "Come on, Denny, I'm sure you have a good reason for trying to kill us. I'd feel better, though, if I knew it *before* the wreck."

She smiled. "You were the one who insisted on coming along."

"So true."

Freewheeling around the next curve, Denver shot down a straightaway and looked back. No headlights. "I got a call tonight from what sounded like a man. He claimed he knows something about Max's murder. He told me to meet him at the fire tower."

"I'm sorry I asked." J.D. let out a breath after Denver successfully maneuvered the Jeep around another sharp curve in the road. "Let me ask you this—are you completely crazy?"

Denver looked over at him for just a second, then back at the road. Yes, she'd been crazy once. Crazy in love. Then just plain crazy when she realized J.D. had walked out of her life and not even looked back. Meeting a possible murderer in the middle of the night was nothing compared to that.

"I know it probably sounds foolhardy to you," she said.

J.D. let out a laugh. "No, it sounds suicidal to me. Have you considered you might be driving right into a trap?"

Why had this made a lot more sense back at the cabin when she was half-asleep? A sudden chill raced up her spine and the first stirrings of real fear made the Jeep seem even colder inside.

The dark pines that lined both sides of the road blurred by blacker than the night. Occasionally the moon broke free of the clouds to lighten the slit of sky where the road made a path through the trees. Her headlights flickered down the long, narrow tunnel of a road.

Behind her, darkness fought the silver-slick reflection of the snow hunkered among the pines.

"If you wanted to kill someone, can you think of a better place than an abandoned fire tower?" J.D. asked.

"No." She reached over to bang on the heater lever; the darned thing wasn't even putting out *cold* air. When she looked up, she saw the reflection of a large mud puddle dead ahead. She tried to avoid it and plowed through a pile of deep slush instead. The windshield fogged over. Hurriedly she rolled down her window. As she wiped a spot clear on the glass with her mitten, she heard what sounded like another vehicle close behind her. Her caller? Or just a reverberation in the trees?

"What's wrong?" J.D. asked, glancing over his shoulder.

"I think we're being followed."

"Great."

Not slowing down, Denver leaned down to rummage under her seat.

"What now?" J.D. asked.

"You don't happen to have a weapon on you, do you?"

"I'm a guitar player, Denny, not a gunslinger."

She dug blindly until she felt the screwdriver, then pulled it out and held it up to the lights from the dash.

"Get serious," J.D. said.

One thought of Max stabbed to death and she tossed the screwdriver back under the seat. She reached under again, the Jeep sliding dangerously around a curve, and pulled out a wrench. It was just a small crescent but it was better than nothing. She handed it to J.D. He groaned.

"Is there any way I can talk you out of this?" he asked as they neared the fire-tower turnoff.

She leveled a look at him.

"I didn't think so."

At the bottom of Horse Butte, Denver took one look at the snowy road zigzagging up into the darkness and shifted into four-wheel drive for the climb. Half a dozen tracks etched the mud and melting snowdrifts, giving little indication as to the last vehicle to climb the single-lane switchbacks up the mountain, or when. Her caller couldn't have picked a more remote spot. Denver glanced down at her wrist. Her watch read 4:19. She hoped she wasn't too late.

A shiver of dread ran through her, followed quickly by growing fear as she began the climb up the mountain. J.D. was right; this was crazy. She rolled down her window to listen. Nothing. If someone had been following them, they weren't anymore.

J.D. glanced back at the darkness. "Only a lunatic would have tried to keep up with you on that road without lights."

"Or someone who knows the road as well as I do."

A gust of wind slammed against the side of the car, rocking the Jeep. In the distance, the wind whirled snow across the frozen surface of Hebgen Lake in the faint moonlight. At the thawed edge of the ice, waves slapped the deserted shore. Air crept in through the cracks around the car door. Denver shivered.

"You suspect you know the caller?" J.D. asked.

Denver nodded as she maneuvered the car up the first of the switchbacks, mud and snow flying. "I think Max's *killer* is someone I know."

J.D. stared at her in shocked surprise.

"Max was stabbed. Cline thinks he got too relaxed around the hitchhiker."

"But you don't."

"Max was too smart for that. I think he knew and trusted the person who killed him." She met J.D.'s gaze for an instant. In the cloudy darkness, his eyes were silver, his beard black as the night. He was more handsome than she remembered.

"And you're afraid you know, and trust, this person, as well?"

Denver nodded and slowed a little as a cloud covered the moon and darkness dropped over the mountaintop. "I'm not sure this is such a good idea."

J.D. laughed, throwing his head back. "I can't believe it. You're actually admitting that we'd be damned fools to come up here in the middle of the night to meet someone who just might be a murderer?"

She frowned at him.

"Well, it's too late to call Cline," J.D. said softly. "And too late to turn around." He motioned to the single-lane road. They wouldn't be able to turn around now until they reached the shortcut fork almost at the top of the mountain. "But once we get up there, I doubt I can get you to leave if you really believe this caller knows something, right?"

She glanced over at him. "You know me better than I thought you did."

"Yeah. And this won't be the first time you and I were fools at this particular fire tower."

She smiled at him. "And we always have our wrench if there's trouble, right?"

J.D. held his breath. He'd done some crazy things in his life; they were nothing compared to this. His heart contracted with each switchback as Denny maneuvered the Jeep up the mountainside. He recognized her apparent calm for what it really was: bravado. She had to be as scared as he was. He couldn't shake the feeling that they were driving into a trap.

And how did Pete fit into this? "Where did you say Pete was?"

"Asleep on my couch," she said matter-of-factly.

"Oh." J.D. touched the lumps on his head tenderly. It had been a long day. While he was glad to hear that Pete was on the couch, he wondered why she hadn't awakened him. Maybe Pete and Denny weren't as close as she was letting on, he thought with a grin. That was the only explanation he could come up with. And it was one he rather liked.

He stared up at Horse Butte. What if someone really knew who had killed Max and would be waiting for them? He let his gaze return to Denny. Then he'd have no reason to stay in West, no reason to hang around this woman. Her hair, dark waves of polished copper, hung free around her shoulders. He imagined the feel of his fingers buried in it.

The image came so sharply and painfully he closed his eyes against it. But it wouldn't go away. Instead, he could see her beside the lake in summer, the sun dying behind Lionshead Mountain, its golden rays spilling over Denny's skin like warm water...his fingers following the path of the sun. He moaned softly and opened his eyes to find Denny staring at him.

"My driving isn't *that* bad," Denver said as she swerved to miss a rock in the middle of the road. The Jeep started to slide in the mud toward the drop-off and the gaping darkness below. The car slipped toward the abyss. She could sense the chasm coming up at her side.

"Denny," she heard J.D. whisper. His hand touched

her thigh. And just when she thought they were going over the side, the car stopped.

"Wanna drive?" she asked, a little breathless.

"I thought you'd never ask."

By the time they reached the fork in the road, Denver had stopped trembling a little. And J.D. wasn't holding on to the steering wheel with white knuckles anymore. The right fork of the road went on up to the fire tower; the left dropped down the far side of the mountain, a shortcut back to the lake cabins. J.D. turned the Jeep up the fire-tower road.

"Wanna change your mind?" he asked.

She shook her head.

"Just checking."

Denver looked at her watch. Four thirty-three. "I hope we're not too late." J.D. didn't answer, and when she looked over at him, he was staring at the fire tower silhouetted in black against the night.

The Jeep's headlights shone on the wooden legs of the tower as he made a sweep of the mountaintop. Only a few wind-warped trees, an old outhouse and the fire tower itself shared the mountain with them. The parking lot was empty with only a few snowdrifts melting at the edge of the road.

J.D. turned the Jeep around and parked facing back down the mountain so they'd be able to see approaching headlights. Only a hint of the lake lay in the blackness beyond. The wind howled across the top of the mountain. An awkward silence grew between them.

"I'm sorry about the last time we were here," J.D. finally said, sounding as young and unsure of himself as he had nine years ago.

"It was just a silly girl thing." Right. She could still

remember every moment, including J.D. telling her he was leaving. The words didn't even register because he'd touched her cheek with his fingers. Her heart had pounded so loudly she didn't hear half of what he'd said. Instead she'd blurted out how she loved him, would always love him. And, impulsively, she'd stood on tiptoes and kissed him. "I got over it."

"Yeah, I noticed."

She took a breath and let it out slowly. "I always knew you'd have to leave one day because of your career. I just had this crazy idea that you'd take me with you."

"You know I couldn't have done that. You were only sixteen. Max would have had my head." His tone softened. "Anyway, all I could think about back then was my music. And you were just a kid who couldn't possibly know what she was saying. I mean offering me your heart—"

"Let's not talk about it," she interrupted. It had been bad enough nine years ago; she didn't need him reminding her how she'd thrown herself at him. "What are you *really* doing here?" she asked.

"Here?" He looked up at the fire tower. "I wish I knew."

"Not here. *Here* in West Yellowstone." She turned on the bench seat to face him. She'd thought it would be different, the two of them on this mountaintop again. It wasn't. She wasn't a kid anymore, but she still wanted this man. Damn him. "What are you doing here with me right now? And don't give me that line about your being worried about me."

J.D. smiled. "I wish you'd just say what you think for

once, Denny." His eyes darkened. "I'm here because I can't let you go after Max's murderer alone."

She stared at him. "Does that mean you're going to help me—or try to stop me?"

"I'd rather talk you out of it—" he held up his hand before she could protest "—but since I know that would be impossible, I guess I'm going to...help you."

She hated herself for being suspicious. "Why do you want to help me after all these years?"

"Let's just say I owe it to Max."

"Oh." Her heart whispered, I told you so. And the wall she'd built around it called for reinforcements. "What makes you think I want your help?"

He laughed. It was a wonderful sound that made her smile. "You're something else, Denver McCallahan. Most women would be anxious for any assistance. Even mine."

"I guess I'm not most women."

His gaze met hers and held it. "No, Denny, I'm beginning to realize that."

He said her name with an intimacy that rattled her. But he seemed serious and it wasn't like anyone else was offering. "If you mean it, then here's the deal," she said, still studying him intently. "No logical arguments. And no trying to protect me from myself."

He grinned and pulled off his glove. "You drive a hard bargain, but you've got yourself a deal," he said, extending his hand.

Reluctantly, Denver pulled off her glove and took his hand. It was warm and soft, but strong. She suspected it would be the same feeling in his arms.

"With a little luck, maybe it will all be over tonight," she said quietly, the memory of his touch still making her hand tingle. If she cared anything about her heart, she had better hope this was over soon. Spending time with J. D. Garrison could definitely be harmful to her health.

J.D. followed her gaze down the mountain. He couldn't believe he'd agreed to help her find Max's murderer. He blamed the late night, his growing exhaustion, the nearness of Denny. But what choice did he have? It was the only way he could stay close to her, the only way he had any chance of protecting her.

Stop deluding yourself, Garrison. You're looking forward to spending time with her. He smiled to himself. While he wanted Max's killer caught soon for Denny's sake, he didn't mind staying around for a while, staying around her. She intrigued him in a way no other woman ever had.

Overhead, the tower swayed in the wind; the clouds ate up the starlight as quickly as it appeared. A light flashed in the distance. J.D. sat up, staring down the mountain. It took him a moment to realize the lights he'd seen were headlights and they were coming up the mountain road. He watched the vehicle inch up the mountainside, then looked over at Denny. He wanted to take her in his arms and hold her, but the look in her eyes warned him that would be a mistake. She didn't trust him anymore.

"Even if this turns out to be nothing, we're going to find Max's killer," he whispered. "Together."

She didn't look convinced. And he wondered what it would take to make her believe in him again. For some reason he couldn't understand, he wanted that more than he'd wanted anything in his life—even his music.

The headlights neared the top of the mountain. J.D.

looked at the lights without seeing them, as he realized it could be Pete Williams coming up that road. As the car came around the second-to-last switchback, he knew he'd do whatever had to be done to protect Denny. No matter who the killer turned out to be.

Then his heart stopped in midbeat as a second set of lights flashed on from the shortcut road. And in the time it took him to take a breath, the second vehicle leaped directly into the path of the oncoming car. The car veered to the left, away from the sudden bright lights, and dropped over the abrupt edge of the road.

"Oh, my God," J.D. breathed. He heard Denver cry out beside him as the car cartwheeled like a toy down the mountainside, its headlights rotating in the darkness.

J.D. jumped from the Jeep and ran to the edge of the road. The second vehicle sped back up the cutoff road, into the twisted pines and disappeared from view. J.D. stared after it for a moment, then looked down to where the car lay at the bottom of the mountainside, its headlights slicing up through the darkness at a frightening angle.

Beside him, Denver began to cry.

Chapter 6

Dawn came with a bloodred sun over Horse Butte Fire Tower. Denver stood huddled in the scratchy wool blanket J.D. had found in the back of the Jeep, his arm around her, warm and reassuring. She couldn't remember J.D. leaving to go to the pay phone at Rainbow Point to call Sheriff's Deputy Cline or him returning to Horse Butte to wait with her for Cline to arrive with the ambulance and wrecker. But the memory of the car being forced off the road kept coming back, a slow-motion nightmare, and the sound of the ambulance wailing into the last of night still clung in the air.

"It's hard to believe," Cline said as he looked back up at the mountain. "You'd think a fall like that would have killed him. Damned lucky kid. Course if he comes to, he's in a pile of trouble."

"What do you mean?" Denver asked.

"Car theft. Not to mention no driver's license."

"He stole the car?" she asked in surprise.

Cline grinned. "Stole it from behind the Elkhorn Café. Probably just forgot to mention to the cook who owns it that he was taking it." The deputy flipped through his notebook. "Okay, let me get this straight. You don't find it strange that a fifteen-year-old kid calls you in the middle of the night and tells you to meet him out here?"

"We've already been over this," J.D. interjected.

Cline ignored him. "And you say you didn't know who it was until you saw him."

"The voice sounded familiar. Then when I saw Davey—" Denver stopped, remembering the horror of finding the boy in the crumpled car. "When I saw him, I realized it was his voice I'd heard on the phone."

Cline smirked at her. "And rather than call me, you decided to meet the kid yourself?"

"The voice on the phone said he wouldn't wait long. All I was thinking about was getting here as quickly as possible. You probably couldn't have gotten here in time anyway."

Cline smiled coldly. "But wouldn't it have been nice if you'd have let me try?"

Denver stomped her feet, trying to warm them, and glanced over at J.D. He looked sick, as if what he'd witnessed last night had hurt something critical inside him. "All I can tell you is that someone tried to murder Davey Matthews. They came out of the shortcut road and forced him off the mountain."

"Now why would anyone want to hurt a high school dropout working as a dishwasher at the Elkhorn Café?

Except maybe the cook whose car he stole," Cline added.

Denver took a calming breath. "Davey told me on the phone that if someone found out he'd called me, that person would try to kill him."

"Someone?" the deputy asked.

She pulled the blanket more closely around her. She was cold and tired, and she didn't want to deal with Cline. Whoever that someone was, he'd stopped Davey from talking to her. Now Davey was unconscious and Denver knew no more than she had yesterday at Max's funeral. "Davey called him a 'he.' Isn't it obvious to you that Davey knew something and that someone tried to keep him from telling me what it was?"

Cline frowned. "How long have you known Davey Matthews?"

She sighed. "I don't really *know* him. He did odd jobs for my uncle. Davey wanted to be a private investigator. Max was trying to get him to go back to high school and graduate. He also used to hang around the band some."

She called up a blurry picture of Davey in her memory: a boy in his teens with large brown eyes and stringy, long brown hair. She immediately felt guilty because she'd never paid much attention to him. Then she remembered him the way he looked when she and J.D. had found him at the bottom of the mountain. At first, she'd thought he was dead. She shivered despite the wool blanket she clutched around her. "I haven't seen him in months."

"What band? The Montana Country Club band?" Cline asked.

Denver nodded. A chill ran through her as she watched the wrecker operator hook onto the demolished car. "Davey would hang around asking questions about drums, guitars, sound systems." She glanced up to find J.D. studying her. He seemed surprised by something she'd said.

The deputy stopped scribbling in his notebook to give each of them a searching glance. "Isn't that the band you started, Garrison?"

"Pete and J.D. started the band," Denver said quickly. "About ten years ago. Pete kept it going when J.D. left."

Cline rubbed his chin. "What happened? You two have a falling-out over something?" He shifted his gaze from J.D. to Denver; a smile played at his lips. "Or over someone?"

"Could we get this over with? It's cold out here," J.D. said.

Cline grinned at Denver but directed his question to J.D. "Your timing's interesting, Garrison. What was it you said brought you *back* to West?"

"Business." J.D.'s gaze narrowed. Denver could feel the heat of anger coming from him. "*Personal* business."

Cline cocked an eyebrow at him. "I'll bet. And how was it you just happened along tonight when you did?"

"I had stopped by Denver's—"

"At four in the morning?" Cline interrupted.

"I was worried about her," J.D. said, his voice deadly soft.

"Worried?"

J.D. nodded.

"And with good reason, it appears," Cline said, slamming his notebook shut.

"When will I be able to see Davey?" Denver asked.

Cline scowled at her. "This is sheriff's department

business now. But I wouldn't put much hope in Davey knowing anything about your uncle's death."

"I guess we won't know until Davey comes to," J.D. said tightly.

"If he does." Cline shoved the notebook into his pocket. "I've got some forms for the two of you to fill out."

"We'll meet you at the office," J.D. said.

Cline seemed about to say something, but apparently stopped himself. He frowned at J.D. "Make sure you do that."

Pete woke to the sound of the phone ringing. He sat up on the couch and immediately grabbed his head. "Damn." He looked around, surprised to find himself not in his apartment but in Denver's cabin. The phone rang again. He stumbled after the sound, confused, head aching. It felt like he had a ferocious hangover, but the last thing he could remember drinking was that awful tea… "Hello?"

"You blew it." The words were little more than a harsh breath but Pete recognized the synthesized voice right away. Midnight. "Your precious Denver could be dead right now."

Panic cramped his stomach. "Denver? What's happened to her?" He glanced up the stairs, realizing that if she were here, she'd have answered the phone. "Where's Denver? Is she all right?"

"*She's* fine. But what the hell happened to you last night?" Midnight demanded.

Pete rubbed his hand over his face, trying to recall. The pills. And the tea. Something clanged, and Pete realized that Midnight was calling from a phone booth. "I…guess the teacups got…switched."

Midnight let out an oath. "And just how did that happen?"

Pete didn't have a clue. He'd been so sure Denver wasn't on to him. "I don't know. But I won't mess up again. You have my word on that."

"Your word?" Midnight laughed. "I have your *life* on that."

So true. "What did you mean, Denver could be dead?"

"Take a look at your pickup."

Pete stepped to the door. He swallowed hard. "It's covered with mud." Mud? The West Yellowstone basin was miles of coarse obsidian sand. Where could he have gotten mud on his truck?

Midnight chuckled. "Don't remember going to Horse Butte last night?"

"Horse Butte?" He rubbed his temples. How many pills had he put in that damned tea anyway? "I couldn't have driven up to Horse Butte last night." But obviously his pickup had.

"I would suggest you wash it before anyone sees it," Midnight said.

"Wash it?" Pete tried to shake off the effect of the pills. His life depended on it, and even drugged, he was smart enough to know that. "Don't tell me you woke me up at this time of the morning to tell me to wash my truck?"

"The question you should be asking is how it got muddy."

Pete stared at his pickup as the puzzling question

wove its way into his hurting head. "How *did* it get muddy?"

Midnight laughed. "You'll find out soon enough." He hung up.

Pete stared at the phone for a moment, then stumbled to the door and pulled on his boots, feeling sick. What the hell *had* happened last night? He had a feeling he didn't want to know.

The phone rang as he was shrugging on his coat. Pete hurried to it, thinking it might be Denver.

"Pete Williams?" a female voice asked.

"Yes." He held his breath.

"This is Helen, the dispatcher at the sheriff's office. Deputy Cline asked me to call you. He said to tell you, and I quote, 'Your girlfriend is on her way to the sheriff's office with J. D. Garrison and maybe you'd better get your butt down there.'"

"What's this all about?" Pete asked, his heart lodged in his throat. Why would Denver and J.D. be on their way to the sheriff's office this time of the morning, together, when the last time he saw her she was headed up to bed alone?

"There was an accident on Horse Butte last night."

Pete darted a look at his pickup. "Horse Butte?" His heart pounded. "Was anyone hurt?"

"I really can't tell you, but I'm sure Deputy Cline will fill you in when you get here."

"I'm sure," Pete said and hung up, his gaze never leaving the muddy pickup. Horse Butte. Looking outside, he could see that Denver's Jeep was gone, but J.D.'s pickup stood back in the pines, mud free.

"What the hell's going on?" he said to the empty

cabin. All he knew for sure was that he had to wash his truck before he went to the sheriff's office.

J.D. seemed lost in thought all the way into town. Denver didn't mind. She didn't want to talk anyway; she kept turning over Cline's questions in her mind. By the time they'd reached the sheriff's office, some of the shock had worn off, making things seem a little clearer to her.

The dispatcher sent them into Cline's office to wait for him. After a good while, the deputy sheriff came in, eating a big gooey doughnut and slurping a giant-sized cup of coffee.

"Why don't you believe someone tried to keep Davey from talking to me?" Denver asked him before he could sit down.

He shoved the last of the doughnut into his mouth and made a place on his desk for the coffee. "Not a very surefire way to shut somebody up permanently, wouldn't you say?" He sat down; the office chair groaned under his weight.

"I told you, the vehicle came off the shortcut road from the far side of Horse Butte. From the angle it came at Davey, his immediate reaction would have been to go to the edge," Denver said.

"She's right," J.D. cut in. "Even an experienced driver might have done the same thing at that spot on the road."

Cline shrugged as he began riffling through a stack of papers on his desk. "Maybe. But let's look at this reasonably. Davey Matthews was driving up the mountain probably to extort money from Miss McCallahan. He'd just stolen a car. And it was pretty dark and spooky out. Then all of a sudden another car appears on the road in front of him. It's no wonder he overreacted."

"We don't know for a fact that Davey planned to extort money from Denver," J.D. reminded him.

"Nor do we know for a fact that the other vehicle purposely tried to run Davey off the road," Cline said, slamming his hand down on his desk. "What we do know is that Davey Matthews is a dropout, a small-time car thief and—"

"I know what I saw," Denver interrupted. And what she knew in her heart. Davey had come up the mountain to tell her who'd killed her uncle. And if Max had trusted Davey to run errands for him, the kid was all right. "I witnessed an attempted murder."

Cline met her gaze. "You witnessed an unfortunate accident." His tone softened. "Look, it's probably only natural that you'd start seeing attempted murders at every turn after what happened to your uncle."

"I am not a hysterical woman," she said, trying to control her anger. "It was four in the morning. Don't you think it odd that another vehicle was even up there, let alone that it used the shortcut road and took off again the same way?"

Cline shook his head. "You both grew up here. I don't have to tell you about the keggers at the old fire tower."

"A kegger this time of year?" J.D. demanded. "And if it was an accident, why didn't the other car stop?"

Cline made a face. "Probably another kid like Davey who wasn't supposed to be up there at that hour and got scared."

Denver stared at him. "Maybe we should contact the sheriff in Bozeman and see what he thinks."

Cline leaned back, folded his hands over his stomach and let out a long sigh. Then his face tightened with anger. "Let's not blow this out of proportion. You were sitting in the dark on top of a mountain with your… friend here." His eyes narrowed. "Maybe you weren't paying a lot of attention at the time, you know what I mean, missy?"

She felt heat radiating from her anger. "It's Denver. Or Ms. McCallahan. Not missy. And I'm sick of your chauvinistic, simpleminded—" She felt J.D.'s hand on her arm.

"Cline, I'd like to talk to you in private," J.D. said.

Cline had his mouth open about to say something to Denver. He looked from Denver to J.D. and back again. "I'd watch my step, *Ms.* McCallahan." He turned to J.D. "And it's *Deputy* Cline to you, Mr. Garrison."

J.D. tipped his hat and followed the deputy into a small room at the back of the sheriff's office.

"You got a problem?" he asked.

J.D. closed the door. "Several. But the only one that concerns you is what I saw at the fire tower last night."

Cline rubbed his jaw. "I already heard this story."

"No, you haven't." J.D. hesitated, wondering if Cline was just a fool or if he could be trusted. "When I saw the lights coming out of the cutoff road, I ran to the edge of the mountainside. I recognized the rig."

Cline chewed at his cheek, his eyes bright with interest. "Why didn't you mention this before?"

"It was Pete Williams's black Chevy pickup. The same one I saw him drive away in from Max's burial service yesterday."

Cline's mouth sagged and he swore loudly. "You don't expect me to believe that?" The deputy pushed past him, started to open the door, then stopped. "I know there's bad blood between the two of you and I know why." He shot a look into the outer office at Denver. "But you aren't going to use me to settle any old scores, Garrison. There are a lot of black Chevy pickups around."

J.D. shook his head. "This one had the fancy running lights Pete had put on. And the matching camper shell."

Cline swore again. "There are probably other trucks like that around. I know Pete Williams. And his family."

"You knew my family," J.D. said, anger building in him like one of the geysers in the park. "Aren't you going to look into what I've told you?"

"I don't have to," Cline said, reaching for the doorknob again. "I know for a fact where Pete Williams was last night. Miss McCallahan is his alibi." Cline grinned. "She said she left him sleeping at her cabin."

"For how long? You'd defend him no matter what. You're his second cousin by marriage and everyone knows that blood always runs thicker than the truth."

Cline turned, eyes blazing. "Watch yourself, Garrison. You're no famous country and western star here. You're just some punk who happened to grow up here." The deputy stormed out, heading straight for Denny. He handed her a stack of forms, tossed another pile on the opposite desk and looked back at J.D. "Be sure you just put down the facts."

J.D. met Denny's gaze as he took a seat.

"What's going on?" she whispered.

"We have to talk, but not here," he said to her. When he thought about the pickup he'd seen at Horse Butte, he realized he should have warned her about Pete last night. Pete Williams was a dangerous man.

Denver had almost finished her paperwork when Pete rushed into the sheriff's office. He came straight to her and pulled her into his arms. "You scared the hell out of me," he declared. "When I heard what happened... What were you doing on Horse Butte?"

She tensed in his arms at the clear reprimand. "Trying to find Max's murderer."

"Smart move." Pete pulled back slowly, anger making his movements tense. "Are you all right?"

"How did you hear about it?" she asked.

"I had my dispatcher call him," Cline said from behind her.

"Hello, Pete," J.D. said. Denver saw something pass between the two of them; she didn't like the look on J.D.'s face.

"Can I speak to you for a moment, Pete?" Cline said. They went into the small room where Cline had taken J.D., and the deputy closed the door. It looked like Cline was doing most of the talking, and not in his usual loud voice, either.

"Remember that phone call you got as you were leaving last night?" J.D. asked. Denver looked up from the form she had just completed. "Could that have awakened Pete?"

"I suppose so," she said cautiously.

"Is there any chance he would have known where you went?"

"I left him a note. Why?"

J.D. ran his fingers through his beard. "Denny, I think I know who may have been driving the vehicle that ran Davey off the road last night."

His words didn't have time to sink in before Cline and Pete came out of the office. Pete closed the door a little harder than necessary, Denver noticed.

"Don't say anything right now," J.D. added in a whisper as Cline and Pete started toward them.

Denver wondered why he wouldn't want Cline to know, but kept silent. Maybe he didn't trust Cline any more than she did. Cline took the forms from her and reached for J.D.'s, not looking all that pleased about doing it.

"If I have any more questions, I'll call you," the deputy said, steering the three of them toward the door. "In the meantime, I'll be keeping my eye on you, Ms. McCallahan, and on your friend."

As Denver walked by the dispatcher, she asked, "Have you heard any word on Davey Matthews's condition?"

Before the woman could answer, Cline came up behind her. "I hope you don't plan to interfere in police business the way your uncle did."

"All I want to know is if Davey's all right," she said evenly.

"You and your friend—" Cline threw a dark look at J.D. "—are treading on thin ice, young lady. Don't get involved. I'm warning you."

"It sounds more like you're threatening her," J.D. said.

Denver could feel tears at the back of her eyes. She was too tired and too emotionally drained to take Cline on, but she was also fed up with his attitude. "The next thing you're going to tell me is that Max wasn't murdered. Maybe he stabbed himself. Suicide." She took a breath, fighting tears. "I would think you'd want to solve this murder as fast as possible. That is unless there's some reason you can't—or don't want to."

"Hold it right there!" Cline took her arm and steered her toward the door, away from the attentive ears of the dispatcher. "I'm warning you about making any wild accusations," he muttered through gritted teeth. "You stay out of my damned investigation or I'll put your little butt behind bars. Is that understood?"

"Let her go," J.D. said, his voice hard and cold as he laid a hand on Cline's arm.

Cline looked down at J.D.'s hand, then carefully removed it. He smiled. "Did your old friend here tell you what he thinks he saw up at Horse Butte?"

A muscle twitched along J.D.'s jawline. "Cline—"

"He says he recognized that vehicle you say purposely ran Davey Matthews off the road," Cline continued, a wide grin stretching his lined face. "He says it was Pete Williams's."

Denver shot a surprised look at J.D. Then at Pete. Pete looked shocked. "How can you be sure?" she pleaded with J.D. "It was so dark and it happened so fast."

"I'm sure," J.D. said softly.

"You're wrong," Pete cried. "I wasn't near Horse Butte last night and Denver knows it. I was asleep at her place."

Denver looked from J.D. to Pete and back again. "There must be another explanation."

"This isn't the time or place to get into this," J.D. said, lowering his voice.

"You're right," Pete agreed. "Denver needs rest."

Denver looked into J.D.'s gray eyes. "Why didn't you mention this last night?"

His gaze caressed her face. "You were already so upset…" He grazed her hand with his fingers. "Denny, there are some things I need to tell you."

"Can't you see how exhausted she is?" Pete demanded. "She needs food and sleep. We can talk about your crazy allegations later." He opened the door and started to usher Denver out into the spring morning.

"I'll be all right," Denver said, surprised by the fear she saw in J.D.'s eyes. Surely he didn't believe it had been Pete on that mountain last night.

J.D. reached for her. "Denny, I can't let you—"

"It's all right," she repeated as Pete led her toward his pickup. "I need to talk to Pete. Alone."

"No, Denny." J.D. tried to get past Cline.

"Not so fast, Garrison," Cline said, blocking his way. "You're not going anywhere. I just thought of some more questions I need to ask you."

J.D. pushed past him and started after Denny.

Cline's hand closed over his arm. "Either we talk now, Garrison, or I can have you held over in jail for the next twenty-four hours for questioning. Which is it going to be?"

J.D. looked down at the hand on his arm, then up at Denny. She'd walked out with Pete to his pickup. The two stood next to it talking but neither looked very happy. Twenty-four hours. J.D. glanced up into Cline's grinning face. The deputy would have liked nothing better than to put him behind bars. "I think we'd better talk now, don't you?" J.D. said.

"Garrison, I suspect you planned to come in here like Rambo and save the damsel in distress," Cline said, rocking back and forth in his large, worn office chair. "Tell me I'm wrong."

"If you're asking if I plan to protect Denver in any way I can, the answer is damned right. And I know what you're up to, Cline. You just detained me to keep me from leaving with Denver."

Cline studied him for a moment. "Let me set you straight on a couple of things. I can do whatever I want in this town. And I'm not going to have any trouble when it comes to you or this case. None. As soon as I find that hitchhiker, this case is going to be closed."

"Wanna bet?" J.D. said.

Cline stopped rocking abruptly and leaned forward. "What did you say?"

"Your killer isn't making tracks down some highway with his thumb out." J.D. got to his feet. "He hasn't even left town. And if you don't believe it, you'd better have a look at Max's office. Someone tore it apart."

"How do you know that?"

J.D. put his palms on Cline's desk and leaned toward him. "You got a murderer loose in your town, Deputy. And you'd better find him soon before someone else gets killed."

"Stick to your guitar playing, son. I know what I'm doing, and if you get in my way—"

J.D. turned and walked out, slamming the door behind him.

Pete's apartment was on the top floor of a two-story log structure in the heart of the town. After he'd put some toast and a glass of cold milk Denver didn't want in front of her, he sat down at the kitchen table. "You realize you could have gotten yourself killed last night. Dammit, Denver, you've got to quit playing Nancy Drew."

Denver broke off a piece of toast, crumbled it and dropped it back on the plate. "I don't want to argue about this. I need to ask you about something else."

"What, that ridiculous claim of J.D.'s?" Pete got up

angrily and poured himself a glass of water. His reaction made it even harder for her to ask him what she had to. But she couldn't forget the worry in J.D.'s eyes.

"Why would J.D. say you were at Horse Butte last night if you weren't?" she asked carefully.

"I don't know." Pete sounded hurt and confused. "I guess there's just bad feelings between us I didn't realize."

"But why?"

Pete frowned as he sat back down. "That's the part I can't understand. Why would he purposely try to hurt me? He has everything he ever wanted."

Denver couldn't argue that; she knew firsthand how much J.D.'s career meant to him. Nothing and no one could ever come before it. He'd made that clear years ago.

"You must have really been tired last night," she said.

She could feel his gaze on her. "Dead to the world," he said. "Why didn't you wake me? Going to Horse Butte alone…" He paused and turned the water glass in his fingers. "But then, you weren't alone, were you?"

"I tried to wake you, but I couldn't," Denver said. "I left you a note. You probably saw it this morning when Cline called. That is where Cline reached you, wasn't it?"

Pete rubbed his temples as if he had a headache. Suddenly he grabbed her shoulders, knocking over his water as he turned her to face him. "Remember me, Denver?" His gaze searched her face, his eyes bright. "I'm your best friend, the guy you grew up with, the one who helped you with algebra, who taught you how to play a guitar, who took care of you when you got your heart broken by J. D. Garrison."

Denver felt tears burn her eyes. "Pete, I—"

He got up and returned with a towel to clean up the water he'd spilled. "Yes, Denver, that's where Cline reached me this morning. He had his dispatcher call. And, no, I wasn't on Horse Butte last night. You know where I was—asleep on your couch." He turned to face her. "The question you should be asking yourself is what the hell J.D.'s doing back here after all these years? It can't be because of Max. He didn't even make the funeral."

"That's something else," she said, voicing her doubts. "J.D. seemed surprised you'd left a message for him about the funeral."

"Where are all these doubts about me coming from?" She watched him wipe up the water and toss the towel onto the kitchen counter. "From you? Or J.D.?"

She stared into Pete's handsome face, the ache in her chest growing. "Why would J.D. lie?"

"Why would *I* lie?" Pete demanded. "Look, Denver, maybe J.D. just didn't see what he thought he did. There's probably a reasonable explanation for all of this." Pete glanced at his watch and groaned. "I was supposed to meet the band to practice an hour ago. I have to go. Stay here, get some rest." On his way to the door, he lifted his white Stetson from the hook on the wall and turned to look back at her.

She brushed distractedly at a dirty spot on her jeans, avoiding his gaze.

"If you care anything about me, Denver, you'll stay away from J. D. Garrison." He turned the hat brim in his fingers. "And if you don't care, then do it for your own good. He hurt you once. He'll do it again. And about Max's murder…" She looked up at him; their gazes met and held. "Keep digging around in it and you'll get yourself killed."

She stared at him, shocked by the threat she heard in his voice, saw in the cool blue of his eyes.

"Get some sleep," he said gruffly. "I'll be back later to make you lunch." He slammed the door on his way out.

Denver pushed back the plate of toast and hurried to the window. As she watched Pete pull away, her stomach did a slow, sick spin. When had he washed his pickup? She remembered it parked in front of the cabin last night; it had been dirty, but not *that* dirty. Pete had to have washed it early this morning *before* he came to Cline's office. Why would he do that? She glanced down at her jeans and the spot she'd been brushing at. Mud. She gripped the windowsill as she remembered brushing against Pete's pickup when she stood outside the sheriff's office with him. Where would Pete get so much mud on his pickup this time of year? Enough to feel the need to get it washed. Denver felt herself turn to ice as she looked at her mud-covered Jeep. Horse Butte.

"I don't like any of this," Maggie said when Denver called her from Pete's. She could hear Maggie relating the story of Max's ransacked office and the incident at Horse Butte to someone in the background, and stopped short of telling Maggie of J.D.'s accusations against Pete. Or her own doubts about his story since seeing the mud on her jeans and Pete's washed pickup.

"Tell me that's not Cline you're talking to," Denver whispered.

Maggie laughed. "No, Taylor's here. He's as worried about you and this mess as I am."

Taylor. Denver was surprised how much he'd been hanging around Maggie since Max's death. She felt jealous for Max's sake, then uncharitable for such thoughts. Of course Taylor was just there because he was Max's friend and was trying to help Maggie get through this. But Maggie was also a nice-looking woman; Taylor would have to be blind not to notice. He'd even mentioned that he might hang around longer than he'd planned.

"I hate to keep repeating myself," Maggie was saying, "but maybe you should stay out of this. Taylor agrees."

"Don't worry. I'm going to Bozeman this afternoon. With a little luck, Davey will be conscious. By this time tomorrow, the murderer could be behind bars."

"I hope so," Maggie said thoughtfully. "In the meantime, please be careful. Max would have a fit if he knew what you were up to. And worse yet, that I'd let you." Maggie seemed to hesitate. "Can you hold on just a second?" Denver could hear her telling Taylor goodbye. "I just wanted to let you know I'm going to Missoula sometime soon," Maggie said. "I have a friend up there whose mother died and she could use some help getting the house ready to sell. Why don't you take down the number where I'll be staying in case you need to reach me."

"Just a minute." Denver looked around for something to write on. Digging in the wastebasket, she found a piece of paper and wrote the number on the back of it.

After she hung up, she glanced at her watch, the watch Pete had given her. It had been such a thoughtful gift. "I just wanted you to know that I was thinking of you," he'd said the morning he'd returned from his gig in Missoula, the morning after Max was found murdered.

She stared at the watch, remembering all the things Pete had done for her over the years. She thought of the tea he'd made her last night, of him passed out on her couch, of the mud that remained on his pickup. There had to be an explanation. Because if she couldn't trust Pete, then whom could she trust?

Chapter 7

Denver knew she couldn't sleep until she talked to Davey Matthews, no matter what Pete said. She took a quick shower and left his apartment.

Once outside in the bright spring sun, she felt a little better. The strong scent of pine and the sun filtering down through the snowy branches promised a new warmer season. She stuffed Maggie's number into her jeans pocket, breathed in the sweet familiarity of the small town and headed for her Jeep. Her steps faltered when she spied the figure leaning against her car. Desire took a trip through her bloodstream at the speed of light.

"Hi," J.D. said, straightening. The sun caught in his eyes, moonlight on water. She fought the urge to wade in, to take even a little dip, no matter how warm and inviting they appeared.

"I'm on my way to the hospital in Bozeman to see Davey Matthews." She dared him to argue with her.

"I'll drive," J.D. offered.

She did a double take. "What, no argument?"

He smiled. It had its usual heart-thudding effect on her. "I believe the deal was no logical arguments. No trying to protect you from yourself. Right?"

"Right. So why did I think you'd change your mind?"

He frowned. "Probably because you don't trust me."

She nodded.

"Give me a chance?" he asked.

His smile warmed something deep inside, thawing the wall of ice around her heart. She looked into his eyes and wanted nothing more than to curl up in his arms.

"Have you heard anything more on Davey's condition?" he asked as he walked her toward his pickup.

"No. I couldn't get any information on Davey from the hospital. At least there, he should be safe."

J.D. opened the door for her. Just as she started to get in, she turned to look behind her, feeling that they were being watched.

Pete leaned against the wall of the building across the street, fighting the sick feeling in the pit of his stomach at seeing Denver and J.D. together. He swore under his breath, his love for Denver almost overwhelming him. He gritted his teeth, wanting desperately to be the one she turned to, the one who would take her in his arms and make love to her. Instead it looked like it would be J. D. Garrison.

That realization squeezed the blood from his heart. For years he'd lived in J. D. Garrison's shadow. Denver had never seen him as anything but a friend. Just recently, he had felt as if he were winning her over.

Now J.D. was back in town.

And as long as J.D. was in the picture, Pete knew he didn't stand a chance. He watched them get into the pale green Ford pickup. If J.D. was gone, Denver would turn to him just as she had years ago. Only this time, he wasn't going to chance J.D. ever coming back again. He'd stop J.D. from ruining everything. And at the same time, get him out of their lives forever.

Denny turned on the radio as J.D. started up the engine. "What's this?" she asked, sounding surprised. "Rock and roll?" She thumbed over to the country and western station. He could feel her studying him out of the corner of her eye.

One of his latest songs, "Heart Full of Misery," came on the radio. He reached over and turned it off. "Denny, we have to talk."

"So what's it really like being a star?" she asked, turning in the bench seat to face him.

J.D. looked over at her, knowing she wanted to talk about anything but Pete—the one thing they really needed to discuss. The sun spilling through the window caught in her still-damp hair, firing it to burnished copper. She smelled of spring, her skin pink from her shower. Just the sight of her made him ache with a need for her like none he'd ever known.

"A star?" he asked, trying to concentrate on the question. He'd never thought of himself as anything but a guitar picker. Certainly not a star. Stars had a tendency to fall. "What's it like? Months on the road playing concerts, months of trying to write new songs, months in a recording studio." He looked into her eyes, the color of a tropic sea, and felt a pull stronger than the tides. "It's not all it's cracked up to be."

"But it's what you always wanted."

He pulled up to a stop sign and looked over at her again, letting his gaze caress her face the way his fingers wanted to do. "Is it?"

"Everything comes at a price," she said.

Didn't he know it. He stared into those aquamarine eyes of hers for a long moment and forced himself to pull away. *You just want to protect her, just like when you were kids.* He laughed softly to himself as he turned onto the highway. *I think it's a little more than that.* Because right now the last thing he was thinking about was protecting Denny. And, boy, did she *need* protecting. But not just from Pete.

"Denny." He took her hand in his. Just the feel of it made him want to stop the car and take her in his arms, to hold her, to feel her body against his. When this was over—"We have to talk about Pete."

She pulled her hand free, closed her eyes and leaned back against the seat.

"I was at Max's burial service yesterday," he said. Her eyes flew open and she turned to look at him. "I met Maggie in that stand of pines overlooking the cemetery."

She narrowed her gaze at him, the old fight coming back into her. "You and Maggie? I don't understand."

He saw her marshal forces against what he was about to say, knowing she understood only too well. "Maggie thinks Pete is somehow involved in Max's death."

Her next words came out controlled, careful, but her gaze crackled like Saint Elmo's fire. "Why would Maggie think that?"

"Max seemed worried in the few weeks before his death, Maggie said." He saw reluctant agreement in

Denny's expression. "The day he died, he told Maggie he was going to see Pete. He was very upset, and told her he had to stop Pete before someone got killed."

"That doesn't mean—"

J.D. told her about the photograph Maggie had found in Pete's coat pocket. Denny started to argue but he stopped her and explained, "When she found it, the photo had been torn. Someone had ripped me out of the picture.

"Hang on, it gets crazier," he continued before she could argue further. "Last night after I left you and Pete at the cabin, I went back to Max's place. I'd seen what looked like a wallet caught between the radiator and the wall in his apartment."

"A wallet?" Denny asked, sitting up a little straighter.

"It was Max's."

She frowned.

"It looks like Max didn't have it with him the day he was killed."

"Then that means Pete could have gotten the photo at any time. Max could have even given it to him."

J.D. nodded.

"Where is the wallet now?" she asked.

"As I was leaving last night, someone relieved me of it." He motioned to the latest lump on his head.

"Are you all right?" she cried.

He smiled, touched by her concern. "I'll live, but this whole thing is getting more dangerous all the time."

She turned to look out the window. A wall of pines, dark green against snow white, blurred past the pickup, throwing her face in shadow. "Pete couldn't kill anyone, especially Max."

They topped Grayling Pass, went by Fir Ridge

Cemetery and dropped into Gallatin Canyon, the road twisting through snowcapped pines and granite cliffs, skirting the Gallatin River. The once-frozen river now flowed around huge slabs of aquamarine ice—another sign that spring was coming.

He could tell that her mind was elsewhere by the way she worried her lower lip with her teeth. "You were right, though," she said softly. "Pete's pickup *was* at Horse Butte last night." She turned a little in the seat to show her backside to him. "Do you see that?"

He slowed down as he stared at her posterior. Oh, yes, he saw that. He'd admired it numerous times lately.

"See it?" she asked, pointing to a spot on the thigh part of her jeans.

He glanced at the highway, then back at the spot on her thigh. "I see some dirt."

"It's mud. I brushed against Pete's pickup this morning and got it on my jeans."

It was the same as the stuff all over Denny's Jeep.

"And that's not all. Pete washed his pickup early this morning." She straightened in her seat. "In his haste, he missed a few spots. He's hiding something, but it's not because he's involved in Max's murder."

"How do you know that?" J.D. demanded. How could she keep defending Pete in light of everything they'd learned?

"I know Pete." Her eyes clouded as she leaned back against the seat, her hair tumbling around her shoulders in a fiery waterfall.

She's in love with him. The thought struck him like a fist. He felt sick. Then shocked that he could feel such pain. *My God, you're falling for her.* He drove on, trying to sort out his feelings. He'd always cared for Denny but not like this. *You just need sleep. And getting hit in the head can't be helping, either.* He laughed to himself, no longer able to blame the way he felt on anything but the truth. He was falling for her like a boulder off a high cliff. All he could think about was taking her in his arms. He'd never wanted to kiss anyone so much in his life.

He realized she was staring at him again. "What about Pete's alibi?" she asked.

Reluctantly he recounted Maggie's story about the barmaid in Missoula.

"So Pete wasn't his usual charming self that night and the barmaid just didn't remember him," she said. "Why wouldn't Pete be there if his band was there?"

She turned those wonderful green eyes on him. He wondered what they would be like fired with desire. And he wondered if he'd ever get the chance to see anything but anger in them.

"And what possible reason could Pete have to kill Max?" she demanded.

"I'm not saying it makes any sense," he said, dragging himself away from her gaze.

Suddenly Denver bolted upright. "Oh, no. Maggie's going to Missoula. She said to help a friend but I'll bet she's going up there to check out Pete's story."

J.D. sighed, wishing Maggie wouldn't do that. "She could be in real danger. Do you know where she's staying?"

Denver dug out a piece of paper from her pocket. "She gave me a number." He watched her turn it in her fingers for a moment as if trying to read something written on it. "No." He watched her bite her lower lip, tears shimmering in her eyes as she fought the tears, and knew whatever was on the paper had upset her deeply.

"What is it?" he asked.

She closed her fingers into a fist, crumpling the paper, and for a moment he thought she wasn't going to tell him. "When I was on the phone with Maggie, I couldn't find anything to write on. I found this in Pete's wastebasket." She held it out to him with shaking fingers. "It's a receipt for the rental of a semitrailer." She closed her fingers around it again.

"Pete rented a semi?" J.D. asked.

Her voice came out a whisper. "A semi almost ran Pete and me off the road on the way back from the funeral yesterday."

"You think Pete rented a truck and hired someone to drive it just to scare you?" he asked, astounded to hear himself defending Pete. "Do you have any idea what it costs to rent a semi?"

"Sounds pretty ridiculous, doesn't it?" She smiled a little. "Also, he was in the pickup with me and could have been killed, too."

J.D. nodded. "Didn't you tell me Pete sometimes does odd jobs around town? He could have rented it for one of his employers."

"That must be what it is," she said, looking relieved as she stuffed the receipt back into her pocket. "And I'm sure there's an explanation for his pickup being on Horse Butte."

"And why he washed it in such a big hurry this morning?" J.D. pressed as they neared the outskirts of Bozeman. The snow-covered Bridger Mountains glowed white gold in the sunlight, a backdrop for the bustling western college town.

"Yes," she said, giving him a hard look. "When did you lose your faith in people?"

He glanced over at her, taken aback by the question. He *had* lost faith in people. And he knew exactly when it had happened. "I'm sure you read in the tabloids about my ex-business manager. I trusted him, Denny. He robbed me blind."

He recognized the determined set of her jaw. She said, "I *know* Pete."

He nodded, afraid just how well she knew him. "I thought I knew my business manager. Sometimes people disappoint you. Even people you care about." And J.D. was afraid Pete Williams was going to disappoint them both. Either way, he intended to keep Pete as far away as possible from Denny.

Davey had regained consciousness. As J.D. pushed open the door, he spotted Deputy Cline beside Davey's bed.

"I figured you two would show up," Cline said, not looking at all pleased. "Don't you ever stay home and clean house or bake cookies or sew or something, Ms. McCallahan?"

"How are you doing?" Denver asked Davey.

"Okay, I guess," he mumbled.

"Don't you have some records to make or something, Garrison?" Cline asked.

Denver flashed J.D. a warning not to take the bait. He just smiled at her. "You don't mind if we visit with Davey for a few moments in private, do you?" she asked Cline.

"This is the sheriff's department's business, Ms. Mc-Callahan," he said, crossing his arms over his belly.

"And I'm the deputy sheriff for West Yellowstone, you might recall. I'm not leaving this room."

J.D. gritted his teeth, but kept his mouth shut, just as he'd assured Denny he would. But it wasn't easy.

"Do you feel up to talking?" she asked Davey as she took the chair beside his bed. He turned his face to the window and chewed at his cheek. "Last night you called me and asked me to meet you at Horse Butte—" she began.

Davey shot a look at Cline. "I don't know what you're talking about."

"What?" Denver exclaimed. J.D. saw the shock on her face. "Are you telling me you didn't call and tell me to meet you at Horse Butte Fire Tower?"

"I'm telling you I don't remember anything. All right?"

Denver stared at the boy. "I don't understand."

"The doc says it's common with concussions," Cline interrupted, sounding almost pleased by the turn of events. "He may never remember what happened."

"Oh, I'm sorry, Davey, I didn't realize..." She touched his hand. He turned it only a fraction, just enough so that J.D. could have sworn it held a small scrap of paper.

"Look, I don't know anything, okay?" Davey insisted.

J.D. watched the boy stealthily slip the scrap into Denver's palm before he turned to the wall. "I just want to be left alone."

"Satisfied?" Cline asked Denver. "Why don't we step out into the hall?"

"I hope you're feeling better soon," she said to Davey, pocketing something as she followed Cline from the room. J.D. took one last look at the boy, then trailed after her.

"Too bad about the kid," Cline said once Davey's door closed behind them. "But I do have a lead on your uncle's murder. You know that hitchhiker Max picked up at the Elkhorn Café just before he was killed?"

Denver made a face. "What about him?"

"Did you know Max gave him a ride out of town?" Cline asked. "Davey saw it. He just told me."

"I thought he couldn't remember anything," J.D. objected.

"Selective memory," Cline said. "I imagine he won't remember stealing that car, either, or trying what I suspect was extortion. I figure he planned to give you the information about the hitchhiker for a price. Of course."

"You think that's all he intended to tell me?" Denny asked.

Cline nodded. "The hitchhiker did it."

"And how do you explain Max's ransacked office?" J.D. asked. Denver shot him an "I-told-you-reporting-it-to-Cline-wouldn't-do-any-good" look.

"This kind of thing happens all the time," Cline said. "Someone gets himself killed, it hits the papers and kids sneak into the dead guy's house and fool around."

"If you thought it was just kids, why did you dust the place for fingerprints?" Denver asked.

"Police procedure."

She glanced back at the boy's room. "I suppose you can also explain why Davey seems…scared—as if he's being threatened not to remember."

Cline's eyes narrowed. "You aren't suggesting—"

"I didn't say *you* were threatening him," Denver quickly amended.

Cline took off his hat and turned the brim in his thick fingers. He glanced over at J.D. "You're being awful quiet." J.D. shrugged and looked away. "It's obvious why the boy's acting the way he is," the deputy said, turning his attention back to Denver. "He's looking at a minimum of a year in Miles City."

Reform school? J.D. glanced back at Davey's room. It all seemed too convenient. When the boy was well, he'd be shipped off. Denny seemed to be thinking the same thing.

"You'll let me know when you pick up this hitch-hiker?" she asked.

Cline grinned. "Trust me. You'll be the first to know." He walked them to J.D.'s pickup and waited until they'd driven away. J.D. watched in the rearview mirror as Cline went back into the hospital.

He looked over at Denny. She sat with one hand in her pocket, the same pocket he'd seen her stick the note from Davey in.

He waited for her to tell him about the note as they started back up the canyon. But when he looked over, she'd fallen into an exhausted sleep. He gently pulled her toward him so that her head rested in his lap. As he studied her angelic face, the first lines of a song came to him, clear and strong, just like they used to. He hummed softly, writing the song in his head as he drove, and Denny slept.

It was the same dream. Denver skipping and singing into the bank. Her parents behind her. The words dying on her lips. Her feet stopping as she saw the people lying facedown on the floor. The silence. Her father calling her name. As she ran back to him, she saw the other policeman on the floor. Her father grabbed her and shoved her down as he reached for his own gun. She hit the floor and slid into the desk leg. The pain made her cry out. Only this time, Denver saw herself crawl under the office desk, felt the cold floor beneath her cheek as she looked out to see the masked man turn, shotgun in his hands. She saw the silver flash, and something flickered in the light as it spun. Her mother screamed. And the room exploded.

Denver sat up with a scream in her throat, her fingers clenched into fists.

"It's all right," J.D. murmured as he drew her to him. He pulled off the road and held her, rubbing her back, soothing her with whispered words. She nestled against him, fighting off the nightmare, feeling safe in his embrace. "Bad dream?" His voice was soft and gentle, like his touch. She nodded. "About Max?"

"No. My parents and the day they were killed." She shuddered and he held her tighter. "I remembered more of it. I saw the bank robber."

"The man who killed your parents?" he asked, sounding not altogether convinced.

"I know it sounds crazy, but ever since Max's death, I've been having the dream again. Each time, I remember a little more. Or maybe I just think I remember. Maybe it's just my imagination. But this time, the robber turned and I saw him. He wore a ski mask but there was something about him…"

J.D. frowned. "I suppose it could be a memory. I can remember things when I was very young." He seemed to hesitate. "Denny, have you ever thought of *trying* to remember? I know Max encouraged you to forget, but what if you got someone to help you bring it all back?"

Her heart pounded; just the idea of reliving it paralyzed her. "Someone?"

"Maybe a psychologist who uses hypnotism."

She stared at the highway ahead, suddenly more afraid than she had ever been. "I'm not sure I could go back to that day, J.D."

"I just thought it might make the nightmare end," he reassured her softly.

"The nightmare will end when we find Max's killer," she said, telling herself she believed it as she snuggled against him. His shirt against her cheek was soft and warm and smelled of J.D., a scent she'd never been able to forget.

"I've always wondered about your parents," he said, sounding cautious.

"I can't remember very much. Max always wanted me to put that part of my life behind me because their deaths had been so violent, and I have so few memories before that. Maybe he was right."

He released her just enough to get the pickup going again. Denver found herself studying J.D. out of the corner of her eye. In broad daylight, he looked even more handsome, strong and muscular from his broad shoulders to his thighs. She mentally shook herself. Being attracted to him was one thing; falling for him was another.

"How are you going to handle our suspicions about Pete?" he asked, back on the road.

Pete. "The more I've thought about it, the more I'm convinced of Pete's innocence," she said, anticipating J.D.'s reaction.

He tensed, and she heard him mutter an oath under his breath. With regret, she moved out of the shelter of his arm and slid across the seat to her side of the pickup. She could see West Yellowstone in the distance.

"You're going to have to be careful with Pete," J.D. said. "If you're wrong and he turns out to be—"

"I know." She stuffed her hands deep into her jeans, not wanting to think about Pete. Her fingers hit the note Davey had slipped her. "Could you drop me by Max's office?" she asked as they entered town.

He shot her a look as he pulled up in front of Max's and started to cut the engine.

"I really need to be alone for a while," she said, opening the door.

"Denny—"

"I'll talk to you later," she said, jumping out and not looking back.

J.D. swore, slamming his fist on the steering wheel. He'd done it again, pushing her away when that was the last thing he wanted to do. He thought about the note he'd seen Davey pass her at the hospital. Damn. Denny hadn't trusted him enough to even tell him about it.

"What do you expect?" he demanded out loud. "The woman has no reason to trust you." *No*, he thought, *instead she trusts Pete. No matter how much evidence piles up against him.*

J.D. headed for Maggie's, thinking of the Denny who'd slept on his lap on the way home and the music that had come back into his head. The music and the words were gone again; just like Denny, they'd slipped away from him.

As he climbed Maggie's steps, he wished he was a detective instead of a musician. A damned good detective could solve this and save Denny from any more sorrow. He knocked, then remembered that Maggie was probably on her way to Missoula. She surprised him by opening the door.

"I was afraid you'd already left."

"Something's come up," she said quietly. She motioned him inside. "Oh, J.D., maybe Max *was* involved in something illegal. A hundred and fifty thousand dollars' worth of illegal."

The words were written in a childlike scrawl. "Gralin Pas. Sunriz. Tommarro. Brng yur karma. And yur skiis."

Denver stared at Davey's note. At first she thought it was in some form of code but soon realized it was just horrendous spelling. "Grayling Pass. Sunrise. Tomorrow. Bring your 'karma'?" Denver moaned. "Bring your camera. And your skis."

Not another one of Davey's secret meeting places! Maybe Cline was right. Davey was just trying to extort money from her. Well, if he thought she was going to meet him at another isolated place, he was wrong. She wadded up the note and threw it into the trash. Davey was in for a surprise. No more games. This time he was going to talk to her.

"Davey Matthews?" the head nurse repeated over the phone.

Denver held her breath. Had Davey gotten worse? Surely he hadn't—

"Are you a relative?" the nurse asked.

"No. I'm a friend. His relatives all live out of state. He's not worse, is he?"

The nurse seemed to hesitate. "Mr. Matthews has left."

"Left? He was released this quickly?"

Silence. "Not exactly. It appears he's run away."

Denver hung up, her hands shaking. Davey had run away, all right, but not to avoid the law, she thought as she looked around Max's ransacked office. Davey was running for his life.

"Oh, Max, what were you working on?" she whispered. The killer was looking for something. But what? Max's office was in a worse mess after Deputy Cline and his fingerprinting team had come through; everything was covered with gray powder.

She began picking up the mountain of papers and putting them into stacks. It was probably fruitless, but right now she needed something to occupy her mind— something besides images of J.D. She thought about the man she'd spent the last twenty-four hours with. Something was desperately wrong. The music industry had acknowledged his talent; his fans had made him rich. He had women falling at his feet. What else would it take to make him happy? she wondered.

Forcing aside the image of J.D. in his snug-fitting jeans, she sat down at the desk and assumed Max's thinking pose. Max had picked up a hitchhiker. They'd gone to the old dump. Not logical, but possible, she supposed. Max liked the place. It was all tall pines and grassy slope now, but years ago it had been the city dump. Many nights she and Max had driven to the edge of the embankment and parked in his Olds wagon above the dump, waiting and listening.

About midnight, Max would snap on the headlights. The beams would shine down the slope, where a handful of black bears scrounged in the day's pickings of people's leftovers. But Max's favorite part was what happened at about two in the morning. The black bears would suddenly get nervous and run off. Then the grizzlies would come out.

Max never tired of watching the grizzlies at the dump. It was a ritual for him. And Denver guessed it was his fascination with the huge, powerful animals and his concern that ordinary people would never get the chance to see a grizzly out of captivity.

Max had taken it personally when the city closed the dump. It wasn't that he wanted the bears munching on tin cans and plastic sandwich bags; he was just sorry to see the grizzlies go when the dump closed. And he missed those late nights, talking, waiting for the grizzlies. So did Denver.

No, it didn't seem strange that Max might go out to the old city dump. Maybe even to meet someone he couldn't meet any other place. That seemed to leave Pete out. Max had no reason to meet Pete secretly as far as she knew. She thought about the hitchhiker. Max would have given him a ride as far as the dump. That was Max. A lover of old city dumps, grizzlies and people in trouble. Maybe when Cline did find the hitchhiker—if he ever did—the man would know something about Max's death. Maybe that was why he was so hard for Cline to find.

She stared at the room and all the work that lay ahead of her. Too many questions still plagued her. And thoughts of J.D. kept pushing in. The way his face softened when he smiled, the way his eyes shone silver— She shook herself, bumping her knee against the desk. It gave out a hollow thud. She stared at the desk, suddenly remembering the secret compartment.

Denver reached under and pushed the worn panel.

It swung inward, and there in the hollow space was the last thing she'd expected to find. Max's gun.

Maggie handed J.D. the bank receipt. "Max deposited 150,000 in his account the day before he died," she said, her voice wavering.

J.D. looked down at it. "Could he have saved that kind of money?"

She shook her head. "Every penny he saved, he put in a special account for Denver. Her account hasn't been touched." Maggie punched the couch as she plopped down onto it. "Dammit, J.D., you have to find out what's going on. Max couldn't have been dirty. Not Max, please."

He took a chair across from her. "I'm trying, Maggie, but none of it makes any sense and Denny—"

Maggie wiped at the tears. "She's going to have to be told."

"It would be better coming from you considering the way she feels about me right now." His suspicion of Pete had driven a wedge between them. He told Maggie about finding Max's wallet.

"It's strange that the attacker took his wallet and not yours," Maggie said after a moment. "Obviously there was something in there the attacker didn't want anyone to find."

"Like what?" J.D. tried to remember the contents. "I wanted Denny to take a look. She might have recognized something significant that I wouldn't." He rubbed his temples. "I feel like I'm making a mess of this."

Maggie smiled at him kindly. "Just think what might have happened if you hadn't been with Denny last night at Horse Butte."

He grimaced. "But she still thinks Pete's a prince and I'm a first-class jerk." J.D. picked up the bank-deposit receipt from the table. "When she hears about this, she isn't going to be happy, Maggie."

"That's why he couldn't be involved in anything illegal," she said. "Max would never hurt Denny."

J.D. hoped Maggie was right about that.

Slowly, Denver pulled the revolver and the box of shells from their hiding place. Then she reached back into the compartment and felt around again. Nothing but dust.

She stared at the gun, angry with Max. Why had he hidden it? If he'd had it, he might still be alive. She rubbed her hand over her tired eyes. Had he left the gun behind because he'd known the person he was meeting at the city dump and felt safe? He would feel safe meeting Pete. Or Deputy Cline, for that matter. Or just about anyone she could think of.

Denver continued to put Max's office back into some kind of order, knowing it was the only way she'd ever be able to make sense of his case files. The files Max had burned nagged at the back of her mind. Had he been trying to protect someone? The same person who'd killed him? She thought about the "Case of the Wandering Husband" Maggie had mentioned and promised herself she'd search for it as soon as she had everything picked up.

Tired and dirty, she lifted the last batch of papers from the floor and made room for them on a corner of the desk. One sheet floated to the floor and she bent under the desk to retrieve it. A noise made her come up too fast and bang her head on the underside of the desk.

"Ouch!" She rubbed her head, staring at the open front door. Sheila Walker stood framed in the doorway, that same goofy hat hanging off the side of her head, that same hungry look in her eyes.

"You and I have to talk, honey," Sheila said. "It's a matter of life and death."

Chapter 8

The reporter strode into the room, shoved papers aside and plopped down on a corner of Max's desk. "I've been doing some digging. Sometimes I get this feeling in my gut. I got that feeling now, honey."

Denver didn't have the foggiest idea what the woman was talking about.

"I heard you were on Horse Butte last night," she said. "Deputy Cline says it was an accident. You buying that?" Denver didn't get a chance to answer. "Me neither."

The woman slipped her large handbag off her shoulder and onto the desk. She got up and stalked around the office.

"What do you think your uncle was hiding?" she asked, poking a finger into one of the holes the burglar had made. When Denver didn't answer, the reporter turned toward her. "You know, they never caught the bank robber who killed your folks. He got away with over a million bucks—and murder. Did you know that?"

Denver felt her head swim. The woman jumped around so fast, it was impossible to follow her line of thinking. "No."

Sheila cocked her head. "Off the record, did your uncle ever talk about the money?"

"What money?"

"I'm on a money trail, honey. And I'm afraid I'm thinking it leads right to your uncle." She came over to the desk to pick up her purse. "Max's murder and that boy being run off the road are just the beginning. A caper this size… Who knows where it will end. Or how many more people are going to die."

Denver stared at her, dumbstruck. What money trail? Surely she didn't think Max—

"Just answer me one question. Did Max leave you a bundle of money?"

"Max never had a bundle of money."

Sheila nodded. "So you're saying you don't know where he stashed the money."

"There is no money."

Sheila Walker smiled. "Take some good advice, honey. Watch your backside. As naive as you are, you're bound to be next."

For a long time after the reporter had left, Denver found herself staring after her. The woman had to be nuts. Did she think Max had something to do with the bank robbery? Max hadn't even been in Billings. She remembered the wait at the police station and a woman police officer finally taking her home to wait until Max arrived. Sheila Walker had to be looking for a connection between the two cases, but if she thought Max was it, she was dead wrong.

Max's pistol lay on the desk beside the box of shells. Sheila's warning that she'd be next ricocheted around in her head. She picked up the pistol and, trying not to speculate on whom she had to fear, loaded it.

Then on impulse she called the Stage Coach Inn and asked for J. D. Garrison. When no one answered in his room, she left a message, then headed home, anxious for the peace of the lake cabin—the healing place Max had given her as a child.

As she left Max's office, she noticed another storm had turned the sky to slate gray. Wasn't spring going to ever come?

The moment Denver opened the front door of the cabin, she knew something was terribly wrong. A cold breeze hit her in the face along with the knowledge that someone had been there. She flicked on the overhead light to find the cabin ransacked, but not as badly as Max's office. She fought between anger and tears; the tears finally won.

Damn the person who had done this. She stepped farther into the cabin, pushing open the laundry room door. Her photography supplies, detergent powder and dirty clothes were scattered everywhere.

What in the world was the person looking for? Did he really think Max would hide a case file in the laundry-detergent box? The thought gave her a sudden chill. A hitchhiker would look in obvious places, but someone who knew Max would look in the detergent.

She strode down the hall to Max's old office and closed the side door to the cabin, cutting off the cold air. His big old rolltop gaped open, everything pulled out onto the floor.

The phone rang. "Hello?" Silence. "Hello?" It hit her that it might be Davey again, but then she heard Taylor's deep voice. Outside, the storm clouds had dropped over the cabin, a dense, dark cover, as dark as her mood.

"Denver?" He sounded almost surprised and she thought for a moment he might have dialed the wrong number. "I'm trying to find Maggie. You don't happen to know where she is, do you?"

"She said she was going to Missoula to help a friend whose mother died, but I'm not sure when she planned to leave."

"Oh, right, Maggie did mention she might go," he said, sounding a little dejected. "I didn't think she'd already left. I didn't even get to tell her goodbye."

"I'm sure she'll be back soon." They talked a little longer, with Taylor asking about her health, if Max's will had turned up, if Cline had found any new evidence. He sounded lonely.

She snapped on a light and began sorting through the mess from Max's desk.

"Are you sure you're all right?" he asked, obviously feeling he had to fill in as her protector now that Max was gone. Did he also feel protective toward Maggie or did he have something more romantic in mind? The thought didn't bother her as much as it had at first.

"Oh, I'm as well as can be expected," Denver said, looking around the ransacked room. She knew if she mentioned what had happened, he'd come out. And as much as she liked him, she didn't know what to say to him. He was so quiet, so different from Max, who would have entertained her while the two of them cleaned up this mess.

She hung up, anxious to get busy. She felt a sudden chill as the side door flew open behind her. An arm locked around her neck and pulled her backward. She fought for breath as the pressure against her throat increased, cutting off her air. A hint of a man's cologne drifted across her senses; the familiarity of it stunned her. Her head pounded as she ripped at the arm around her throat with her fingers. Panic seized her as black spots danced before her eyes. She felt the darkness coming up for her and realized he planned to kill her. She kicked frantically behind her, connecting with a shin, and got a loud curse.

Then the lights went out. Literally.

"Get out!" She heard a man yell from down the hallway, the voice muffled as if behind a mask. "Now."

Her attacker let go, shoving her forward. She stumbled into Max's desk and hurriedly groped for the pistol in her purse. She could hear her attacker stumbling down the dark hall. She pulled out the gun, planning to go after him, when a wave of cold air hit her, then a body. The body hurled her to the floor. The pistol went flying.

"Stay down. And keep quiet," the man on top of her commanded.

Denver moaned as she recognized the voice. "Great timing, Garrison." The cologne scent was gone, along with the man who wore it.

"I knew you couldn't keep quiet," J.D. growled, rolling off her. In the other room, the front door slammed. "Stay here!"

She heard J.D. run down the hall toward the living

room. He knocked over something large, swore loudly as it rumbled to the floor, then a door opened again, followed by silence.

Denver felt around for the pistol and, not finding it, got to her feet and made her way to the dark living room. The front door stood open, cold air rushing in; snow had begun to fall, making the day even darker. She tried the light switch, then when it didn't come on, felt around on top of the fireplace mantel for a flashlight.

"J.D.?" Denver called as she stepped outside into the storm. "J.D.?"

A car engine cranked over, its headlights cutting a swath of light through the snowflakes. Denver could make out two shadowy figures wrestling in the snow near the edge of the road. J.D. and...another man. Denver ran back to the cabin, grabbed the poker from the fireplace and ran toward the two, screaming at the top of her lungs.

The sight of her, or maybe it was just the sound of her, made them both look up. One man stumbled to his feet and ran toward the waiting car. The other kneeled in the road, an arm over his face as the car turned around, roaring away in a tidal wave of ice shards and chunks of frozen obsidian sand. As the car's taillights died away in the pine trees, J.D. slowly got to his feet.

"Are you all right?" Denver called out.

"I thought I told you to stay where you were," he snarled as he started back toward the house.

"And miss seeing you get killed?"

J.D. pushed Denver through the open doorway and slammed the door behind them. Denver flicked the beam of her flashlight over him. He took it from her hand, along with the poker she still carried, and laid both on the hearth.

"Did you get a look at him?" she asked.

"No." She heard him snap the light switch. "How about you? Did you recognize him or the car?"

"Just his cologne." She could hear J.D. stumbling over things in the living room. She told herself that anyone could buy the same designer cologne Pete wore, anyone with money, but it didn't help ease the sick feeling in her stomach.

"Where's the breaker box?" J.D. asked as if he hadn't heard her. He seemed to be running on straight anger and she wasn't sure how much of it was aimed at her.

She took the flashlight from the hearth. "In the laundry room. I'll get it."

J.D. followed her into the multipurpose room. Denver held the flashlight on the electrical box behind the wall calendar near the door, while J.D. flipped the breakers. The lights came on.

She caught sight of J.D.'s face. "My God." She stared at him, the ransacked room and the assailant quickly forgotten. "J.D., you're hurt."

Gingerly he touched his left eye with his fingers. "Just a lucky punch, that's all. I'm fine." But Denver was already running warm water in the laundry tub. She reached into the overhead cabinet and took out a washcloth.

"Come here," she said, motioning for him to sit down on a footstool. She touched the washcloth gently to his face. "What about these cuts?"

"It was just a little gravel," he mumbled. "Ouch."

"Hold still." Her fingers found a bump on the side of his head, probably where she'd hit him with the lamp.

The tears came without warning. Denver bit her lip and tried to step away from him. "I'll get some antiseptic for those cuts."

He caught her hand and pulled her into his arms. She clung to him, feeling his strength, his warmth, the steady beat of his heart against her breast. He hugged her tightly against him as if he needed her in his arms as much as she needed to be there.

"You could have been killed," she whispered.

"I'm all right, Denny." He cradled her head with one hand, her back with the other. "I'm fine."

She brushed at her tears, pulling back a little to look at him, but didn't move from his arms. "What do you think they wanted?"

"I wish I knew because you won't be safe until we do," he said, pushing back a strand of her long hair from her face. His gaze shifted to her neck. "Oh, Denny, your throat."

She touched it gingerly with trembling fingers. "I don't know what would have happened if you hadn't come along when you did."

He pulled her against him, cradling her in his arms, rocking her. "It's all right, baby. It's all right now."

The room seemed to shrink, pressing them even closer. Denver fought for breath as J.D. held her. She could feel his heart pick up a beat next to hers, feel his breath against her cheek become ragged. Warning signals began to go off in her head. *Dangerous territory! Red alert!* Except she couldn't move.

He pulled back a little; his look flamed her cheeks and sent her temperature skyrocketing. She watched his gaze touch her lips as tenderly as a kiss. And as he stole up to her eyes again, she felt her heartbeat go from a two-step to a cowboy jitterbug.

"I should get the antiseptic," she whispered, but didn't move.

The phone rang. She stared at it, not wanting to leave his arms but knowing if she didn't—

"You get the phone. I'll get the antiseptic," J.D. said, his voice thick with emotion.

Reluctantly she stepped from his arms; he didn't seem any more anxious to let her go than she was to leave. As she answered the phone, she put the washcloth to her face and fought to quiet her thundering pulse. She heard J.D. draw in a ragged breath. "Hello?" she said. Silence. Then a click.

"Who was it?" J.D. asked behind her.

She shook her head as she ran more cold water over the cloth and put it to her still burning cheeks. "They hung up."

"Probably just a wrong number."

Under normal circumstances, Denver would have agreed. But before her caller had hung up, she'd heard the distinct opening of a phone-booth door. She couldn't shake off the feeling that whoever it was had been calling from just up the road—and that that person had just tried to kill her.

She flung the washcloth over the tub and took the antiseptic from J.D.'s hand. He didn't even flinch as she touched it to his scrapes and scratches. Instead, he kept his gaze on her face.

"Thanks," he said softly. He was so near her she could feel the heat of his body.

"I guess I'd better start putting this place back together." She put the antiseptic away, then knelt to pick up the pistol. After stuffing it back into her purse, she stepped past J.D. He threw her completely off guard.

"What were these, Denny?" he asked. He was holding several long strips of exposed film. A couple of the cassettes still hung from the ends of the film.

"Just some promo shots I was doing for a free-lance project."

"Doesn't it seem odd that the burglar destroyed them?"

All she could think about was that she'd have to re-shoot them.

"What else have you been working on that someone might find interesting?" J.D. prodded.

Denver shrugged. "I've got some shots of celebs for the free-lance writers I work with. Montana's hot right now, you know. Lots of movie stars and TV moguls moving here."

"I heard."

"And there's some film I was getting ready to soup for a travel brochure I've contracted to do." She grumbled under her breath as she picked up more strips of exposed film dangling out of film cassettes. "I guess I'll have to shoot these again, too."

"Nothing more?" J.D. asked.

"Just Max's birthday party. That's it."

"Max's birthday?" he asked, taking the film from her. "Do you think any shots can be saved?"

"Not of the film that's out of the cassettes. If there's any shots still inside…maybe."

"Let's take a look," J.D. said, hitting the light.

"Sorry there isn't more," she said later as she hung up the processed film to dry. Only a few photos in three of the rolls had survived.

"That's all right. It was a long shot anyway, but it just seems strange that they'd destroy your film." There were several pictures of the buffalo jump near Three Forks and a nice scenic landscape of Big Sky with Lone Mountain Peak. On the other roll, three shots of Max's birthday party had turned out.

"Damn," Denver said, holding the frames up to the light. "These are the last photos of Max and most of them are ruined."

"Can we put these on your light table?" J.D. asked.

"What are we looking for?" Denver asked as she spread out the negatives.

J.D. picked up the loupe and bent over to study them.

"See anything?" she asked.

He handed her the loupe. "Here, take a look. At the back of the room by the fireplace."

Denver bent over the negatives. "I think we'd better blow this up."

A few minutes later, she held up the photograph from Max's birthday for J.D. to see. It was a wide-angle shot of the entire party; the photo as well as the cabin overflowed with people. But now she could see the two people at the rear clearly. Pete Williams was having a very serious conversation with Cal Dalton.

"It almost looks like Pete and Cal are arguing," J.D. said.

"I wonder what they have to argue about? I didn't even know they knew each other." Her gaze skimmed the rest of the photo. "Oh, my God, look," she said, pointing to the right-hand side of the picture.

"Max is just washing up some dishes," J.D. said, sounding confused.

Denver shook her head. "See how he's carefully

wrapping up that glass in a towel?" Her gaze met J.D.'s. "I've helped him collect evidence before to send to the crime lab in Missoula. He's getting someone's fingerprints from the party."

J.D. stared at her. "Why would Max run a fingerprint check on anyone at the party?"

"I know it doesn't make any sense. We knew everyone who attended the party." She shivered. "But it would mean that even two weeks ago he suspected someone close to him."

"Come on," J.D. said, taking her hand, "I'm going to build a fire so you can warm up." He pulled a chair up to the fire for her and began pulling kindling and old newspapers out of the wood box. "Why would Max take one of the guest's fingerprints? It's not like most people's fingerprints are on file somewhere, right?"

"Unless the person had been arrested before or worked in a high-security job that required them," Denver agreed, sitting forward. "Or Max might have needed the prints to compare to some he'd picked up at a crime scene."

While J.D. got the fire going, Denver went to the phone. He listened while she called the crime lab in Missoula.

"They received a fingerprint request from Max," she said after she hung up. "But they can't give me any other information. They did say that their findings have been mailed." She picked up one of her framed photographs from the floor. "Another dead end unless we can dig them up at Max's office."

"You were very lucky this time, Denny," J.D. said as he joined her and hung the photo back on the wall.

"Whoever tried to strangle you obviously meant business."

"Speaking of luck, you must have gotten my message right after I called."

"You called me?" He sounded pleased to hear that.

She had stooped down to pick up a stack of spilled magazines; now she looked over at him. "If you didn't get my message, how did you—"

"Just luck." He smiled that all-too-familiar sexy smile of his. She wished he wouldn't do that when she was feeling vulnerable, then realized that around him she was *always* vulnerable.

"There seems to be a lot of luck going around," she said quietly.

"I followed you out of town," he confessed with a shrug and a sheepish grin. "I just thought—"

"That I might need help again." She laughed and shook her head at him in amazement. "You *do* know me, don't you." He knew her in a way no other man ever had; he'd seen into her heart and she'd invited him in. She quickly looked away from those knowing gray eyes of his.

"You said you recognized the guy's cologne?"

Denver picked up a couch cushion and put it back in place. So he *had* heard her. She hugged herself but couldn't shake off the cold chill as she looked over at him. His gaze was so filled with compassion she thought she would cry if she kept looking at him.

"It was the kind Pete wears," she said, realizing J.D. had probably recognized it, too.

"That's what I thought."

She waited for him to say, I told you so. He didn't. "Thanks for coming to my rescue."

His laugh was low, directly behind her. "A knight in armor I'm not, Denny. In fact…" His fingers touched her shoulder and his voice dropped.

"You were doing fine without me," she said, realizing she could mean both the fight in the driveway or his life in California.

"Don't kid yourself. I needed you."

Her body stirred beneath the warm touch of his fingers. His voice found its way to her heart and chipped away at the wall of ice she kept trying to build against him. Slowly she turned and looked up into his eyes. His gaze softened. How had she ever forgotten the depth of emotion in those eyes?

"You're scared to death it's Pete, aren't you?" He caressed her face, tracing his fingers along her cheek.

"Pete's been my best friend for years."

His fingers stopped short of her lips. "He's asked you to marry him?"

She nodded reluctantly.

He pulled his hand away. "Have you given him an answer yet?"

How could she tell J.D. that he'd been the only man who'd ever interested her let alone had a chance with her heart? "Yes. I can't marry Pete when I gave my heart to another man years ago—" The words caught in her throat.

"Denny," he said, his voice low and soft.

How many times had she wondered if J.D. ever regretted leaving West Yellowstone—and her? He looked as if all he wanted to do was kiss her, as if his lips wanted nothing more than to touch hers. But then he stepped back over to the fire.

"I'm never going to hurt you again," he said, making

her wonder if he was telling her—or reminding himself. He tossed another log onto the fire. "We'd probably better have a look upstairs to see how much damage
was done."

She stood, staring at his strong, muscular back, his
slim hips, wanting him in ways she'd never even imagined at sixteen. Then she followed him upstairs.

Her intruder had obviously started his search upstairs. Clothing hung out of dresser drawers; closet
doors stood open, their insides tumbled about. With
J.D.'s help, she quickly put things away. Then she saw
her old cloth doll on the floor. Denver picked it up; she
held it against her chest fighting tears of joy to see that
it hadn't been damaged.

"At least they didn't destroy the house as badly as
they did Max's office," she said, unable to let go of
Hominy. She touched the doll's worn face, thinking of
Max. And her parents. She couldn't remember if it had
been Max or her parents who'd given her Hominy. She
thought she remembered her mother giving her the doll
on her birthday but she couldn't be sure. Maybe she just
wished her mother had given it to her. She had so little
left of that life.

"You think this all ties in with Max's death?" she
asked.

"It seems likely, don't you think?" J.D. replied,
watching her. "Come on, let's clean up the other bedroom."

When they finished the bedroom, J.D. led the way
back downstairs. Denver picked up a throw pillow and
replaced it. When she turned, she caught the expression on J.D.'s face.

"What is it?" she asked. Her legs turned wobbly

under her and she gripped the back of a chair J.D. had righted. "You're scaring me."

"I'm sorry, I didn't mean to," he said, going to her. He led her over to the hearth and sat down beside her.

"Tell me what's wrong," she pleaded. "You didn't just come out here tonight because you were worried about me, did you?"

He shook his head. "Look around this room, Denny. Look at the bruises on your neck. You have to be straight with me if you want me to help you find Max's killer." Firelight caught in his eyes, making them bright as winter moonlight on new snow.

Automatically Denver reached for her mother's locket at her throat as she got up and walked to the window facing the lake. The glow of the fire flickered behind her, searing her silhouette to the glass.

"You're right not to trust me with your heart," he said. "But you have to trust that I'm here to help you."

She was right not to trust him with her heart? The words made her ache inside. Didn't he realize that trusting him meant surrendering not only her heart to him? There was no half way, no possibility of compromise, not between them. They could never just be friends. At least she couldn't.

"I saw Davey slip you a note, Denny." The hurt in his voice tugged at her heart.

She turned slowly, searching for the words. "I needed to open that note alone." Her desperation to find the name of Max's killer printed on that scrap of paper in that boy's young hand had pushed her away from J.D., the one man she longed to be close to. The fire danced wildly behind him, throwing his face in shadow. "It wasn't you. It was me." She began picking books up off the floor without even realizing she was doing it.

"Denny..." She continued gathering up things from the floor. Pictures from the walls, pillows, an over-turned chair. Suddenly she felt J.D.'s hand on her arm. "Talk to me, Denny." She looked up and saw some of her own fears mirrored in his eyes. J.D. pulled her to him and held her with a force that comforted her as nothing else had since Max's death. She pressed her cheek against his shirt, listened to his heart thunder next to her ear. "Talk to me, please."

She breathed in the scent of him. "I feel like my world is falling apart, like nothing is real—or ever was."

He stroked her hair, his hand sure and strong. "I'm going to help you put it back together. I'm not going to let anyone hurt you, Denny. I promise you that. But you have to trust me. No more secrets."

She struggled to find solid ground beneath his silver gaze. Instead, what she saw deep in his eyes made her heart dance to a beat she'd never known before. Over-whelming desire. It raced through her blood, melting the wall of ice around her heart. "Did I destroy any chance of you ever trusting me?" he asked, his eyes darkening like the storm outside.

She shook her head and looked away. "I'm just afraid your music will call you back before we can find Max's murderer."

He took her face in his hands; his eyes met hers. "I won't leave, Denny, until you no longer need me."

Then you will never leave, she thought.

Chapter 9

"Here," Denver said, handing him the note. "And don't bother to say it."

J.D. read the words, then looked up at her. "Say what? That you'd be a fool to meet him in an even more isolated place than the fire tower—that is, if he bothers to show up, if he has any information for you, if it's not a trap, if he could even spell?"

"That about covers it." She dropped into a chair by the fire. He could see the day's events had taken their toll on her, but a steely determination still burned in those incredible eyes.

"But you're going to do it anyway, aren't you?"

As she curled her feet up under her, she met his gaze. "You saw him at the hospital. He's obviously scared. Why would he have run if he didn't know something?"

J.D. hadn't the heart to tell her that the kid might have

taken off just to avoid reform school. "I'm going with you."

She smiled. "I had a feeling you'd say that."

God, she was beautiful. The firelight played in her hair, igniting it. And her eyes. Light, mysterious eyes. He wanted nothing more than to drown himself in them.

"As long as I'm being truthful, I guess there's something else you ought to know. I found Max's pistol and a box of shells he'd hidden in a compartment in his desk. If it's some kind of message to me, I don't know what it could be."

He felt his heart expand, his desire for her growing with the trust she was putting in him. She was still as defiant, stubborn and fiery spirited as anyone he'd ever known, only now there was an elegance to it that made her all the more fascinating. The last thing he wanted to do was hurt this woman. He promised himself he'd protect her—not only her life—but her heart.

He thought about his music. He'd come home, running scared. Nothing had mattered. Or hadn't until he'd seen her standing over him holding a lamp base.

Denver brushed a strand of hair back from her face. "The only lead I have to go on is a case Maggie said he was working on before his death. He'd been trailing a possible cheating husband and spending late long hours following the man."

"Any chance Max would have cross-referenced his files?"

She laughed. "You knew Max."

"It was just a thought." J.D. wondered if either of them really knew Max. "Denny…" Her gaze held a warning, almost convincing him it would be better if she found out from Deputy Cline. Almost. "Max made a rather large deposit in his account the day before he was murdered."

"How large?" she whispered.

"One hundred and fifty thousand dollars."

"Where would he get that kind of money?"

"I was hoping you might know."

She shook her head, her eyes filled with dread. "There's this reporter in town from the *Billings Register*. She stopped by Max's office earlier. She asked me where Max got his money and insinuated he'd been in on the bank robbery."

J.D. swore. "That's ridiculous. Your parents were killed during that robbery."

Denver shook her head. "The woman didn't know Max." She took a breath and let it out slowly. "But it doesn't look very good for him, does it?"

"No, it doesn't."

Denver buried her face in her hands for a moment. "He's innocent, J.D.," she murmured sadly, lifting her gaze. "But then, I want to believe Pete is innocent, don't I?"

With very little prompting, Denver agreed to spend the night in town at Maggie's. J.D. knew she was running from all the evidence building against Max, from her dreams about her parents, her worries about Davey, her fears about Pete. Max looked like a crook, and that, J.D. knew, was much more frightening to her than anything else that was happening.

As Denver gathered her ski gear for their meeting with Davey and her overnight bag to go to Maggie's, the phone rang.

It was obvious from the frown on her face that she

444   Odd Man Out

wasn't delighted about what was being said on the other
end of the line. Nor was that person letting her say much.

J.D. watched, suddenly frightened, knowing Pete
was on the other end of that line. And that Pete wasn't
happy about something. It scared him.

What bothered him most was the 150,000. Did the
reporter really suspect something, or was she just following up on the rumors?

"I don't want to talk about this right now," Denny
was saying, irritation in her tone. She twisted the phone
cord around her fingers. "Fine, I'll see you then."

He didn't like to hear that last part. "Everything all
right?"

"Pete just wants me to stop by the Stage Coach. The
band's playing there tonight."

J.D. nodded. "Denny, you wouldn't—"

"Don't worry, I haven't forgotten," she said, touching the bruises on her neck.

He wanted to say something to take the hurt from her
eyes. "Until we find out who killed Max, we're going
to suspect everyone."

She nodded and glanced toward the window. It had
stopped snowing and the first stars had popped out over
the mountains.

"You still want to go dig through Max's files? I'll
help you."

They split a pile of Max's papers in the middle of
the floor. And began sorting through them looking for
the "Case of the Wayward Husband," as J.D. called it,
as well as the fingerprint results from the crime lab.
She was glad for the company and even happier that
he'd suggested it.

"I love Max's system," J.D. said, holding up a file marked RoadKill. "What do you think goes in here?"

Denver shook her head. "Knowing Max, it could be anything." She read a file name. "How about this one— Rock 'n' Roll." They laughed together, their gazes locking. "I guess we'll have to rename the files."

J.D. nodded. "We could even use last names. What do you think?"

His hand brushed hers as he reached for more papers. Her pulse took off running. Her heart yearned to go chasing after it. His touch earlier seemed like an appetizer and she was one starved woman.

"Hungry?" J.D. asked.

She blinked at him. "What?"

"You just said you were starved."

"I did?" She ducked her head to hide her embarrassment.

J.D. got to his feet. "Why don't I get us something? I'll be right back. Want me to surprise you?"

"Great." Not that anything could surprise her after that. She sat in the middle of the floor trying to still her panic as she listened to his pickup leave. When was she going to learn not to say what she was thinking? She could just imagine what she'd say one of these days if she continued to hang around J. D. Garrison, feeling the way she did about him.

J.D. returned with two chili dogs loaded, fries and large Coke floats.

"You remembered," Denver said when she saw the food.

"Who could forget what you like?" he joked. "Not that many women like jalapeños and tortilla chips on their chili dogs."

"I have an odd appetite," she admitted, studying him through her lashes. As much as she loved chili dogs, right now all she really wanted was J.D.

He groaned softly, a smile playing at his lips, as he sat down beside her. "You know, I've always admired your appetite. Among other things." When he looked at her, she could have sworn he was reading her mind.

They wolfed down the food, then leaned against the wall to finish their Coke floats. Denver idly thumbed through a stack of Max's papers, thinking more about J.D.'s long legs than the words on the pages. One word jumped out at her. *Affair.* She plucked the sheet from the pile and checked the date. The last entry was less than a week ago.

"This is it!" she cried, sitting up straighter.

J.D. moved closer to read it with her. "Lester Wade? Is that the one I know?"

Denver nodded, momentarily mute from the scent of him. "Lester still plays in the band." She read down the page through a series of surveillance times and dates, all late at night even after the bars had closed. "That's strange. He had to be cheating on his wife, Lila. What else would he be doing out at this hour every night?"

"Not so." J.D. pointed to the last notation on the page. It read simply: "No other woman."

They looked at each other. "You don't think—"

Denver flipped the page. Written in Max's scrawl was the comment:

Informed wife Lila, Lester not having an affair.
Paid in full.

"Well, I guess that takes care of that," Denver said,

then squinted at the notation Max had made at the bottom of the page:

Bil 69614. Pearl file.

"Pearl file?" J.D. asked. His leg touched hers; the jolt rivaled any faulty toaster she'd ever known. "Do you know anyone named Pearl?"

Denver shook her head.

"How about the numbers?" J.D. asked.

She shook her head again. He was so close she thought for sure he'd kiss her. He must have thought the same thing because he moved over and got to his feet.

"Maybe it's some kind of billing code," J.D. suggested.

She groaned at the loss she felt when he moved away from her. "With Max, they could be just about anything." But she wrote them down, noticing it was late. "I didn't see a Pearl file, did you?"

"No. I didn't see anything with Bil on it, either," J.D. assured her. "Our burglar could have taken it, too, I suppose."

"That and the fingerprint results," Denver reminded him. She glanced at her watch. "I told Pete I'd stop by the Stage Coach."

The closeness she'd felt with J.D. all evening disappeared in one blink of his gray eyes. "I don't think that's a good idea, Denny. If you say anything to him—"

"I know," she interrupted. "I'll be careful."

As they were leaving, Denver reached into the mailbox, amazed she hadn't thought to check it before. She thumbed through the stack of bills and junk mail, then thumbed through again, this time paying closer attention. The return address of the crime lab in Missoula caught her eye. She plucked it from the pile and handed it to J.D. with trembling fingers. He took one look at it and tore it open.

"Who?" she asked, her voice no more than a whisper.

"I don't know. The prints belong to a man named William Collins. Do you have any idea who that is?"

"J.D., I knew everyone at Max's party. Whoever this William Collins is, I know him. I just don't know him by that name."

When they walked into the Stage Coach Inn's bar, Pete spotted them right away. The band was just finishing a number and Pete looked up. Just the sight of J.D. seemed to make him angry.

"Why don't you wait for me at the bar," Denver said.

"You're calling the shots." His gaze warned her to be careful. "But if you need me, I won't be far away." He strode off into the bar, where a group of fans was already on their feet with pens and paper in hand.

Denver felt as if someone had dumped a bucket of ice water on her as she watched the women huddle around J.D. for autographs. Sometimes she forgot about his fame.

Pete said nothing as he came toward her but grabbed her arm and propelled her out of the bar to the lobby.

"Where have you been?" he demanded as he pulled her over to the side of the wide, sweeping staircase. "I asked you to wait at the apartment for me."

Denver jerked free of his hold and glared at him. "I had to talk to Davey Matthews."

"Davey Matthews? When is this going to end?"

"When Max's killer is caught," she said.

"I'm trying to protect you. Can't you see that? And what is J.D. trying to do?" He pulled off his hat and raked his fingers through his blond hair. "You still believe that I hurt that kid up at Horse Butte?" Pete looked toward the lounge, anger in his eyes.

"I don't know what to believe." The sweet scent of his cologne was the same as the man's who'd attacked her at the lake cabin, but in her wildest imagination, she couldn't conceive of Pete trying to kill her. She could hear J.D.'s warnings but she couldn't stop herself. She'd worn a turtle-necked sweater to hide the bruises on her neck. Now she pulled the collar down so Pete could see her neck.

He let out an oath; his eyes filled with shocked horror. "Who did this to you?" he demanded.

She shook her head. "There were two men. They ransacked the cabin." She stared at him, remembering the feel of the man's arm around her throat. Anyone could buy the same cologne as Pete's—anyone with money, she reminded herself again. And yet she'd never wondered until that moment where Pete got the money to buy expensive cologne or new pickups or live the way he did. He certainly didn't make a lot playing with the band. But his family had money, she reminded herself, sick at the doubts she was having. "One of the men tried to kill me," she said, needing to get it all out. "He wore the same cologne you wear."

Pete rocked back as if he'd been slapped. "What are you saying? That you believe I could do this to you?"

Tears rushed to her eyes. This was a man who'd professed his love for her, who'd asked her to marry him. "I think the person who hurt me wanted me to believe it was you."

"Why?" He looked pale under the hotel's lights. Pale and sick. "Why would someone do that?"

"I don't know." She felt as if she'd been punched. "I thought maybe you would know."

He looked away for a moment, and she had the strongest feeling he knew more than he was telling her. His gaze softened as he turned back to her. "Remember when we were kids on the lake?"

She nodded. It had always been the three of them and Max. "Do you remember the tree house we built?" She wanted those times back. They'd been so close. Like family.

"The tree house." Pete looked up at the ceiling. "I'd forgotten about the tree house."

"You and J.D. didn't always agree, but we pulled together and we got it built," she said, memories flooding her heart. "Remember how it was? We were all best friends."

"Times change," Pete said, jamming his hands into his jeans.

"You and I have always been friends."

"Yeah, friends." He grimaced; it had never been enough for him.

She bit her lip, knowing she shouldn't say any more, but needing to know, and more than anything, wanting to give him a chance. "The day Max was murdered, you were in Missoula with the band." She studied him, thinking of the years they'd shared. The words caught in her throat. "Were you, Pete?"

He closed his eyes for a moment, then looked toward the bar again. "You want me to write it in blood? Because I'm sure my word won't be enough."

"Tell me about the photograph," she whispered, her

voice as lost as the look in his eyes. This was Pete. Pete Williams, a man she'd always trusted.

"The photograph?" Pete sighed as he pushed his hat back on his head. In the other room, the band started up again, only it was J.D. singing instead of Pete. And it was one of the songs that had made J.D. famous— "Good Morning, Heartache."

"Max called me and said he had to see me before I left for Missoula," Pete said slowly. "I knew something had been going on with him but he'd never wanted to talk about it before."

Denver held her breath, afraid of what Pete was going to say.

"But when I got to his office, he wasn't there." Pete looked her in the eye. "The photograph was on his desk."

"You took it and ripped J.D. out of the picture." It seemed like such a childish thing to do.

Pete shrugged. "He has it all, Denver. Everything. Including you. I'd let him have all his success and more if I could just have you."

Her heart ached at his words. In the next room, J.D. sang in that voice that had haunted her every dream for years.

"I'm sorry," she said quietly.

He nodded and touched a tear on her cheek with his fingertip. "Yeah, I know you are. But you're making a big mistake with him. He's back here, probably thinking you're what he needs." She could feel Pete's gaze on her face. "With J.D., nothing will ever be enough. Not even you."

Pete's words hit a chord in her. J.D. hadn't found happiness with his music. Did he see her as just another goal to be reached? The thought battered her heart.

"Haven't you ever asked yourself where J.D. got his start nine years ago?"

Denver caught her breath.

"Max." Pete spit out the word. "J.D. made a deal with Max. Money for the promise that he'd never come back for you. Max bought him off, and J.D. took the money and ran."

She let the air slip from her lungs, her wounded heart fighting to keep beating. "I don't believe you." Max wouldn't demand such a deal, and surely J.D. would never—

"You want to know what happened to that photo?" he asked as he started to walk away from her. "I ripped J.D. out just like I'd like to rip him from your heart."

As she watched Pete stalk away, she felt a fear, heart-deep, and an emptiness as cold and dark as a winter night. She staggered to the doorway of the lounge, stunned by Pete's jealousy of J.D. as much as by his claim that Max paid J.D. never to come back. Was J.D. that sure he would never want to come back, that he could never love her?

On stage, Pete announced that he and the famous J. D. Garrison were going to sing a song they had written together as teenagers. Anyone in the audience would have thought they were still the best of friends.

Their voices blended beautifully. Tears of sadness stung Denver's eyes. She'd known Pete harbored some envy when it came to J.D., but she had never realized how much. And it had nothing to do with music.

She stumbled down the hallway to the ladies' room and stared into the mirror. "Oh, Max." She washed her hands and splashed the achingly cold water on her face. She would get to the truth, she told herself as she left the room. Her resolve wavered, however, when she saw Deputy Cline in the shadows beside the stairway in the lobby. The music had stopped. And Cline was in deep conversation with J.D. They seemed to be arguing.

"What's wrong?" she asked, joining them.

Both men quit talking abruptly. Cline stepped back and pulled off his hat. There was a weariness about him as if he hadn't had much sleep lately.

"Denny," J.D. said, "it seems the deputy has frozen your uncle's assets until a deposit for 150,000 can be explained." His look warned her to be careful.

She frowned at Cline. "Why would you do that?"

The deputy attempted a sympathetic smile. "The money might have been acquired illegally."

"That's ridiculous," she snapped at him.

"Are you saying Max squirreled away that much?" Cline asked.

Money had never meant much to Max. "Obviously someone put it in his account to cast doubt on his character."

"One hundred and fifty thousand dollars?" Cline chuckled. "I wish someone would cast that much doubt on my character." He sobered. "Know anyone with that kind of money who hated your uncle enough to do that?"

Denver shook her head. Max didn't have any enemies that she knew of, let alone rich ones.

"It could be a smoke screen," J.D. interjected. "To lead you in the wrong direction."

Cline stood for a moment looking from one of them to the other. "Well, until we get to the bottom of it, that money stays right where it is. The Great Falls police have picked up a hitchhiker matching the description of the one seen with Max. They're holding him until I can drive up and talk to him."

Denver stared at Cline. "You can't still believe a hitchhiker killed my uncle. Not after this 150,000 has turned up. Unless you think the hitchhiker put it in Max's account."

Cline scratched his red neck. "I'm just covering all my bets. Maybe this hitchhiker didn't kill your uncle. But he might have seen who did."

"So you think that's a possibility?" Denver asked, amazed Cline had thought of it.

He grinned. "Anything's possible."

"When will you be talking to him?" she asked.

"First thing in the morning."

"I can't wait to hear what he has to say." Finally, maybe they'd have a lead. "Have you found Davey?" she asked, and realized belatedly that either way he would be a sore point with Cline.

"No, as a matter of fact, I have more important things to do than worry about a fifteen-year-old runaway," he snapped. "And one more thing, Ms. McCallahan. The next time you withhold information from my department, you're going to be the guest of the county. Got that?" He tipped his hat to J.D. and stomped off.

Denver turned her glare on J.D. "You told him about my ransacked cabin and the man who jumped us?"

"Someone had to. This is a homicide investigation, remember?"

"And a lot of good it did telling Cline," Denver said, daring him to argue with her. "Look what he came up with at Max's office. Nothing. He isn't going to solve this case and you know it."

"We can't be sure of that."

Tears rushed to her eyes. "I'm not sure of anything— or anyone. Not anymore." She turned to leave, but he grabbed her arm.

"You told Pete, didn't you?" he demanded.

She jerked away; her gaze snapped up to his. "I don't expect you to understand. I needed answers and I owed Pete that much."

J.D. slammed his fist against the wall. "Dammit, Denny, you may have just made the biggest mistake of your life."

"No, J.D., I did *that* the day I fell in love with you." She turned, tears blinding her, and ran.

Chapter 10

J.D. caught her just outside the door and pulled her into his arms. He kissed her the way he'd wanted to from the moment he saw her with that lamp in her hand at Max's apartment. An electricity danced between them. Her body felt as wonderful as he'd expected it would. But nothing prepared him for the sweet taste of her or the desire that swept through him as they kissed. All the memories of the past melded with the present, shocking him with one simple earthshaking fact: he'd never felt this way about a woman before. They both stumbled back from the kiss. Denver looked as dazed as he felt.

"And what was that all about?" she demanded, her voice as shaky as his knees.

"I just wanted to kiss you," he answered truthfully.

She nodded as if she'd expected as much from him. "Answer one other question then. Where did you get the money to go to California nine years ago?"

He knew where this had come from. Pete.

"Did Max give you money?" she asked, her eyes begging him to say no.

J.D. looked her in the eye. "Yes."

"And you made a deal with him that you would never come back into my life, right?"

"Denny, you were just a kid when I left."

"I see." She started to turn away from him.

He grabbed her arm and pulled her to him again. "No, you don't see. But you're going to." He led her to his pickup. "Get in. And this time, Denny, don't argue."

With a regal air, she climbed into the cab, slamming the door behind her. He joined her from the driver's side. The neon of the Stage Coach Inn sign flickered across the windshield. He could hear her angry breathing and feel his own pulse accelerate out of fear. He'd found Denny again and he didn't want to lose her.

"I *did* take money from Max," he said. "He offered it to me to give me a start. I later paid it back with interest. But there was no deal." He touched her shoulder, her heat rushing through his fingers and into his blood. The effect this woman had on him!

"Max obviously wanted you out of town as badly as you wanted to go." He heard what could have been a laugh—or a sob—come from her. She turned her face toward the side window away from him.

"Denny, all I ever promised Max was that I'd never hurt you. He just wanted you to be happy," he said, his hand gently rubbing her shoulder. "And he knew that couldn't happen if you quit school and took off with me. I had nothing to offer you. I didn't even know where I'd be sleeping or eating or—" His laugh was low and self-deprecatory. "No, the big thing was, I didn't know if I had talent. I was betting everything on a talent I wasn't even sure existed. I couldn't have asked you to go with me even if we hadn't been kids, even if—" she turned to look at him "—you'd been in love with me?"

He felt her gaze warm his face and he smiled wryly. "I was too full of myself to know how I felt about anyone."

Denver's answering smile was as sad as the knowing look in her eyes.

"That day at the fire tower, I didn't realize what you were offering me," he said softly. "I do now."

They sat in silence for long minutes. "It's getting late," she said. "I'd better get to Maggie's."

"I'll drive you."

"No." She started to open the door, but he stopped her.

"Dammit, Denny, can't we stop fighting each other?" She met his gaze and held it, the hurt in her eyes softening.

"I need to be alone to think," she whispered.

He wanted to kiss her again right now. Her lips looked full and soft, her eyes shimmered, and it was all he could do not to take her in his arms. "You'd better get out of here before I kiss you," he said.

She opened the pickup door, then leaned back in to kiss him. He grabbed her and pulled her into his arms. The first kiss had been sweet and stunning; this one started a fire in him he knew could never be put out. He drew her closer, pressing his lips and body to hers, feeling a bond that filled the holes in his heart.

She pulled away first. "I have to think," she mumbled as she slipped out of the pickup.

He watched her go, surprised by what he found himself wishing for.

* * *

The night air mingled with memories. J.D. grinning at her, holding her, threatening to kiss her. Denver forced herself to relive those first few months after his sudden departure. The hurt that had holed up inside her for so long finally moved on. Her heart soared, a kite in a strong wind, flying high into the night, free. She felt tears sting her eyes as the memories overwhelmed her. Memories of J.D. and Pete and Max. They'd always been connected, always been part of the happiest time of her life. Growing up on the lake with Max and the boys. Loving J.D. for as far back as she could remember.

Had Max really been trying to buy J.D. off, or had he just wanted J.D. to have a chance at reaching his dream? Max had always been proud of him. And Max had always known how Denver felt about J. D. Garrison.

She stopped on Maggie's steps recalling the kisses, the feel of his lips, the way her heart had pounded and her limbs had turned liquid. Just the touch of him made her insides ache. The night caressed her, clear and cold, while the dark velvet sky, splattered with a shower of silver as silver as J.D.'s eyes, smiled down on her. She breathed in the night air, savoring it the way she savored J.D.'s kisses. A laugh escaped her lips; she hugged herself, smiling. The past suddenly gave her a sense of peace. And the future?

J.D. still had a hold on her as strong as ever. He'd warned her not to trust him with her heart. What did he know that she didn't? No, the future held no peace, only a restlessness that she knew wouldn't end with the capture of Max's killer. It wouldn't end as long as J. D. Garrison had her heart. And she realized now that that would be forever.

Denver opened the door to find Maggie standing in the middle of a ransacked living room.

"Look what they've done," Maggie cried. "What in God's name was Max involved in?"

J.D. sat in his rented pickup down the street from the Stage Coach Inn waiting for Pete. He fought to quell his anger at Pete for lying about the reason why Max had given him money and why he'd taken it. Was there nothing Pete Williams wouldn't do to keep Denny? What frightened J.D. was not knowing Pete's motives. Was it only out of love for Denny? Or was he trying to hide his role in Max's death? As much as J.D. had first fought the idea, he now considered Pete Williams a prime suspect.

The back door of the Stage Coach opened and Pete came out and climbed into his pickup. It was parked next to an old school bus. The entire bus had been painted black, including the side windows, and the name Montana Country Club had been slapped on the side in an array of colors. J.D. remembered a bus he'd driven during his early touring days that looked a lot like it. Instantly he felt guilty for his success.

J.D. waited, then fell in behind at a safe distance, following Pete north out of town. He wasn't even a little surprised when Pete turned onto the Rainbow Point road. He was headed for Denny's cabin. J.D. turned out his lights, letting the bright sky overhead keep him on the road between the tall lodgepole pines, probably much like Pete had done that night on his way to the shortcut road on Horse Butte.

J.D. parked at the edge of a snowbank, not far from where Pete had left his pickup, and followed, keeping the thin beam of Pete's flashlight flickering through the trees ahead of him in sight. It took J.D. a moment to realize where Pete was headed—to the large tree house the three of them had built one summer when they were kids.

J.D. moved closer. The flashlight beam bounced with each step as Pete climbed up the makeshift ladder. Then the light went out for a moment as Pete disappeared inside the tree house. Through the cracks in the walls, J.D. saw the light come on again and heard Pete rummaging around, apparently searching for something.

J.D. sneaked to the bottom of the tree and climbed up as quietly as he could. As he reached the trapdoor, he wished he had a gun. He didn't like guns. But right now, holding heavy, cold steel in his hand would have given him a real feeling of security. He slipped through the open trapdoor.

Denver helped Maggie clean up the house. Like hers, it hadn't been ransacked as badly as Max's office and apartment. Just enough to make her and Maggie both feel violated.

"Are you sure you're okay?" Denver asked after they'd finished. Maggie had built a fire in the fireplace and collapsed in front of it.

"I'm just mad now," she said. "I want these people stopped."

"I was hoping you'd say that. There's someone I need to talk to—Lila Wade. She's the woman Max was working for right before his death."

"Yes, that's the one who suspected her husband of cheating on her," Maggie returned.

Denver explained what she and J.D. had discovered in the file, including the notation at the bottom. "I'm hoping Lila might be able to shed some light on it. Mind if I borrow your car? J.D. and I left my Jeep at the lake."

"Of course not." Maggie handed her the keys. "Are you sure you don't want me to come with you?"

Denver shook her head. "I don't want her to feel like we're ganging up on her."

Pete stood over an old box that had once doubled as a bench, leafing through a manila file folder by flashlight. The smell of the old wooden tree house flooded J.D. with memories of the three of them and the club they'd formed to protect their treetop fort. Just kids. Silly kids.

"Interesting reading?" J.D. asked.

Pete jumped, the file folder snapping shut in his hands. "I thought you'd be with Denver."

"Did you? Is that why you told her about Max giving me money?"

Anger showed in Pete's eyes and in the tight set of his jaw. "You forced me to do that because you wouldn't stay out of things. Your interference is causing me a lot of headaches."

J.D. sighed, suddenly tired. And afraid. "What's going on, Pete? I assume that's the case file everyone's been looking for. What's so important about it?"

Pete glanced at the folder in his hands. "You don't know how badly I need this. When I was talking to Denver tonight, she reminded me of the tree house."

Max had hidden it where he thought Denny would find it. Had he forgotten about Pete? Or had he trusted Pete so much it got him killed? "There was a time when we were best friends, when we trusted each other," J.D. said.

Pete gripped the file tighter. "That was before Denver fell in love with you and stayed in love with you."

"This doesn't have anything to do with Denny and me," J.D. said, realizing it probably had more than he knew to do with them. "Let me see the file."

Pete ran the back of his hand across his mouth. "I can't do that." His hand dropped to his jacket pocket.

J.D. swore as he stared at the pistol Pete pulled, then looked up at his friend's face. "Tell me you didn't kill Max."

"Would it do any good?"

"I don't believe you're a murderer."

"Why not? You already know I'm a liar."

"But not a killer," J.D. said with more confidence than he felt.

"Oh, I wouldn't bet your life on that, old buddy," Pete said, moving toward the trapdoor, the gun pointed at J.D.'s chest.

J.D. held his ground. "The name of Max's murderer is in that file, isn't it? Who are you protecting, Pete?"

"How do you know I'm not just protecting myself?" They stood only a few feet apart; J.D. could taste the tension between them. He estimated the distance and wondered whether he could reach Pete, take the gun away and not get either of them killed.

"Don't do it, J.D. There's been enough bloodshed."

"If you care about Denny, tell me what's in that file. She isn't going to give up looking for Max's killer and you know it."

Pete swore. "Can't you make her see how dangerous this is?"

"Just how dangerous is it, Pete?"

"It could get her killed."

J.D. shook his head. "Turn the file over to Cline."

Pete seemed amused by that idea. "Cline?" He

glanced down at the folder. "This is about a lot more than just who killed Max, don't you realize that? Stay out of it, old buddy. And keep Denver out."

They stood staring at each other, across the years and the choices that separated them.

"Is that file worth dying over?"

Pete smiled. "Or killing over? Yes." He edged toward the door. "If this landed in the wrong hands..." He shook his head. "Take care of Denver. I can't protect her anymore. But don't break her heart again, old buddy. Not again." The gun leveled at J.D.'s heart, Pete stepped to the trapdoor and waited for J.D. to move so he could slip through it.

J.D. moved back, but at the last moment grabbed his arm. "Dammit, Pete, I can't let you leave with the file."

Pete shook off J.D.'s hold. "But the only way you can stop me is to take this gun away from me, and I can't let you do that. Trust me on that, J.D."

J.D. looked from the pistol to Pete's face. Would Pete really shoot him? "Tell me I'm not a fool to trust you."

Pete smiled, his eyes as blue as they'd been in his youth and just as hard to read. "Oh, you're a fool, all right, J.D.," he said, and dropped through the hole into the night.

J.D. stood in the tree house, praying he hadn't made a fatal mistake.

Lila Wade answered the door of her doublewide trailer in a hot pink chenille robe and fuzzy bunny slippers. Most of her short brown hair was still trapped in curlers; some had escaped and stood on end, giving her a comical look.

"Yes?" she muttered, squinting as she held the door open.

Denver introduced herself.

"I know who you are." Lila had partaken of at least a few beers this night. "What can I do for you?"

"I'd like to talk to you about my uncle," Denver said, hoping they wouldn't be forced to have this discussion on the front steps. "It will just take a moment."

Lila made a face but opened the door wider for Denver to enter. "Lester's going to be home soon, you know."

Denver didn't know. Lila motioned toward the couch, and Denver sat down, dropping deeper than she expected into the worn-out cushions. "I'm checking into some recent cases my uncle was working on before his murder." She tried to work her way to the edge of the couch but gave up. "You hired him a few weeks ago to follow your husband."

Lila let out a snort as she picked up a bottle of bright red fingernail polish and continued what Denver had obviously interrupted. "Don't ask me why I did it. I was telling Clara—Clara Dinsley, you know her—"

"She's the beautician at ClipTop."

Lila nodded, the polish brush dangling from her fingers. "I was telling her I thought that damned Lester was chipping around on me. And she suggested hiring Max. I guess she'd hired him once." She waved that away as another story. "So I did. It was just plain silly. Lester with another woman! He can't even handle the one he has." She let out a brittle laugh as she screwed the lid down tight on the polish.

"Where was Lester those nights you thought he was with another woman?" Denver asked.

Lila's face stiffened as if a mud mask she'd applied had suddenly dried. "Just foolin' around with the boys. Drinkin', stuff like that." She got to her feet, careful not to touch her nails. "Lester will be home soon. I don't want him finding you here."

Denver nodded as she pushed herself out of the couch. "Well, thank you."

"No problem. I hope I helped you some." Lila closed the door behind her. Denver walked to Maggie's car and, as she climbed in, turned to look back. She caught Lila peeking out the curtains. And she wondered just what Lester Wade had been doing those late nights. And why Lila had lied for him.

The call from California came just before J.D. showed up at Maggie's door. It was from a member of his band who'd tired of leaving messages at the Stage Coach and was trying to track J.D. down. Denver took the message. She handed it to J.D. when he came in. It read:

> I hope things are going better, that you're writing some new songs, and that you've changed your mind. Hurry back.

J.D. read it, then crumpled the note and threw it into the fireplace. Denver saw the dark frustration in his eyes and doubted he'd written any new songs. He'd been too busy helping her. But what did "hope…you've changed your mind" mean?

"I understand if you have to go back—"

"You'd better get some sleep," he said, cutting her off. "We have to be at Grayling Pass before daybreak. I'm going to spend the night here with you and Maggie just in case—"

She nodded and went down the hall to the linen

closet to pull out sheets and blankets for him. "Can't you tell me what it is, what's wrong?"

"Nothing's wrong." He turned his back to her and began making himself a bed on the couch with the bedding she handed him.

"Fine. Nothing's wrong. Everything's great." She spun on her heel and started down the hall.

"Denny."

She turned to find him silhouetted against the firelight.

"You don't understand." His voice, soft as a caress, tugged at her.

"No, I don't," she said, closing the distance between them. "Why don't you tell me? It's being here with me, isn't it? It's hurting your career."

He let out an oath and took her shoulders in his hands. "It's not you. It's the songs. They're gone." He dropped his hold on her and moved over to the fire.

She stared at his back. "What do you mean they're gone?"

"The music has been in my head ever since I can remember." He turned to look at her. "Then one day, I woke up and it wasn't there anymore. And I didn't care." His gaze met hers and held it. "Until I saw you again."

She stepped into his arms and he held her. The fire crackled behind them.

"Go to bed," he said softly, kissing the top of her head. "We need to get some rest."

She nodded and moved away, knowing nothing she could say would erase the pain in his eyes. Behind her, she heard J.D. collapse on the couch.

She stopped in Maggie's room to tell her goodnight, then went into the guest room, stripped down and crawled into bed. For so long, her heart broken, she'd focused all her thoughts and energy on losing J.D. Now as she lay staring up at the ceiling, she felt only his hurt, his pain. If she followed her heart, she knew exactly where it would lead. To the man on the couch in the other room. She didn't care where J.D.'s heart was headed. He needed her. While she wasn't sure how to help him, as she drifted off to sleep, she promised herself when the time came, she'd be there for him.

Chapter 11

Long before sunrise, J.D. pulled off Highway 191 into a plowed area not far from Grayling Pass on the far side of Fir Ridge. "What's wrong?" he asked as the darkness settled around them.

Denver glanced back at the highway. "Nothing."

"I don't think we were followed, if that's what's worrying you."

She looked behind her again and he could tell she didn't believe that. "It's nothing," she said again. "Probably just the heebie-jeebies."

J.D. knew those well. He'd lain awake last night thinking about Denny. As he studied her face in the shadowy darkness, he wondered what the future held for them. That old spark of hope he'd thought dead stirred in his heart. For a while, he'd forgotten about liars and murderers; he'd even forgotten about Pete and the case file.

"Denny, last night, after you left the Stage Coach, I followed Pete out to your cabin. He went to that tree house we built."

"The tree house?"

"He found the case file Max had hidden there."

"So there *was* a case file." She grumbled softly under her breath. "Why didn't I think of the tree house? Only Max would hide it there. What was in the file?"

J.D. chewed at his cheek. "I don't know. Pete wasn't in the mood to show me."

"What?"

"He had a gun," J.D. explained. "But that was only one reason I didn't try to stop him."

He heard her chuckle. "So which one of us is the bigger fool?"

He grinned. "I'd say it's a toss-up." He rubbed his whiskered jaw and stared out into the dark. "What are the chances I can talk you into staying here and letting me get the information from Davey?"

Her laugh was low as she climbed out of his pickup. He concentrated on the dark for a moment, wondering if they were just as foolish to trust Davey, then followed her.

The faint starlight did little to illuminate the pre-dawn sky. Denver fingered the tiny flashlight in her jacket pocket, but quickly rejected the idea. As J.D. handed down her cross-country skis and backpack from the pickup, she felt the blackness envelop her and the memory of Davey's wreck on Horse Butte came back in vivid detail like an omen. Her fingers shook as she snapped her boots into the bindings; she told herself it was just the cold.

She swung the backpack on, automatically pulling her long braid out from under the strap. Bending down to put on his rental skis, J.D. was an ebony-etched shadow in the night beside her. She was getting used to having him around.

It had snowed during the night. The earth lay cloaked in a soft white mantle. Away from the shadow of the trees, the snow glowed, clean and cold, a virgin tapestry. Denver skied to the top of the ridge and turned to watch J.D. glide toward her. Something in the way he crossed the snowfield tugged at her. His smooth, fluid grace. The power behind his gentle movements as he joined her on the ridge line.

"Where to, Sunshine?" he whispered, just inches from her. Blame it on the quiet seclusion of the hillside. Or the cold air that seemed to suspend them in time. Or the fact that J. D. Garrison hadn't called her Sunshine in years. Suddenly all she wanted was to be wrapped in his arms. To feel his warm breath on her neck. To have him kiss away the cold—and the fear.

Even in the dull light, she was afraid he had seen what she was thinking and quickly turned away. But too late. His gloved hand clasped her shoulder and turned her to him. In an instant, she was in his arms, her skis entwined with his. His lips grazed hers tentatively. His kiss last night had been urgent, then soft, sweet and loving. This was a combination of the two. His lips caressed hers, his tongue explored the warm wetness of her waiting mouth. She melted into him, surrounded by his strong arms and the warmth of his body, the wondrous feel of his mouth on hers. His tongue touched hers, teasing, tempting, then plunged into her again, seeking, savoring. Slowly he pulled back to look at her, his breath as ragged as her own.

"Oh, J.D."

He smiled ruefully and pointed to a large pine tree. "I think we'd better find a place to wait for Davey."

They crouched in the windblown hollow under the huge pine, hiding in the shadowy darkness beneath it. Denver focused her binoculars on the crest of the ridge. It was still too dark to make out anything but patterns of black. She rubbed her mittened hands together. Her breath came out in frosty white puffs.

"Cold?" J.D. whispered.

"A little." Just the closeness of him was enough to fog up her binoculars.

"Well, I'm freezing." He put his arm around her and gently pulled her to him. "You wouldn't let me freeze, would you?" She snuggled against him without protest and fought the sharp pang of desire that swept through her. His breath stirred the hair at her temple. She closed her eyes to the dark and listened to the rapid beat of his heart, her own answering with a thunder as she snuggled against him to wait for sunrise.

The sound of a semi coming up Grayling Hill woke her up. Denver sat up under the tree, banging her head on a limb and sending a shower of new snow cascading down on her. In the silence after the truck topped the hill, she heard another sound. The soft click of a car door closing. She glanced over to find the spot under the tree beside her empty. J.D. was gone.

Swearing, she raised her binoculars and scanned the wide stretches along the highway through the barren limbs of the aspens. The sky had lightened but not enough to distinguish much more than shapes. Then she saw them. Two figures, dressed in heavy coats and hats, unloading large packs from a light-colored van parked beside the highway. It was still too dark to recognize them, but one towered over the other. Could Davey be the smaller one? Denver scanned the hillside again. Where was J.D.?

After a moment, the van drove away, and she watched the two finish loading their equipment onto a sled. Something glinted in the waning darkness, then the skiers covered the sled with a tarp and started east along the ridge line toward Yellowstone National Park, the larger man pulling the sled behind him.

Denver watched with growing interest. These skiers were taking an awful lot of gear if they only planned to make the Fir Ridge Trail Loop through forest-service land and part of Yellowstone Park, ending on the outskirts of West Yellowstone. It was only a half-day loop, certainly not long enough for all the supplies and equipment they were carrying.

She lowered her binoculars. They could be planning to go into the back country of the park and camp for a few days. Except... She brought the binoculars up to her eyes again. Except that it was spring, a bad time for a long ski trip, what with the snow rotting in sunny places on the mountainsides and with the grizzly bears coming out of hibernation in hungry, ill-tempered moods.

Another semi downshifted for the long climb up the hill as the sky began to lighten over the dark purple of Mount Holmes peak. Denver cursed J.D. as she struggled to get out of her hiding place under the tree. How could he wander off now, of all times?

"You have such a way with words," said a voice above her. Strong arms pulled her easily from the shel-

ter beneath the pine boughs, then dropped her unceremoniously in the snow. She stumbled and almost fell.

"Where have you been?" Denver demanded.

"Keep your voice down," J.D. whispered. "I just
wanted to take a closer look."

"And?"

"And nothing. Just two men. Davey wasn't one of
them. Let's go home."

Denver watched the silhouettes of the two figures
move across the ridge line as she reached for her skis.
"I'm going to follow them."

"I beg your pardon?"

"Shh. Something isn't right here and you know it."

"I know there's another storm coming in, Davey
tricked us into getting up early, he's probably robbing
your cabin right this moment, and at best, I know following these two men could be a waste of time. At
worst—" His gaze locked with hers, warming her deep
inside.

"Are you trying to tell me you don't think there's
anything suspicious about those two?"

He glanced after the skiers. "Too much equipment,
too early in the morning and too late in the season?"

She nodded. "Want to try to convince me it's a coincidence that Davey told me to be here at the same time
those two showed up?"

"No."

She slipped on her pole straps, grinning at him.
"Then I'm going after them."

"I never doubted it for a moment."

"Then why did you argue with me?" she demanded
in a hoarse whisper.

"Habit?" He gave her a shrug and a grin. The grin

made her want him to hold her again more than ever. "Maybe you ought to go back and let someone know what's going on."

"Nice try," she said.

As they skied after the pair, Denver wondered what would happen when they all arrived at their destination. She thought of Max's pistol in her backpack. It seemed little consolation as she skated her skis to gain speed, trying to catch sight of the men. She skied parallel to the trail and the men, keeping a good fifty yards to the south. Ahead of her, she watched J.D.'s back, his skis making a steady swish across the snow. She just hoped they weren't being drawn into a trap.

Not far up the trail, Denver realized they'd lost the skiers. The ridge line glistened in the silvery light of daybreak as she traced the horizon through her binoculars from Highway 191 across the gossamer-smooth snowfields to a thick stand of aspen several hundred yards ahead. Beyond the aspen grove, mountains cloaked in dense pines climbed toward the heavens. The nearest road to the east was thirty miles away. Someone could get lost in this remote part of the country forever, she thought as she turned to search again among the bare aspen limbs etched against the skyline. She'd just lost two of them.

"See 'em?" J.D. whispered beside her.

"No." She handed J.D. the binoculars and surveyed the countryside with her naked eye. "They couldn't just disappear," she whispered back. "They should be on the ski trail. Unless..." She glanced over at J.D.

He lowered the binoculars. "Unless they knew we were following them. Or they have some reason not to take the trail."

Denver scoured the ridge line again. "They couldn't have seen us. And this isn't the Bermuda Triangle. They didn't have that much lead time. They couldn't have just vanished." She reached for her poles to ski farther up the trail. Then she saw it.

A movement. In the aspens. She motioned to J.D. Suddenly a figure glided from the trees, a sleek silhouette of arms and legs in stride as he skimmed across the snowy opening. In an instant, another skier burst from the trees.

Denver gave J.D. a thumbs-up sign. "We have them now," she said softly, watching the men head east toward Yellowstone Park and directly into the pines and the approaching storm. They were making their own trail as they went.

J.D. grunted. "Or they have us."

"Don't try to change my mind," she advised.

"I'm smarter than that."

Denver gave him a look that said she doubted it, as she tucked her binoculars into the backpack next to her camera, survival gear, including her hairbrush, and Max's loaded pistol. As she zipped the top of the pack closed again, she eyed the approaching storm.

"It's pretty dangerous to ski into a storm, especially a spring storm," he said quietly.

A spring storm could drop several feet of snow in a matter of hours. People got lost every year; they went to sleep after wandering in circles and died of hypothermia. She and J.D. were breaking not one but two cardinal rules—they were skiing into a storm and they were alone. No one knew they were there. Except Davey. Wherever he might be.

Denver swung the pack onto her back and smiled at

J.D. "Why worry about a little old spring storm? I'll bet those men are more dangerous than any storm you've ever run across."

He laughed. "Got your logic from Max, didn't you?"

Just the mention of Max made them look solemnly at one another for a moment, then up the trail after the skiers.

"Okay, Denny," J.D. acceded. He touched her cheek, his gaze assuring her that he was willing to take the risk with her, because of her. "Let's go get 'em."

Winter had wrapped the earth in a cold and silent package of white, and spring had done little to release its hold here in the high mountains. Picking up the ski tracks left by the men, she and J.D. followed at a safe distance, gliding their skis across the silken snow in a rhythmic swish. The air tasted cold and wet; the breeze played at the loose strands of hair that had escaped from her braid and her hat. She didn't look back as they skied away from the highway and deeper and deeper into the mountains. Instead, she concentrated on the skiers ahead. And J.D. directly in front of her. Whatever trouble might lie up the trail, she was taking J.D. into it with her. That, she realized, worried her more than her own safety.

Daylight came slowly. First, flickers of gray rimmed the mountains, then filtered up into the atmosphere. The snow absorbed the light, then radiated it. But the new day brought problems; they could no longer follow as closely and had to drop back. The men were moving fast, probably rushed by the storm that now inched across the peaks toward them.

"You know something, Denny?" J.D. remarked at her side. They'd stopped for a moment along a hillside; their quarry had also stopped. The day had broken and was spilling around them, gray as the coming storm. "You've turned into quite the woman. I'm proud of you." He looked away. "They're moving again," he said, skiing off.

She smiled, then followed him.

A half mile up the trail, J.D. came to a sudden stop. "Get down!" He pushed Denver behind a snow-covered pine, but not before she'd seen the skier below them. He stood at the bottom of a ravine, his rifle raised, looking through the scope. In her direction.

"Tell me that wasn't a rifle," Denver whispered.

"It was a rifle."

She glared at him.

He shrugged in reply. "Something tells me we're not dealing with your average armed cross-country skiers here."

"Firearms are prohibited in Yellowstone Park," she said. "And they're headed for the park."

He glanced over at her and smiled. "Well, Denny, when we catch up to those two, I think you'd better tell them that."

She mugged a face at him. "Do you think he saw us?"

J.D. pulled her deeper into the shelter of the pine tree. "I don't know." She could see the worry on his face. "You have to admit that the chances are good these guys could be dangerous."

She cupped his bearded jaw in her gloved hand. "Convince me it's a coincidence that Davey told me to be here at sunrise."

He smiled at her. "I've never had any luck convincing you of anything." His gaze caressed her face. "You realize, of course, if that skier saw us, he's probably working his way back up the hill toward us."

"Or rounding up his friend to come get us," she whispered back.

"You always know just what to say to make me feel better." His look turned grim. "Seriously, Denny, this is a risky business. I think we're out of our league here."

"But we're on to something. You feel it, too. If we turn back now, we may never find out what's going on." He held her gaze. My God, did J.D. really believe Max was involved in something illegal? She looked at the mountains ahead, suddenly afraid of what they might discover there.

"If that skier didn't see us, he's going to be moving again," J.D. warned. Denver shifted and peered around the trunk of the tree.

"Damn. He's gone." Denver scanned the trees and the white snowy expanse ahead. "You all right?" she asked, adjusting her backpack. J.D. hadn't moved.

He looked at her with a straight face. "We're miles from the highway, heading into a snowstorm, following two men with guns. Of course I'm all right."

She tugged his ski hat down over his face, then poled after the skiers, following the tracks in the snow.

They'd lost valuable time and the thought of losing the skiers now was unbearable. Ahead she saw the clear-cutting that marked the Yellowstone Park boundary. At first she didn't see the man. Then she caught a glimpse of movement as white as the snow. He crossed the clearing, his dark-colored coat hidden under what looked like a white bed sheet, and was quickly sucked up in the pines on the other side. Yellowstone Park.

"Did you see that?" Denver pulled her camera from

her pack. Her fingers trembled as she snapped on the telephoto lens. She had a feeling she was about to take some of the best photographs she'd ever taken in her life. The second skier crossed the clearing—also covered with a white sheet. Denver focused, then hit the motor drive, capturing the second skier's movements on film like an evasive ghost.

"Kinda makes you think they don't want anyone to see them enter the park," J.D. muttered. He stood watching her, a frown creasing his forehead. There was no turning back now, and Denver could see that in J.D.'s expression.

Denny slipped the camera back into her coat.

"You realize if there was some way I could protect you—"

"I've been protected too much in my life, as it is." She squared her shoulders and brushed a gloved finger along his bearded jawline. "From now on, I'm going to make my own mistakes. And by the way, I have Max's pistol. We're just as illegal as those two."

"Thanks for warning me."

The storm dropped over the tops of the pines like a thick drape, snuffing out the light, making the new day appear to dissolve into twilight. The air settled around them, heavy with moisture. Denver threw her pack over her shoulders again and adjusted it, then she and J.D. headed after the men. Time was running out.

She could feel the men's driving need to get somewhere. Her arms and legs ached to the point of numbness as the hours passed and she wondered how much farther she could go.

Not far into the park, the skier in front of them dropped down a hillside and stopped. Denver and J.D.

skied into a stand of small pines. Denver slipped her camera from its shelter in her coat and handed J.D. her binoculars. As she focused on the skier they'd been trailing, Denver saw the larger skier join him and push back his ski mask, giving her a clear view of his face. She swore as she recognized him.

"It's Cal Dalton!" She snapped his photo, then focused on the other man. He still wore his ski mask, but he looked vaguely familiar. "Can you tell what they're doing?" she asked J.D.

Cal tugged at something and a camouflaged tarp fell away from a huge pile of what looked like limbs, tree limbs.

She focused the telephoto lens on the pile. They weren't limbs. They were antlers. Elk antlers. Denver moaned.

"Horn hunters," J.D. said, peering through the binoculars. "Looks like they've come for their cache."

The other skier stepped into view, his ski mask now pushed back as he started to load the horn onto the sled.

Denver's heart lurched. "It's Lester Wade."

Chapter 12

Pete had never liked Earthquake Lake, didn't like meeting here and wasn't thrilled about the feeling he'd had all day that something was wrong, terribly wrong. As he stood at the empty visitors center, he tried to focus his thoughts on Midnight. The boss had finally agreed to meet him face-to-face. No more having to deal with that crazy Cal.

But not even finally meeting Midnight could keep him from feeling uncomfortable here. He stared at the lake, trying to decide what it was about it that bothered him. A feeling of death hung suspended over the long narrow lake. Maybe it was all the dead trees, still standing like aging sentinels chest-deep in the icy water. Or maybe it was the ghosts of the people who'd died here that night in 1959 when the earth shook down a mountain on top of them, while behind the fallen mountain, the Madison River pooled like blood to form the lake.

The phone rang, making him jump. He stared at it, realizing that Midnight had tricked him again.

"You're late," the synthesized voice said on the other end of the line.

"I thought you said you'd meet me here," Pete complained.

Midnight let out that synthesized laugh Pete had come to hate. "You sound tense. Has something happened?"

"No." Pete tried to relax. "Everything's fine."

"You have Denver under control?" he asked.

"Sure." He only wished. He'd been trying to reach her all morning and there'd been no answer. Where in the hell was she? And more importantly, what kind of trouble were she and J.D. cooking up? At least he had the file now.

"What about the kid?" Midnight asked. "We find him yet?"

"Davey won't be doing any talking."

"Then everything is just as we planned?"

"Yeah." Pete was relieved when Midnight didn't ask him any more about Denver, but got straight to business. He'd stashed Davey at a friend's—not quite as permanent as Midnight would have liked, but Pete didn't have the stomach for more bloodshed.

"I have a buyer," Midnight said. "Wants a trophy elk and a deer. The guy's willing to pay 16,000 a piece. And we need more bear. Our Oriental entrepreneurs are paying 4,000 a pound for bear gallbladders. The little suckers are so damned easy to transport inside film canisters—let's hit them hard."

"Bear bladders," Pete muttered, mentally adding them to the list. He wondered where Midnight was calling from. Someplace safe, no doubt, the way he was running off at the mouth.

"Can you imagine wolfing down dried bear bladders?" Midnight pretended to gag. "Some aphrodisiac, if you ask me. Kind of like that stuff they make out of the horns—wapiti love potion, my behind. Supposed to have a rejuvenating property like ginseng, keeps you from aging or something. All I know is sliced-up elk horns and all those strange grasses they throw in and boil up make for some pretty vile brew. It sure didn't do anything for me as far as the ladies are concerned, but then I never needed it to start with." Midnight chuckled. "*You* might want to try it, though, Pete." He tried to contain his laugh and failed. "Or maybe give a little to Denver."

At times like this, Pete wished he'd never gotten involved with this operation. Or this man. But he had to admit Midnight was damned good at this business; that's why no one had ever caught him.

"And my buyer will take all the bear-paw pads you can get," Midnight continued. "They eat 'em, you know. Bear-paw pads." He groaned. "Can you believe that?"

The shadows running ahead of the storm collected in the dead pines. Pete wished they could hurry. He felt nervous and tired; all he wanted was for this to be over so he could go find Denver.

"Anyone seen any griz yet?" Midnight asked.

"Yeah, Cal got treed the other day."

Midnight swore. "Tell him to shoot the damned things instead of letting them run him up a tree. Jeez. We need more griz and bear claws for our jewelry customers, too." He chuckled. "That damned Cal. He's crazy, you know that?"

Unfortunately, Pete did. And he wondered if Midnight had ordered the hit on Denver the other night or if Cal had just improvised on his own. Another scare tactic.

Pete could hear Midnight's admiration for crazy Cal resonating in his counterfeit voice. "How is the shed-horn shipment coming? We can't miss the deadline or the price will fall."

"There won't be any delays." At least Pete hoped there wouldn't be. He could feel Midnight listening closely to him and tried to sound enthusiastic. "Cal says it's like the ultimate Easter-egg hunt out there this year. They're picking up a thousand dollars' worth of horn in about thirty minutes."

"My kind of sport!" Midnight declared. "You don't seem all that excited about business, though. I mean, we're making more money than the president of the United States and it's as easy as robbing an unguarded bank." Midnight laughed.

"I'm not sure Max would have agreed with that."

The laugh died. "Just get me the merchandise. And don't sound so damned unhappy about raking in money. It makes me nervous."

"When am I going to meet you?" Pete asked before Midnight could hang up. "Don't you think it's time we quit playing this little electronic phone game?"

Silence. "We will meet soon enough. In the meantime, make sure Denver doesn't become any more of a problem. And you know that case file you found of Max's?"

Pete held his breath. "Yes?"

"It felt like some of the information was missing."

Pete's heartbeat echoed, ricocheting against his chest

so loudly he almost couldn't hear Midnight when he spoke.

"You wouldn't hold out on me, would you, Pete?"

"If you'd tell me exactly what it is you're looking for—"

But Midnight had already hung up. Pete swore. He didn't like working for a synthesized voice at the end of a phone line; it was time Midnight showed himself.

As Pete walked back to his pickup, snow began to drift down from the grayness overhead. He thought about the case file and the information he'd taken out. A little insurance. Then he thought about Max hiding the file, probably thinking it was his insurance. Max's death still bothered him, gave him nightmares even in the daylight. Maybe there was no insurance against a man like Midnight.

He returned to his more immediate problem. Denver. Where was she and what was she doing? He didn't even want to consider the possibilities.

Poachers. Cal Dalton and Lester Wade. Denver groaned as she watched Cal raise binoculars and point them toward a wind-scoured slope across the ravine. At the edge of the storm clouds on the opposite mountainside, she could see a bull elk feeding on the snow-bare slope. The area was a winter elk range. And it didn't take an Einstein to figure the two below her had been collecting the antlers shed by the elk in hopes of smuggling them out of the park—a highly profitable but equally illegal enterprise.

"It all makes sense now," Denver said as she remembered Max's scribbles at the bottom of Lester Wade's file. "Pearl. Oh, J.D., don't you see? That's what Max meant. The Oriental Pearl, the brow of the elk, the elixir of the Orient. The elk horn." She stared at him, her eyes widening. "Max was referring to the poaching operation."

"That would explain a lot," J.D. agreed. "Like why he was spending time with Cal Dalton. And what Lester Wade was doing late at night when his wife thought he was chasing other women."

"And why Lila lied," Denver added. "I'm sure she and Lester could use any extra money he made. She was probably just relieved Lester wasn't running around on her."

"Most people don't consider picking up shed horns—even in a national park—much of a crime," J.D. remarked.

Denver focused the camera on Cal near another cache of horns and snapped his photo; the motor drive hummed as she captured the two on film as they loaded the sled.

"Davey must have reason to suspect Max's death is connected to the poachers," she said, lowering the camera. "Why else would he tell me to be here this morning?"

"He could have known Max was investigating Lester Wade and found out about the poaching."

She looked over at J.D. as she dropped the exposed film into her backpack. Maybe it was just the way he said it or the way he wouldn't meet her gaze. "That explains everything except the 150,000 in Max's account."

"Yeah."

She began reloading the camera. Her fingers trembled with anger. And fear. "Poaching has become very profitable. Newly shed horns can go for more than ten dollars a pound. But not *that* profitable." She bit her lip, and shifted her gaze at him. "Max wasn't involved in poaching horn."

J.D. put his arm around her. "You won't get an argument from me. Poaching wasn't Max's style."

She leaned into him and gave him a quick kiss. "Thank you."

His eyes sparkled as if he liked the idea of her kissing him for whatever reason. "Still, ten dollars a pound doesn't seem like much money for the risk involved."

"That's the problem. There isn't much risk. Right now, the number of rangers in the park is at an all-time low. It's estimated thirty tons of elk antlers are being shipped to the Orient every year from the twenty thousand head of elk in this great Northern Yellowstone herd. The park's too large and there aren't enough rangers to stop the poaching."

"Well, it looks like Max tried," J.D. said.

She took more shots, getting Mount Holmes in the background so there was no mistaking where the horns—and the horn hunters—were. "With poaching laws so lenient, I just find it hard to believe that anyone would kill Max over a few shed horns. Even if they're caught, these guys would probably never see jail time. Just a fine."

Cal and Lester had taken off their skis and now wandered through the pines on the southern-exposed bare areas of the mountain. Both had their rifles slung over their shoulders. Denver kept photographing as they collected more shed horn.

J.D. scanned the hillside with the binoculars. "Denny, doesn't this look like an awfully large horn-hunting operation?"

She nodded. "Most are just a couple of guys carrying out a few days' horn on their backs after dark." She snapped more photos of the poachers and close-ups of the antlers, chocolate brown with ivory tips.

"If Max was investigating this poaching ring—"

"Then the case file is probably the one Pete found in the tree house." She turned to face him. "Pete could be covering for Lester, one of his band members, instead of himself."

"That's a possibility, I suppose. It doesn't explain Pete's pickup at Horse Butte, though."

"No, it doesn't." She wished he hadn't reminded her of that. He must have seen the disappointment on her face because he pulled her into his arms. She leaned into him, feeling his strength and warmth.

"Denny, I think we'd better get that film to the authorities."

She didn't want to move out of his embrace. But she knew she should get more photographs, enough to nail Cal and Lester but good.

The report of a rifle made her jump. She and J.D. scrambled to look around the tree. Cal was standing still, holding his rifle. Not ten yards away, a small black bear lay dead.

"Why the hell did you do that?" Lester demanded, his voice coming up the hillside.

"It's a bear. We're supposed to kill bears, remember?" Cal snapped.

"Not in the park in broad daylight! You're going to get us in trouble." Lester stomped back to the cache of antlers and worked to remove it by himself.

Denver lifted her camera, taking a couple of shots

of Lester and the horn, then turning it on Cal. He stood over the dead bear, a knife in his hand…

Then the storm came, in a rush. The sky blurred chalky white in front of her camera lens and snow-flakes cascaded down from the heavens, obliterating everything in front her.

In the shelter of her coat, she reloaded the camera, stuffing the exposed roll into her pocket for safekeeping, then put her camera back in the pack.

"Ready?" J.D. whispered. Denver started to move from the shelter of the pines. She saw Lester glance up in their direction.

"Up there!" he yelled. "I just saw something."

J.D. pulled Denver down behind the bushy pine but through the branches she could see Lester pointing to the pines where they crouched. "There's never a dull moment being with you," J.D. whispered. "You ready to leave *now*?"

She nodded and grabbed her ski poles. The snow-laden pines would provide only minimal protection. In a moment, Lester would be making his way up the hill and he'd see their tracks. Even if they found a better hiding place, their ski tracks would lead the two men directly to them.

"Head down the mountain keeping to the south," Denver whispered. "When you hit Duck Creek follow it west to the summer cabins, then head to the high-way for help."

J.D. grinned at her. "And where are you going to be?"

"I'm going to stay here and—"

He shook his head. "No way. You're going first." She started to argue. "I'll be right behind you, Sunshine. Covering your backside. Now git."

She swung the pack over her shoulder.

"Go on," J.D. urged. "And Denny—"

She looked into his eyes and for an instant had the feeling that this might be the last time. The thought tore at her heart.

"If we get separated, don't double back. Keep going. You hear me. You have to get that film to the rangers. And...be careful." He grabbed her and kissed her hard. Then gave her a shove.

Denver dived from the pines, skiing across the opening to where the mountainside dropped down toward the valley below. It wasn't the fastest way back to the highway and safety, and it definitely wasn't the safest escape route, but right now it was the only way out. Straight down.

She could hear voices behind her, and the sound of her skis on the snow. Neither Lester nor Cal could have reached the top of the hill yet, she told herself. Slightly off to her left, she saw J.D. skiing through the trees. A few more minutes and the horn hunters wouldn't be able to see them because of the storm. She heard the sharp crack of a rifle shot. Terror filled her.

She raced down the mountainside at the edge of her control, turning only to miss a stump, a fallen tree or a standing one. Out of the corner of her eye, she caught glimpses of J.D.'s dark ski jacket. Then nothing. Worry stole through her. She wished she had never gotten J.D. involved in this mess, wished he were still safe in California. "Stay with me, J.D.," she pleaded. "Stay with me."

Her vision blurred as the snow beat against her face and often blinded her completely. At best, she could make out the shapes of trees; at worst, she saw nothing but white.

She dipped down into a small gully and poled frantically up the other side, her heart pounding loudly in her ears. Off to her right, she heard the sound of a tree limb breaking and a grunt. Without taking time to think, she skied toward the sound. She tasted the metallic sourness of fear. What if J.D. had fallen? What if—Her skin went clammy and cold. What if they'd shot him? The thought ricocheted inside her head, out of control.

Denver stopped and pulled Max's pistol from her pack, listening. Silence. Large white flakes fell all around her, insulating the land in a cold, protective shell. She tucked the pistol into her coat and traversed the hillside, heading once more in the direction of the sound.

The wind whirled snow around her like a plastic-bubble winter scene from a five-and-dime store. She wondered how she'd ever find J.D. in this swirling white curtain of cold. Then Denver heard it. The faint swish of fabric against pine needles. "J.D.?" she called fearfully. "J.D.?"

Cal came out of the trees from her left. She went for the pistol in her coat. He lunged for her, ripping the gun from her fingers as his other gloved hand came around from behind to cover her mouth before she could scream.

"Well, well, well, if it isn't Denver McCallahan," he sneered. "We finally meet again. And on my turf."

Chapter 13

Pete Williams pulled the pickup over to the side of the road and adjusted the tracking equipment on the seat next to him. He didn't want to believe it. He stared at the faint green beep, then out his window. Damn. How could this have happened? He slammed his fist against the steering wheel. He should have known. Stopping Denver McCallahan was like trying to lasso a runaway train. Especially now that she had J.D. as a running mate. But how had she found out? A leak somewhere. He remembered Davey and moaned. The little snot-nosed kid *had* talked before Pete got to him. Damn.

For a few moments, Pete sat staring at the falling snow, wondering what he'd be doing right now if Max McCallahan were still alive. He drove down the road to the phone booth at the old Narrows resort and dug out a quarter. Midnight was right about one thing. Denver was a problem.

He dialed the number he'd been given for emergencies. "It looks like I'm going to need some help."

"Where?"

"Grayling Pass at Fir Ridge."

Whiteout. J.D. stopped for a moment, hearing nothing. Snowflakes fell around him, cold and lacy white. The poachers had turned back, he told himself as he tried to see ahead. Nothing. Nothing but a solid white wall of snow. He'd lost sight of Denny. By now she could already have reached Duck Creek and the summer cabins. *Denny is a good skier. She can take care of herself.*

The words sounded hollow even to him. Fear filled his chest to overflowing. He couldn't lose Denny. Not now. He pushed off again, skiing down the hill, knowing sooner or later he'd hit Duck Creek. Then he'd find her. He refused to believe anything else as he skied forward.

The snow obliterated everything in his path. He couldn't see more than a few feet in front of him. Trees would appear suddenly and without warning. Rocks and stumps came at him out of the snow, large white mounds he had to dodge at the last moment. Just a little farther and he'd be off the mountain. "Denny." He whispered her name like a prayer.

The land before him seemed to flatten out and he thought the worst part was over. Then the earth dropped out from under him.

"Don't scream or I'll hurt you," Cal muttered harshly against her temple. Slowly he pulled his gloved hand away from her mouth.

Denver's first instinct was to scream bloody murder.

She squelched it, though, fighting for a calm she didn't feel, because she knew now that Cal Dalton was capable of anything. If she screamed, it could bring Lester. Or worse yet, J.D. She didn't doubt Cal would shoot him.

"You're a pretty clever broad," Cal said. "What did you do, follow us from town?" A strange kind of admiration glowed in his blue eyes. "Take off your pack, sweetheart. I think I'd like to see what you've got in there."

Denver slipped the pack strap from her shoulders as slowly as possible, her mind racing. He had his rifle slung over his back with a leather strap and Max's pistol stuck in the waist of his pants. She knew he could get to either before she had a chance to escape. "Why don't you tell me what horn hunting had to do with my uncle's murder?"

Cal shook his head as he planted his ski poles in the snow and reached for the pack. "Horn hunting? I don't know what you're talking about." He opened the backpack. She knew in a moment he'd see the camera, and even as dense as Cal was, he'd figure out she'd taken photos of the poaching operation.

"You know, what you really want isn't in there."

He looked up, a smile slowly lighting his eyes as he let the pack slip from his fingers. "No?"

"No," she said softly.

He moved closer. "It's about time you came around."

She swung one of her poles, hoping to knock him off balance and into the snow. It might give her enough time—

Cal grabbed her wrist and twisted. The pole dropped into the snow at their feet. "You think I'm a fool?" he demanded hoarsely. One hand captured her face; the other dragged her to him. "I'm tired of playing games with you." He shoved her down into the snow and fell on her, his fingers tearing at the zipper on her coat. "You're about to find out what a real man is like." He laughed as he jerked her coat open. She didn't put up a fight as his hands slipped beneath her sweater. "And you're in for a treat, sweetheart."

She knew he planned to rape her. And then what? Kill her? With shaking fingers, she began to unzip his coat.

J.D. fell over the edge of the cornice, dropping through snowflakes and cold air, then hitting the snow-field and somersaulting. A branch slapped him; a rock dug into his ribs. He lost all perception as he tumbled downward. There was no sense of distance, or depth, only that endless falling sensation and a brilliant suffocating whiteness.

And just when he thought it would never end, he slammed into a snowbank and stopped. For a few moments, he lay still, crumpled and cold, his breath ragged. He brushed at the snow on his face and beard, simply breathing and trying to get his bearings. Then he felt the unmistakable pain in his left ankle.

First he'd escaped two rifle-toting horn hunters. Then he'd survived a fall off a cliff. And now his ankle was broken. He groaned. And where was Denny? Right now, all he wanted was to see her smiling face. To hear her laugh or speak his name. He closed his eyes. But that old sharp stab of fear that Denny was in trouble hit him hard between the eyes and he opened them again.

The snow fell around him. Quiet. Like death. He leaned over to survey the damage the fall had done to his ankle. He didn't even bother to worry about the scratches, scrapes and gouges. It was the ankle that would mean the difference between getting out of here and finding Denny or dying in a snowdrift.

It didn't hurt as badly as it had at first. But he wasn't sure if that was a sign he was about to freeze to death. Hypothermia. Good night, Irene. He untied his boot and felt along the ankle. He felt again, unable to believe his good luck. At least it wasn't a compound fracture. Maybe it was just a bad sprain, not even broken. It didn't hurt enough to be broken, he assured himself. He tied his boot up again and tried getting to his feet.

Bad idea. Pain raced up his leg. He fell back into the snow. Damn. If he couldn't even get to his feet to try to ski for help... No, he didn't want to think about that. Instead, he thought of Denver. That did the trick. He took his ski poles and determinedly worked his way up onto the one good leg. Carefully he put a little weight on his bad ankle and knew two things: his ankle wasn't broken, but he wasn't going far.

Denver slid her hand under Cal's shirt. She sank her other hand deep into the snow.

Cal leered at her. "Finally see the light, huh?" He laughed as he leaned down to kiss her.

Denver wrapped her fingers around a cold hard chunk of granite she'd dislodged under the snow. She brought the rock up with one swift movement and slammed it into the side of Cal's head. He looked confused for an instant. Then she gave him a shove and he fell over into the snow. His eyes slowly closed as if he needed a little nap.

"Finally see the light, huh?" Denver said, getting

to her feet and zipping up her coat again. She snapped
on her ski bindings Cal had so helpfully released, anxious to find J.D. as quickly as possible. She pulled the
rifle from the snow where it had fallen next to Cal and
slung it over her shoulder, but didn't take the time to
look for Max's pistol somewhere in the snow. She heard
Cal moan and was relieved she hadn't killed him. Then
she picked up her ski poles and skied down the mountain through the falling snow.

J.D. pointed himself what he guessed to be south.
The land dropped away at a gentle slope. He hoped
there were no more cliffs. The next thing he wanted to
stumble into was Denny. And Duck Creek. Together
they could find a cabin and take shelter from the storm.

Using the poles as crutches, he slid one ski forward,
then the other. Pain. It beaded up perspiration on his
forehead even in the cold. More than ever he wanted to
lie down and sleep. His brain tempted him to do so. The
thought of Denny kept him moving. He had to tell her
something. And when he saw her it was the first thing
he was going to do, tell her. *If* he ever saw her again.

"Denny." He realized he'd said her name out loud.
And worse yet, he thought he heard her voice on the
wind. He told himself he had to be delirious.

As he stumbled clumsily along in the storm, the wind
whirled around him, giving him only teasing seconds
of sight. Then he saw it.

He blinked with disbelief. A mirage rising from the
desert! But instead of tall, cool shade palms and a pool
of clear water, he thought he'd seen the side of a cabin
in the woods. His eyes were playing dirty tricks on him,

tormenting him. Could he really have reached the first of the cabins along Duck Creek?

The storm was a living force he had to battle to reach the mirage. He concentrated on Denny, her smile, her laugh, the defiance and determination that so often burned in her eyes, instead of the pain, fatigue and icy-cold wetness that enveloped him as he lumbered forward. It took all his powers of concentration to keep his legs moving.

He was so preoccupied that he almost collided with the corner logs of the building. A cabin. It had to be one of the summer homes along the creek. That would mean shelter and probably a fireplace. Surely he could find something to burn to make a fire. The thought of a warm, dry place—and Denny—pushed him on. Just a few more feet.

Hope soared, but quickly fell as he rounded the corner and saw that the structure was nothing more than part of an old cabin wall. He held on to the corner of the rotting logs. There would be little shelter in the crumbling edifice, little chance of keeping a fire going in the wind.

As if the wind were aware of his dilemma, it swirled snow around him in a low growl. He tucked his head down against its freezing sharpness. For a moment, he thought he heard Denny's voice on the wind again. Calling to him. The wind continued to whip the snow in tiny eddies. He raised his head to see the outlines of two other buildings looking like a ghost town in a desert sandstorm. The cabins disappeared again in the storm—or in his mind. He feared they had only been in his mind. Just like the sound of Denny's voice.

When Denver reached Duck Creek and the first boarded-up summer cabins, she stopped. Snow circled around her. Cold and tired, she urged herself to go on to the highway for help. But her heart wouldn't let her. J.D. If he'd made it to the highway, he'd already be getting help. And if he hadn't…

She peered into the storm, then, making up her mind, she skied to the larger of two cabins. The door was locked. But with a piece of firewood from the stack beside the cabin, she pried open a shutter, broke the window and let herself in. She thought about J.D. out in the cold and debated building a fire. The smoke could lead Cal and Lester right to her door. But she knew that if the two men made it as far as the cabins, they'd find her anyway. And she wanted the place to be warm if she found J.D. *When* she found him. She refused to consider any other possibility.

Hurriedly she got a fire going in the old stone fireplace, warmed her hands, then went back out in the storm to look for J.D.

Smoke. J.D. thought for a moment he could smell smoke coming from one of the cabins that had appeared miraculously from out of the storm. He'd gone a few feet when he saw what had to be another mirage. A figure was coming out of the storm toward him. At first he thought it might be one of the horn hunters. He stopped, the cold and the pain freezing all thought. The sweet scent of smoke tantalized him; the wind whistled across the cabin's roof, dying in a low howl off the eaves. Then he heard her voice calling his name.

"Denny?" Snow whirled around him. The cabin was gone. So was Denny. A mirage. Only a mirage. He stumbled and fell into the snow. Too tired to move, he closed his eyes, remembering the feel of her in his arms. "Denny," he whispered and smiled. "I love you."

Chapter 14

"Denny," J.D. whispered, snuggling deeper into the couch. She wrapped her arms around him, giving him her warmth. He still shivered from the cold. She tried not to think about what could have happened if she hadn't found him when she did. "I love you, Denny."

"Sure you do," she said, her voice breaking. She held him, wondering if it was the pain or the cold that was making him delirious. "I love you, too, J.D.," she whispered, knowing he couldn't hear her. A lock of his hair curled down over his forehead. She pushed it back and touched his forehead. Hot. The fire beside them murmured in hushed tones; outside, the storm canceled out any thought of escape.

Denver studied J.D.'s face in the firelight and felt a sudden chill of worry. What if the horn hunters found them here now, with J.D. so sick? She'd considered going for help, but couldn't leave him alone. They were safe from the poachers as long as the storm continued, she assured herself. But once it let up, Cal would be looking for them again. Looking for her especially.

She pressed her lips to J.D.'s forehead; his heat seared them. If only his fever would pass. Then, if he could ski on his hurt ankle. If… There were too many ifs.

He sighed in his sleep. "…love you."

Tears came to her eyes. "Oh, J.D."

She slipped from his arms and knelt to tuck more blankets around him. In the cabin's tiny kitchen, she rummaged through the cabinets and came up with an old can of coffee and some powdered milk. Not much, but better than nothing. Outside, she scooped up a pan full of snow, then set it on the wood stove to heat. She felt so tired. From fueling the fires all afternoon. From skiing for miles. From running. Running scared. She still felt scared. For J.D. For them both.

Denver leaned over the counter and watched the storm through a crack in the boarded-up window. Snow stacked silently higher; by morning everything would be obliterated. Through the chink she spotted an old shed. Hope fought back her exhaustion. She gulped down a cup of the horrible coffee, then pulled the pot to the edge of the stove. Quickly she threw on her coat and boots, picked up Cal's rifle, took one last look at J.D. to be sure he was still covered, and left.

The snow was now knee-deep. Denver stumbled through it to the weathered shed only to find the door locked. With the butt of the rifle, she broke the padlock, promising herself she would find the owner of the cabin and pay him for all the damage she'd done. Then she pushed open the door of the shed and peered into the shadowy, frigid darkness. As her eyes adjusted to the dim light, she smiled.

The one thing that might save them hunkered in the back of the shed, big, old and ugly—an ancient Ski-Doo snowmobile, much like one Max used to have. But what made it such a welcome sight was that it didn't require a key, only mixed fuel. She found a gas can, half-full, and several quarts of oil.

Denver wanted to start the snowmobile to make sure it ran, but knew that wouldn't be smart. If Cal and his friends were anywhere near, they'd hear it. No, she'd have to wait until the storm broke and just hope it would get her and J.D. to the highway. She mixed some fuel in one of the gas cans and filled the vehicle's tank, then left, closing the door firmly behind her. She and J.D. stood a chance. If the snowmobile still worked.

Trudging through the snow to the cabin, Denver held the rifle, ready for the slightest movement from out of the storm. All the way back, she expected Cal or Lester to appear. Smoke curled up from the chimney to blend with the grayness of the storm. On the porch, she took one last look out into the falling snow, then slipped inside.

J.D. had drifted off to sleep, no longer shivering. After checking the door to make sure it was bolted and the shutter was firmly nailed back over the broken window, Denver curled up on the couch beside J.D., Cal's rifle on the floor next to her, and waited for sleep to take her. She didn't have to wait long.

J.D. woke to find a fire blazing in the fireplace and Denny asleep beside him on the couch. The heat made his eyelids heavy and he started to drift back into the fairyland of sleep. A flash of memory—skiing, the whiteout, Denny—forced his eyes open again. He pushed himself up on one arm and looked down at her. Strands of hair had come loose from her braid. They curled around her face, fiery red in the firelight. He brushed one back with his finger and glanced down to see that she'd found them both dry clothes. His fit better than the large old T-shirt and baggy jeans she'd scavenged up for herself. He thought about her undressing him and felt a heat that had nothing to do with the fire. Through a crack in the boarded-up windows, he could see the snow that still fell into the night.

He glanced around the sparsely furnished room, trying to put the scattered pieces of memory together. The handcrafted log furniture gave him the eerie impression that he'd been dropped into another time. The old couch frame was built of slim lodgepole pines, stripped of bark and coated with varnish to a yellowed sheen. Even the rocking chair by the fireplace was handmade. An old guitar leaned against the wall by the fireplace. Behind him, a wall divided the cabin, but he could smell coffee and knew the kitchen was on the other side.

He slipped from the couch, careful not to wake Denny. The moment he put his left foot to the floor, he remembered his ankle. Swollen and bruised, it balked at holding his weight. Denver had wrapped it. He glanced down at her again, touched by her strength and courage. And her tenderness toward him. A man who had done nothing but hurt her. He took one of the fire tools and limped his way into the kitchen.

He poured himself a cup of coffee and looked at his watch, wondering if he'd lost hours or days. It wasn't even nine at night. But what night? Then he remembered what had woken him. A song. It played on the edge of his memory. He dug through the kitchen drawers until he found a pencil and some scratch paper. Taking his coffee with him, he went back into the living room and sat down on the hearth in front of the fire.

It took only a moment to tune the old guitar. He ran his fingers across the worn wood, wondering who owned it. Then he softly strummed a few chords, the song he'd heard in his dream coming back. He strummed some more, then scribbled notes hurriedly, afraid the music would escape.

Denver woke to music, soft and sweet as the warm flicker of the fire. She remained perfectly still, watching J.D. Completely lost in the music, he didn't notice. As he began to sing softly, Denver let the sound lull her. The words, as gentle as a caress, brought tears to her eyes. Did he really mean the lyrics he sang? Would he truly give up everything just to be with her? She pushed herself up on one elbow to watch him play.

He stopped abruptly, killing the sound with his hand across the strings, when he realized she was awake.

"You wrote a new song," she whispered into the quiet that followed.

He nodded, his gaze polished silver as he put down the guitar and came to kneel beside her. "It's about you. It's called 'On My Way Back to Denver.'"

Her heart jitterbugged. "You're feeling better?"

"Yes." His look heated her face hotter than the fire.

"You were delirious earlier." From the way he was staring at her, she wondered if he still wasn't. "Talking crazy."

He grinned. "Was I? What did I say?"

She looked away. "Not much."

His hand cupped her chin and turned her face to his. "Did I say I loved you?" The firelight caught in his eyes. "When I was in the middle of that storm, I realized—"

She touched a finger to his lips. "Don't say anything you'll regret later."

He smiled sadly. "Oh, Denny, I already have so many regrets. I can't stand to add another one. I love you." He cradled her face in his hands. "I love you, Denver McCallahan. I've always loved you in some way. But now…"

Tears filled her eyes to overflowing. She pulled away, getting up to go stand in front of the fireplace. Behind her, she heard J.D. sigh. She picked up her hairbrush from the hearth where she'd left it earlier and stared down at it. "We've been through a lot the past few days. This kind of danger sometimes makes people—"

He laughed softly. "Face how they really feel about each other?"

"'Confused,' is the word I would have chosen." She turned. Just the sight of him made her weak.

"Come here, Denny."

The fire burned hot, radiating heat across the room. She stood before the flames, her braid partially undone, her hair curled around her face. Firelight shone through the thin, worn T-shirt. She breathed raggedly, her eyes dark, her face in shadow.

J.D. caught a glimpse of the expression on her face and fought for breath. "Come here, Denny," he said again, sliding up to sit on the couch.

She took an unsteady step toward him, his name on her lips, and dropped to the floor to kneel at his feet. He touched her hair, soft and warm. Slowly he began to unbraid it. The strands parted beneath his fingers, silken and smooth. He freed them and took the hairbrush from her hand. She turned her back to him and he began to brush the shimmering auburn waves in long, slow strokes. Again and again he ran the bristles from her scalp through the dark crimson tapestry to where her back curved to jeaned bottom. He heard her moan or maybe it was the sound of his own desire.

She leaned back into him with each stroke. Her hair fanned across his thighs; his fingers ran through the strands of liquid fire. "Denny," he whispered. She arched back to look at him; her breasts stretched against the thin cotton T-shirt. Nipples hardened into dark points beneath the cloth. He buried his hand in her hair and pulled her head back. His mouth dropped to hers, first tentatively tasting the wetness between her lips, then plunging into the warm, moist darkness. He felt heat where the back of her head rested and told himself he should stop. As much as he loved her, he didn't know what would happen to them tomorrow. He wanted to promise her happiness with him, but he couldn't. He didn't know what his own future held.

He lifted his lips from hers. Her eyes closed; she moaned softly and reached for him. Reason evaded him. He bent to take one nipple in his mouth. His tongue moistened the thin cloth. He captured the nipple gently between his teeth.

Her body jerked, making his heart pound like beats on a drum. He pulled away to look into her eyes. The fire that had been simmering in his groin burst into flame. If he was going to stop, he'd better stop now. If he slid the T-shirt up over her breasts, if his mouth touched her bare skin, he would never be able to.

"Damn, you're so beautiful, so desirable," he murmured. The wanting in her eyes mirrored his own and they begged him not to stop. Slowly he inched the T-shirt up over her firm, flat stomach, then over the smooth, rounded breasts, nipples silhouetted rosy pink in the firelight. He tossed the T-shirt aside and pulled her into his arms. Her hair spilled out like a dark red river across the icy whiteness of her shoulder to her breasts. He buried his hands in it and tilted her head as he pulled her down into a kiss.

Denver opened her mouth for J.D.'s demanding kiss and moaned as his lips devoured hers. She reached for the buttons on his shirt, wanting desperately to feel his chest against her naked breasts. He groaned as she began unbuttoning his shirt.

She freed the last button and slid the shirt off his shoulders. He pulled her to him. Her breasts pressed against his warm chest, setting her skin on fire as his mouth savored hers again. He dropped a kiss at a time to her neck, then her breast. She shuddered as his mouth closed over her nipple.

His eyes flamed in the firelight; her body glistened from his kisses. "Please, J.D.," she cried, needing him inside her, needing to feel his body on hers.

"Oh, Denny, you're so beautiful," he whispered as he covered her mouth with his, her body with his.

With a cry, she felt him fill her. He came to her like the storm, slowly at first, like tentative snowflakes drifting earthward from the swollen clouds above. Kisses fevered and wet-slick. Bodies burning, slithering touches, cries and caresses. Then stronger, a pulsating need, a pressing and probing like the wind at the windows. The clouds opened. She rose with him, again and again, a gale of sensations wracking her body.

"J.D., oh, J.D.," she moaned. The storm swept her along in a blinding whiteout until she cried out beneath him, felt his body pulse and tremble with the first shock of their combined passion and thought she would burst from the joy of loving him.

Bodies gleaming in the firelight, the snowstorm raging outside the cabin, she reached the zenith of another storm, heard the thunder within her. She wrapped her arms around him and held her to him as the storm subsided. He smiled down at her; her heart filled like a helium balloon.

"Never in my life have I felt anything like this," he whispered at her temple. He raised his head to press a kiss to her swollen lips. "Never," he said, locking onto her gaze. "I love you, Denny."

She pulled him down to her again, smiling as she kissed him, leisurely exploring his mouth.

"You knew that day at the fire tower, didn't you?" he asked, trailing his fingers across her skin.

"That I loved you and would never love another man the way I did you?" She smiled. "Yes."

He shook his head, his eyes dark with his need for her. "I thought for so many years that all I needed was my music. But something was missing. I just didn't know what it was until I saw you again."

She lay in his arms, more contented than she'd ever thought possible. His skin felt warm and smooth against hers. She glanced toward the window, wishing they never had to leave this cabin. The snow still fell thick and white against the darkness.

"We're safe here," he said, caressing the silken skin at the base of her throat.

"Until the snow stops."

The fire popped softly. Shadows danced across the ceiling to a music Denver had never heard before, but had unknowingly longed for. She looked up at him, her eyes soft and dark. He smiled as he bent to kiss her. This time the music started slowly, then caught time with the beat of her heart as she came to him again.

Later, they lay wrapped in each other's arms as the fire died down. J.D. stared up at the shadowy darkness, listening to Denny breathing gently beside him, trying not to think about poachers or murderers. Instead, he closed his eyes and concentrated on the soft, warm feel of her skin against his, rather than on what they would have to do once the sun rose over the mountains and the storm ended.

Chapter 15

April 19

At first she thought it was the steady beat of her heart. Or a flushed grouse coming out of the brush in a flutter of frantic wings. She thought she was dreaming again.

Denver sat up and looked around, forgetting for a moment where she was, but not who she was with. She smiled down at J.D. asleep beside her on the couch. The firelight played on his peaceful face, across the expanse of his chest, his skin golden in the glow. He stirred, eyes opening, his gaze as loving as his body had been as it drifted over her. Then he, too, heard the sound and sat up abruptly.

Through the crack in the shutter, Denver could see it was still dark out. But the storm had stopped and the fallen snow shone like freshly minted silver. The sound grew stronger, a steady throbbing now.

J.D. swore as he jumped up and hopped to the window to peer through the broken shutter. "A helicopter."

"Maybe it's someone looking for us?" she asked as she joined him, clutching a blanket around her.

"Who knows we're here, Denny?" He pulled her into his arms and stroked her hair, his hold fierce and protective. Tears sprang to her eyes as he wrapped the blanket around them both. Yes, who did know they were here? Davey? Cal. Lester.

"If the horn hunters have a helicopter..." she began.

"Then this is quite a sophisticated poaching operation."

Denver looked up into his face, thinking about other horn hunters she'd read about. Greedy poachers, who shot down the elk to cut off the newly grown more potent and prized antlers still in velvet, leaving the elk to bleed to death. Dangerous men. Like Cal.

"That means they have unlimited resources, Denny."

The sound of the helicopter grew louder. "Think there's a chance they won't find us?" she asked hopefully.

J.D. raised an eyebrow.

"That's what I thought."

She hurried back to the couch and began to dress in her ski clothes. When she looked up, J.D. was still standing by the window.

"You go," he said, limping over to her. "I'll just slow you down."

"I'm not going anywhere without you," she said, stopping to meet his gaze. They stared at each other, the fire crackling softly, the steady *whoop whoop* of the chopper moving nearer.

He smiled, shaking his head at her. "Why do I keep forgetting just how determined you are?"

"I don't know." She returned his smile. "I found a snowmobile in the shed. I'm not sure if it runs, but either way, we're leaving here together."

He closed the distance between them. Eyes wistful, he wrapped his arms around her and kissed her hard, taking her breath away. As he pulled away to dress, Denver assured herself it wouldn't be their last kiss.

J.D. helped Denny out the back of the cabin through a window, then leaned against the building in the deep snow. His ankle ached with each step; he balanced on his good foot, knowing he wouldn't be going far if the snowmobile didn't run. He'd have to force Denny to go on without him because there was little doubt in his mind what the occupants of the chopper had in mind. Darkness still hung over the treetops but the new snow shone bright as moonlight on water.

"Why haven't they landed?" Denver whispered.

The chopper made another pass over the cabin, backtracking west. Through the trees, J.D. could see other cabins along the creek. "I think they can't figure out which one we're in." He pointed up. The smoke from their fire formed a gray haze that stretched all along the creek. And the storm had obliterated all their tracks in the snow. The pilot of the chopper didn't know where to land. Yet. "You ready?"

Denver nodded. He could see the fear in her eyes and knew it had nothing to do with her own safety.

"Let's go," he whispered.

They broke through the drifts to the shed. In the distance, they could hear the helicopter heading back.

J.D. pulled the shed door open just enough for them to squeeze through, then slipped into the darkness after Denver, and pulled the door shut behind him.

It took a moment before he spotted the large old Ski-Doo at the back of the shed. He handed Denver his pack and the rifle. "It's now or never," he said, feeling something in his heart pull like fingers on a guitar string.

The sound of the chopper grew louder. A beam of bright light cut through a break in the haze like a laser, skittering across the outside of the shed. "They've got a spotlight," she said. "If the smoke clears—"

J.D. grabbed the handle on the rope starter and pulled. The Ski-Doo engine coughed once. The helicopter hovered overhead. He pulled again. The engine coughed a couple more times. He choked it. The steady beat of the chopper grew louder and closer.

"They're putting down," Denver cried.

He gave the starter another yank, putting all his weight into it. The engine sputtered, rumbled to life, coughed a few times, but kept rumbling. He released a breath. The Ski-Doo's headlight flickered on, illuminating the tiny shed.

"Ready?" he asked.

Denver nodded and smiled. It sent his heart soaring, and he promised himself that if they ever got out of this, he'd make her smile like that the rest of her life.

Denver pushed open the shed door. Through the trees, he could make out the silhouette of the chopper touching down in a clearing not far away and knew they had seen the snowmobile light. He gave the throttle a twist, and Denver jumped on behind him, wrapping her arms around him as they roared out of the shed. The chilling spray of new snow showered them as the snowmobile broke through the first deep drifts and headed west.

J.D. spotted Pete running from the chopper, a rifle in his hands, saw Pete's mouth open but didn't hear the words over the high-pitched whine of the snowmobile's engine. But he knew Pete was yelling for them to stop. J.D. knew Denny saw Pete, too. He felt her tighten her hold on him. J.D. gave the Ski-Doo all the throttle there was to give and they burst through the snow and into the pines, the single light on the vehicle cutting a swath through the darkness and the trees.

J.D. glanced back, afraid of what he'd find. But Pete was pushing through the deep snow headed back to the chopper. "I'm sorry, Denny," J.D. yelled over the roar of the snowmobile. She hugged him tighter, burying her face against his back.

Damn Pete. Damn him for hurting Denny. J.D. could only hope that Pete wasn't the one who killed Max. He feared that would destroy her.

Denver fought the anger and disappointment that pulled at her mind and body. Pete. Pete with a rifle trying to stop them. For an instant back there, she thought maybe he'd come to rescue her. But how could he have known they might be in one of the cabins along Duck Creek? Only if Cal had told him.

She tried not to think how it all fit together as she and J.D. sped west toward the highway. The snowmobile broke through the deep new drifts, sending snow flying. Its headlight punched a bobbing hole in the darkness, while behind them she knew the chopper would be coming. She huddled against J.D.'s back, feeling his warmth and his love. It gave her strength. She tried to imagine living without him again. And couldn't.

She felt J.D. turn around and knew the helicopter must be tracking them.

"We have to kill that headlight," he yelled. She nodded against his back as he brought the snowmobile to an abrupt stop, the engine putt-putting, and climbed off. They'd have to break it; the light wouldn't shut off except when the engine did. She handed J.D. the rifle. He limped around to the front. In one swift movement he brought the rifle butt down into the headlight. The darkness settled around them. They both turned at the sound of the chopper coming up quickly behind them.

Hurriedly, J.D. jumped back on and hit the throttle. They shot into the darkness of the pines. The spotlight from the chopper flickered across the treetops, then flashed off. The steady *whoop whoop* of the blades disappeared in the roar of the Ski-Doo's engine as they raced through the snow, zigzagging in the night shadows, trying to lose the helicopter. Denver tried not to think about what had happened to the idyllic Montana life Max McCallahan had given her. Instead, she held tight to J.D. and the love they'd shared.

"Dammit." Pete leaned back against the chopper seat as he surveyed his latest disaster. "What's that over there?" He pointed off to his right.

"Looks like another snowmobile light," the pilot said.

Pete swore again. They'd lost Denver in the trees and the dark. And now someone else had joined in the hunt. "It's got to be Cal. I should have known he wouldn't stay out of this." Cal had skied out for a snowmobile, convinced he could find Denver before Pete did. Now he was backtracking, trying to pick up Denver's trail, and it looked like he had.

"I better radio the boss." The pilot reached for the radio, but Pete stopped him.

"No. I'll handle this." The pilot looked skeptical. "Just follow Cal. He's going to lead us straight to Denver. And then I'll take care of her."

"I really think—"

Pete shifted the rifle in his lap. "Don't think. Just do what I tell you." The pilot hesitated. "Denver should have been stopped a long time ago. I'm going to do it now before she and that damn J. D. Garrison blow everything. Trust me. You'll probably get a bonus."

The pilot laughed at that, but banked the chopper back over the lone snowmobile headlight. Pete watched it bob through the trees; Cal was following Denver's snowmobile tracks, hunting her like a rabid dog. The vast snowfield glowed virgin white in the darkness. Only the pines provided shaded sanctuary. Denver was out there somewhere. Denver and J.D. Pete gripped his rifle and waited for Cal to track them down.

Denver saw the light fluttering high in the trees ahead of her. It took her a moment to realize what it was. Another snowmobile. She tightened her hold on J.D. as he set about outracing it. She estimated they were no more than five miles from the highway; all they needed was a fighting chance. But with a helicopter overhead and a snowmobile following in their tracks, she entertained little hope of that. The vehicle behind them was also gaining quickly. Newer and faster, it probably carried one rider; she could guess who it was.

The light flickered over them as the other snowmobile drew closer. J.D. turned, his lips brushing her ear.

"I'm going to jump off. You keep going. Will you do that for me, Denny?"

She heard the pleading in his voice. This was no time to argue. They couldn't outrun the other machine. She nodded.

The light grew brighter as it neared. The poachers had no intention of letting them reach the authorities. Denver felt J.D. shift his weight; then he was gone. She held the throttle down and kept going.

J.D. tumbled off, rolled a few times in the snow, but came up with the rifle strap still snug across his chest. He eased it off, then crouched low behind a small pine adjacent to Denny's snowmobile tracks. The approaching light bobbed across the white expanse from a pocket of darkness along the edge of the pines; its engine screamed. J.D. stayed down, the rifle ready. In those few seconds before the snowmobile came alongside him, his brain tried to convince him that the driver was someone Davey had sent for them. Maybe Maggie or Taylor. Even Deputy Cline. He couldn't shoot before he was sure. But as the rider roared up, there was no mistaking him. J.D. raised the rifle to fire, but there wasn't enough time. Swearing, he grabbed the barrel end and swung as Cal Dalton roared past.

The rifle hit Cal in the chest with a blow that sent him flying backward from the snowmobile and shattered the rifle stock. The machine sputtered a few feet without its rider holding down the throttle, then stopped. J.D. limped over to Cal and picked him up by the front of his coat.

"All right, you bastard," he said as Cal's eyes flickered open. "Denny told me what you tried to do to her. You have one chance to tell me who's behind this."

A sneer curled Cal's lips as the sound of the helicopter drew closer. "I'll have Denver yet."

J.D. glanced at the snowmobile idling a few feet away, its light shining like a beacon. He slammed Cal down into the snow, making the man grimace with pain and his breathing come out in a wheeze. He pushed his boot into Cal's chest. "Who killed Max?"

The wheezing grew louder. Cal tried to push off the boot but finally gave up. "Pete." He closed his eyes; his arms dropped to his sides. "Pete Williams." J.D. gave him a shove with the boot and limped over to the snowmobile. He could hear the helicopter, see the spotlight slicing through the darkness ahead as it searched for Denny. He wished he hadn't sent Denny on ahead, worried he might have sent her into worse danger. As he started to gun the engine and catch up with her, he heard the unmistakable sound in the pines close by.

The old snowmobile came out of nowhere, bursting through the snow-filled branches of the pines, airborne. Denny landed the Ski-Doo just inches from Cal's inert body. For the first time, J.D. was glad she hadn't listened to him. He stumbled through the snow, his ankle be damned, to pull her off the machine and into his arms. He kissed her, crushing her lips as well as her body against his.

"Boy, am I glad to see you," he murmured in her ear.

She clung to him for a moment, her only answer, and he saw her looking at Cal, lying passed out cold in the snow. "Did he say anything—"

"No," he lied. Not now. He'd tell her later, after they'd gotten away.

He listened for the helicopter, surprised he couldn't hear it. Hurriedly he picked up the broken rifle from the snow and Denny followed him to the newer snowmobile. He smashed the light and climbed on in front of her.

They had sped through the snow for a few hundred yards when J.D. brought the vehicle to a stop. He pointed ahead to a spot where the terrain narrowed down to only a trail between Duck Creek and a granite bluff. Beyond it he could see a set of headlights flash along Highway 191. "Is there another way out of here?"

Denver shook her head. He could feel her trembling and knew it wasn't from the cold. "Not without crossing the creek. Why, what's wrong?"

He couldn't put his finger on it. The heebie-jeebies. "Nothing." He gave the snowmobile gas and raced toward the bluff.

They'd almost reached the narrow trail wedged between water and rock when Pete stepped out, blocking the road and their escape. He held a pistol in his hand. The barrel pointed at J.D.'s heart. And ultimately Denver's.

Denver let out a cry as Pete stepped in front of the snowmobile. She saw the pistol and the expression on Pete's face. She thought for a fleeting moment that J.D. wouldn't stop. That he'd run into Pete and plunge him into the creek or into the wall of granite. But not before Pete had gotten off at least one shot.

J.D. brought the snowmobile to a skidding halt. And Pete reached over the windshield to turn off the engine, the gun still trained on them.

"I knew you couldn't run me down," Pete said to J.D. He sounded tired and he looked worse than he sounded. "At least I hoped you couldn't." Pete shifted his gaze to Denver.

"Let us go, Pete," J.D. said, his voice as cold as the morning. "It's all over. We know about the poaching. We know who killed Max."

Denver wondered for an instant if J.D. was bluffing. Then she realized what Cal had told him back there in the snow. That Pete had killed Max. "Pete, no."

Pete looked her in the eye. "Don't believe it, Denver." He sighed and rubbed his face with his hand, fatigue showing in every line of his body. "We don't have much time, so please listen. I wish I could tell you everything but I can't. You have to trust me." His gaze settled on Denver again. "You have to give me a few days."

"You can't possibly expect us to trust you," Denver cut in. "Not after everything that's happened."

Pete glanced behind him where the chopper was probably waiting for him, then back at her. "Isn't saving your lives enough reason to give me a couple of days?"

"What difference could a few days make except to give you time to get your damned horn shipment out?" Denver demanded. "J.D.'s right, Pete. It's over. Turn yourself in. Don't make me—"

Pete shook his head. "I wish it was that simple. Give me the film, Denver."

She swallowed the lump in her throat. "What film?"

"You'd never go anywhere without your camera— especially not after what Davey must have told you about the operation. Just give me the film, okay?"

When she didn't move, he jerked the pack from her back and, still holding the pistol on her, opened it. He dug around, slipping a completed roll of film into his coat pocket, then cracked open the camera and ripped out the partially exposed film. He studied Denver while he felt around in the bottom of the pack for more.

"J.D. told me about Max's case file you found in the tree house," she said. "It was the horn-hunting case, wasn't it? But why kill Max?"

"Give me a few days and I'll tell you everything. Right now, I don't have any more answers than you do."

"I want to believe you, Pete." She felt tears rush to her eyes. "But I can't. Not anymore. You've lied to me too many times."

He stared at her for a moment, then handed back the pack. "I told you not to look for Max's murderer. You should have listened to me, Denver. Now you leave me no choice." He pulled a two-way radio from his coat pocket. Static filled the air. "Come on in. Let's get this over with."

With a slow *whoop whoop*, the chopper's blades whirled to life on the other side of the bluff. In seconds, the helicopter rose over the treetops, then moved toward them. Snow whipped at them as sharp and cold as ice shards. *It's now or never*, J.D. thought, and instantly felt Denny's fingers on his waist, warning him to be careful. Under different circumstances, it would have been funny, *her* warning him.

He looked into Pete's face, searching for some hope, finding none. What he found there was more frightening than the pistol Pete had trained on them. Defeat. A dangerous combination when mixed with the gun in Pete's hand.

Shooting for speed, J.D. pulled the starter on the snowmobile and the throttle. Unlike the antiquated machine, this one started in a heartbeat, the roar of its engine drowned out by the deafening whir of the chopper. The snowmobile leaped forward.

Pete had only an instant to make up his mind. J.D. saw his decision in those speeding seconds. He pulled the trigger, but the shot went wild, ricocheting off the rocky bluff. He dived into the icy creek as the snowmobile just missed barreling over him. J.D. didn't look back; he pointed the snowmobile northwest, toward Grayling Pass and his pickup. The helicopter thrummed behind them. Over the tops of the trees, daybreak pried at the darkness.

Chapter 16

Denver didn't expect the pickup to run. She sat shivering as J.D. hurriedly cleaned the snow from the windshield and slid in behind the wheel.

"Cross your fingers," he said, pulling her to him before he reached for the key.

"They had to have tampered with the engine." She watched the shadows pooling beneath the pines in the first light of day and wondered where the helicopter was.

"If it doesn't run, we take the snowmobile and go on into town."

She nodded, doubtful how far they'd get. Pete was out there somewhere. And Cal. Even a fool like Cal would know they'd head for town if the pickup didn't run. And not even the pickup was a match for a helicopter.

The engine made a slow, sluggish attempt to turn

over. J.D. tried it again. He grinned at her as it started, but neither the grin nor the running engine reassured her. Why hadn't Pete disabled the pickup? Because he hadn't expected them to escape?

She watched J.D. test the brakes, knowing he, too, was questioning their luck. If the pickup was going to blow up, wouldn't that have happened right away? He backed the truck up to the highway. She stared out the window, expecting to see Cal's face—or Pete's—appear without warning.

The promise of dawn danced across the mountainside, playing hide-and-seek among the shadowed pines. No helicopter spotlight poured from the gray sky overhead. No snowmobile came flying out of the trees.

"Where are they?" Denver wondered aloud.

J.D. pulled her closer. "We have two choices. We can run or we can go to the Feds. It's up to you, Denny."

She nodded, feeling time slip like sand through her fingers. Emotions stirred within her. Anger pushed at the cold and exhaustion, at the disappointment and disillusionment. Not Pete, her brain kept arguing. No, not Pete. "I want to stop them." She glanced up at J.D. "We can't chance going into West Yellowstone, but there's a district ranger who has a weekend place down by Hebgen Dam." Tears blurred her eyes; she fought them back as he pulled her to him.

He kissed her, a warm, soft, reassuring kiss, then he hugged her closer. "I just want you to be safe, that's all, Denny." He pulled onto the highway and headed south. "Who is this ranger?"

"Roland Marsh."

"Roland Marsh?" J.D. asked with a frown. "Denny, I've heard that name before. It's unusual enough—" He hit the steering wheel with the palm of his hand. "That's it. I saw that name and a telephone number written on a piece of paper in Max's wallet."

Denver looked out into the waning darkness. "Maybe Marsh was his government contact person." But if that was the case, Max hadn't been very careful, carrying that note around in his wallet. But Max had been terrible at remembering phone numbers.

"Let's see if Marsh is at his cabin, and then we'll go to Ennis on the Quake Lake road," J.D. said. "I don't think they'll expect that, do you?"

She shook her head, more interested at that moment in the road ahead. She could tell J.D. didn't want to pass Fir Ridge any more than she did. As the pickup climbed the far side of the hill, Denver held her breath. She imagined the helicopter sitting in the middle of the road.

But when they topped the crest, there was nothing there. Their headlights caught the leafless quaking aspens and the gravestones as the cemetery slipped by in a flash of headlights. Then they were past, the pickup rolling toward the Duck Creek Y. No snowmobiles chased after them. No helicopter was waiting.

"They must have given up," J.D. said. "Pete has the photographs—he probably feels safe now."

Denver closed her eyes, not believing that any more than she knew J.D. did. Whatever was going on wasn't over.

J.D. took her hand in his, squeezing it as if he thought he could squeeze the warmth back into her, could squeeze out the pain. "I'm sorry about Pete, Denny."

Tears stung her eyes. "How could he get mixed up in poaching, especially with someone like Cal?"

J.D. sighed. "I've asked myself that same question."

She squeezed his hand back. He brought her hand to his lips and kissed her palm. "Thank you," she said, letting her gaze settle on his handsome face. "For being here."

He grinned. "My pleasure."

The white world outside glistened as the new day continued to break around them. She leaned against J.D.'s strong shoulder and closed her eyes. Pete. His face came to her, so clearly she almost reached out to him. But it wasn't the face she'd seen in the middle of the trail in front of the snowmobile. It was the face of her friend—Pete Williams. Smiling at her. Promising to help her forget about J.D. Telling her to trust him. How could she have been so wrong about him? She opened her eyes. If they gave the death sentence for deception, Pete Williams would get the chair.

The highway remained empty, just a stretch of snow-packed pavement splashed in daylight. J.D. drove up the mountainside to Roland Marsh's cabin. It sat pushed back into the mountain, the front windows looking out over the still-frozen dam arm of Hebgen Lake. The drapes were closed, everything quiet, but smoke was curling out of the chimney. Denver felt a chill she couldn't explain. Why hadn't Pete or Cal tried to stop them? Because without the photographs, they had no proof. She was certain that Pete and Cal would move the caches of antlers as quickly as possible. It would be her word and J.D.'s against theirs.

As they walked up to the house, Denver could tell that J.D.'s ankle hurt him. Her heart wrenched watching him. This had to end. She pulled his arm over her shoulders and tried to take some of his weight.

As they stumbled up the not-yet-shoveled steps to

the front door, Denver had the feeling that they were being watched again. Was she losing her mind or had they been followed? J.D. tapped at the door. If Pete had somehow followed them here, why didn't he make his move now? What was he waiting for? She pushed her hands deeper in her coat pocket; her fingers touched something slick and cold. A roll of exposed film. Then she remembered. She'd put a completed roll of film she'd taken of the poachers in her pocket. Pete hadn't stolen all the film after all.

"J.D., I forgot this last roll—"

Just then the porch light flashed on and the door opened.

Ranger Roland Marsh tugged at his faded blue bathrobe and squinted at the bright light. Slim, with graying short hair and a cropped silvery mustache, Marsh looked to be in his late fifties. Sleepy blue eyes blinked from behind angular wire-rimmed glasses. "Yes?"

"We're sorry to bother you this early," J.D. said, glancing over his shoulder at the highway below.

Marsh blinked again, the last of the slumber leaving his eyes. "Please, come in," he said, stepping aside. He smiled as he motioned for them to sit down. "J. D. Garrison. My wife's not going to believe this. She's quite a fan of yours. She'll never forgive herself for not being here."

J.D. sat down on the edge of the couch. Denver joined him.

"And Denver McCallahan." Marsh beamed at her. "This is an unexpected surprise."

"I didn't think you'd remember me," Denver said. A year ago, she'd done some photography for a park-service brochure.

He took a chair across from them. "I was so sorry to hear about your uncle. A terrible loss."

Denver clung to the couch with a feeling of relief soaking in. He knew Max. That could explain his name being in Max's wallet. Solid ground. Finally they had someone who would help them.

"Now, what can I do for the two of you?" Marsh asked, still smiling as if he expected their visit to be a social one.

"We've stumbled across a poaching ring," J.D. said.

Marsh frowned.

"We followed two horn hunters into Yellowstone Park at Fir Ridge," Denver added.

"Horn hunters?"

"They're part of what we suspect is a very large poaching ring," J.D. said.

Marsh shook his head. "I've never heard of a horn operation on this side of the park. Gardiner, yes, with all the elk that winter-range in that area, but not West Yellowstone. You're sure about this?"

"I was hoping you knew about this poaching ring," Denver said, near tears. "I was hoping Max—"

"We think Max found out about the poachers," J.D. finished for her. "We thought he might be working with you because your name and number were in his wallet."

Marsh shook his gray head, his brows furrowed. "This is the first I've ever heard of such a thing. I've seen residents this time of year picking up horn along the park boundary, but—"

"These are huge caches of antlers *in* the park," Denver explained, giving him the location. "We saw one of the poachers shoot a bear. Unfortunately, the poachers saw us, too."

"They tried to kill us," J.D. added.

Marsh stared at him. "You can't be serious."

"They tried to keep us from getting out of the mountains with the information," Denver assured him.

"I'm sorry if I sound skeptical," Marsh said quickly, "but with the low fines poachers get if they're caught... I mean, why would they try to...kill you?" He looked shocked. "I can't believe this."

J.D. took Denver's hand. His fingers moved slowly, reassuringly over her palm. She concentrated on his touch.

"We have proof," Denver said, reaching into her pocket with her free hand.

"Proof?" Marsh asked.

"Photos of the antler caches, the horn hunters and one of them standing over the bear he shot," she said, and handed him the roll of film.

He stared down at it for a moment, then pushed himself up from his chair and started for the kitchen. On his way he dropped the film into his robe pocket. "Let me get us some hot coffee or tea."

Denver pulled her hand free of J.D.'s and followed the ranger. "I'm sure they'll try to move the antlers as quickly as possible."

Marsh stopped in the kitchen doorway so abruptly she almost collided with him. "As you have the men on film, does that mean you also recognized them?"

Denver swallowed. She didn't want to tell him about Pete but she knew she had to. "As you'll see in the photographs—" Through the kitchen door, she spotted something that stopped her heart in midbeat and silenced her tongue. Then she found her voice again.

"The storm blew in and the visibility wasn't great. Then they saw us."

Denver turned to find J.D. staring at her in puzzlement. She fought the tears that burned her eyes, feeling more weak and tired than she'd ever been in her life.

"Of course, the storm," Marsh said. "So we might not have a positive ID of the men on this film?" He studied her with an intensity that made her heart pound with fear; he had to know she was lying. Would he try to keep them from leaving? "You must be exhausted," he said as he shifted in the doorway. "You could stay here if you like."

"No, thank you. I want to go back to my place at the lake and wait there," she said, feeling like a mechanical doll as she moved toward J.D. He got up and limped to her side, his arms encircling her with what should have given her a feeling of safety. Her eyes felt full of sand; her muscles ached. She wondered if she'd ever feel safe again. "You'll call when you've found the antlers?" she asked.

Marsh nodded, looking relieved. "I'll be in touch with you by this afternoon."

"Thank you so much for your help, Mr. Marsh," J.D. said as they made their way to the door. Denver reached for the doorknob.

"Just a moment," Marsh said behind them. Denver stopped, her heart pounding. She turned, afraid of what she'd find. Marsh was holding out a scratch pad and a pen. "Would you mind giving me your autograph for my wife?"

J.D. took the pad and pen. "What's your wife's name?"

"Annabelle." Denver watched J.D. scribble on the

pad. He handed it to Marsh, who read it and smiled. "You two be careful," he said as they left. "And don't worry. I'll take care of everything."

"I'm sure you will," Denver said as J.D. took her arm. They walked quickly toward the pickup, J.D. limping at her side.

"What in the world was that all about?" he demanded the moment they were out of earshot.

"Just keep walking. The sooner we get out of here, the better. *If* we get out of here."

J.D. shot her a look of surprise. "Were we followed?"

"No." They reached the pickup and climbed in. "That's just it. We weren't followed." She tried to laugh but it came out a sob.

J.D. looked at her as if she'd gone mad as he started the pickup and headed down the mountain.

"We walked right into a trap." She leaned back against the seat and closed her eyes, fighting fresh tears of pain and frustration. "Pete's hat. I saw it on the counter in Marsh's kitchen." She opened her eyes. "Pete was there."

J.D. stared at her. "How could he have known where we were going? How could Pete have beaten us there?"

"Marsh's lake place was the closest, and he *is* the district ranger."

J.D. glanced in the rearview mirror, then at the highway ahead. "They'll be watching us. If we turn toward Ennis, they'll know we're double-crossing them. We have to head back toward town to make it look as if we're going to the lake cabin."

"But at the Duck Creek Y, we'll go north to Bozeman," Denver said, sitting up straighter. "We'll go to

Bozeman and then…" She looked over at J.D. "Then what?"

He put his arm around her and pulled her closer. "It looks like we're on our own, Sunshine."

"J.D.," Denver said thoughtfully, "How *did* Pete find us at the cabin on Duck Creek? And beat us to Marsh's? Are you thinking what I'm thinking?"

He swore. "A tracking device. They've got us wired."

"Not *us*," Denver said, looking down at her wrist and the watch Pete had given her the day after Max's death.

Chapter 17

The moment Pete left Marsh's, he turned on the tracking unit. He held his breath as he watched the monitor. The last thing he'd expected Denver to do was go to her cabin and stay out of trouble. But the steady beep verified that J.D. and Denver were on their way toward West Yellowstone and the Rainbow Point turnoff to the lake.

He smiled and relaxed a little. Maybe everything would work out after all. He doubted they'd cause any more trouble for a while. And right now, he had more urgent worries. Such as saving his own neck. Midnight hadn't told him where they'd be loading the last of the shed horn for the shipment. Pete hoped this oversight wasn't personal, that Midnight just mistrusted everyone. But it made him worry. He didn't like working for a man he'd never met; it would be too easy for Midnight to double-cross him.

* * *

Denny woke crying.

"It was just a dream," J.D. said, pulling over to the side of the road and taking her in his arms. "Just a bad dream."

She snuggled against him. "It was so real."

"Dreams are like that sometimes." He thought of his own nightmares in strange motel rooms in the wee hours of the morning. They were more real than life. And because of that, much more frightening.

She sat up and looked around as if she didn't recognize the countryside. They were just coming out the Gallatin Canyon. The early-morning sun hung over the Bridger Mountains, glazing the new snowfall in blinding brightness.

They'd flagged down a bread truck at Duck Creek Y on its way into West Yellowstone. Denver knew the driver and asked him to take the watch to the sheriff's office *after* he'd made his delivery rounds. If he thought the request strange, since he had to make a large loop through the lake area before going into town, he didn't say anything. J.D. had then headed the pickup for Bozeman, and Denver had fallen into an exhausted sleep.

"Was the dream about your father and mother again?" he asked.

She nodded. "But this time, the past and present were all mixed up. You were there, and Maggie." She shook her head. "And Cal Dalton. Like I said, it was all mixed up."

He reached over to push a wisp of hair back from her cheek and kissed the spot. She seemed to avoid his gaze.

"You said you were in this for the long haul."

"I am," he assured her, taking her hand.

"Then... I think it's time I find out about this dream." She searched his face. "I was thinking I might try hypnosis like you suggested. There is something in that dream that keeps bothering me and has ever since Max's murder. The bank robber was wearing a ski mask but there is something about him, something I just can't put my finger on. I keep thinking if I could just see it a little more clearly..." She glanced toward the foothills glowing in the sun. "I keep seeing something silver spinning in the man's hands." She shook her head and smiled at him. "I know it doesn't make any sense. I just feel the answers are in that dream. But I promised Max I'd leave it alone, that I'd never try to remember."

"Sometimes there are good reasons to break a promise," he said, hoping that was true as he turned his attention to the highway ahead. "What do you say to a hot bath, some new clothes. And breakfast first?"

She nodded. "I want to call Maggie, too. You don't think she went to Missoula after we warned her not to, do you?"

"Are you asking if she's as stubborn as you and Max?"

She elbowed him gently in the ribs.

"And don't forget Cline. He's probably gotten that hitchhiker to confess by now," J.D. said.

This time she elbowed him a little harder.

After a large breakfast, Denver used the phone at a gas station on the east end of Bozeman. When Maggie didn't answer at the Missoula number or at her home in West, Denver called Taylor at the Three Bears.

"Maggie?" Taylor said, sounding a little surprised. "I guess she hasn't come back from Missoula."

Denver shot J.D. a look. So she'd gone to check out Pete's alibi on her own. Denver swore under her breath. Maggie had probably picked up that stubbornness from all those years around Max.

"I think she just needed to get away for a few days," Taylor said, confirming her suspicions that Maggie hadn't even told him what she was up to. "I'll tell her you called when I see her."

When he saw her. "So you're staying around for a while?" she asked.

He chuckled softly. "It looks like it. I was thinking I might buy a business here."

Denver couldn't help smiling. She'd resented his attentiveness to Maggie at first, but only because she felt as if he was cutting in on Max. But Max was gone. And Maggie was alone. She supposed if Taylor wanted to settle in West, it would be all right.

"I'm going to be out of town for a few days myself," she told him. "I'll catch Maggie when she gets back."

Then she dialed Cline's number. The dispatcher said he wouldn't be back until later in the day.

Pete stared at the tracking monitor for a few moments, then at the sheriff's office, and swore. Denver had done it. Somehow she'd realized the tracking device was in the watch he'd given her. He swore again. She'd suspected him of being a liar and a murderer, and now she knew just how low he'd go.

The two-way radio squawked and Cal's voice filled the pickup's cab. "Come in, Cowboy."

Pete could tell by the tone of Cal's voice that he'd told Midnight about what had happened and Midnight wasn't pleased. He picked up the headset. "What do you want?"

Static. "Somebody wants to talk to you. Now."

Great, Pete thought. And what was he going to say when Midnight asked him, "Where is Denver McCallahan?"

Good question. He wished to hell he had the answer.

J.D. left Denver sleeping on the queen-size bed that took up most of the motel room. They'd both spied the bed the moment they walked into the room. He'd taken one look at her and knew she wanted him as badly as he did her. He'd waited until she fell asleep before he'd gotten up and gone into the bathroom to shave off his beard. For a long time, he stood in front of the mirror staring at himself, wondering how long he'd been hiding beneath the beard.

"Oh, J.D.," Denver cried when he came back into the bedroom. She jumped up to take his face in her hands. She studied him for a long moment, her eyes brimming with tears, and then she kissed him. "I'd forgotten what a wonderful face you have."

They made love again in the big, soft bed, then reluctantly got dressed in their new clothes for the appointment with the psychologist they'd found in the yellow pages. The doctor specialized in hypnotherapy.

Trembling, Denver leaned against the wall as they took the elevator up to his office on the third floor of the old Bozeman Hotel building. The other night when the man in her cabin had tried to choke her, she'd known fear, but she'd never experienced sheer terror. J.D. gave her hand a reassuring squeeze as they entered Dr. Rich-

ard Donnley's office. "I'm here for you," he said. She
smiled in answer, hoping that would always be the case.

The doctor was a tall, thin man with kind eyes and a
soft voice. His office was much like him, with a soft and
peaceful feeling. Denver sank into a comfortable, overstuffed love seat. J.D. sat beside her, holding her hand.

"It's true that dreams can be a way for the subconscious to communicate with us," Dr. Donnley said carefully after Denver explained about the nightmares.

"Does that mean that under hypnosis I might be able
to remember more?" she asked.

"Sometimes you can access a memory through hypnosis," he agreed. "But the whole area of memory retrieval is very controversial."

"Controversial?" J.D. asked.

"It's rare that you get a pure memory," the doctor explained, steepling his fingers against his chin. "It will
only be *your* perception of what happened."

"Does that mean what I recall under hypnosis won't
be real?" she asked in surprise.

"It will be the way you remember that day, which
may not be exactly the way it was," he replied.

"I saw the robber's face when he turned. He wore a
mask and he had something in his hand…"

"Even if you recognized him, it wouldn't be admis-
sible in court," he said.

J.D. squeezed her hand. "Her memory isn't enough
to have him arrested—let alone convicted, right?"

"Exactly." Dr. Donnley brushed a speck of lint from
his pant leg. "There is another point to consider. You
may not be able to see the man's face in your dream because you couldn't see it that day in the bank."

"But I feel so certain the dream is trying to tell me

something," Denver cried. "It must be the identity of the murderer."

"Not necessarily so," the doctor said. "It's not unusual in a case like this for you to want so desperately to recognize him that you start believing you can. We won't know until we hypnotize you. And there is a good chance that if it's too painful, your subconscious might not *let* you remember."

"So what do you think, Sunshine?" J.D. asked. He smiled at her, a lock of his hair hanging down over his forehead. "You still want to do this?"

She nodded. "I have to. I have to know."

Denver leaned back in the chair, eyes closed, hands curled in her lap. She felt herself drifting in the darkness. The feeling was not unpleasant. It soothed, as did Dr. Donnley's softly spoken words. Deeper and deeper. Her body felt heavy; her breathing slowed until she feared she'd forget to take a breath. Then she forgot to worry about it as she floated in the peaceful darkness, content.

"Let's go back to that day when you were five," Dr. Donnley said. "You and your parents were going to the bank. Do you remember?"

Denver nodded, although she didn't feel her head move.

"What did you do before you went to the bank?"

"We picked up my father from work." Her voice sounded far away. "He's a policeman."

"So he's still in his uniform when you go into the bank. Tell me what you're doing as you go into the bank."

"Skipping. And singing." She sang softly, the words

still there after all these years. "You are my sunshine, my only sunshine…"

"Where are your parents?"

"They're behind me. I stop skipping."

"Why?"

"There are people on the floor. Something is wrong. I turn around to tell my parents. But I can't."

"Why?"

"I see the other policeman."

"What other policeman?"

"The one on the floor. He's reaching for his gun. It's still in his holster. And I hear my father call my name. I run back to him. I'm afraid."

"What's happening now?" Dr. Donnley asked.

The words poured out as she watched it happening in her head. "My father pulls his gun. He grabs my shoulder with his other hand and pushes me hard. It hurts. He pushes me as he yells at my mother to get down. I hit the floor and slide. The floor is cold and hard. I hit my chest on the desk leg. It hurts so bad."

"You're all right, Denver," the doctor assured her.

"It hurts. I can't breathe." Denver felt tears rolling down her face, then the fear, the panic. "I can't breathe!"

"You're all right. You're not there. It's just a memory. Take a deep breath. There now. What do you see?"

"Nothing. I'm on the floor by the desk. I can't see anything." She sobbed quietly for a moment. "I hear my mother scream. I crawl under the desk. I can see the robber. He's standing by the counter. He turns. He has a shotgun in one hand and something in the other. It's shiny. I can't tell what it is. I look at my father. All I can see is his legs. But I can see the other policeman on the floor. He has a gun in his hand. He's pointing it at my father. I hear the gunshots."

Dr. Donnley kept talking, his voice soft and reassuring. "What is happening now?"

"I hear people screaming. Now I hear the shotgun go off. My father is on the floor beside me. His eyes are open. There is blood on the floor. Blood everywhere. People are crying. I'm crying. I slide farther under the desk and watch the robber leave. He stops for a moment beside the desk."

"Can he see you?"

"No."

"Can you see what he has in his hand?"

She shook her head. "He leaves. And I see my mother. She's on the floor, too." The sobs rose from deep inside her, a well of sorrow. "A lady helps me out from under the desk. She hugs me and tells me my parents are dead."

"It's all right to be sad. It's all right to cry."

Denver cried until there were no more tears, until she could hear the music and feel her mind drifting in the darkness again.

"Think back, Denver. Are you sure you don't know the man wearing the mask?"

She shook her head, remembering only the mask and the flash of silver she'd seen in his hand. But as she looked into the darkness, she saw another face. "I know the other one."

"What other one?"

Denver focused on the darkness. She stared into the man's face. Into those bottomless eyes. Her heart seemed to race out of her chest. She couldn't catch her breath. "Ooohh."

"You're all right, Denver."

Her eyes flew open. She jerked up, pushing herself back into the chair as her gaze darted around Dr. Donnley's office. "I saw him!" she cried. He'd been younger then, not much more than a teenager, and thinner. But there was no mistake about that hair, those eyes or that awful, cold look of his. "It was Cal. Cal Dalton. He was the cop on the floor. But he's dead."

J.D. held Denny. The sun poured into the front seat of the pickup. She felt good against him, warm and safe in his arms. He stroked her back, his chin resting on the top of her head.

"It was Cal," she whispered. She'd been saying it over and over again. "But he was on the floor of the bank, surrounded by blood. He was dead. How could that be?"

J.D. hugged her to him. "I don't know."

Dr. Donnley had warned her again about the questionability of memory retrieval. The man she'd seen might have been someone she connected with evil, he'd explained. She'd said herself that this man had tried to rape her. It would be understandable that she'd put his face on a man who might have killed her parents.

But Denver had argued that she'd recognized him as he was more than twenty years ago. Was that possible? she'd asked him.

Dr. Donnley had smiled sympathetically and told her there was much they didn't know about the mind and warned her not to take much stock in the things she'd remembered. He'd suggested further hypnosis.

J.D. believed Denny had seen Cal's face, but like the doctor, he was skeptical as to what it meant. She'd been through so much lately. It didn't seem impossible she should put Cal's face on a dead man's.

"I can't explain it, but I know I saw Cal," Denver insisted now as she leaned back to look into J.D.'s eyes.

"Maybe it was someone who looked like him," J.D. said reasonably. "Maybe even a…relative."

"I never thought of that." She smiled.

He knew that smile. "Let me guess, we're going to Billings to investigate a robbery?"

They drove into the Magic City, the sun high overhead, the city's famous rock rims drenched in warm sunlight against a clear blue Montana sky. The largest city in the state, Billings sprawled across the valley, jumping the Yellowstone River, then running south as far as the eye could see. Denver had been quiet all morning, and he knew she was anxious about what they'd find. She nestled against him, her face set in an iron-willed determination that constantly amazed him.

The library was a huge brick building just off a one-way street downtown. They waded through the 1969 city directory—the same year as the bank robbery—then the years before and after. Denver's disappointment showed in her eyes when they didn't turn up even one Dalton in the years before or after.

"We just keep hitting one dead end after another," she complained, slamming shut the 1971 directory. "So much for the relative theory."

On impulse, J.D. flipped through the 1969 directory again, only this time to the *C*'s. He ran his finger down a column.

"Take a look at this, Sunshine," he said, turning the directory so she could see. "William Collins."

She stared at him, then at the name. The one that matched the fingerprints Max had taken at his birthday party. "You don't think—"

"There's only one way to find out."

Denny slid into his arms, pressing her lips against his neck, before they walked to the pickup. She felt warm, her familiar scent making him want nothing more than to be alone with her.

The *Billings Register* was in a large old brick building on the south side of the city, which was part of a city renewal plan. As soon as they walked in, J.D. still limping, heads turned. Denver seemed confused at first as to why everyone was staring at them, and then realized they were staring at J. D. Garrison, country and western star.

"I keep forgetting just how well-known you are," she said.

At that moment, J.D. wished he wasn't. The woman at the front desk asked him for his autograph. Denver insisted he give it to her. "We need the morgue," J.D. said. The woman dragged her eyes away from J.D. to point down the hallway.

They pulled out the roll of microfilm from 1969 and sat down. J.D. held Denver's hand for just a minute. It was cool and he could feel it trembling.

"The summer of 1969?"

She nodded.

The pages blurred by. He wanted to hold her, to make this easier on her, but he doubted there was anything he could do to lessen her anxiety.

The first story about the robbery came up on the screen and Denver covered his hand on the knob to freeze it.

A masked bandit killed two people and wounded
a third during a holdup that netted more than a
million dollars at State Bank this morning.

Denver's grip on his hand tightened; she took a
ragged breath. "Wounded a third?"

Chief of Police Bill Vernon said the male robber wearing a ski mask came into the bank shortly
after it opened. At gunpoint, he forced bank per-
sonnel onto the floor while one teller sacked the
money.

A spokesman for the bank said this branch
doesn't normally have that much cash on hand
but was transferring money from the oil fields.

The shootings occurred when an off-duty police officer, still in uniform, came into the bank
with his family. The police officer was killed,
along with his wife, and a security guard was
wounded during the shoot-out that followed.

"Oh, J.D., the guard wasn't killed," Denver cried.
"Does it give his name?"

J.D. shook his head as he scanned down the rest of
the article.

The robber escaped with more than one million
dollars. No arrests have been made. Chief Vernon
said the investigation is continuing.

J.D. started to scroll to the next story when Denver
stopped him. "Look," she said, pointing to the date of
the first article.

He stared at the numbers and felt a sudden chill. "June 14, 1969. It's the number from Max's notation at the end of the Wade file."

"The date of the robbery article in the *Billings Register*," Denver said. "Bil 69614. He'd already connected the poaching and the robbery or at least suspected a connection. Better make a copy of the stories," Denver added.

J.D. nodded, dropped in a dime and hit the copy button. Then he turned to the next robbery story.

Police Chief Bill Vernon confirmed today that the victims of the State Bank holdup last week were Timothy McCallahan and his wife, Linda. Both were shot during the robbery, which netted more than one million dollars.

He felt her tremble and pulled her closer. "Are you sure you want to read this, Denny?"
She nodded.

Timothy McCallahan, a Billings police officer, was off duty at the time of the robbery, but still in uniform. Witnesses say he entered the bank and, realizing what was happening, went for his gun.

Also wounded during the shootout was bank guard William Collins. Collins is in satisfactory condition at Billings Deaconess Hospital.

Denver let out a cry. "William Collins?"
But J.D. had already scanned ahead to the next robbery story and the accompanying photograph. A young

Cal Dalton smiled at the photographer from his hospital bed. "Just what we thought."

"William Collins is Cal Dalton!" Denver exclaimed. "We were right!"

J.D. pulled her into his arms and swung her around in a circle, hopping on his one good leg. She laughed, her head thrown back, her eyes bright, and he yearned to see that kind of happiness in her face always. Then he kissed her. At first lightly, then with a need that made him weak with wanting her. He released her when an older woman came into the morgue. They both sat back down at the microfilm table and waited innocently for the woman to leave, then they looked at each other and burst out laughing.

After a moment, they turned their attention back to the photograph of William Collins a.k.a. Cal Dalton. Cal was much younger but there was no doubt that William Collins and Cal Dalton were one and the same. "Do you realize what this could mean? If you were right about Cal being the bank guard, then there's a good chance you were right about Cal shooting at your father, instead of the masked bank robber."

Denver moved in closer to read the story. "You're saying it was an inside job?"

"That would explain why Cal still had his gun."

"This could be what we've been looking for," she said. "It could explain why Max was hanging around Cal, why he'd run a fingerprint check on him."

"But Max never got the results," J.D. observed.

Denver tilted her head up in speculation. "I wonder if Max knew something or was just suspicious? I guess it doesn't matter. If Cal even *thought* Max was on to him..."

He nodded, thinking the same thing. "It could have been enough to get Max killed."

They quickly scanned later newspapers for news of the robbery. The articles became shorter and shorter as the weeks went by. Both the bandit and the money still had not been found. William Collins a.k.a. Cal Dalton recovered from his gunshot wound and was released from the hospital. Then the robbery just died away.

"I'd sure like to talk to this Chief Vernon," Denver said as they put the microfilm away.

He smiled as he took her hand. "Then I guess we'd better find him."

At the police station, a young lieutenant told Denver that Chief Bill Vernon had retired. "But if it's an old case, he'll remember it." He wrote down an address on the west end of town.

Bill Vernon was a tall, silver-haired man with an arrow-straight back and keen gray eyes. "The State Bank robbery in '69." He nodded his head. "Remember it well." He offered them chairs and coffee. They turned down the coffee but sat down on the couch. "Want to tell me what makes you interested in such an old case?"

J.D. covered Denver's hand with his own. "Denver's father and mother were killed in the robbery."

Vernon's eyebrows shot up; his expression softened with sympathy. "You're the little girl?"

Denver nodded, feeling like that frightened little child again. Chief Vernon had the answer she needed. Who had killed her parents? She'd always believed it was a stranger. Now there was a possibility she knew the man.

"Timothy McCallahan was one fine policeman," Vernon said.

Tears welled in her eyes. "Thank you."

"A terrible tragedy." Vernon shook his head, his gaze distant. "That was one case I wanted to crack more than any other in my career. We knew there was someone on the inside but couldn't prove it."

Denver stole a look at J.D. "We think William Collins was the inside man."

Vernon nodded. "I still do, too. The gunshot wound should have proved it."

"The gunshot wound?" J.D. asked.

"Collins was shot with a standard-issue police revolver," Vernon said. "He said he was in your father's line of fire and was shot by accident."

"Then my father did shoot him?" Denver asked. "I remember the guard pulling his gun and pointing it at my father, and then I heard the shots."

Vernon rubbed the back of his neck, studying her. "So you do remember some of it?"

"Some. I'm just not sure how much of it is real," she said, thinking of the flashing silver.

"We knew the guard had to be in on it, but he wasn't the brains behind the holdup. He wasn't smart enough," Vernon said.

That certainly fit Cal Dalton a.k.a. William Collins, she thought.

"The case was never solved?" J.D. asked.

Vernon shook his head. "Got away free as a bird. Money and all."

Denver thought of the memories that had surfaced during her hypnosis session. "There's something I need to know. Did William Collins kill my parents?" she asked, bracing herself for the answer.

Vernon shook his head. "They were both killed by the bank robber. Witnesses said the man carried a sawed-off shotgun. That is consistent with the pathologist's findings."

Denver took a deep breath and let it out. In the park across the street, two young boys worked to get a Ninja Turtle kite airborne. "Is there any way to trace the money from the robbery?" she asked, thinking of the 150,000 in Max's account.

Vernon shook his head.

"And if you could prove William Collins was in on the robbery?" J.D. asked.

"Accessory to murder." The old police chief smiled. "Fortunately, there's no statute of limitations on murder, and there is nothing I'd like better than to nail Collins."

Denver thanked him. As she got up to leave, she noticed a photograph of several policemen on the wall. She moved closer, recognizing a younger version of Chief Vernon. Then her gaze took in a young policeman on his right. Her pulse thundered in her ears. "Who is that man?" she asked, her voice cracking.

Vernon stepped up behind her. "That's Bill Cline. He and I went to the academy together."

"He didn't happen to work for the Billings Police Department in 1969, did he?" Denver asked, holding her breath.

Vernon frowned. "Bill? No, he was never on the force here."

"Just a thought," Denver said, breathing again.

Vernon opened the door for them. "No, in 1969, Bill Cline was working in security."

"Here in Billings?" J.D. asked.

Vernon shook his head. "Up in the oil fields. He was an armored-car driver for Interstate West, a company that transferred oil money."

Chapter 18

"I'm telling you he's our bank robber," Denver argued as they left Vernon's.

"Cline?" J.D. started the pickup and headed back into the city. "He's a lot of things—"

"He's an obnoxious redneck, male-chauvinist, know-it-all jerk," she said, daring him to disagree.

J.D. laughed. "Yes, he's all of that and probably a lot more you're just too polite to name."

She grinned at him.

"But a bank robber and murderer? Let alone the brains behind a million-dollar heist?"

That stopped her. She'd never thought of Cline as smart, but maybe she'd misjudged him. Maybe all that redneck bluster was an act. "Think about it, J.D. Cline called Pete the morning after Davey's accident on Horse

Butte to warn him. And Cline would have known about a large oil-money transfer to the bank."

"So would a lot of other people," J.D. countered. "And Cline likes Pete and he isn't that wild about me."

"Are you going to tell me it isn't strange that Cline and Cal Dalton ended up in the same town?"

"Cline's been the deputy sheriff in West Yellowstone for years," J.D. said reasonably. "Dalton or Williams or whoever he is has only been in town how long?"

"A few months," Denver admitted. "But maybe he went there because of Cline."

J.D. pulled up to a light and looked over at her. "Isn't it more likely that he went there because of the horn?"

"He could have come for both," she muttered under her breath.

"The question now is, what are we going to do?" he asked.

"About Cal?"

"About food." He grinned at her. "I'm starved."

She laughed, snuggling against him. "You're always starved."

"Always starved for *you*," he said, planting a kiss on the top of her head. Her hair smelled clean and fresh and made him want her more than food.

He drove into an older neighborhood in the south end of town and found an authentic-looking Mexican café. They took a booth by the window and ordered two combination plates and two beers.

"Sheila Walker thinks she's traced the money trail to Max," Denver said after the waitress left. "If that money in his account is from the robbery, then the person who put it there has to be someone involved in the crime."

"Or someone who knew where the money was hidden."

Denver frowned. "I never thought of that."

"Or the money might be from horn hunting," J.D. said. "It might have been put in his account just to make Max look guilty."

The waitress put two frosty mugs of beer down in front of them. The place was empty at this time of day. J.D. felt safe for the first time in days and knew Denny did, too. He didn't want to talk about murder or robbery or horn poaching. He just wanted to look at Denny sitting across from him. He pressed his leg against hers under the table. She responded in kind with a smile, took a sip of beer and flipped through the robbery stories they'd photocopied.

J.D. reached across the table to take her hand. With his thumb he traced her life line. Then her love line.

"What do you see?" she asked, pushing the newspaper stories aside.

"I see a long, interesting life filled with adventure," he said, and she laughed. "And lots of children."

She raised one eyebrow and grinned at him. "Lots?"

"At least two."

"Two's a nice number. And is there a man in my life?"

"Of course." He frowned. "Well, I hope so."

"Is he tall, dark and handsome?" she asked, looking down at her palm.

"He'll pass."

Her eyes glinted with mischief. "Then maybe I already know him."

The waitress came back with a bowl of chips and salsa and J.D. reluctantly let go of Denver's hand.

She took another sip of her beer and licked the foam from her lips as she looked out the window. "You un-

derstand that I have to find Max's killer before I can—"
She turned to him.

"Yes, but what if that person's never found, Denny?
How long are you willing to put your life on hold?"

She picked up the newspaper accounts of the robbery again. "Don't ask me that, J.D. You know this is
something I have to do. I owe Max." He watched her
leaf through the newspaper articles. If she couldn't clear
Max's name—Suddenly she stopped in midmotion, her
fingers trembling as she clutched an article in her hand.
"Look at this."

J.D. leaned over to see the page she was gripping.

"Sheila Walker," Denver whispered. "That reporter
who keeps wanting to talk to me. She covered the robbery. No wonder she thinks she's found the money."

"I'm scared," Denver said to J.D. as she hung up the
phone. He leaned against the doorway of the phone
booth. Just the sight of him made her heart go pitter-
patter. She ran her fingers through the curly hair at his
nape and breathed in the heady scent of him.

"You didn't reach Maggie?" he asked.

She shook her head. "She should have been back
from Missoula by now. As much as I don't want to do
it, I have to call Cline and see if he's heard anything."
She dialed, then spoke to the dispatcher, who put the
deputy sheriff on immediately.

"Where the hell have you been?" he demanded. "I've
been trying to get ahold of you for two days."

Her heart leaped up into her throat. It was Maggie,
she thought. "Why? Has something happened?"

"We've caught your uncle's murderer."

Denver fought for breath. "What?" J.D. stared at her face, concern making his eyes the color of pewter.

"The hitchhiker," Cline said with obvious satisfaction.

"The hitchhiker?" she repeated, dumbstruck.

"He had the murder weapon on him and he confessed. Case closed." Cline let out a long I-told-you-so sigh. "And as far as that other little detective work you and Garrison did," Cline continued, "Roland Marsh and I went back in to the park, where you said you saw those elk-horn caches."

She gripped the phone. "You and Marsh?"

"No horn. No sign of any poaching. No dead bear. If I were you, I'd stick with that photography hobby of yours."

She started to hang up, but Cline's next words stopped her.

"And by the way, I'm not your damned secretary, missy. Everybody and their brother have been calling here."

"Who's everybody?" she asked, hoping there'd be a message from Maggie.

"Pete. I told him to wait until the dance tonight and if you didn't show up…"

She'd forgotten she'd promised to go with Pete. The Montana Country Club band was playing for the Spring Fling at the old railroad station. It seemed like a lifetime ago when she'd made the date.

"Pete said to call him. Something about Maggie."

"Maggie?"

"And that reporter woman," Cline said distastefully. "Sheila Walker. You're to call her at Max's office. Said it's a matter of life and death." He let out an irritated sigh. "Get an answering machine, will ya?" He hung up.

Denver stared at the phone, then quickly dialed Maggie's number. No answer. She rang Pete's. Still no answer. Finally she called Taylor. "I'm trying to find Maggie," she said carefully.

"Isn't everyone?" Taylor said, not sounding all that happy. "I've been looking for her myself. I thought she'd call me when she got back."

"Then she *is* back?"

"That's what Pete told me. But I have to tell you. I'm worried about her. Pete sounded like she might be in some sort of trouble."

"I'll keep trying Pete's number," she said, fighting panic. "If I hear anything, I'll get back to you."

"Wait a minute, where are you?" she heard him ask, but she broke the connection and dialed Max's office number. What if Sheila really had found out something? The phone rang and rang. No Sheila. Denver hung up and stepped from the booth into J.D.'s arms.

She fought her growing fears as she recounted first the conversation with Cline, then the one with Taylor. "Pete has Maggie. I'm sure of it. She must have found out Pete wasn't in Missoula the day Max was killed." She made a face. "Cline said he and Marsh went to look for the horn. Said they didn't find it or a trace of the dead bear. What does that tell you?"

He ran a hand through his hair and looked up at her. "That we're going back to West Yellowstone."

"If Pete has Maggie and we can't trust Cline—" J.D. swore and pulled Denver into his arms. "We have no choice but to go back," she agreed.

"I was hoping you'd say that."

Chapter 19

Maggie sat in a chair by the fire pretending interest in the flames. She reviewed her options, wondering what Max would have done under the same circumstances, reminding herself that she'd never had Max's flair for the dramatic—or his total disregard for danger.

· "How long do you plan to hold me here?" she asked the man beside her, trying to keep the fear from her voice.

Lester Wade smiled in answer. He was small, with soft brown eyes, but Maggie couldn't miss the hard edge to him. Or the pistol he cradled in his lap.

Maggie had gotten back from Missoula anxious to share her news with Denver. She'd verified at The Barn that Pete Williams hadn't been in Missoula the afternoon of the murder with the rest of the band. But when she'd rushed to Denver's cabin, she'd found the barrel of a gun—held by one of Pete's band members—waiting for her.

"Where's Denver?" Lester had demanded.

Maggie wished she only knew. Worrying about Denver made her feel braver.

Lester jumped when the phone rang. He picked it up. "Yeah?" He listened, frowning, then hung up. "Lucky for you, lady. They've found Denver. It sounds like she's headed back."

"Headed back here?" Maggie felt sick. Was she being used as a decoy to get Denver to the cabin?

"Don't worry about it," Lester said, sitting across from her. "Everything's going as planned now."

"What a relief," she said, but Lester didn't get the sarcasm. The plan seemed to be that Lester and some others would be skipping town tonight with enough money to retire someplace warm. She'd overheard that much when Lester was on the phone earlier. "Do you mind if I stretch my legs?"

Lester looked worried. "Stay in this room, don't touch anything and don't move too fast."

"I'm too old to move too fast."

The man had no sense of humor, Maggie thought as she got to her feet. She caught a movement outside the window in the growing darkness. A figure popped up for a moment and disappeared again. She moved to block Lester's view as best she could. A scraggly boy in his teens with large brown eyes peered into the window. He motioned for her to keep quiet and disappeared again. It wasn't exactly the cavalry but it was help. Possibly.

"Could I have a glass of water, please?" she asked.

Lester eyed her suspiciously.

"I promise not to try to drown myself in it."

He shot Maggie a humorless smile and moved cautiously into the kitchen. All the time he let the tap water run, he kept the pistol trained on her. She wandered away from the window, pretending to warm her hands in front of the fire. Lester filled a glass and brought it to her. He put it down on the hearth and stepped back as if he thought she'd try to jump him. He must think that kind of behavior ran in the family.

He headed back to his chair, but never reached it. His head jerked around at a sound in the hallway, the pistol raised ready to fire. Maggie caught a glimpse of the young man's head and knew Lester had, too. Quickly grabbing a log from the wood box, Maggie closed her eyes and swung. A gunshot whined through the cabin, echoing off the walls, and someone screamed.

From the top of Grayling Pass, J.D. could see the lights of West Yellowstone glowing in the distance like a small aurora borealis. He let up on the gas as they topped the hill in the van they'd rented in Bozeman and began the drop down into the wide valley.

"About this plan of yours…" he said, glancing over at Denver.

"The blueberry syrup plan?" She shrugged. "It's biodegradable and environmentally safe. That's about all I can say about it."

She'd had him stop in Bozeman, rent a van, and buy four gallons of blueberry syrup, a bottle opener and some wire.

J.D. looked over at her, his gaze softening at just the sight of her. "I hope this works."

"Have a little faith, Garrison," she said.

Out of the corner of his eye, he watched her chew at her lower lip and smiled at the familiarity of it. When he wasn't touching her, he loved looking at her. Her bravado right now made him love her all the more. But offered little reassurance. They were driving straight into a trap and she knew it.

J.D. honked as they crossed the Madison River bridge, making Denver smile. "I have to tell you these past few days with you have been—"

"Paradise?" she asked, laughing up at him.

He grinned. "Being chased by killers, hit on the head with hard objects, shot at with big-game rifles. Yes, Denny, it's been a little bit of heaven."

"Don't forget that fall into the bathtub."

"How could I?"

"If you're trying to say I'm not boring, I thank you," she teased, her gaze on the highway ahead.

"Boring?" He laughed. "Oh, Denny, you are anything but boring." His heart ached. "No matter what happens tonight—"

She touched her finger to his lips. "I know."

He pulled her hard against him. "This has to work."

They drove into West Yellowstone at one-thirty in the morning. Summer's Coming, read a sign at the Conoco station. If there were any signs of summer in this still-hibernating tourist town, J.D. couldn't see them.

He turned up Geyser Street. "J.D." Her hand squeezed his arm; he followed her gaze down the block to Max's office. "There's a light on. Sheila must be there."

"We don't have much time," he said as he parked the van. He felt a sense of urgency; they had to be at the dance before two. "Let's find out what she's got to say."

A chill crawled around his neck as they walked up the steps. J.D. took Denver's hand. The light was on only in the apartment above; it spilled down the stairs into the office, giving the room an eerie glow. No sounds came from inside. Nothing looked amiss. Except for the front door. It stood open, letting the night in.

"I don't like this," Denver whispered.

"No kidding."

It took Maggie a moment to realize where the screaming was coming from.

"Hey, lady! Are you nuts?" the young man in front of her yelled. She closed her mouth, swallowing the last of the scream, and nodded. She'd never been more nuts in her life.

"Thanks," the kid said, uncovering his ears. "That's quite a set of lungs you've got."

"I used to scream professionally," Maggie told him.

He grinned at her. "You must have made a fortune."

Maggie smiled. "You have to be Davey."

"You've heard of me?" He sounded pleased.

Maggie noticed then that the front door stood open and Lester was gone. In the distance, she could hear the roar of an engine dying away down the road. Davey picked up the pistol from the floor.

"Max told me about you," she said, taking the gun from him as if it was a dirty diaper. He was the kind of kid Max had always loved to take under his wing; she suspected he was a lot like Max had been at that same age. "And of course your reputation for trouble precedes you."

"Oh, yeah?" He grinned, obviously pleased. "You want me to go after that guy?"

"No," Maggie assured him as she went to the phone. "I want you to stay here with me in case he comes back. And I want you to tell me who killed Max."

Davey shrugged. "Sure. A guy Cal calls Midnight."

"Midnight?"

He shrugged again. "Yeah, he offed Max to keep him from dropping a dime on him and Cal."

She remembered Max taking a stack of old detective-story paperbacks up to his office. "I've got this kid working for me. I'm just trying to help him with his reading," Max had said.

"Dropping a dime, huh?" she said to Davey.

"You know, dropping a dime—making a call to the cops," he replied.

"I know. And how did you find out all this about Midnight and Cal?"

He grinned. "I hang out. I listen. I do what Max did. I've been tailing Cal ever since Max bought it."

"You're lucky you didn't get yourself killed. And what else do you know about this Midnight person?" she asked.

"He's running a poaching ring here and sending illegal stuff all over the world. Lester and Cal have been stealing antlers and animal stuff out of Yellowstone Park for him. You wanna hear about the animal stuff? It's pretty gross."

She declined and picked up the phone to drop her own dime.

Davey looked uncomfortable. "You're not going to call the cops, are you?"

Maggie dialed the number. "I won't mention your name."

He nodded and headed for the fridge. "I hope you have better food than the place where they were keeping *me*."

The moment Deputy Cline came on the line, Maggie poured out what little information she had based on what Davey had told her, adding the part about her own kidnapping by Lester Wade. She didn't mention Davey. Cline listened without saying a word.

"Stay there," he said when she'd finished. "Lock the doors, don't let anyone in and don't answer the phone." He hung up. She stared at the phone, hoping she'd done the right thing by calling Cline. But she couldn't throw off the uneasy feeling Cline had given her. Why hadn't he seemed more surprised by the information?

She dialed Taylor's number. He answered on the first ring, and she quickly recounted what had happened.

"Are you sure you're all right?" he asked.

She assured him she was fine.

"Where is this Lester person now?"

"I don't know. Deputy Cline sounded like he might know, though."

"You called Cline?"

She couldn't miss the worry in his voice. "You don't think—"

"I'm sure you did the right thing." Taylor didn't sound sure at all. "I'll keep an eye on Cline. Just stay there."

She hung up, relieved she'd called Taylor. Max had once told her the reason he didn't get along with the deputy was because Cline bent the law when it suited him. But not even Cline would bend the law to protect a murderer, would he? Unless *he* was the murderer.

Just as she finished locking the doors, Davey came out of the kitchen with a large bag of chips, a jar of salsa, a couple of turkey and cheese sandwiches and two Cokes.

"Hungry?" he asked with a grin.

Denver expected Max's files to be ransacked again. But as she stepped in, she realized it looked just as it had the last time she and J.D. had been here.

"Sheila?" Denver called out.

A sheet of silence as thick as ice lay over the house. Not even a breeze stirred the pines outside. Denver followed J.D.'s gaze to the stairs and felt him squeeze her hand. As she trailed after him, her pulse thundered in her ears. The stairs creaked under their weight as they climbed slowly into the light above.

On the landing at the top, Denver slipped and would have fallen if J.D. hadn't caught her. "What is it?" he whispered.

"Something's on the floor." She moved her foot to find a dark stain. She bent down to touch it gingerly with a finger, knowing what it was before she felt the sticky substance. "I think it's blood."

J.D. let out a groan; his hand tightened on hers. "Stay here."

She watched him cautiously push open the door to Max's apartment. He swore angrily.

"Tell me it's not Maggie!" she cried, hurrying up behind him.

"It's not Maggie," J.D. assured her, trying to hold her back. She pushed past him and stared down at the figure on the floor.

Sheila Walker lay on her side in a pool of blood. She was very dead.

J.D. dialed the Sheriff's office. Denver stood at Max's office window staring out into the night. When the dispatcher came on the line, she informed him that Deputy Cline wasn't in and couldn't be reached by radio right now. Was there a message?

"Tell him there's been a murder at Max McCallahan's. Upstairs. Her name's Sheila Walker."

Denver headed for the front door as J.D. hung up. "Where are you going?" he demanded, following her out to the porch.

"I don't want to be here when Cline gets here. He'll try to stop us. We have to fix the band's rigs and find Maggie."

J.D. checked his watch. He couldn't believe he was going along with her blueberry-syrup plan. "We still have time." He pulled her into his arms, cradling the back of her head in his hand. Just the touch of her hair brought back the memory of them together. His heart ached with worry that he might lose her.

"I can't quit now," she whispered against his shirt. In the distance, J.D. could hear the wail of a siren.

"I know." He released her; she stepped back and looked up at him. Her expression tore at his heart. They would never find happiness until Max's killer was caught.

J.D. took her hand and they ran across the street to the van. His ankle still hurt but felt stronger, he realized. With the headlights off, he quickly turned down the alley into the dark pines. Moments later, a patrol car came to a screeching halt in front of Max's office. The blue light on top spun, flickering against the night sky. J.D. pulled the van to the end of the alley and, heading toward the old depot, turned on the headlights.

Denver could hear the music from the dance as J.D. pulled the van under a large pine on a logging road behind the depot and killed the engine. The festive sounds of the party drifted on the cool night air, belying the danger.

Denver glanced at the dashboard clock. It was 1:48 a.m. "Wanna flip for the bus or the pickup?"

J.D. shook his head. "You can have the bus. You'd probably cheat on the coin toss anyway."

She started to open her door, but he pulled her into his arms. His kiss promised her things she could not bear to think about. The feel of his lips, the taste of him, made her crave more. When he released her, she looked into his eyes, seeing the love she'd always dreamed of. How badly she wanted to forget this mess and just take off with him. But she knew Max's murder would always haunt her. And she had to find Maggie.

"I'll see you in a few minutes," she whispered and kissed him quickly. "For luck."

Then, pulling two gallons of the blueberry syrup, wire and a pair of pliers from the back, she headed for the band's old school bus before she could talk herself out of it.

It felt like a lark, something she and Pete and J.D. would have done when they were kids. But she neared the bus cautiously, only too well aware of what was at stake. The bus was parked behind the depot-turned-community center, secluded by virtue of the darkness and the large pines that loomed over it. Denver stopped for a moment to look back at J.D. He carried the same equipment she did, only he was working his way toward Pete's pickup parked around front, and she realized why he'd given her the bus. It was safer.

Laughter rippled on the breeze, mixing with voices. But no music. The band must be on a break. A few partygoers stood on the back steps of the old railroad depot, smoking and talking. It was too dark to see their faces—only the glow of their cigarettes was visible.

She hung back in the shadows until they returned inside when the music started up again. Taking one last look around, she climbed under the bus.

J.D. crawled beneath Pete's pickup, pulling the supplies with him. The sounds of the dance drifted around him. He listened for closer sounds as he checked his watch. Almost 2:00 a.m. The dance would be over soon. He reached for the first plastic gallon of blueberry syrup and the wire. Cutting a piece of wire, he tied the container to the undercarriage of the pickup, then carefully made a small hole in the plastic. The syrup began to drip. He reached for another gallon and attached it with more wire to the first in piggyback fashion, making a hole between the two gallon jugs. He watched the slow, steady drip of syrup for a moment, and smiled. He'd laughed at Denny's idea in the beginning.

"Well, it might not be as good as Hansel and Gretel leaving bread crumbs," Denny had said. "But at least the syrup should leave a trail we can follow on a snow-packed highway in the dark."

J.D. listened to the night sounds for a few seconds, thinking he'd heard a noise nearby. Nothing. He slipped out, brushed snow from his jeans and turned to find himself staring down the barrel of a shotgun.

Denver finished "syruping" the bus and looked around for J.D. Not seeing him, she headed back to the van according to plan. Her heart jackhammered at the thought that their plan might actually work. Now it was up to the FBI to stop the poachers; she'd called them from Billings and told them about the blueberry-syrup trail she planned to leave for them. But she couldn't be sure they'd taken her seriously. She'd warned them not to contact Marsh or Cline, and that could have been a mistake.

Now she couldn't wait to get back to the van—and J.D. More than ever, she wanted this whole thing to be over so they could be together. Once Maggie was safe—

Something moved ahead of her. Denver slowed, searching the pools of blackness beneath the pines and the shadows that sprawled across the aging snowbanks.

"J.D.?" she whispered.

A large dark shadow stepped from the trees. Just in time she caught the scream that rose in her throat. "Deputy Cline!" Her heart thundered against her ribs. "What are you doing here?"

"I believe that's my line. You're the one sneaking around in the dark." He nodded to the wire and pliers. "Like to tell me exactly what you've been up to?"

She took a step back in the snow, but he restrained her with a hand on her arm. "A hitchhiker didn't kill my uncle."

"Don't you think I know that?" he demanded. He motioned toward his patrol car parked in the pines down the road behind the depot. "You're coming with me." His fingers bit into her flesh.

"You're behind all of it?" Denver burst out, jerking her arm free of Cline's grasp as she tried to get her wobbly legs to move.

"You fool woman!" he snarled, reaching for her again.

She stumbled back. He grabbed her shoulder and spun her into him. She heard the metal clink of handcuffs and his mumbled curses as she fought to escape, but she didn't stand a chance against his strength.

Denver didn't hear the other person approach. It wasn't until Cline's grip loosened and he crumpled to the ground, that she realized she'd been saved. Again. She looked up to see Taylor looming over her. She fell into his arms, tears overflowing at the mere sight of him. "We have to quit meeting like this," she said on a sob.

He laughed softly. "I guess you're all right if you see any humor in this," he said, holding her at arm's length.

"This is twice that you've come to my rescue." Then she heard it. The rumble of the bus engine. Through the pines, she could make out two distinct figures. Cal was forcing someone into the back of the bus. "Oh, my God, they've got J.D."

Chapter 20

"I have to help J.D.," Denver cried, turning back toward the depot as the bus started to pull away.

Taylor caught her arm. "That won't help him, Denver. That could get him killed."

She spun around to face him. "You don't understand."

"Yes, I do. I talked to Maggie and she told me all about the poaching ring."

Relief rushed through her. "Maggie's all right?"

"Davey Matthews is with her at your cabin."

"Davey?" She felt like she'd fallen down a well.

Taylor looked at the unconscious Cline. "Davey told her about the poaching ring and some guy called Midnight, who he thinks killed your Uncle Max."

"Midnight?"

"Unfortunately, Maggie also called Deputy Cline

and gave him the same information. That's why I've been following him. I've never trusted him."

She nodded, feeling a weight come off her shoulders. Taylor hadn't believed Cline's killer hitchhiker theories, either. No wonder he'd been hanging around Maggie's. She stared at the deputy, trying to imagine his face covered with a ski mask. It would explain a lot of things. Max would have trusted Cline. And the deputy had done everything to make it look like a hitchhiker was the murderer in order to keep her from looking for the real culprit.

"What can we do?" she pleaded as the band's bus pulled away from the old stone depot.

"One thing we can't do is let the deputy tip off the poachers. Help me move him."

They dragged Cline over to a tree, where Taylor gagged and handcuffed him.

"Come on." Putting his arm around her shoulders, Taylor led her to his Suburban. "We've got to call someone for help. How about the district ranger?"

"Roland Marsh?"

J.D. sat helpless in the back of the bus while Lester taped his wrists and ankles. Cal leaned against the opposite wall, holding a shotgun on him.

"Is that necessary?" Pete yelled back.

Cal swore. "Just drive."

J.D. tried to talk through the tape already covering his mouth.

"Worried about Denver?" Cal asked, guessing his concern. "We're taking good care of her." He laughed, then leaned over to check the job Lester was doing on

J.D.'s ankles. "Use more tape. We don't want any trouble out of him."

J.D. noticed Pete looking at the road behind them in the rearview mirror as if he expected company. Cal must have noticed it, too.

"You got a problem, Williams?"

"I just want this night to be over."

Cal glanced back down the main drag. "Don't we all."

Just before they'd left the parking lot, Cal had checked the bus with an electronic device for detecting bugs. All the time he was doing it, he was watching Pete as if he thought Pete might have bugged the bus. J.D. could feel the tension between the two of them. Nothing like a falling-out among thieves, he thought. And here he was right in the middle of it. But where was Denver?

He caught a glimpse of the community church off to his left and realized they were headed north out of town. He prayed that Cal was wrong, that Denny was all right and that she'd gotten away.

"You're sure the boss is going to show?" Pete hollered as he got the old bus rattling down the highway.

"You worry too much," Cal yelled back. "By now, Midnight's got Denver and he's taking her to the semi." He smiled at J.D.'s reaction. "You don't like the idea of him having your girlfriend?"

J.D. felt his heart collapse from the sudden weight of worry on his chest. Denny with a man called Midnight. The leader of a poaching ring at best. At worst, a murderer.

"Stop that or I'll stop you," Cal said when he caught J.D. fighting the tape on his wrists.

Lester finished taping J.D.'s ankles. Cal inspected the job, then the two of them moved up to the front of the bus.

J.D. strained to hear their conversation. They seemed to be arguing but he couldn't be sure about what. He looked around for something to use to cut the tape.

"We can't go to marsh," Denver said, climbing into the passenger side of the Suburban. The band's bus turned at the corner and headed north. "He's working with the poachers."

Taylor swung around to face her. "Are you sure?" She nodded and he swore, then apologized for it. "This whole thing is totally out of control."

"We have to follow the bus," Denver said. "I'm sure they plan to move the horn tonight. There's a tracking device on the bus. It's not as high-tech as the one Pete used on me, but hopefully it will work."

Taylor looked puzzled.

"I'll tell you all about it on the way," Denver assured him.

"Are you sure you want to do this?" he asked, checking the two rifles on the rack behind their heads.

"Yes, they have J.D. And who is there we can trust?"

"No one, I guess." He reached under the seat and pulled out a .38. He laid it on the console between them without a word, then turned onto the street, heading in the same direction as they'd last seen the bus going. "I think you'd better start at the beginning," Taylor said.

She filled him in. Starting with Lila Wade hiring

Max to see if Lester Wade was cheating to the cryptic words at the bottom of Lester's case file, and all the way to the *Billings Register*'s morgue and Sheila Walker's murder. "Anyone who's gotten too close is dead," she finished.

Taylor didn't say anything. Instead, he studied her face, a frown creasing his brow. "It's all so hard to believe. You say Pete and this district ranger are in on it?"

She stared at the empty highway ahead, trying to pick up the blueberry-syrup trail, trying desperately not to think about her disappointment in Pete. "Pete used some sort of tracking device to follow me to Marsh's."

Taylor looked at her and swore, this time not apologizing for it. "Does J.D. know all this?" She nodded. "Then his life is in as much danger as yours is."

She thought of J.D. in the hands of murderers, and dread made her heart pound so that each breath was a labor. She picked up the syrup trail in the Suburban's headlights on the outskirts of town. A thin, dark blue line of drops along the snowpack shone in the lights; somewhere ahead, the band's bus lumbered down Highway 191 headed north.

"No wonder Pete and Cline tried so hard to dissuade me from looking for Max's killer," Denver said, seeing everything more clearly.

"So Davey's the one who tipped you off about the poaching ring," Taylor said, shaking his head. "Awfully brave kid, huh, especially after he was almost killed on Horse Butte that night. Then tonight he rescued Maggie from this Lester Wade character."

"I don't know what we would have done without him. I wouldn't have found out about the poaching and

Cal and put it all together." They dropped over the hill past Baker's Hole Campground. There was no sign of the bus's taillights, just the steady line of blueberry syrup down the center of the lane.

"And you think it's all tied in with a 1969 bank robbery?" Taylor asked, sounding incredulous.

"Cal's the connection, although his real name is William Collins." She explained what she'd seen under hypnosis and what she later learned from Chief Vernon. "I think Sheila Walker figured it out and that's what got her killed."

He shook his head. "It's hard to believe Deputy Cline is this Midnight person."

"I know," Denver agreed, thinking about the small cabin he lived in at the edge of town. "I wonder what he did with the money from the robbery."

"Maybe he has it hidden somewhere for the time when he retires," Taylor suggested. They crossed Grayling Pass and dropped down the other side, the syrup drops growing smaller and farther apart. "Your blueberry-syrup trail just ended, kid."

Denver stared at the road for a moment, then behind her. "Didn't we pass a side road back there?" she asked, looking into the darkness. "They must have turned off."

"Or your syrup ran out."

She didn't even want to consider that possibility.

Taylor turned the Suburban around and pulled off on what looked like an old fishing-access road, nothing more than a snowy, narrow dirt road leading into the trees. But more than one set of dual tire tracks had already broken through the snowdrifts.

Taylor turned off his headlights and followed the

tracks in the snow along the river. On a rise above a wide clearing, he stopped and killed the engine. Denver stared at the snowy meadow in front of them and the semitrailer sitting in the middle of it. The rear doors of the trailer were open, and in the faint glow of a lantern's light, she could see that the refrigerated trailer was only half-full. Huge piles of antlers waited to be loaded.

Parked in the pines off to the right was the band's bus. Where was J.D.?

A sudden chill stole up her spine as she looked over at Taylor.

He'd picked up a quarter from the tray on the dash and was spinning it between two fingers. It shone silver, flickering in a blur of light.

In the back of the bus, J.D. strained to hear. Pete had brought the bus to a rattling halt, and the three of them had climbed out, slamming the doors behind them, still arguing about, of all things, grizzly bears. Cal opened the back door of the bus, checked the tape on J.D.'s ankles, then slammed the door again. A few moments later, J.D. heard the thump of something hard on metal not far from the bus. He pulled himself up. In the golden glow of lantern light, J.D. watched the three men load elk antlers into the back of an open semitrailer.

He eased himself down to work on the tape wrapped around his wrists, only to stop a few minutes later to listen again. He could have sworn he heard another vehicle coming up the road. The boss and Denver? He thought of the blueberry syrup; he only hoped it had worked and the FBI would be able to find them. He fell to work on the tape again, running it back and forth against the dull ridges in the metal floor—the sharpest things he'd found in the rear of the bus.

She stared, spellbound by the spinning silver, stunned by its significance.

"Max would have been proud of you, Denver," Taylor said as he looked at the scene in the clearing. She noticed he touched the brake pedal with his foot twice. The coin spun around and around his fingers, a shiny blur. "You're a damned good investigator."

In the clearing below, three men came out of the trailer for more antlers. Denver recognized Pete, Cal and Lester. She stared at them, her heart racing, then looked over at Taylor.

"I never would have thought your blueberry-syrup trail would work," he said, shaking his head.

Denver went for the pistol between them and quickly turned it on Taylor, her hand shaking. "I remember," she whispered as the earth seemed to cave in beneath her. He caught the coin in his fist and looked surprised she had the pistol on him. She stared at him, two nightmares playing in her mind. In each she saw the strange light, the spinning silver. "It was you," she said. Just the other day at Maggie's, she'd watched him spin a toothpick and thought it a nervous habit. Why hadn't she realized then what it meant? "You were the masked robber. You were the one who killed my parents."

Taylor feigned shock. "Whatever would make you say such a thing?"

"The coin."

He looked at the quarter in his hand. "The coin? It's just a silly habit."

Denver nodded, the pistol wavering but still aimed in the general direction of his heart. "You picked up a coin from the counter that day at the bank and stood spinning it while you were waiting for the teller to bag the money. I saw you do it the other day at Maggie's with a toothpick."

He gave her a slight bow. "Very astute."

She watched him glance in the rearview mirror at the road they'd just come down. Was he expecting someone? Denver darted a glance at the trio loading antlers, then at the bus. "Where's J.D.?"

"He's not in the bus, if that's what you're thinking. I instructed Cal to tie him up and leave him in the woods. Only when the horns are safely on their way to the coast will I let the authorities know where to find you both."

"You've thought of everything," she said softly, not sure she believed him. He'd killed everyone who'd tried to stop him; he wouldn't let her and J.D. live. Not now.

She considered getting out to search the bus herself, but knew the pistol in her hand or even the rifles behind her wouldn't be enough to hold off four men. She just had to believe that wherever J.D. was, he was safe. And wait for the FBI to follow the same syrup trail she had.

"You were never in the army with Max, were you?"

He shook his head. "Everyone in town has heard Max's army stories. It was easy enough to find out what I needed to know and bluff my way into your confidence."

"And the robbery? What did you do with the money?"

A smile twisted his lips as he began to spin the coin again. "I spent it, of course."

Tears filled her eyes. "You killed my parents because of money." She felt her finger tighten on the trigger; Taylor's eyes narrowed for a moment.

"No one would have been hurt if your father hadn't come in when he did." He actually sounded as if he believed that.

"And Max? Was he to blame for his own death, also?" she demanded, fighting tears of pain and anger.

"Max found out about the poaching. Cal realized it was just a matter of time before Max put it all together and realized that he was really William Collins, the former bank guard. Cal got panicky, and rather than have him turn state's evidence against me, I took care of Max. I needed Cal to finish my work here in West Yellowstone."

Her heart ached as she stared at him. "Max must have trusted you to let you get so close that day at the dump."

He smiled. "For a few moments there, even Max believed we'd been in the army together."

"You tricked him into meeting you at the dump and then you killed him. After you'd put the money in his account."

He shrugged. "I thought with a few rumors and some money, Deputy Cline would think Max was the leader of the poaching ring." The coin spun in a silver blur. "I fed Sheila Walker enough information to make her think maybe Max pulled off the bank job or at least was in on it."

Denver tried to steady the heavy pistol. "Anyone who knew Max knew he was too honest for that."

"Not all plans turn out the way you hope they will."

Denver caught him looking in the rearview mirror again. The pile of antlers was shrinking. Was he expecting someone? Roland Marsh? Or Deputy Cline? "Suggesting going to Marsh was just a test, huh? And Deputy Cline is—"

Taylor grinned. "A chauvinist and a fool, but certainly not a man smart enough to operate a poaching ring the size of mine." He watched as Cal picked up a large rack and added it to the pile in the truck. "This is only part of a huge smuggling network. I set Cal up here just to keep an eye on him. And it has its moments. Did you know a bear is worth more dead than alive? It's like selling the parts from an expensive car."

With horrifying clarity, Denver realized Taylor was only telling her this because he planned to kill her, as well. She glanced down at the pistol in her hand.

"Right again," he said, smiling at her. "It isn't loaded. You are very good at this."

She let him take the pistol from her trembling fingers. Taylor reached into his pocket and brought out six shells and began to insert them into the empty chambers, watching her closely. Slowly she dropped her hands to her sides in defeat. He relaxed a little and she saw her chance. She grabbed the door handle and pushed, throwing herself from the Suburban. The momentum sent her sprawling into the wet snow. She kicked the door shut and scrambled to her feet. On the other side, she heard Taylor yell at Pete and Cal as he climbed hastily out of the driver's side of the Suburban. Denver ran toward the bus hoping to reach it before Taylor could fire at her.

She was almost past the semi when someone tackled her from the darkness. She screamed as she fell with a force that knocked the air from her lungs.

"I got her," Cal Dalton called as he held her down. "I got her."

Denver looked over her shoulder to see Pete standing above her, a rifle in his hands. The expression on his face was one of total fury.

Chapter 21

J.D. pushed himself up the back of the bus seat. He swore in frustration as he saw what was happening. He dropped back down, working harder at the thick tape around his ankles. Just a little—The fibers in the thick, sticky tape finally gave way...

Just as a shot exploded in the spring night.

It happened so fast, Denver wasn't sure at first that she'd seen it.

Pete pointed the rifle at Cal. "Get away from her." His voice sounded far away. Cal looked up at him, no doubt expecting the rifle barrel to be aimed at her instead of his back.

Taylor came into view behind Pete; in those split seconds, Denver saw him raise the pistol. She screamed a warning but the explosion drowned it out.

Pete flew forward, hitting the ground hard. He rolled onto his side. Cal kicked the rifle away from him and Denver saw the bright red stain spreading across Pete's right shoulder.

He looked up at Taylor, resignation in his expression. "It's all over, Midnight," he said, his voice filled with pain. "The Feds will be here any minute. Do you think I trusted you enough to believe the location you gave me? I put a tracking device on the semi."

Taylor smiled. "Cal swept the bus and the semi. Forget about the Feds." He glanced toward the bus. "Where's Garrison?"

"Tied up in the back," Cal said. "Pete wouldn't let me dump—"

"You stupid—" Taylor swung the pistol on Cal, then seemed to change his mind. "Go get him. Lester, you keep loading horn." Denver started to get up but Taylor waved her back down with the pistol. "That would be very foolish, my dear. I realize now that it would have been a lot easier if I'd killed you at the bank years ago."

Denver leaned over Pete. His shoulder glowed bright red, a flower bursting into bloom from between his fingers as he gripped it. Pain deformed his handsome face. She pulled off her gloves and placed them on the wound beneath his hand. He smiled faintly, tears in his blue eyes.

"Move out of the way, Denver," Taylor ordered.

She glanced over her shoulder at him. "You aren't going to kill him."

Taylor looked pained to say he was. "He's working with the government, my dear. Obviously part of a sting operation if Roland Marsh is involved."

"Oh, Pete, I'm sorry," she said, realizing she had helped give him away by telling Taylor about Marsh.

Pete smiled ruefully. "He planned to murder us all in the end anyway. Once those antlers were loaded he was going to kill us. He's too greedy to share any of the wealth, especially now that things have gone badly."

"How true." Taylor raised the pistol, and shoved Denver aside. "Any dying request?"

At that moment, Cal came from out of the darkness, running hard, breathing heavily as if he were being chased.

"What the hell is it?" Taylor demanded.

"J.D.'s gone."

"What?" Taylor glanced frantically around the clearing. "He can't have gone far. Find him."

Cal didn't move. Instead, he stared at the night, a look of fear coating his face as thick as any mask.

"What's wrong with you?" Taylor demanded. "I said go find him."

Cal licked his lips, his eyes darting into the darkness of the pines. "She's out there. I heard her."

Taylor followed Cal's gaze to the shadows beyond the semitrailer. "What the hell are you talking about?"

Pete's laugh was low.

Taylor swung around to face him. "What's going on?"

"The mama grizzly," Pete grunted, grimacing from the pain. "Cal killed a cub this morning on the other side of that stand of trees and wounded the sow. When he found out this was the shipment location…" Pete coughed, closing his eyes for a moment. "He's convinced she's coming back to get him."

Taylor picked up Pete's rifle from the snow and

tossed it to Cal. Then he grabbed the man's coat collar
and shoved him hard. Cal fell to one knee, then awkwardly got to his feet again. "Find J. D. Garrison or *I'll*
kill you." Cal looked from the pistol in Taylor's hand to
the dark woods, and then back.

"Bears aren't like people," Taylor said, his voice almost compassionate. "They don't hold grudges, Cal.
There's only one danger out there in those woods and
that's J. D. Garrison."

Cal swallowed hard, glancing furtively into the trees.
"That sow was the biggest I've ever seen, and wounded
like that—"

"She crawled off somewhere and died," Taylor persisted, looking at his watch. "Just find me Garrison,
then I'll give you…" He looked around. "… Denver.
She's yours." Cal's eyes widened and he grinned, then
he crept off into the darkness.

Denver moved closer to Pete, hoping to shield him
from Taylor. "Run, J.D., run," she whispered. Beside
her, Pete took her hand, motioning for her to be careful. She stared at him, startled when he led her fingers
to the hunting knife in the top of his boot. He looked
almost apologetic for suggesting it. She nodded and
slipped the knife into the top of her own boot before
Taylor turned around. "You can't possibly believe you
can get away with this," Denver said to him, trying to
block a straight shot at Pete.

Taylor looked almost sad, and for a moment she
thought he might regret what he'd done. "I'll get away
just like I did last time." He settled his gaze on her. "Except this time I won't leave any loose ends."

A scream tore open the night. Cal screamed again
from the darkness beyond the semi. It was a terrified

howl that made Taylor jerk Denver to her feet and hold her like a shield in front of him. He pointed the pistol in the direction the sound had come from, his hand shaking. "Cal? Cal!" Taylor swore as he dragged her around the back of the semitrailer. Lester wasn't in sight. Taylor released her just long enough to extinguish the lantern.

After a moment or two, Denver could make out shapes. One was too black, too big and moving too fast to be human. "The mama grizzly," she whispered in horror as she realized the bear had Cal down in the snow. With horrifying clarity, she could hear the low growls between Cal's screams. Taylor tightened his hold on her as he yelled for Lester to close the doors on the trailer. "You have to help Cal," she pleaded.

"I have to get this shipment to the coast."

Another figure moved among the pines. Denver saw J.D. lift a rifle to his shoulder and fire three quick shots in succession at the huge grizzly. Silence followed.

"J.D.?" Taylor called, pressing the barrel of the pistol against Denver's temple. "Come out where I can see you or I'll have to kill your girlfriend." Denver held her breath as J.D. stepped from the trees, Taylor's rifle from the Suburban in his hands. She felt Taylor's arm tense as he recognized the weapon. "Fool, there were only three bullets in that rifle and you wasted them on Cal!" He swung the pistol to fire at J.D.

"No!" Denver screamed and lifted her boot for the knife. She grabbed it and drove the blade into Taylor's thigh. The pistol exploded in her ears, the shot going wild. Taylor shoved her away as he grabbed for the knife stuck in his leg. Denver fell, hit the snowy ground and rolled away from him.

After that, everything happened so fast, and yet she

would always remember it in slow motion, a flashing sequence of motor-drive shots, each in focus, each as permanent as a photograph. Taylor pulling the knife from his thigh and cursing, throwing the knife into the darkness and turning the pistol on her again. A shot-gun report roaring in her ears. Taylor spinning around in surprise to find J.D. holding a sawed-off shotgun in his hands. Then Taylor staring down at his trouser legs and the bright red flow of blood, his words a cry in the night—"You should have made it count, Garri-son." Taylor smiled as he brought the pistol up again, trying to steady it as he staggered on his wounded legs. First pointing it at J.D. and then swinging it on Denver again. Next, stumbling back, his legs refusing to hold him. His eyes widening as he saw the cache of antlers still beside the semitrailer. Swearing, then laughing as he must have realized what was going to happen. J.D. running for him. Taylor squeezing the trigger as he fell. The shot hitting somewhere in the trees overhead. J.D. reaching for Taylor but not being able to keep him from falling. And Taylor impaling himself on one large sharp tine in the pile of illegal antlers.

Denver watched it all in horror. Right to the end when Taylor looked over at her, the pistol slipping from his fingers, and smiled at the irony.

J.D. swept Denver up from the snow and carried her to the Suburban. Her hands were ice-cold, but she didn't seem to notice. And he realized she'd been running on pure adrenaline. He could only guess what Taylor had told her, but whatever it was had her wired long before the terror of the night had even begun. "Are you all right?" he asked, knowing better.

She nodded. "Pete—"

"He's going to make it."

Denver looked around her as if blinded by the night. In the distance, he could hear the whine of a siren headed their way. He took off his coat and wrapped it around her.

"It's over, Denny," he murmured. The sirens grew closer and lights flickered in the trees as the first of the park-service four-wheel-drive vehicles pulled into the clearing.

Marsh jumped out, picked up Pete's white hat from the trampled snow. Behind him, Cline swore. Denver began to cry. J.D. pulled her into the protective circle of his arms. "It's going to be all right now," he whispered. "It's finally going to be all right."

Epilogue

When J.D. and Denver entered Pete's hospital room
they found District Ranger Roland Marsh and Deputy
Bill Cline beside his bed.

"We were just talking about you, Miss McCallahan,"
Marsh said, and smiled. "You're quite the heroine this
morning." He paused. "Pete says you saved his life last
night."

She met Pete's blue-eyed gaze. "I think it was the
other way around." He looked pale and older, as if his
boyish good looks had taken on a sudden maturity.

"Thank you," Pete said, his voice weak. His gaze
moved to J.D. standing behind her. "You, too, J.D. I
owe you my life."

Cline grumbled under his breath. "They both almost
got *me* killed."

Marsh laughed. "You're lucky all you got was a bump on your head, Bill. If Taylor hadn't been afraid of blowing his cover in front of Denver, you'd have been dead right now," he reminded the cop.

"How's Cal?" Denver asked.

"He'll live to stand trial," Cline said. "In the meantime, he's been very talkative. So was Lester after we found him."

"And Taylor?" she asked.

Marsh shook his head. "He was dead when we got there."

Denver stepped to the side of Pete's bed. Marsh and Cline moved down to the end. "How are you?" she asked Pete.

"I'll live. Roland was just telling me about the blueberry-syrup trail they followed to find us last night."

"We thought it was oil at first," Marsh said.

"Not biodegradable," J.D. answered. "Denny's idea."

Marsh smiled over at her. "That was smart, calling the FBI. We'd have been there sooner but we got a false lead from Taylor. I'm sorry we couldn't have confided in you, but we didn't know who was behind the operation and we couldn't take any chances."

"So you were in on it from the beginning?" J.D. asked.

Marsh nodded. "When Max found out about the poaching ring, he turned it over to us. With Pete on the inside, we went after the leader. We knew it wasn't Cal Dalton."

"And I suppose it was Max's idea for Pete to go under cover?" Cline asked.

"No, Pete volunteered for the job," Marsh said. "It

was fairly easy for him to get in once Pete knew Lester was involved. Max was dead set against it. He tried to stop Pete that morning—"

"Well, that explains why Max was so upset," J.D. said.

"Why *did* you take that chance?" Denver demanded of Pete.

"I overhead Max on the phone with Marsh one afternoon at Maggie's." Pete avoided her gaze. "I thought I could make some brownie points with you—as well as with Max." He coughed, grimacing with pain. "But my infiltrating the ring didn't help Max."

"Meanwhile, Max continued to investigate Cal," Marsh said. "I didn't know he'd run a fingerprint check on him. Unfortunately, Max made Cal nervous, and when Cal got nervous, Taylor got *real* nervous."

"Taylor was worried that if Max found out about the 1969 robbery, he might get Cal to turn state's evidence," Denver confirmed. "So he came here pretending to be an old friend and killed Max."

"I imagine we were easily deceived because there were dozens of Max's old friends turning up for his funeral," Pete said.

"And Pete had just gotten into the poaching ring. He hadn't met Midnight yet," Marsh continued. "So we had no idea it was Taylor. But Max must have been pretty nervous himself about Cal, because he hid the case file."

"Then why didn't he take his gun that day?" Denver demanded.

"From what we can gather, Max thought he was meeting Pete at the dump that day," Marsh said. "Or at least Pete and some old friend."

"I just don't understand how Taylor hoped to get away with killing Max?" J.D. asked.

Marsh chuckled. "Well, for starters, he didn't realize what a tenacious young woman Denver is. And secondly, he'd already gotten away with robbery and murder in Billings. He probably didn't think anyone could stop him, especially a small-town deputy like Cline here."

"I beg your pardon?" Cline objected.

They all laughed. "You know what I mean," Marsh amended. Cline didn't look as if he did. "When Cline started looking for the hitchhiker, Taylor thought he was home free. Then, Denver, you started investigating Max's death."

"Any one of you could have stopped me," she cried. "Why didn't you tell me the truth?"

"Believe me, I wanted to," Pete said. "But we knew whoever this Midnight person was, he'd be suspicious if you *didn't* try to find Max's killer."

"So Cline was in on it the whole time?" J.D. asked.

The deputy nodded, beaming as if he'd just won an Oscar.

J.D. frowned. "If Pete wasn't at Horse Butte—"

"It was Cal," Cline said. "Taylor sent him out to Denver's to help Pete look for the file. Cal found Pete passed out on the couch, saw Denver's note and called Taylor. Taylor told him to use Pete's pickup to get Pete in so deep they wouldn't have to worry about his loyalties."

"And I didn't realize what had happened until the next morning when I got a call from Midnight," Pete said. "I'm sorry about trying to drug you, Denver. By then, I *was* in deep."

"And the hitchhiker?" Denver asked.

"He existed," Cline said. "We just invented the one who confessed. And we were looking for him in case he witnessed anything. He didn't."

"I assume Cal tore up Max's office, my cabin and Maggie's," Denver said.

"He and Lester," Cline added.

"But I smelled your cologne that night at my cabin," Denver said to Pete.

He nodded. "It seems Lester and Cal also searched my apartment. Cal helped himself to some of my cologne." He took her hand. "No wonder you were so afraid of me."

"So it was probably Cal who hit me on the head that first night at Max's," J.D. said.

"It's a good thing you have such a hard head, Garrison," Cline commented, but Denver detected an almost grudging compliment in the remark.

She closed her eyes for a moment. Her head swam. "That sawed-off shotgun J.D. found under Taylor's rear seat—"

"It's the same one that killed your parents," Marsh confirmed.

J.D. turned from the window. "What kind of fool would keep a murder weapon?"

"A lot of criminals like to keep a souvenir," Marsh said. "And I'm sure he saw some poetic justice in killing the daughter with the same gun more than twenty years later."

Silence filled the room to overflowing. Marsh took the hint and excused himself to make a phone call. Unfortunately, Cline didn't; the ranger almost had to drag him out of the room.

"I still think women should stay in the kitchen," Denver heard Cline say as he left. She smiled to herself. Right now, staying in J.D.'s kitchen, raising his children, baking cookies and doing the wash sounded wonderful, not that her camera bag would ever be far away.

"I owe the two of you an apology," Pete said, motioning for J.D. to come closer. "I did everything I could to keep you apart. You were right. I never called J.D. about the funeral."

Denver took his hand. "Pete—"

"Let me finish. I thought that you'd eventually get over J.D." He glanced at J.D., who had come to stand beside his bed. "I realize now that is never going to happen." Pete offered his uninjured left hand. "Friends?"

J.D. took his hand. "Friends." He turned to Denver. "I'll be outside."

She stood for a moment listening to the sound of birds singing beyond the open hospital window. "Thank you for trying to help Max."

Pete waved her thanks away. "I did it for all the wrong reasons." He took a breath and let it out slowly. "J.D.'s the right man for you, you know."

She smiled as she leaned over to plant a kiss on Pete's cheek. "Some day you're going to meet a woman who'll knock you off your feet and you'll wonder what you ever saw in me."

He laughed softly. "That's going to have to be *some* woman."

"She will be."

"Denver…" Pete pulled some folded papers from the

table beside his bed. "I found this in Max's Oldsmobile. It's his will." She stared at the papers. "He wrote you a letter, too." Pete grinned. "Wishing you and J.D. happiness. Max knew you'd end up together, I guess." He met her gaze. "Be happy."

She smiled, tears in her eyes. "I'm going to try, Pete."

J.D. found her sitting on a bench in a courtyard at the north end of the hospital. He stood for a minute just looking at her, marveling at everything they'd been through. Quietly he sat down on the bench beside her and looked out at the Bridgers. The sun brightened the pines still laden with snow and brushed the rocky cliffs to gold. The air smelled of spring, and he realized, like the day, he held new hope for the future.

"I can't believe it's finally really over," Denver said, glancing at him.

"Are you all right?"

She nodded as she looked at the city of Bozeman sprawled below them. "Pete gave me Max's will." She handed him the letter. It was short and to the point. "He hopes the two of us will be happy. And he wants us to name one of our kids after him."

J.D. laughed as he handed back the letter. "We do make quite the team, don't we?"

She nodded. "Max would have been impressed, wouldn't he?" Tears welled in her eyes. "I miss him so much."

"I know." He took her hand; his thumb gently caressed the tender skin of her palm. "But I have a feeling he's still watching over you."

She brushed at her tears with her free hand and

smiled. "I swear sometimes I can almost smell those awful cigars he smoked when he was working on a case."

The breeze stirred her hair; her lower lip trembled with emotion. J.D. touched her lip with his fingertips, wanting to make the same journey with a kiss. He pulled his hand back. "Denny." It came out a tortured groan. "How can I ask you to give up your life here, knowing how much you love it?"

"Because a long time ago you promised Max you'd do what was best for me," she whispered.

He said nothing; he didn't even dare breathe.

She cupped his jaw with her hand. "I think you know what's best for me."

He brushed her hair back from her temple. "You realize that means being on the road for months at a time and—"

She stopped him with a kiss. "Do you really think it matters where we are, as long as we're together?"

He took her face in his hands and kissed her eyelids, her cheeks, her lips. "I want you so much, Denny. I've never wanted, needed anything so badly." She raised an eyebrow; he grinned. "No, sweetheart, not even the music."

She laughed. "That's good, J.D., because I hate playing second fiddle to a guitar."

He held her for a moment, just breathing in the familiar scent of her. Was it possible? Was it really possible? "What about your camera shop and the cabin?" he asked with apprehension.

He watched Denny look toward Gallatin Canyon, the way home to West Yellowstone and the place she loved. "Maggie's taking Davey on to finish raising. The two of them have offered to run the shop for me. And the cabin will always be there for us." When she turned to him again, she smiled. "As for Max…well, he'll always be with me, too, J.D., no matter where I am." She leaned up to kiss him gently, her lips warm and inviting. "And it's not like I'm going to put my cameras away. I'm going to start a photo book."

"A photo book?" he asked, seeing that old adventurous glint in her eye.

"For our children. It's going to be photographs taken of their father's tours in the years before they were born. I want them to know right from the very beginning that their father is a musician."

He swallowed hard. "Our children." How he loved the sound of that. "They're going to love the lake." As much as we did, he thought. And he could see them, tanned by the sun, standing in front of the cabin Max had built for Denny, smiling into the camera. "We'll be back."

She smiled. "I know."

He kissed her then, putting as much of his love as he could into only a kiss. The sun warmed his back and caught in her eyes, making them sparkle. "Marry me, Denny," he whispered. "Say you'll marry me before you come to your senses."

Her laugh filled the spring air, the most beautiful music he'd ever heard, strong as their love and just as lasting. She looked to the heavens as if listening for a voice to guide her. Then she smiled and nodded.

It was the first time he'd ever seen her at a loss for words, and he knew it wouldn't last. He swept her into his arms and kissed her. The future waited on the horizon, beckoning them with promises like none he'd ever dreamed. His heart filled with songs yet to be written as he took her hand in his, and together they walked into the new day.

* * * * *

We hope you enjoyed reading

THE WATERFALL

by *New York Times* bestselling author

CARLA NEGGERS

and

ODD MAN OUT

by *New York Times* bestselling author

B.J. DANIELS

Both were originally MIRA and
Harlequin Intrigue® stories!

You crave excitement!
Harlequin Intrigue® stories deal in serious
romantic suspense, keeping you on the edge
of your seat as resourceful, true-to-life women
and strong, fearless men fight for survival.

INTRIGUE

EDGE-OF-YOUR-SEAT INTRIGUE, FEARLESS ROMANCE.

Look for six *new* romances every month from
Harlequin Intrigue!

Available wherever books and ebooks are sold.

www.Harlequin.com

NYTHRS1017

Get 2 Free Books,
Plus 2 Free Gifts –
just for trying the Reader Service!

STRS17R

She prayed for sleep, but her mind kept returning to that time in the Sahara. Being part of the expedition had been such a privilege. She remembered the way they'd all felt when they'd broken through to the tomb. Satima Mahmoud—the pretty Egyptian interpreter who had so enchanted Joe Rosello—had been the first to scream when the workers found the entry.

Of course, Henry Tomlinson was called then. He'd been there to break the seal. They'd all laughed and joked about the curses that came with such finds, about the stupid movies that had been made.

Yes, people had died during other expeditions—as if they had been cursed. The Tut story was one example—and yet, by all accounts, there had been scientific explanations for everything that'd happened.

Almost everything, anyway.

And their find…

There hadn't been any curses. Not written curses, at any rate.

But Henry had died. And Henry had broken the seal…

No mummy curse had gotten to them; someone had killed Henry. And that someone had gotten away with it because neither the American Department of State nor the Egyptian government had wanted the expedition caught in the crosshairs of an insurgency. Reasonably enough!

But now…

For some reason, the uneasy dreams that came with her restless sleep weren't filled with mummies, tombs, sarcophagi or canopic jars. No funerary objects whatsoever, no golden scepters, no jewelry, no treasures.

Instead, she saw the sand. The endless sand of the Sahara. And the sand was teeming, rising up from the ground, swirling in the air.

Someone was coming…

She braced, because there were rumors swirling along with the sand. Their group could fall under attack—there was unrest in the area. Good Lord, they were in the Middle East!

But she found herself walking through the sand, toward whomever or whatever was coming.

She saw someone.

The killer?

She kept walking toward him. There was more upheaval behind the man, sand billowing dark and heavy like a twister of deadly granules.

Then she saw him.

And it was Micah Fox.

She woke with a start.

And she wondered if he was going to be her salvation…

Or a greater danger to her heart, a danger she hadn't yet seen.

Don't miss
SHADOWS IN THE NIGHT,
available November 2017 wherever
Harlequin® Intrigue books and ebooks are sold.

www.Harlequin.com

HIEXP1017

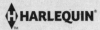

HARLEQUIN®

INTRIGUE

EDGE-OF-YOUR-SEAT INTRIGUE, FEARLESS ROMANCE.

Save $1.00

on the purchase of ANY Harlequin® Intrigue book.

Available wherever books are sold, including most bookstores, supermarkets, drugstores and discount stores.

Save $1.00

on the purchase of any Harlequin® Intrigue book.

Coupon valid until December 31, 2017.
Redeemable at participating outlets in the U.S. and Canada only.
Not redeemable at Barnes & Noble stores. Limit one coupon per customer.

`52614978`

Canadian Retailers: Harlequin Enterprises Limited will pay the face value of this coupon plus 10.25¢ if submitted by customer for this product only. Any other use constitutes fraud. Coupon is nonassignable. Void if taxed, prohibited or restricted by law. Consumer must pay any government taxes. Void if copied. Inmar Promotional Services ("IPS") customers submit coupons and proof of sales to Harlequin Enterprises Limited, P.O. Box 3000, Saint John, NB E2L 4L3, Canada. Non-IPS retailer—for reimbursement submit coupons and proof of sales directly to Harlequin Enterprises Limited, Retail Marketing Department, 225 Duncan Mill Rd., Don Mills, ON M3B 3K9, Canada.

U.S. Retailers: Harlequin Enterprises Limited will pay the face value of this coupon plus 8¢ if submitted by customer for this product only. Any other use constitutes fraud. Coupon is nonassignable. Void if taxed, prohibited or restricted by law. Consumer must pay any government taxes. Void if copied. For reimbursement submit coupons and proof of sales directly to Harlequin Enterprises, Ltd 482, NCH Marketing Services, P.O. Box 880001, El Paso, TX 88588-0001, U.S.A. Cash value 1/100 cents.

® and ™ are trademarks owned and used by the trademark owner and/or its licensee.

© 2017 Harlequin Enterprises Limited

HIBJDCOUP1017

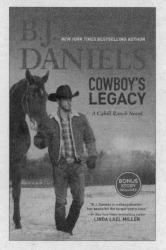